This is for
PHILIP SPITZER AND JOEL GOTLER
Great advisors and agents, but most of all
great friends.

The critics on Michael Connelly

'An excellent thriller that puts Connelly firmly in the frame as one of the stars of American crime writing' *Sunday Times*

'The real thing, and the best of its kind since *Silence of the Lambs* . . . An unputdownable masterclass in thriller writing' *Time Out*

'A cracker . . . it fairly coruscates with all that goes to make a good crime thriller' *Irish Times*

'Most impressive . . . rich in detail, strong on character, with a fascinating plot that functions on several emotional levels . . . Connelly has, with great skill, given us a detective who inhabits a world filled only with torment, fear and danger' *People Magazine*

'Impressive . . . convincing ambience, a mass of procedural detail, authentic dialogue, a speeding plot and a flawed hero' *The Times*

'His methods of killing and eluding detection are infernally ingenious, adding an intellectual charge to the visceral kick of the hunt' *New York Times*

'One of the most authentic pieces of crime writing I've ever read. It is an extraordinary story, one that engages the reader on the first page and never lets go' James Lee Burke

'In-depth knowledge informs every turn of a wonderfully Byzantine plot . . . If you are an aspiring crime writer, buy this bravura display of technique' *Sunday Times*

'Intensely clever, entirely credible . . . thrilling, suspenseful and securely anchored in procedure and purpose. Not a false note; deeply satisfying stuff' *Literary Review*

A former police reporter for the *Los Angeles Times*, Michael Connelly is the author of fourteen acclaimed and bestselling novels. He lives in Florida. Visit his website at www.MichaelConnelly.com.

By Michael Connelly

MICHAEL CONNELLY

THE
POET

With an Introduction
by Stephen King

ORION

An Orion paperback

First published in Great Britain in 1996
by Orion
This paperback edition published in 2004
by Orion Books Ltd,
Orion House, 5 Upper St Martin's Lane,
London WC2H 9EA

A CIP catalogue record for this book is available
from the British Library.

ISBN 0 75286 391 6

Typeset by Datix International Limited, Bungay, Suffolk

Printed and bound in Great Britain by
Clays Lts, St Ives plc

INTRODUCTION
by Stephen King

Whether you are the reader or the writer, it can be extremely hard to start a novel. No one in the book is your friend yet, and all the places are strange; hence, starting to read feels like a forced act of intimacy. A hooker can help in this regard. I'm not talking about a prostitute but a good first line. I'm a sucker for good first lines, collect them in a little notebook the way some people collect stamps or coins, and the first line of *The Poet* is a blue-ribbon winner. *Death is my beat*, Jack McEvoy writes, and we are immediately hooked and pulled in. It's not a cheat-line, either, but one that perfectly sets the tone: dark, brooding, just plain scary. It also serves to immediately distance *The Poet* from the four other novels Connelly had written up to that time. Those books are about a series character. I can imagine Harry Bosch (of *The Concrete Blonde*, et cetera) saying something like 'Death is my beat,' but not until much further along the arc of his disillusionment.

The first thing you need to know about this novel is that it's a marvelous and sustained piece of storytelling, an absolute joy to read if you like tales of suspense. The book is full of incident and stuffed with characters, many of them colorful; I counted twenty-eight 'speaking parts' and know I didn't even come close to getting them all. Still, you won't get lost because Jack is almost always there, anchoring the tale, and 'Death is [his] beat.'

The second thing you need to know about *The Poet* is that it's genuinely terrifying. We all know the corny old cliché about reading with all the lights on (as if you could get much reading done with them all turned out), but the first time I read *The Poet* – this was in Boulder, Colorado, less than forty miles from the place where Sean McEvoy's life comes to an end – I did indeed find myself calling for wattage backup as the story wound toward its climax inside and the dark drew down outside. I think of myself as relatively case-hardened to make-believe terrors, but the further I followed Jack into the Poet's world, the more frightened I became. I don't believe I will ever again listen to the high-pitched cry of mating modems without thinking of this novel. And Connelly achieves his scares the old-fashioned way, by actual *storytelling*. There's plenty of blood for the gorehounds among you – an attractive college student found in two pieces, for starters – but it's never ladled out simply to pump up a flagging plot. Because the plot of *The Poet* doesn't flag. Let me repeat that it's a *novel*, not a trick, and brings with it all the novel's old, delicious pleasures.

Connelly's writing is by turns elegant and matter-of-fact. It pulls the reader into a tale that works as a classic mystery story (howdunit as well as who, in this case), and at the end, after a series of surprises that go off like well-placed dynamite charges, the reader can look back and see how carefully (and how craftily) the entire work was put together. I repeat, there is no cheating. Writers of this kind of book want us to be surprised – even shocked – when the truth comes to light in the last two chapters. (Think of how you felt the first time you discovered who *really* killed Roger Ackroyd.) After a lifetime of Ellery Queen, John D. MacDonald, Elmore Leonard, Ngaio Marsh, Ruth Rendell, and a raft of others, we hardly ever are. But at the end of *The Poet*, I *was* surprised. Shocked, as well. This is a good deal more than a mystery, but Michael Connelly has paid close attention to the mystery story's rather strict rules of logic just the same. The result is a book with true depth and texture, one that bears rereading, not just twice but perhaps thrice.

This is the best work Michael Connelly, a prolific writer, had done up to this point (1996) and marked him as an important voice in the genre at the turn of the century. I do not use the word *classic* lightly, but I believe that *The Poet* may well prove to be one. Sometimes a novelist sends us a wonderful message between the lines: 'I am capable of much more than I thought.' *The Poet* is that sort of book, long and rich, multi-layered and satisfying. I wish you all the joy of finding out what lies beyond 'Death is my beat.'

Stephen King
October 18, 2003

I

....

Death is my beat. I make my living from it. I forge my professional reputation on it. I treat it with the passion and precision of an undertaker – somber and sympathetic about it when I'm with the bereaved, a skilled craftsman with it when I'm alone. I've always thought the secret of dealing with death was to keep it at arm's length. That's the rule. Don't let it breathe in your face.

But my rule didn't protect me. When the two detectives came for me and told me about Sean, a cold numbness quickly enveloped me. It was like I was on the other side of the aquarium window. I moved as if underwater – back and forth, back and forth – and looked out at the rest of the world through the glass. From the backseat of their car I could see my eyes in the rearview mirror, flashing each time we passed beneath a streetlight. I recognized the thousand-yard stare I had seen in the eyes of fresh widows I had interviewed over the years.

I knew only one of the two detectives. Harold Wexler. I had met him a few months earlier when I stopped into the Pints Of for a drink with Sean. They worked CAPs together on the Denver PD. I remember Sean called him Wex. Cops always use nicknames for each other. Wexler's is Wex, Sean's, Mac. It's some kind of tribal bonding thing. Some of the names aren't complimentary but the cops don't complain. I know one down in Colorado Springs named Scoto whom most other cops call Scroto. Some even go all the way and call him Scrotum, but my guess is that you have to be a close friend to get away with that.

Wexler was built like a small bull, powerful but squat. A

voice slowly cured over the years by cigarette smoke and whiskey. A hatchet face that always seemed red the times I saw him. I remember he drank Jim Beam over ice. I'm always interested in what cops drink. It tells a lot about them. When they're taking it straight like that, I always think that maybe they've seen too many things too many times that most people never see even once. Sean was drinking Lite beer that night, but he was young. Even though he was the supe of the CAPs unit, he was at least ten years younger than Wexler. Maybe in ten years he would have been taking his medicine cold and straight like Wexler. But now I'll never know.

I spent most of the drive out from Denver thinking about that night at the Pints Of. Not that anything important had happened. It was just drinks with my brother at the cop bar. And it was the last good time between us, before Theresa Lofton came up. That memory put me back in the aquarium.

But during the moments that reality was able to punch through the glass and into my heart, I was seized by a feeling of failure and grief. It was the first real tearing of the soul I had experienced in my thirty-four years. That included the death of my sister. I was too young then to properly grieve for Sarah or even to understand the pain of a life unfulfilled. I grieved now because I had not even known Sean was so close to the edge. He was Lite beer while all the other cops I knew were whiskey on the rocks.

Of course, I also recognized how self-pitying this kind of grief was. The truth was that for a long time we hadn't listened much to each other. We had taken different paths. And each time I acknowledged this truth the cycle of my grief would begin again.

My brother once told me the theory of the limit. He said every homicide cop had a limit but the limit was unknown until it was reached. He was talking about dead bodies. Sean believed that there were just so many that a cop could look at. It was a different number for every person. Some hit it early.

Some put in twenty in homicide and never got close. But there was a number. And when it came up, that was it. You transferred to records, you turned in your badge, you did something. Because you just couldn't look at another one. And if you did, if you exceeded your limit, well, then you were in trouble. You might end up sucking down a bullet. That's what Sean said.

I realized that the other one, Ray St. Louis, had said something to me.

He turned around in his seat to look back at me. He was much larger than Wexler. Even in the dim light of the car I could make out the rough texture of his pockmarked face. I didn't know him but I'd heard him referred to by other cops and I knew they called him Big Dog. I had thought that he and Wexler made the perfect Mutt and Jeff team when I first saw them waiting for me in the lobby at the *Rocky*. It was like they had stepped out of a late-night movie. Long, dark overcoats, hats. The whole scene should have been in black and white.

'You hear me, Jack. We'll break it to her. That's our job, but we'd just like you to be there to sort of help us out, maybe stay with her if it gets rough. You know, if she needs to be with somebody. Okay?'

'Okay.'

'Good, Jack.'

We were going to Sean's house. Not the apartment he split with four other cops in Denver so in accordance with city regs he was a Denver resident. His house in Boulder where his wife, Riley, would answer our knock. I knew nobody was going to be breaking anything to her. She'd know what the news was the moment she opened the door and saw the three of us standing there without Sean. Any cop's wife would know. They spend their lives dreading and preparing for that day. Every time there's a knock on the door they expect it to be death's messengers standing there when they open it. This time it would be.

3

'You know, she's going to know,' I told them.

'Probably,' Wexler said. 'They always do.'

I realized they were counting on Riley knowing the score as soon as she opened the door. It would make their job easier.

I dropped my chin to my chest and brought my fingers up beneath my glasses to pinch the bridge of my nose. I realized I had become a character in one of my own stories – exhibiting the details of grief and loss I worked so hard to get so I could make a thirty-inch newspaper story seem meaningful. Now I was one of the details in this story.

A sense of shame descended on me as I thought of all the calls I had made to a widow or parent of a dead child. Or brother of a suicide. Yes, I had even made those. I don't think there was any kind of death that I hadn't written about, that hadn't brought me around as the intruder into somebody's pain.

How do you feel? Trusty words for a reporter. Always the first question. If not so direct, then carefully camouflaged in words meant to impart sympathy and understanding – feelings I didn't actually have. I carried a reminder of this callousness. A thin white scar running along my left cheek just above the line of my beard. It was from the diamond engagement ring of a woman whose fiancé had been killed in an avalanche near Breckenridge. I asked her the old standby and she responded with a backhand across my face. At the time I was new to the job and thought I had been wronged. Now I wear the scar like a badge.

'You better pull over,' I said. 'I'm going to be sick.'

Wexler jerked the car into the freeway's breakdown lane. We skidded a little on the black ice but then he got control. Before the car had completely stopped I tried desperately to open the door but the handle wouldn't work. It was a detective car, I realized, and the passengers who most often rode in the back were suspects and prisoners. The back doors had security locks controlled from the front.

'The door,' I managed to strangle out.

The car finally jerked to a stop as Wexler disengaged the security lock. I opened the door, leaned out and vomited into

4

the dirty slush. Three great heaves from the gut. For a half a minute I didn't move, waiting for more, but that was it. I was empty. I thought about the backseat of the car. For prisoners and suspects. And I guessed that I was both now. Suspect as a brother. A prisoner of my own pride. The sentence, of course, would now be life.

Those thoughts quickly slipped away with the relief the physical exorcism brought. I gingerly stepped out of the car and walked to the edge of the asphalt where the light from the passing cars reflected in moving rainbows on the petroleum-exhaust glaze on the February snow. It looked as if we had stopped alongside a grazing meadow but I didn't know where. I hadn't been paying attention to how far along to Boulder we were. I took off my gloves and glasses and put them in the pockets of my coat. Then I reached down and dug beneath the spoiled surface to where the snow was white and pure. I took up two handfuls of the cold, clean powder and pressed it to my face, rubbing my skin until it stung.

'You okay?' St. Louis asked.

He had come up behind me with his stupid question. It was up there with *How do you feel?* I ignored it.

'Let's go,' I said.

We got back in and Wexler wordlessly pulled the car back onto the freeway. I saw a sign for the Broomfield exit and knew we were about halfway there. Growing up in Boulder, I had made the thirty-mile run between there and Denver a thousand times but the stretch seemed like alien territory to me now.

For the first time I thought of my parents and how they would deal with this. Stoicly, I decided. They handled everything that way. They never discussed it. They moved on. They'd done it with Sarah. Now they'd do it with Sean.

'Why'd he do it?' I asked after a few minutes.

Wexler and St. Louis said nothing.

'I'm his brother. We're twins, for Christ's sake.'

'You're also a reporter,' St. Louis said. 'We picked you up because we want Riley to be with family if she needs it. You're the only –'

'My brother fucking killed himself!'

I said it too loud. It had a quality of hysteria to it that I knew never worked with cops. You start yelling and they have a way of shutting down, going cold. I continued in a subdued voice.

'I think I am entitled to know what happened and why. I'm not writing a fucking story. Jesus, you guys are . . .'

I shook my head and didn't finish. If I tried I thought I would lose it again. I gazed out the window and could see the lights of Boulder coming up. So many more than when I was a kid.

'We don't know why,' Wexler finally said after a half minute. 'Okay? All I can say is that it happens. Sometimes cops get tired of all the shit that comes down the pipe. Mac might've gotten tired, that's all. Who knows? But they're working on it. And when they know, I'll know. And I'll tell you. That's a promise.'

'Who's working it?'

'The park services turned it over to our department. SIU is handling it.'

'What do you mean Special Investigations? They don't handle cop suicides.'

'Normally, they don't. We do. CAPs. But this time it's just that they're not going to let us investigate our own. Conflict of interest, you know.'

CAPs, I thought. Crimes Against Persons. Homicide, assault, rape, suicide. I wondered who would be listed in the reports as the person against whom this crime had been committed. Riley? Me? My parents? My brother?

'It was because of Theresa Lofton, wasn't it?' I asked, though it wasn't really a question. I didn't feel I needed their confirmation or denial. I was just saying out loud what I believed to be the obvious.

'We don't know, Jack,' St. Louis said. 'Let's leave it at that for now.'

The death of Theresa Lofton was the kind of murder that gave people pause. Not just in Denver, but everywhere. It made anybody who heard or read about it stop for at least a moment to consider the violent images it conjured in the mind, the twist it caused in the gut.

Most homicides are little murders. That's what we call them in the newspaper business. Their effect on others is limited, their grasp on the imagination is short-lived. They get a few paragraphs on the inside pages. Buried in the paper the way the victims are buried in the ground.

But when an attractive college student is found in two pieces in a theretofore peaceful place like Washington Park, there usually isn't enough space in the paper for all the inches of copy it will generate. Theresa Lofton's was no little murder. It was a magnet that pulled at reporters from across the country. Theresa Lofton was the girl in two pieces. That was the catchy thing about this one. And so they descended on Denver from places like New York and Chicago and Los Angeles, television, tabloid and newspaper reporters alike. For a week, they stayed at hotels with good room service, roamed the city and the University of Denver campus, asked meaningless questions and got meaningless answers. Some staked out the day care center where Lofton had worked part-time or went up to Butte, where she had come from. Wherever they went they learned the same thing, that Theresa Lofton fit that most exclusive media image of all, the All-American Girl.

The Theresa Lofton murder was inevitably compared to the Black Dahlia case of fifty years ago in Los Angeles. In that case, a not so All-American Girl was found severed at the midriff in an empty lot. A tabloid television show dubbed Theresa Lofton the White Dahlia, playing on the fact that she had been found on a snow-covered field near Denver's Lake Grasmere.

And so the story fed on itself. It burned as hot as a trash-can fire for almost two weeks. But nobody was arrested and there were other crimes, other fires for the national media to warm itself by. Updates on the Lofton case dropped back into the inside pages of the Colorado papers. They became briefs for the digest pages. And Theresa Lofton finally took her spot among the little murders. She was buried.

All the while, the police in general, and my brother in particular, remained virtually mute, refusing even to confirm the detail that the victim had been found in two parts. That report had come only by accident from a photographer at the *Rocky* named Iggy Gomez. He had been in the park looking for wild art – the feature photos that fill the pages on a slow news day – when he happened upon the crime scene ahead of any other reporters or photographers. The cops had made the callouts to the coroner's and crime scene offices by landline since they knew the *Rocky* and the *Post* monitored their radio frequencies. Gomez took shots of two stretchers being used to remove two body bags. He called the city desk and said the cops were working a two-bagger and from the looks of the size of the bags the victims were probably children.

Later, a cop shop reporter for the *Rocky* named Van Jackson got a source in the coroner's office to confirm the grim fact that a victim had come into the morgue in two parts. The next morning's story in the *Rocky* served as the siren call to the media across the country.

My brother and his CAPs team worked as if they felt no obligation to talk to the public at all. Each day, the Denver Police Department media office put out a scant few lines in a press release, announcing that the investigation was continuing and that there had been no arrests. When cornered, the brass vowed that the case would not be investigated in the media, though that in itself was a laughable statement. Left with little information from authorities, the media did what it always does in such cases. It investigated the case on its own, numbing the reading and television-watching public with assorted details about the victim's life that actually had nothing to do with anything.

Still, almost nothing leaked from the department and little was known outside headquarters on Delaware Street; and after a couple of weeks the media onslaught was over, strangled by the lack of its lifeblood, information.

*

I didn't write about Theresa Lofton. But I wanted to. It wasn't the kind of story that comes along often in this place and any reporter would have wanted a piece of it. But at first, Van Jackson worked it with Laura Fitzgibbons, the university beat reporter. I had to bide my time. I knew that as long as the cops didn't clear it, I'd get my shot at it. So when Jackson asked me in the early days of the case if I could get anything from my brother, even off the record, I told him I would try, but I didn't try. I wanted the story and I wasn't going to help Jackson stay on it by feeding him from my source.

In late January, when the case was a month old and had dropped out of the news, I made my move. And my mistake.

One morning I went in to see Greg Glenn, the city editor, and told him I'd like to do a take out on the Lofton case. That was my specialty, my beat. Long takes on the notable murders of the Rocky Mountain Empire. To use a newspaper cliché, my expertise was going behind the headlines to bring you the real story. So I went to Glenn and reminded him I had an in. It was my brother's case, I said, and he'd only talk to me about it. Glenn didn't hesitate to consider the time and effort Jackson had already put on the story. I knew that he wouldn't. All he cared about was getting a story the *Post* didn't have. I walked out of the office with the assignment.

My mistake was that I told Glenn I had the in before I had talked to my brother. The next day I walked the two blocks from the *Rocky* to the cop shop and met him for lunch in the cafeteria. I told him about my assignment. Sean told me to turn around.

'Go back, Jack. I can't help you.'

'What are you talking about? It's your case.'

'It's my case but I'm not cooperating with you or anybody else who wants to write about it. I've given the basic details, that's all I'm required to do, that's where it stays.'

He looked off across the cafeteria. He had an annoying habit of not looking at you when you disagreed with him. When we were little, I would jump on him when he did it and punch him on the back. I couldn't do that anymore, though many times I wanted to.

'Sean, this is a good story. You have –'

'I don't have to do anything and I don't give a shit what kind of story it is. This one is bad, Jack. Okay? I can't stop thinking about it. And I'm not going to help you sell newspapers with it.'

'C'mon, man, I'm a writer. Look at me. I don't care if it sells papers or not. The story is the thing. I don't give a shit about the paper. You know how I feel about that.'

He finally turned back to me.

'Now you know how I feel about this case,' he said.

I was silent a moment and took out a cigarette. I was down to maybe half a pack a day back then and could have skipped it but I knew it bothered him. So I smoked when I wanted to work on him.

'This isn't a smoking section, Jack.'

'Then turn me in. At least you'll be arresting *somebody*.'

'Why are you such an asshole when you don't get what you want?'

'Why are you? You aren't going to clear it, are you? That's what this is all about. You don't want me digging around and writing about your failure. You're giving up.'

'Jack, don't try the below-the-belt shit. You know it's never worked.'

He was right. It never had.

'Then what? You just want to keep this little horror story for yourself? That it?'

'Yeah, something like that. You could say that.'

In the car with Wexler and St. Louis I sat with my arms crossed. It was comforting. Almost as if I were holding myself together. The more I thought about my brother the more the whole thing made no sense to me. I knew the Lofton case had weighed on him but not to the point that he'd want to take his own life. Not Sean.

'Did he use his gun?'

Wexler looked at me in the mirror. Studied me, I thought. I wondered if he knew what had come between my brother and me.

'Yes.'

It hit me then. I just didn't see it. All the times that we'd had together coming to that. I didn't care about the Lofton case. What they were saying couldn't be.

'Not Sean.'

St. Louis turned around to look at me.

'What's that?'

'He wouldn't have done it, that's all.'

'Look, Jack, he –'

'He didn't get tired of the shit coming down the pipe. He loved it. You ask Riley. You ask anybody on the – Wex, you knew him the best and you know it's bullshit. He loved the hunt. That's what he called it. He wouldn't have traded it for anything. He probably could have been the assistant fucking chief by now but he didn't want it. He wanted to work homicides. He stayed in CAPs.'

Wexler didn't reply. We were in Boulder now, on Baseline heading toward Cascade. I was falling through the silence of the car. The impact of what they were telling me Sean had done was settling on me and leaving me as cold and dirty as the snow back on the side of the freeway.

'What about a note or something?' I said. 'What –'

'There was a note. We think it was a note.'

I noticed St. Louis glance over at Wexler and give him a look that said, you're saying too much.

'What? What did it say?'

There was a long silence, then Wexler ignored St. Louis.

'Out of space,' he said. 'Out of time.'

'"Out of space. Out of time." Just like that?'

'Just like that. That's all it said.'

The smile on Riley's face lasted maybe three seconds. Then it was instantly replaced by a look of horror out of that painting by Munch. The brain is an amazing computer. Three seconds to look at three faces at your door and to know your husband isn't coming home. IBM could never match that. Her mouth formed into a horrible black hole from which an unintelligible sound came, then the inevitable useless word: 'No!'

'Riley,' Wexler tried. 'Let's sit down a minute.'

'No, oh God, no!'

'Riley . . .'

She retreated from the door, moving like a cornered animal, first darting one way and then the opposite, as if maybe she thought she could change things if she could elude us. She went around the corner into the living room. When we followed we found her collapsed on the middle of the couch in an almost catatonic state, not too dissimilar from my own. The tears were just starting to come to her eyes. Wexler sat next to her on the couch. Big Dog and I stood by, silent as cowards.

'Is he dead?' she asked, knowing the answer but realizing she had to get it over with.

Wexler nodded.

'How?'

Wexler looked down and hesitated a moment. He looked over at me and then back at Riley.

'He did it himself, Riley. I'm sorry.'

She didn't believe it, just as I hadn't. But Wexler had a way of telling the story and after a while she stopped protesting. That was when she looked at me for the first time, tears rolling. Her face had an imploring look, as if she were asking me if we were sharing the same nightmare and couldn't I do something about it. Couldn't I wake her up? Couldn't I tell these two characters from a black and white how wrong they were? I went to the couch, sat next to her and hugged her. That's what I was there for. I'd seen this scene often enough to know what I was supposed to do.

'I'll stay,' I whispered. 'As long as you like.'

She didn't answer. She turned from my arms to Wexler.

'Where did it happen?'

'Estes Park. By the lake.'

'No, he wouldn't go – what was he doing up there?'

'He got a call. Somebody said they might have some information about one of his cases. He was going up to meet them for coffee at the Stanley. Then after he ... he drove out to the lake. We don't know why he went there. He was found in his car by a ranger who heard the shot.'

'What case?' I asked.

'Look, Jack, I don't want to get into –'

'*What case?*' I yelled, this time not caring about the inflection of my voice. 'It was Lofton, wasn't it?'

Wexler gave one short nod and St. Louis walked away shaking his head.

'Who was he meeting?'

'That's it, Jack. We're not going to get into that with you.'

'I'm his brother. This is his wife.'

'It's all under investigation but if you're looking for doubts, there aren't any. We were up there. He killed himself. He used his own gun, he left a note and we got GSR on his hands. I wish he didn't do it. But he did.'

2
....

In the winter in Colorado the earth comes out in frozen chunks when they dig through the frost line with the backhoe to open up a grave. My brother was buried in Green Mountain Memorial Park in Boulder, a spot not more than a mile from the house where we grew up. As kids we were driven by the cemetery on our way to summer camp hikes in Chautauqua Park. I don't think we ever once looked at the stones as we passed and thought of the confines of the cemetery as our own final destination, but now that was what it was to be for Sean.

Green Mountain stood over the cemetery like a huge altar, making the small gathering at his grave seem even smaller. Riley, of course, was there, along with her parents and mine, Wexler and St. Louis, a couple dozen or so other cops, a few high school friends that neither Sean nor I nor Riley had stayed in touch with and me. It wasn't the official police burial with all the fanfare and colors. That ritual was reserved for those who fell in the line of duty. Though it could be argued that it was still a line-of-duty death, it wasn't considered one by the department. So Sean didn't get the Show and most of the Denver police force stayed away. Suicide is believed to be contagious by many in the thin blue line.

I was one of the pallbearers. I took the front along with my father. Two cops I didn't know before that day, but who were on Sean's CAPs team, took the middle, and Wexler and St. Louis were on the back. St. Louis was too tall and Wexler too short. Mutt and Jeff. It gave the coffin an uneven cant at the back as we carried it. I think it must have looked odd. My mind wandered as we struggled with the weight and I thought of Sean's body pitching around inside it.

I didn't say much to my parents that day, though I rode with them in the limousine with Riley and her parents. We had not talked of anything meaningful in many years and even Sean's death could not penetrate the barrier. After my sister's death twenty years before, something in them changed toward me. It seemed that I, as the survivor of the accident, was suspect for having done just that. Survived. I am also sure that since that time I have continued to disappoint them in the choices I have made. I think of these as small disappointments accruing over time like interest in a bank account until it was enough for them to comfortably retire on. We are strangers. I see them only on the required holidays. And so there was nothing that I could say to them that would matter and there was nothing they could say to me. Aside from the occasional hurt-animal sound of Riley crying, the inside of the limo was as quiet as the inside of Sean's casket.

After the funeral I took two weeks of vacation and the one week of bereavement leave the paper allowed and drove by myself up into the Rockies. The mountains have never lost their glory for me. It's mountains where I heal the fastest.

Headed west on the 70, I drove through the Loveland Pass and over the peaks to Grand Junction. I did it slowly, taking three days. I stopped to ski; sometimes I just stopped on the turnouts to think. After Grand Junction I diverted south and made it to Telluride the next day. I kept the Cherokee in four-wheel drive the whole way. I stayed in Silverton because the rooms were cheaper and skied every day for a week. I spent the nights drinking Jagermeister in my room or near the fire-place of whatever ski lodge I stopped in. I tried to exhaust my body with the hope that my mind would follow. But I couldn't succeed. It was all Sean. Out of space. Out of time. His last message was a riddle my mind could not put aside.

For some reason my brother's noble calling had betrayed him. It had killed him. The grief that this simple conclusion brought me would not ebb, even when I was gliding down the slopes, the wind cutting in behind my sunglasses and pulling tears from my eyes.

I no longer questioned the official conclusion but it had not been Wexler and St. Louis who had convinced me. I did that on my own. It was the erosion of my resolve by time and by facts. As each day went by, the horror of what he had done was somehow easier to believe and even accept. And then there was Riley. On the day after that first night she had told me something that even Wexler and St. Louis hadn't known yet. Sean had been going once a week to see a psychologist. Of course, there were counseling services available to him through the department, but he had chosen this secret path because he didn't want his position to be undermined by rumors.

I came to realize he was seeing the therapist at the same time I went to him wanting to write about Lofton. I thought maybe he was trying to spare me the same anguish that the case had brought him. I liked the thought that that was what he was doing and I tried to hold on to that idea during those days up in the mountains.

In front of the hotel room mirror one night after too many drinks, I contemplated shaving my beard off and cutting my hair short like Sean's had been. We were identical twins – same hazel eyes, light brown hair, lanky build – but not many people realized that. We had always gone to great lengths to forge separate identities. Sean wore contacts and pumped iron to put muscle on his frame. I wore glasses, had had a beard since college, and hadn't picked up the weights since high school basketball. I also had the scar from that woman's ring in Breckenridge. My battle scar.

Sean went into the service after high school and then the cops, keeping the crew cut as he went. He later got a CU degree while going part-time. He needed it to get ahead in the department. I bummed around for a couple of years, lived in New York and Paris, and then went the full-time college route. I wanted to be a writer, ended up in the newspaper business. In the back of my mind I told myself it was just a temporary stop. I'd been telling myself that for ten years now, maybe longer.

That night in the hotel room, I looked at myself in the mirror for a long time but I didn't shave off my beard or cut my hair. I kept thinking about Sean under the frozen ground and I had a crushed feeling in my stomach. I decided that when my time came I wanted to be burned. I didn't want to be down there under the ice.

What hooked me deepest was the message. The official police line was this: After my brother left the Stanley Hotel and drove up through Estes Park to Bear Lake, he parked his department car and for a while left the engine running, the heat on. When the heat had fogged the windshield he reached up and wrote his message there with a gloved finger. He wrote it backward so you could read it from outside the car. His last words to a world that included two parents, a wife and a twin brother.

Out of space. Out of time.

I couldn't understand. Time for what? Space for what? He had come to some desperate conclusion, yet he never tested us on it. He had not reached out to me, nor to my parents or Riley. Was it up to us to reach for him, not even knowing of his secret injuries? In my solitude on the road, I concluded that it was not. He should have reached. He should have tried. By not doing so he had robbed us of the chance to rescue him. And in not doing so he had left us unable to be rescued from our own grief and guilt. I realized that much of my grief was actually anger. I was mad at him, my twin, for what he had done to me.

But it's hard to hold a grudge against the dead. I couldn't stay angry with Sean. And the only way to alleviate the anger was to doubt the story. And so the cycle would begin again. Denial, acceptance, anger. Denial, acceptance, anger.

On my last day in Telluride I called Wexler. I could tell he didn't like hearing from me.

'Did you find the informant, the one from the Stanley?'

'No, Jack, no luck. I told you I'd let you know about that.'

'I know. I just still have questions. Don't you?'

'Let it go, Jack. We'll all be better off when we can put this behind us.'

'What about SIU? They already put it behind? Case closed?'

'Pretty much. I haven't talked to them this week.'

'Then why are you still trying to find the informant?'

'I've got questions, just like you. Just loose ends.'

'You changed your mind about Sean?'

'No. I just want to put everything in order. I'd like to know what he talked about with the informant, if they even talked. The Lofton case is still open, you know. I wouldn't mind nailing that one for Sean.'

I noticed he was no longer calling him Mac. Sean had left the clique.

The following Monday I went back to work at the *Rocky Mountain News*. As I entered the newsroom I felt several eyes upon me. But this was not unusual. I often thought they watched me when I came in. I had a gig every reporter in the newsroom wanted. No daily grind, no daily deadlines. I was free to roam the entire Rocky Mountain region and write about one thing. Murder. Everybody likes a good murder story. Some weeks I'd take apart a shooting in the projects, telling the tale of the shooter and the victim and their fateful collision. Some weeks I'd write about a society murder out in Cherry Hill or a bar shooting in Leadville. Highbrow and lowbrow, little murder and big murder. My brother was right, it sold papers if you told it right. And I got to tell it. I got to take my time and tell it right.

Stacked on my desk next to the computer was a foot-high pile of newspapers. This was my main source material for stories. I subscribed to every daily, weekly and monthly newspaper published from Pueblo north to Bozeman. I scoured these for small stories on killings that I could turn into long take outs. There were always a lot to choose from. The Rocky Mountain Empire had a violent streak that had been there since the gold rush. Not as much violence as Los Angeles or Miami or New York, not even close. But I was never short of source material. I was always looking for something new or different about the crime or the investigation, an element of gee whiz or a heart-tugging sadness. It was my job to exploit those elements.

But on this morning I wasn't looking for a story idea. I began looking through the stack for back issues of the *Rocky* and our competition, the *Post*. Suicides are not normal fare for newspapers unless there are unusual circumstances. My brother's death qualified. I thought there was a good chance there had been a story.

I was right. Though the *Rocky* had not published a story, probably in deference to me, the *Post* had run a six-inch story on the bottom of one of the local pages the morning after Sean died.

DPD INVESTIGATOR TAKES LIFE IN NATIONAL PARK

A veteran Denver Police detective who was in charge of the investigation into the slaying of University of Denver student Theresa Lofton was found dead of an apparent self-inflicted gunshot wound Thursday in the Rocky Mountain National Park, officials said.

Sean McEvoy, 34, was found in his unmarked DPD car, which was parked in a lot at Bear Lake near the Estes Park entrance to the rugged mountain park.

The body of the detective was discovered by a park ranger who heard a shot about 5 P.M. and went to the parking lot to investigate.

Park services officials have asked the DPD to investigate the death and the department's Special Investigations Unit is handling the matter. Detective Robert Scalari, who is heading the investigation, said preliminary indications were that the death was a suicide.

Scalari said a note was found at the scene but he

refused to disclose its contents. He said it was believed that McEvoy was despondent over job difficulties, but also refused to discuss what problems he was having.

McEvoy, who grew up and still lived in Boulder, was married but had no children. He was a twelve-year veteran of the police department who rose quickly through the ranks to an assignment on the Crimes Against Persons unit, which handles investigations of all violent crimes in the city.

McEvoy was currently head of the unit and had most recently directed the investigation into the death of Lofton, 19, who was found strangled and mutilated three months ago in Washington Park.

Scalari refused to comment on whether the Lofton case, which remains unsolved, was cited in McEvoy's note or was one of the job difficulties he may have been suffering.

Scalari said it wasn't known why McEvoy went to Estes Park before killing himself. He said the investigation of the death is continuing.

I read the story twice. It contained nothing that I didn't already know but it held a strange fascination for me. Maybe that was because I believed I knew or had the beginnings of an idea why Sean had gone to Estes Park and driven all the way up to Bear Lake. It was a reason I didn't want to think about, though. I clipped the article, put it in a manila file and slid it into a desk drawer.

My computer beeped and a message printed across the top of the screen. It was a summons from the city editor. I was back at work.

Greg Glenn's office was at the back of the newsroom. One wall was glass, enabling him to look out across the rows of pods where the reporters worked and through the windows along the west wall to the mountain line when it wasn't hidden by smog.

Glenn was a good editor who prized a good read more than anything else about a story. That's what I liked about him. In this business editors are of two schools. Some like facts and cram them into a story until it is so overburdened that practically no one will read it to the end. And some like words and never let the facts get in the way. Glenn liked me because I could write and he pretty much let me choose what I wrote about. He never hustled me for copy and never badly dinged up what I turned in. I had long realized that should he ever leave the paper or be demoted or promoted out of the newsroom, all of this most likely would change. City editors made their own nests. If he were gone, I'd probably find myself back on the daily cop beat, writing briefs off the police log. Doing little murders.

I sat down in the cushioned seat in front of his desk as he finished up a phone call. Glenn was about five years older than me. When I'd first started at the *Rocky* ten years earlier, he was one of the hot shot writers like I was now. But eventually he made the move into management. Now he wore a suit every day, had one of those little statues on his desk of a Bronco football player with a bobbing head, spent more time on the phone than on any other activity in his life and always paid careful attention to the political winds blowing out of the corporate home office in Cincinnati. He was a forty-year-old guy with a paunch, a wife, two kids and a good salary that wasn't good enough to buy a house in the neighborhood his wife wanted to live in. He told me all of this once over a beer at the Wynkoop, the only night I'd seen him out in the past four years.

Tacked across one wall of Glenn's office were the last seven days of front pages. Each day, the first thing he did was take the seven-day-old edition down and tack up the latest front page. I guess he did this to keep track of the news and the continuity of our coverage. Or maybe, because he never got bylines as a writer anymore, putting the pages up was a way of reminding himself that he was in charge. Glenn hung up and looked up at me.

'Thanks for coming in,' he said. 'I just wanted to tell you

again that I'm sorry about your brother. And if you feel like you want some more time, it's no problem. We'll work something out.'

'Thanks. But I'm back.'

He nodded but made no move to dismiss me. I knew there was something more to the summons.

'Well, to business then. Do you have anything going at the moment? As far as I remember, you were looking for your next project when ... when it happened. I figure if you are back, then maybe it would be good for you to get busy with something. You know, dive back in.'

It was in that moment that I knew what I would do next. Oh, it had been there all right. But it hadn't come to the surface, not until Glenn asked that question. Then, of course, it was obvious.

'I'm going to write about my brother,' I said.

I don't know if that was what Glenn was hoping I would say, but I think it was. I think he had had his eye on a story ever since he'd heard the cops had met me down in the lobby and told me what my brother had done. He was probably smart enough to know he didn't have to suggest the story, that it would come to me on its own. He just had to ask the simple question.

Anyway, I took the bait. And all things in my life changed after that. As clearly as you can chart anyone's life in retrospect, mine changed with that one sentence, in that one moment when I told Glenn what I would do. I thought I knew something about death then. I thought I knew about evil. But I didn't know anything.

3

········

William Gladden's eyes scanned the happy faces as they moved past him. It was like a giant vending machine. Take your pick. Don't like him? Here comes another. Will she do?

This time none would do. Besides, their parents were too close by. He'd have to wait for the one time one of them made a mistake, walked out on the pier or over to the snack window for cotton candy, leaving their precious one all alone.

Gladden loved the carousel on the Santa Monica Pier. He didn't love it because it was an original, and, according to the story in the display case, it took six years to hand-paint the galloping horses and restore it to its original condition. He didn't love it because it had been featured in lots of movies that he had seen over the years, especially while in Raiford. And he didn't love it because it brought to mind memories of riding with his Best Pal on the merry-go-round at the Sarasota County Fair. He loved it because of the children who rode on it. Innocence and abandonment to pure happiness played on each one's face as it circled again and again to the accompaniment of the calliope. Since arriving from Phoenix he had been coming here. Every day. He knew it might take some time but one day it would eventually pay off and he would be able to fill his order.

As he watched the collage of colors his mind jumped backward as it had so often since Raiford. He remembered his Best Pal. He remembered the black-dark closet with only the band of light at the bottom. He huddled on the floor near the light, near the air. He could see his feet coming that way. Each step. He wished he were older, taller, so that he could reach the top shelf. If only he were, he would have a surprise waiting for his Best Pal.

Gladden came back. He looked around. The ride had ended and the last of the children were making their way to waiting parents on the other side of the gate. There was a line of more children ready to run to the carousel and pick their horse. He looked again for a dark-haired girl with smooth brown skin but saw none. Then he noticed the woman who took the tickets from the children staring at him. Their eyes met and Gladden looked away. He adjusted the strap of his duffel bag. The weight of the camera and the books inside it had pulled it down on his shoulder. He made a note to leave the books in the car next time. He took a last look at the carousel and headed for one of the doors that exited onto the pier.

When he got to the door he casually looked back at the woman. The children screamed as they ran to the wooden horses. Some with parents, most alone. The woman taking tickets had already forgotten about him. He was safe.

4

....

Laurie Prine looked up from her terminal and smiled when I walked in. I was hoping she'd be there. I came around the counter and pulled an extra chair away from an empty desk and sat down next to hers. It looked like a slow moment at the *Rocky* library.

'Oh no,' she said cheerfully. 'When you come in and sit down, I know it's going to be a long one.'

She was referring to the extensive search requests I usually made in preparation for stories. A lot of the crime stories I wrote spiraled into wide-ranging law enforcement issues. I always needed to know what else had been written about the subject and where.

'Sorry,' I said, a feigned contrition. 'This one might keep you with Lex and Nex the rest of the day.'

'You mean, *if* I can get to it. What do you need?'

She was attractive in an understated way. She had dark hair I had never seen in anything other than a braid, brown eyes behind the steel-rimmed glasses and full lips that were never painted. She pulled a yellow legal pad over in front of her, adjusted her glasses and picked up a pen, ready to take down the list of things I wanted. Lexis and Nexis were computer databases that carried most major and not so major newspapers in the country, as well as court rulings and a whole host of other parking lots on the information highway. If you were trying to see how much had been written on a specific subject or particular story, the Lexis/Nexis network was the place to start.

'Police suicide,' I said. 'I want to find out everything I can about it.'

Her face stiffened. I guessed she suspected the search was for personal reasons. The computer time is expensive and the company strictly forbids its use for personal reasons.

'Don't worry, I'm on a story. Glenn just okayed the assignment.'

She nodded but I wondered if she believed me. I assumed she would check with Glenn. Her eyes returned to her yellow pad.

'What I'm looking for is any national statistics on occurrence, any stats on the rate of cop suicide compared to other jobs and the population as a whole, and any mention of think tanks or government agencies that might have studied this. Uh, let's see, what else . . . oh, and anything anecdotal.'

'Anecdotal?'

'You know, any clips on cop suicides that have run. Let's go back five years. I'm looking for examples.'

'Like your . . .'

She realized what she was saying.

'Yes, like my brother.'

'It's a shame.'

She didn't say anything more. I let the silence hang between us for a few moments and then asked her how long she thought the computer search would take. My requests were often given a low priority since I was not a deadline writer.

'Well, it's really a shotgun search, nothing specific. I'm going to have to spend some time on it and you know I'll get pulled when the dailies start coming in. But I'll try. How about late this afternoon, that be okay?'

'Perfect.'

As I went back into the newsroom I checked the overhead clock and saw it was half past eleven. The timing was good for what I needed to do. At my desk I made a call to a source at the cop shop.

'Hey, Skipper, you going to be there?'

'When?'

'During lunch. I might need something. I probably will.'

'Shit. Okay. I'm here. Hey, when'd you get back?'

'Today. Talk to you.'

I hung up, then I put on my long coat and headed out of the newsroom. I walked the two blocks over to the Denver Police Department headquarters, flipped my press pass at the front counter to a cop who didn't bother to look up from his *Post* and went on up to the SIU offices on the fourth floor.

'I've got one question,' Detective Robert Scalari said after I told him what I wanted. 'Are you here as a brother or as a reporter?'

'Both.'

'Sit down.'

Scalari leaned across his desk, maybe, I guessed, so I could appreciate the intricate hair-weaving job he had done to hide his bald spot.

'Listen, Jack,' he said. 'I have a problem with that.'

'What problem?'

'Look, if you were coming to me as a brother who wanted to know why, that would be one thing and I would probably tell you what I know. But if what I tell you is going to end up in the *Rocky Mountain News,* I'm not interested. I've got too much respect for your brother to let what happened to him help sell newspapers. Even if you don't.'

We were alone in a small office with four desks in it. Scalari's words made me angry but I swallowed it back. I leaned toward him so he could see my healthy, full head of hair.

'Let me ask you something, Detective Scalari. Was my brother murdered?'

'No, he wasn't.'

'You are sure it was suicide, right?'

'That is correct.'

'And the case is closed?'

'Right again.'

I leaned back away from him.

'Then that really bothers me.'

'Why is that?'

'Because you're trying to have it both ways. You're telling me the case is closed, yet I can't look at the records. If it is closed, then I should be allowed to look at the case because he was my brother. And if it's closed, that means that, as a reporter, I can't compromise an ongoing investigation by looking at the records, either.'

I let him digest that for a few moments.

'So,' I finally continued, 'going by your own logic, there is no reason why I shouldn't be able to look at the records.'

Scalari looked at me. I could see the anger working behind his cheeks now.

'Listen to me, Jack, there are things in that file better left not known, and certainly not published.'

'I think I'm a better judge of that, Detective Scalari. He was my brother. My twin. I'm not going to hurt him. I'm just trying to make sense of something for myself. If I then write about it, it will be to finally put it in the ground with him. Okay?'

We sat there staring at each other for a long moment. It was his turn and I waited him out.

'I can't help you,' he said finally. 'Even if I wanted to. It's closed. Case is closed. The file went to records for processing. You want it, go see them.'

I stood up.

'Thanks for telling me at the beginning of the conversation.'

I walked out without saying another word. I had known Scalari would blow me off. I went to him because I had to go through the motions and because I wanted to see if I could learn the location of the file.

I went down the stairs that mostly only cops used and into the office of the department's administrative captain. It was fifteen minutes past twelve so the desk in the reception area was empty. I walked past it, knocked on the door and heard a voice tell me to enter.

Inside, Captain Forest Grolon sat behind his desk. He was such a large man that the standard issue desk looked like child's furniture. He was a dark-complected black man with a shaven head. He stood to shake my hand and I was reminded that he topped out above six and a half feet. I figured a scale would have to have 300 on its dial if it were going to take his full measure. I shook his hand and smiled. He had been a

28

source of mine since I was on the daily police beat six years earlier and he was a patrol sergeant. We had both risen through the ranks since then.

'Jack, how's it going? You say you're just back?'

'Yeah, I took some time. I'm okay.'

He didn't mention my brother. He had been one of the few at the funeral and that made it clear how he felt. He sat back down and I took one of the chairs in front of his desk.

Grolon's job had little to do with policing the city. He was in the business end of the department. He was in charge of the annual budget, hiring and training. Firing, too. It had little to do with police work but it was all part of his plan. Grolon wanted to be police chief one day and was gathering a wide variety of experience so when the time came he'd look best for the job. Part of that plan was also to keep contacts in the local media. When the time was right, he'd count on me for a positive profile in the *Rocky*. And I would come through. In the meantime, I could count on him for things as well.

'So what am I missing lunch for?' he said gruffly, which was part of the routine we played. I knew that Grolon preferred meeting me at lunch when his adjutant was out and there was less chance that he would be seen with me.

'You're not missing lunch. You're just getting it late. I want to see the file on my brother. Scalari said he already sent it to get filmed. I thought maybe you could pull it and let me look at it real quick.'

'Why do you want to do that, Jack? Whyn't you let sleeping dogs lie?'

'I've gotta look, Captain. I'm not quoting from it. I just want to look at it. You get it now and I'll be done with it before the microfilm folks even get back from lunch. Nobody will know. Except you and me. And I'll remember it.'

Ten minutes later, Grolon handed me the file. It was as thin as the year-round residents phone book for Aspen. I don't know why but I had expected something thicker, heavier, as if the size of the investigative file bore some resemblance to the significance of the death.

Inside on top was an envelope marked PHOTOS which I put to the side of the desk without opening. Next there was an autopsy report and several standard reports that were paper-clipped together.

I had studied autopsy reports often enough to know that I could skip the pages of endless description of body glands, organs and general condition and go to the last pages, where conclusions were written. And there were no surprises here. Cause of death was a gunshot wound to the head. The word suicide was circled below it. Blood scans for commonly used drugs showed traces of dextromethorphan hydrobromide. Following this entry a lab tech's notes said 'cough suppressant – glove box.' It meant that other than a shot or two of cough syrup from a bottle kept in the car, my brother was stone cold sober when he put the gun in his mouth.

The forensic analysis report contained a subreport labeled GSR, which I knew meant gunshot residue. It stated that a neutron activation analysis of leather gloves worn by the victim found particles of burned gunpowder on the right glove, indicating he had used that hand to fire the weapon. GSR and gas burns were also found in the victim's throat. The conclusion was that the barrel had been in Sean's mouth when the gun discharged.

Next in the packet was an evidence inventory and I saw nothing unusual here. After this I found the witness statement. The witness was Park Ranger Stephen Pena, who was assigned to a one-ranger substation and information booth at Bear Lake.

Witness stated he did not have a view of the parking area while working in the booth. At approx. 4:58 P.M. witness heard a muffled report he identified from experience as a gunshot. He identified the origin as the parking lot and immediately went to investigate the possibility of illegal hunting. At this time there was only one vehicle in the lot and through the partially fogged windows he saw the victim slumped back in the driver's seat. Witness ran to the vehicle but could not open the door because it was locked. Looking closely through the fogged windows he determined that the victim appeared to be deceased because of the massive damage to the rear of the head. Witness then returned to the park booth where he immediately notified authorities and his supervisors. He then returned to the victim's car to await the arrival of authorities.

Witness states that the victim's vehicle was within his sight no more than five seconds after he heard the shot. The car was parked approx. 50 yards from the nearest forest cover or structure. It is believed by the witness to have been impossible for someone to have left the victim's car after the shooting and gotten to the cover without the witness seeing him.

I returned the statement sheet to its place in the packet and glanced through the other reports. There was a page titled Case Report that detailed my brother's last day. He reported to work at 7:30 A.M., had lunch with Wexler at noon and signed out at 2 P.M. to go to the Stanley. He did not tell Wexler or anyone else whom he was going to see.

Attempts by investigators to determine if Sean had actually gone to the Stanley were unsuccessful. All waitresses and busboys in the hotel's restaurant were interviewed and none recalled my brother.

There was a one-page report in the file summarizing Scalari's interview with Sean's psychologist. Somehow, maybe through Riley, he had found out that Sean was seeing the Denver therapist. Dr Colin Dorschner, according to Scalari's report, said Sean was suffering from acute depression brought about by job stress, in particular his failure to close the Lofton case. What was not contained in the interview summary was whether Scalari ever asked Dorschner if he had thought my brother was suicidal. I wondered if Scalari had even asked that question.

The last sheaf of papers in the package was the investigating officer's final report. The last paragraph was Scalari's summary and conclusion.

Based upon physical evidence and the eyewitness account of the death of Detective Sean McEvoy, I/O concludes that the victim died of a self-inflicted gunshot wound after writing a message on the inside of the fogged windshield. The victim was known by colleagues, including I/O, and his wife and psychologist Colin Dorschner to be emotionally burdened by his unsuccessful efforts to clear by arrest the Dec. 19 homicide of Theresa Lofton (case no. 832). It is believed at this time that this disturbance may have led him to take his own life. DPD psychological consultant Dr Armand Griggs said in an interview (2/22) that the message – Out of space – Out of time – written on the windshield could be considered a suicide-style farewell consistent with the victim's state of mind.

At this time, there is no evidence conflicting with the conclusion of suicide.

Submitted 2/24 I/O RJS D-II

Clipping the reports back together, I realized there was only one thing left that I hadn't looked at.

Grolon had decided to go to the cafeteria to pick up a sandwich to go. I was left alone in his office. Probably five minutes passed in stillness while I considered the envelope. I knew that if I looked at the photographs they would become the lasting image in my mind of my brother. I did not want that. But I also knew that I needed to see the photos to know for sure about his death, to help disperse any last doubts.

I opened the envelope quickly so as to not change my mind. As I slid the stack of 8 × 10 color prints out, the first image that greeted me was an establishing shot. My brother's detective car, a white Chevy Caprice, alone at the end of the parking lot. I could see the ranger shack up a low hill from it. The lot had been freshly plowed, a four-foot embankment of snow around the edges.

The next photo was a close-up of the windshield from the outside. The message was barely legible, as the steam had dissipated from the glass. But it was there and through the glass I could also see Sean. His head was snapped back, his jaw up. I went to the next photo and I was inside the car with him. Taken from the passenger side front, his whole body visible. Blood had worked its way like a thick necklace around his neck from the back and then down over the sweater. His heavy snow coat was open. There was spatter on the roof and back side window. The gun was on the seat next to his right thigh.

The rest of the photos were mostly close-ups from various angles. But they did not have the effect on me I thought they would. The sterile lighting robbed my brother of his humanity. He looked like a mannequin. But I found nothing about them as upsetting as the fact that I had once more convinced myself that Sean had indeed taken his own life. I admitted to myself then that I had secretly come with a hope and that it was gone now.

Grolon came back in then. He looked at me with curious eyes. I stood up and placed the file on his desk as he maneuvered around it to his seat. He opened a brown paper bag and removed a plastic-wrapped egg salad sandwich.

'You okay?'

'I'm fine.'

'You want half?'

'No.'

'Well, how do you feel?'

I smiled at the question because I had asked the same thing so many times. It must have thrown him off. He frowned.

'See this?' I said, pointing to the scar on my face. 'I got that for asking somebody that same thing once.'

'Sorry.'

'Don't be. I wasn't.'

5
········

After viewing the file on my brother's death I wanted the details of the Theresa Lofton case. If I was going to write about what my brother did, I had to know what he knew. I had to understand what he had come to understand. Only this time Grolon couldn't help me. The active homicide files were kept under lock and Grolon would see more of a risk than a benefit in attempting to get the Lofton file for me.

After I checked the CAPs squad room and found it emptied for lunch, the first place I looked for Wexler was the Satire. It was a favored place for cops to eat – and drink – at lunch. I saw him there in one of the rear booths. The only problem was, he was with St. Louis. They didn't see me and I debated whether it would be better just to withdraw and try later to get to Wexler alone. But then Wexler's eyes stopped on me. I walked over. I could see by their ketchup-smeared plates that they had finished eating. Wexler had what looked like a Jim Beam and ice on the table in front of him.

'Would ya look at this?' Wexler said good-naturedly.

I slid into the wide booth next to St. Louis. I chose his side so I would be looking at Wexler.

'What is this?' St. Louis mildly protested.

'It's the press,' I said. 'Howzit going?'

'Don't answer,' St. Louis said quickly to Wexler. 'He wants something he can't have.'

'Of course I do,' I said. 'What else is new?'

'Nothing is new, Jack,' Wexler said. 'Is what Big Dog says true? You want something you can't have?'

It was a dance. Friendly patter designed to ferret out the basic nut of information without specifically asking for it and confronting it. It went with the nicknames cops used. I had danced like this many times and I was good at it. They were finesse moves. Like practicing the three-man weave in high school basketball. Keep your eyes open for the ball, watch the other two men at once. I was always the finesse player. Sean was the strength. He was football. I was basketball.

'Not exactly,' I said. 'But I am back on the job again, boys.'

'Oh, here we go,' St. Louis whined. 'Hold on to your hats.'

'So, what's happening on the Lofton case?' I asked Wexler, ignoring St. Louis.

'Whoa there, Jack, are you talking to us as a reporter now?' Wexler asked.

'I'm only talking to you. And that's right, as a reporter.'

'Then no comment on Lofton.'

'So the answer is nothing is happening.'

'I said no comment.'

'Look, I want to see what you've got. The case is almost three months old now. It's going into the dead case file soon if it isn't already there and you know it. I just want to see the file. I want to know what hooked Sean so deep.'

'You're forgetting something. Your brother was ruled a suicide. Case closed. It doesn't matter what hooked him about Lofton. Besides, it's not known as fact that it had anything to do with what he did. It's collateral at best. But we'll never know.'

'Cut the crap. I just saw the file on Sean.' Wexler's eyebrows raised a subliminal amount, I thought. 'It's all there. Sean was fucked up over this case. He was seeing a shrink, he was spending all of his time on it. So don't tell me we'll never know.'

'Look, kid, we –'

'Did you ever call Sean that?' I interrupted.

'What?'

'Kid. Did you ever call him kid?'

Wexler looked confused.

'Nope.'

'Then don't call me it, either.'

Wexler raised his arms in a hands-off manner.

'Why can't I see the file? You're not going anywhere with it.'

'Who says?'

'I do. You're afraid of it, man. You saw what it did to Sean and you don't want it to happen to you. So the case is stuck in a drawer somewhere. It's got dust on it. I guarantee it.'

'You know, Jack, you're seriously full of shit. And if you weren't your brother's brother, I'd throw you outta here on your ass. You're getting me pissed. I don't like being pissed.'

'Yeah? Then imagine how I'm feeling. The thing of it is, I am his brother and I think that cuts me in.'

St. Louis gave a smirking type of laugh meant to belittle me.

'Hey, Big Dog, isn't it about time you went out and watered a fire hydrant or something?' I said.

Wexler burst out with the start of a laugh but quickly contained it. But St. Louis's face turned red.

'Listen, you little fuck,' he said. 'I'll put you –'

'All right, boys,' Wexler intervened. 'All right. Listen, Ray, why don't you go outside and have a smoke? Let me talk to Jackie, straighten him out, and I'll be out.'

I got out of the booth so St. Louis could slide out. He gave me the dead man's stare as he went by. I slid back in.

'Drink up, Wex. No sense acting like there isn't any Beam on the table.'

Wexler grinned and took a pull from his glass.

'You know, twins or not, you're a lot like your brother. You don't give up on things easy. And you can be a smart-ass. You get rid of that beard and the hippie hair and you could pass for him. You'd have to do something about that scar, too.'

'Look, what about the file?'

'What about it?'

'You owe it to him to let me see it.'

'I don't follow, Jack.'

'Yes, you do. I can't put it behind me until I've looked it all over. I'm just trying to understand.'

'You're also trying to write about it.'

'Writing does for me what you got in that glass does for

you. If I can write about it, I can understand it. And I can put it in the ground. That's all I want to do.'

Wexler looked away from me and picked up the check the waitress had left. Then he downed the rest of his drink and slid out of the booth. Standing, he looked down at me and let out a heavy breath redolent of bourbon.

'Come back to the office,' he said. 'I'll give you one hour.'

He held his finger up and repeated himself in case I was confused.

'One hour.'

In the CAPs squad room I used the desk my brother had used. No one had taken it yet. Maybe it was a bad-luck desk now. Wexler was standing at a wall of file cabinets looking through an open drawer. St. Louis was nowhere to be seen, apparently choosing to have nothing to do with this. Wexler finally stepped away from the drawer with two thick files. He placed them in front of me.

'This everything?'

'Everything. You got an hour.'

'C'mon, there's five inches of paper here,' I tried. 'Let me take it home and I'll bring it –'

'See, just like your brother. One hour, McEvoy. Set your watch, because those go back in the drawer in one hour. Make that fifty-nine minutes. You're wasting time.'

I stopped belaboring the point and opened the top file.

Theresa Lofton had been a beautiful young woman who came to the university to study for an education degree. She wanted to be a first-grade teacher.

She was in her first year and lived in a campus dorm. She carried a full curriculum as well as working part-time in the day care center at the university's married-housing dorm.

Lofton was believed to have been abducted on or near the campus on a Wednesday, the day after classes ended for the Christmas break. Most students had already left for the holiday. Theresa was still in Denver for two reasons. She had her job; the day care center didn't close for the holidays until the end of the week. And there was also the problem of her car. She was waiting for a new clutch to be put into the old Beetle so she could make the drive home.

Her abduction was not reported because her roommate and all her friends had already gone home for the holidays. No one knew she was missing. When she didn't show up for work at the day care center on Thursday morning, the manager thought she had simply gone home to Montana early, not completing the week because she wasn't due to return to the job after the Christmas break. It would not be the first time a student pulled this kind of stunt, especially once finals were over and the holiday break beckoned. The manager made no inquiry or report to authorities.

Her body was found Friday morning in Washington Park. The investigators traced her last known movements back to noon on Wednesday when she called the mechanic from the day care center – he remembered children's voices in the background – and he told her the car was ready. She said she would pick it up after work, first stopping at the bank. She did neither. She said good-bye to the day care center manager at noon and went out the door. She was not seen alive again. Except, of course, by her killer.

I only had to look at the photos in the file to realize how the case could have grabbed Sean and put a leash around his heart. They were before-and-after photos. A portrait shot of her, probably for the high school yearbook. A fresh-faced young girl with a whole life ahead of her. She had dark wavy hair and crystal-blue eyes. Each reflected a small star of light, the flash of the camera. There was also a candid of her, in shorts and a tank top. She was smiling, carrying a cardboard box away from a car. The muscles of her slender, tan arms were taut. It looked as though it was a slight strain for her to stand still with the heavy box for the photographer. I turned it over and read in what I guessed was a parent's scrawl: 'Terri's first day on campus! Denver, Colo.'

The other pictures were taken after. There were more of these and I was struck by the number. Why did the cops need so many? Each one seemed like some kind of a terrible invasion, even though the girl was already dead. Theresa Lofton's eyes had lost their brilliance in these photographs. They were open but dull, webbed in a milky caul.

The photos showed the victim lying in about two feet of brush and snow on a slight incline. The news stories had been correct. She was in two pieces. A scarf was tightly wrapped around her neck and her eyes were sufficiently wide and bugged to suggest this was how she died. But the killer apparently had more work to do afterward. The body had been hacked apart at the midriff, the bottom half then placed over the top half in a horrific tableau suggesting that she was performing a sex act on herself.

I realized that Wexler was at the other desk watching me as I looked at the gallery of ghastly photos. I tried not to show my disgust. Or my fascination. I knew now what my brother was protecting me from. I had never seen anything so horrible. I finally looked at Wexler.

'Jesus.'

'Yeah.'

'The stuff the tabs said about it being like the Black Dahlia in L.A., it was close, wasn't it?'

'Yeah. Mac bought a book about it. He called some old horse in the LAPD, too. There were some similarities. The chop job. But that one was fifty years ago.'

'Maybe somebody got the idea from that.'

'Maybe. He thought of that.'

I returned the photos to the envelope and looked back at Wexler.

'Was she a lesbian?'

'No, not as far as we could tell. She had a boyfriend back up in Butte. Good kid. We cleared him. Your brother thought the same thing for a while. Because of what the killer did, you know, with the parts of the body. He thought maybe somebody was getting back at her for being a lezzie. Maybe making some kind of sick statement about something. He never got anywhere with it.'

I nodded.

'You've got forty-five minutes left.'

'You know, that's the first time I've heard you call him "Mac" in a long time.'

'Don't worry about it. Make that forty-four minutes.'

The autopsy report was pretty much anticlimactic after the photos. I noticed that the time of death was set on the first day of Lofton's disappearance. She had been dead more than forty hours when her body was found.

Most of the summary reports dealt with dead ends. Routine investigations of the victim's family, boyfriend, friends on campus, coworkers and even parents of children she cared for, turned up nothing. Almost all were cleared through alibis or other investigative means.

The conclusions in the reports were that Theresa Lofton had not known her killer, that her path had somehow intersected with his, that it had simply been bad luck. The unknown killer was always referred to as a male, though there was no positive proof of this. The victim had not been sexually assaulted. But most violent murderers and mutilators of women were men, and it was believed it would have taken a physically strong person to cut through the body's bone and gristle. No cutting weapon was ever found.

Though the body had nearly completely bled out, there were indications of postmortem lividity, which meant some time had passed between the victim's death and the mutilation. Possibly, according to the report, as long as two or three hours.

Another peculiarity was the timing of when the body was left in the park. It was discovered approximately forty hours after investigators believed Theresa Lofton had been killed. Yet the park was a popular running and walking spot. It was unlikely that the body could have been in place in the open park field for that long without being noticed, even though an early snow considerably cut down on the number of people who passed through. In fact, the report concluded that the body had been in place no more than three hours when it was spotted after dawn by an early morning jogger.

So where was it all that time? The investigators couldn't answer that question. But they had a clue.

The fibers analysis report listed numerous foreign hairs and cotton fibers that had been found on the body and combed out of the hair. These would primarily be used to match a suspect to the victim, once a suspect became known. One particular section of the report had been circled. This section dealt with the recovery of a specific fiber – kapok – found on the body in large quantity. Thirty-three kapok seed hairs had been removed from the body. The number suggested direct contact with the source. The report said that while similar to cotton, kapok fibers were uncommon and primarily found in materials requiring buoyancy, such as boat cushions, life vests and some sleeping bags. I wondered why this section had been circled on the report and asked Wexler.

'Sean thought the kapok fibers were the key to where the body had been during the missing hours. You know, if we found a spot where we found that fiber, which isn't all that common, then we'd have the crime scene. But we never found it.'

Because the reports were in chronological order I could see how theories were considered and discarded. And I could sense a growing desperation in the investigation. It was going nowhere. It was clear that my brother believed Theresa Lofton had crossed paths with a serial killer, the toughest criminal to track. There was a return report from the FBI's National Center for the Analysis of Violent Crime containing a psychological profile of the killer. My brother had also kept a copy in the file of a seventeen-page checklist survey of aspects of the crime he had sent to the bureau's Violent Criminal Apprehension Program. But the VICAP computer's response to the survey was negative. The Lofton killing did not match any other killings across the country in enough details to warrant further attention from the FBI.

The profile the bureau had forwarded was produced by an agent listed on the report as Rachel Walling. It contained a host of generalities that were largely worthless to the investigation because while the characterizations were in depth and possibly even on target, they did not necessarily help the detectives winnow down the millions of men who might qualify as suspects. The profile projected that the killer was most likely a white male, twenty to thirty years old, with unresolved feelings of inadequacy and anger toward women, hence the gross mutilation of the victim's body. He was probably raised by a domineering mother and his father probably was not present in the household or was absorbed in earning a living and forfeited child rearing and development to the mother. The profile classified the killer as 'organized' in his methodology and warned that his seemingly successful completion of the crime and escape from detection could lead him to try further crimes of a similar nature.

The last reports in the first file were investigative summaries of interviews, tips that were checked out and other details from the case that might have meant nothing at the moment they were typed up but could be pivotal later. Through these reports I could chart Sean's growing attachment to Theresa Lofton. In the initial pages she was always referred to as the victim, sometimes Lofton. Later on, he began referring to her as Theresa. And in the last reports, those filed in February before his death, he called her Terri, probably having picked up the diminutive name from her family and friends, or maybe from the back of the photo of her first day on campus. The happy day.

With ten minutes left I closed the file and opened the other one. This one was thinner and seemed to be filled with a hodgepodge of investigative loose ends. There were several letters from citizens offering theories on the killing. One letter was from a medium who said Theresa Lofton's living spirit was circling somewhere above the ozone layer in a high-frequency sound belt. She spoke in a voice so fast that it sounded like a chirp to the untrained ear, but the medium could decipher the chirping and was willing to ask her questions if Sean wanted to. There was no indication from the file that he did.

A supplemental report noted that Theresa's bank and auto repair shop were within walking distance of the campus. Three times detectives walked the routes between her dorm room, the day care center, the bank and the repair shop but came across no witnesses who remembered seeing Theresa on the Wednesday after classes ended. Despite this, my brother's theory – outlined in another supplemental – was that Lofton had been abducted sometime after calling her mechanic from the day care center but before she got to the bank to get money to pay him.

The file also contained a chronological record of the activity of the investigators assigned to the case. Initially, four members of the CAPs squad worked the case full-time. But as little headway was made and more cases came up, the investigative effort was winnowed down to Sean and Wexler. Then just Sean. He wouldn't let it go.

The last entry in the chronological record was made on the day he died. It was just one line: 'Mar. 13 – RUSHER at Stanley. P/R info on Terri.'

'Time.'

I looked up and Wexler was pointing to his watch. I closed the file without protest.

'What's P-slash-R mean?'

'Person Reporting. It meant he got a call.'

'Who is Rusher?'

'We don't know. There's a couple people in the phone book with that name. We called them, they didn't know what the fuck we were talking about. I ran something on NCIC but with just a last name didn't get anything to work with. Bottom line is, we don't know who it was or is. We don't even know if it's a man or woman. We don't know if Sean actually met anybody or not. We found nobody at the Stanley who saw him.'

'Why would he go to meet this person without telling you or leaving some kind of record about who it was? Why'd he go alone?'

'Who knows? We've gotten so many calls on that case, you could spend all day just writing notes. And maybe he didn't know. Maybe all he knew was that someone wanted to talk to him. Your brother was so caught up on this one, he would have gone to meet anybody who said they knew something. I'll let you in on a little secret. It's something that's not in there because he didn't want people around here thinking he was loony. But he went to see that psychic – the medium – that's mentioned in there.'

'What did he get?'

'Nothing. Just some bullshit about the killer being out there wanting to do it again. I mean, it was like – yeah, no kidding, thanks for the tip. Anyway, that's off the record, the psychic stuff. I don't want people thinking Mac was a flake.'

I didn't bother to say anything about the stupidity of what he had just said. My brother had killed himself and yet Wexler was engaged in trying to limit the damage his image might suffer if it was known he had consulted a psychic.

'It doesn't go past this room,' I said instead. After a few moments of silence I said, 'So what's your theory on what happened that day, Wex? Off the record, I mean.'

'My theory? My theory is he went out there and whoever it was who'd called him didn't show. It was another dead end for him and it tipped the scale. He drove up to that lake and he did what he did ... Are you going to write a story about him?'

'I don't know. I think so.'

'Look, I don't know how to say this but here goes. He was your brother but he was my friend. I might've even known him better than you. Leave it alone. Just let it go.'

I told him I would think about it but it was only to placate him. I had already decided. I left then, checking my watch to make sure I had enough time to get out to Estes Park before dark.

6
....

I didn't get to the parking lot at Bear Lake until after five. I realized it was just as it had been for my brother, deserted. The lake was frozen and the temperature was dropping quickly. The sky was already purple and going dark. It wasn't much of a draw for locals or tourists this late in the day.

As I drove through the lot I thought about why he had picked this place to come. As far as I knew it had nothing to do with the Lofton case. But I thought I knew why. I parked where he had parked and just sat there thinking.

There was a light on in the ceiling of the overhang above the front of the ranger shack. I decided to get out and see if Pena, the witness, was there. Then another thought struck me. I slid over to the passenger side of the Tempo. I took a couple of deep breaths, then opened the door and started running for the woods where they grew closest to the car. As I ran I counted by thousands out loud. I was at eleven thousand by the time I had gotten over the snowbank and reached the cover.

Standing there in the woods, a foot deep in snow without boots on, I bent over and put my hands on my knees as I caught my breath. There was no way a shooter could have gotten into the woods to hide if Pena had been out of the shack as quickly as he had reported. I finally stopped gulping the air and headed toward the ranger's shack, debating how to approach him. As a reporter or a brother?

It was Pena behind the window. I could see the nameplate on his uniform. He was locking a desk when I looked through the window. He was calling it a day.

'Can I help you, sir? I'm closing up.'

45

'Yes, I was wondering if I could ask you a few questions.'

He came out, eyeing me suspiciously because I obviously wasn't dressed for a hike in the snow. I had on jeans and Reeboks, a corduroy shirt beneath a thick woolen sweater. I had left my long coat in the car and I was very cold.

'My name is Jack McEvoy.'

I waited a moment to see if it registered. It didn't. He had probably only seen the name written in reports he had to sign, or in the newspaper. Its pronunciation – Mac-a-voy – didn't jibe with its spelling.

'My brother . . . he was the one you found a couple weeks ago.'

I pointed toward the lot.

'Oh,' he said, understanding. 'In the car. The officer.'

'Uh, I've been with the police all day, looking at the reports and stuff. I just wanted to come out and take a look. It's hard, you know . . . to accept it.'

He nodded and tried to hide a quick glance at his watch.

'I just have a few quick questions. You were inside there when you heard it? The shot?'

I spoke quickly, not giving him the chance to stop me.

'Yes,' he said. He looked like he was trying to decide something and then he did. He continued. 'I was locking up just like tonight, 'bout to go home. I heard it. It was one of those things, I kinda knew what it was. I don't know why. Really what I thought was that it might be poachers after the deer. I came out pretty quick and the first place I looked was the lot. I saw his car. Could see him in there. All the windows were fogged up pretty good but I could see him. He was behind the wheel. Something about the way he was leaning back, I knew what happened . . . Sorry it was your brother.'

I nodded and studied the ranger's shack. Just a small office and storage room. I realized that five seconds was probably a long estimate from the time Pena heard the shot until he saw the lot.

'There was no pain,' Pena said.

'What?'

'If it's something you want to know. There was no physical

pain, I don't think. I ran to the car. He was dead. It was instant.'

'The police reports said you couldn't get to him. The doors were locked.'

'Yeah, I tried the door. But I could tell he was gone. I came back up here to make the calls.'

'How long do you think he was parked there before he did it?'

'I don't know. Like I told the police, I don't have a view of the lot. I'd been in the shed – I got a heater in there – oh, I'd say at least a half hour before I heard the shot. He could have been parked there the whole time. Thinking about it, I guess.'

I nodded.

'You didn't see him out on the lake, did you? You know, before the shot.'

'On the lake? No. Nobody was on the lake.'

I stood there trying to think of something else.

'Did they come up with any reason why?' Pena asked. 'Like I said, I know he was an officer.'

I shook my head no. I didn't want to get into it with this stranger. I thanked him and started back to the lot while he locked the shack door. The Tempo was the only car in the plowed lot. I thought of something and turned back.

'How often do they plow?'

Pena stepped away from the door.

'After every snow.'

I nodded and thought of something else.

'Where do you park?'

'We've got an equipment yard a half mile down the road. I park there and walk up the trail in the morning, down at quitting time.'

'You want a ride?'

'Nah. Thanks, though. The trail will get me there quicker.'

The whole way back to Boulder I thought of the last time I had been to Bear Lake. It was also winter then. But the lake wasn't frozen, not all the way. And when I left that time, I felt just as cold and alone. And guilty.

*

47

Riley looked as if she had aged ten years since I had seen her at the funeral. Even so, I was immediately struck when she opened the door by what I hadn't realized before. Theresa Lofton looked like a nineteen-year-old Riley McEvoy. I wondered if Scalari or anybody else had asked the shrinks about that.

She asked me in. She knew she looked bad. After she opened the door she casually raised her hand to the side of her face to hide it. She tried a feeble smile. We went into the kitchen and she asked if I wanted her to make coffee but I said I wasn't staying long. I sat down at the kitchen table. It seemed that whenever I visited we would gather around the kitchen table. Even with Sean gone that hadn't changed.

'I wanted to tell you that I'm going to write about Sean.'

She was silent for a long time and she didn't look at me. She got up and started emptying the dishwasher. I waited.

'Do you have to?' she finally asked.

'Yes . . . I think so.'

She said nothing.

'I'm going to call the psychologist, Dorschner. I don't know if he'll talk to me, but now that Sean's gone I don't see why not. But, uh, he might call you for permission . . .'

'Don't worry, Jack, I won't try to stop you.'

I nodded my thanks but I noted the edge to her words.

'I was with the cops today and I went up to the lake.'

'I don't want to hear about it, Jack. If you have to write about it that's your choice. Do what you have to do. But my choice is that I don't want to hear about it. And if you do write about Sean, I won't read that, either. I have to do what *I* have to do.'

I nodded and said, 'I understand. There is one thing I need to ask, though. Then I'll leave you out of it.'

'What do you mean, leave me out of it?' she asked angrily. 'I wish I could be left out of it. But I'm in it. For the rest of my life I'm in it. You want to write about it? You think that's a way to get rid of it? What do *I* do, Jack?'

I looked down at the floor. I wanted to go but didn't know

how to exit. Her pain and anger radiated toward me like heat from a closed oven.

'You want to know about that girl,' she said in a low, calmer voice. 'That's what all the detectives asked about.'

'Yes. Why did this one . . . ?'

I didn't know how to phrase the question.

'Why did it make him forget about everything good in his life? The answer is I don't know. I don't goddamn know.'

I could see anger and tears welling in her eyes again. It was as if her husband had deserted her for another woman. And here I was, as close a flesh and blood approximation of Sean as she would ever see now. No wonder she was venting her anger and pain at me.

'Did he talk about the case at home?' I asked.

'Not especially. He told me about cases from time to time. This one didn't seem that different except for what happened to her. He told me what the killer did to her. He told me how he had to look at her. After, I mean. I know it bothered him but a lot of things bothered him. A lot of cases. He didn't want anybody to get away. He always said that.'

'But this time he went to see that doctor.'

'He'd had dreams and I told him he should go. I made him go.'

'What were the dreams?'

'That he was there. You know, when it happened to her. He dreamed he saw it but couldn't do anything to stop it.'

Her comment made me think of another death a long time ago. Sarah. Falling through the ice. I remembered the helpless feeling of watching and being unable to do anything. I looked at Riley.

'You know why Sean went up there?'

'No.'

'Was it because of Sarah?'

'I said I don't know.'

'That was before we knew you. But that was where she died. An accident . . .'

'I know, Jack. But I don't know what it had to do with anything. Not now.'

49

I didn't, either. It was one of many confusing thoughts but I couldn't let it go.

Before heading back to Denver I drove over to the cemetery. I don't know what I was doing. It was dark and there had been two snows since the funeral. It took me fifteen minutes just to find the spot where Sean was in the ground. There was no stone yet. I found it by finding the one next to it. My sister's.

On Sean's there were a couple of pots of frozen flowers and a plastic sign sticking out of the snow with his name on it. There were no flowers on Sarah's. I looked at Sean's spot for a while. It was a clear night and the moonlight was enough for me to see. My breath came out in clouds.

'How come, Sean?' I asked out loud. 'How come?'

I realized what I was doing and looked around. I was the only one in the cemetery. The only one alive. I thought about what Riley had said about Sean not wanting anybody to get away. And I thought about how I didn't even care about such things, as long as it made a good thirty-inch story. How had we separated so completely? My brother and I. My twin. I didn't know. It just made me feel sad. Made me feel like maybe the wrong one was in the ground.

I remembered what Wexler had said that first night when they came for me and told me about my brother. He talked about all the shit coming down the pipe finally being too much for Sean. I still didn't believe it. But I had to believe something. I thought of Riley and the pictures of Theresa Lofton. And I thought of my sister slipping through the ice. I believed then that the girl's murder had infected my brother with the most desperate kind of hopelessness. I believed he became haunted by that hopelessness and the crystal-blue eyes of the girl who had been cut in half. And since he didn't have his brother to turn to, he turned to his sister. He went to the lake that took her. And then he joined her.

I walked out of the cemetery without looking back.

7

· · · · · · · · ·

Gladden posted himself at a spot along the railing on the other side from where the woman took the tickets from the children. She couldn't see him. But once the great carousel began turning, he was able to study each child. Gladden pushed his fingers through his dyed blond hair and looked around. He was pretty sure everybody else regarded him as just another parent.

The ride was starting again. The calliope was grinding out the strains of a song Gladden could not identify and the horses began their bobbing, counterclockwise turn. Gladden had never actually ridden on the carousel, though he had seen that many of the parents got on with their children. He thought that it might be too risky for him to do it.

He noticed a girl of about five clinging desperately to one of the black stallions. She was leaning forward with her tiny arms wrapped around the candy-striped pole that came up through the painted horse's neck. One side of her little pink shorts had ridden up the inside of her thigh. Her skin was coffee brown. Gladden reached into his duffel and brought out the camera. He amped up the shutter speed to cut down on movement blurring and pointed the camera at the carousel. He focused and waited for the girl to come around again.

It took him two revolutions of the carousel but he believed he got the shot and brought the camera back down. He looked around just to be sure he was cool and he noticed a man leaning on the railing about twenty feet to his right. The man hadn't been there before. And most alarming, he was wearing a sport coat and tie. The man was either a pervert or a policeman. Gladden decided he'd better leave.

Out on the pier the sun was almost blinding. Gladden shoved the camera into the duffel and pulled his mirrored shades out. He decided to walk out further on the pier to where it was crowded. He could lose this guy if he had to. If he was actually being followed. He walked about halfway out, nice and steady, acting cool. Then he stopped along the railing and turned and leaned back against it as if he wanted to catch a few rays. He turned his face up toward the sun but his eyes, behind the mirrors, took in the area of the pier he had just come from.

For a few moments there was nothing. He didn't see the man in the sport coat and tie. Then he saw him, jacket over the arm, sunglasses on, walking along the front of the arcade concession, slowly moving toward Gladden.

'Fuck!' Gladden said out loud.

A woman sitting on a nearby bench with a young boy looked at Gladden with baleful eyes when she and the boy heard the exclamation.

'Sorry,' Gladden said.

He turned and looked around the rest of the pier. He had to think quickly. He knew cops usually worked in pairs while in the field. Where was the other one? It took him thirty seconds but he picked her out of the crowd. A woman about thirty yards behind the man in the tie. She was wearing long pants and a polo shirt. Not as formal as the man. She blended in, except for the two-way radio down at her side. Gladden could see that she was trying to hide it. As he watched, she turned so that her back was to him and began talking into the two-way.

She had just called for backup. Had to be. He had to stay cool but come up with a plan. The man in the tie was maybe twenty yards away. Gladden stepped away from the railing and started walking at a slightly faster pace toward the end of the pier. He did what the woman cop had done. He used his body as a shield and pulled the duffel bag around so that it was in front of him. He unzipped it and reached in and grabbed the camera. Without pulling it out, he turned it over until he found the CLEAR switch and erased the chip. There wasn't much on there. The girl on the carousel, a few kids at the public showers. No big loss.

That done, he again proceeded down the pier. He took his cigarettes out of the bag and, using his body as a shield, turned around and huddled against the wind to light one. When he had the smoke lit, he looked up and saw the two cops were getting closer. He knew they thought they had him bottled. He was going to the dead end of the pier. The woman had caught up to the man and they were talking as they closed in. Probably deciding whether to wait for the backup, Gladden thought.

Gladden quickly walked toward the bait shop and the pier offices. He knew the layout of the end of the pier well. On two occasions during the week he had followed children with their parents from the carousel to the end of the pier. He knew that on the other side of the bait shop were stairs that led to the observation deck on the roof.

As he turned the corner of the shop out of sight of the cops, Gladden ran down the side to the back and then up the steps. He could now look down on the pier in front of the shop. The two cops were there below, talking again. Then the man followed Gladden's path and the woman stayed back. They weren't going to take a chance on letting him slip away. A question suddenly occurred to Gladden. How did they know? A cop in a suit just doesn't happen by the pier. The cops had gone there for a purpose. Him. But how did they know?

He broke away from those thoughts to the situation at hand. He needed a diversion. The man would soon figure out he wasn't with the fishermen at the end of the pier and come up to the observation deck looking for him. He saw the trash can in the corner by the wooden railing. He ran to it and looked in. It was almost empty. He put the duffel bag down, lifted the trash can over his head and with a running start moved to the railing. He threw it out as far as he could, then watched it go over the heads of two fishermen below and down into the water. It made a large splash and he heard a young boy yell, 'Hey!'

'Man in the water!' Gladden yelled. 'Man in the water!'

He then grabbed the duffel bag and quickly moved back to the rear railing of the deck. He looked for the woman cop. She was still there below him but had clearly heard the splash and his yelling. A couple of children ran around the side of the bait shop to see what the yelling and excitement were about. After what seemed to be a physical hesitation, the woman followed the children around the corner of the building to the source of the splash and ensuing commotion. Gladden hooked the duffel over his shoulder and quickly climbed over the railing, lowered himself down and then dropped the final five feet. He started running down the pier toward land.

About halfway to land Gladden saw the two beach cops on bikes. They wore shorts and blue polo shirts. Ridiculous. He'd watched them the day before, amused that they even considered themselves cops. Now he ran right toward them, waving his hands to make them stop.

'Are you the backup?' he yelled when he got to them. 'They're at the end of the pier. The perp's in the water. He jumped. They need your help and they need a boat. They sent me to get you.'

'Go!' one of the cops yelled to his partner.

As one started pedaling away, the other pulled a two-way off his belt and started radioing for a lifeguard boat.

Gladden waved his thanks for their speedy reaction and started walking away. After a few seconds he looked back and saw the second cop pedaling toward the end of the pier. Gladden started his run again.

On the crest of the bridge from the beach up to Ocean Avenue, Gladden looked back and could see the commotion at the end of the pier. He lit another cigarette and took his sunglasses off. Cops are so stupid, he thought. They get what they deserve. He hurried up to the street surface, crossed Ocean and walked down to the Third Street Promenade, where he was sure he could lose himself in the crowds at the popular shopping and dining area. Fuck those cops, he thought. They had their one chance and blew it. That's all they get.

On the promenade he walked down a corridor that led to several small fast-food restaurants. The excitement had left Gladden famished and he went into one of these places for a slice of pizza and a soda. As he waited for the girl to warm up the pizza in the oven, he thought of the girl on the carousel and wished he hadn't cleared the camera. But how could he know he'd so easily slip away?

'I should have known,' he said angrily out loud. Then he looked around to make sure the girl behind the counter hadn't noticed. He studied her for a moment and found her unattractive. She was too old. She could practically have children herself.

As he watched, she used her fingers to gingerly pull the slice of pizza out of the oven and onto a paper plate. She licked her fingers afterward – she had burned them – and put Gladden's meal on the counter. He took it back to his table but didn't eat it. He didn't like other people touching his food.

Gladden wondered how long he would have to wait until it was safe to go back down to the beach and get the car. Good thing it was in an overnight lot. Just in case. No matter what, they must not get to his car. If they got to his car, they would open the trunk and get his computer. If they got that, they would never let him go.

The more he thought about the episode with the cops, the angrier he became. The carousel was now lost to him. He couldn't go back. At least not for a long time. He'd have to put out a message to the others on the network.

He still couldn't figure out how it had happened. His mind bounced along the possibilities, even considering someone on the net, but then the ball stopped on the woman who took the tickets. She must have made the complaint. She was the only one who saw him each of the days. It was her.

He closed his eyes and leaned his head back against the wall. In his mind he was at the carousel, approaching the ticket taker. He had his knife. He was going to teach her a lesson about minding her own business. She thought she could just –

He sensed someone's presence. Someone was looking at him.

Gladden opened his eyes. The two cops from the pier were standing there. The man, drenched in sweat, raised his hand and signaled Gladden to stand up.

'Get up, asshole.'

The two cops said nothing of value to Gladden on the way in. They had taken the duffel bag, searched him, handcuffed him and told him he was under arrest but they refused to say what for. They took his cigarettes and wallet. The camera was the only thing he cared about. Luckily, he hadn't brought his books with him this time.

Gladden considered what was in the wallet. None of it mattered, he decided. The Alabama license identified him as Harold Brisbane. He had gotten it through the network, trading photos for IDs. He had another ID in the car and he'd kiss Harold Brisbane good-bye as soon as he got out of custody.

They didn't get the keys to the car. They were hidden in the wheel well. Gladden had been prepared for the eventuality that he might be popped. He knew he had to keep the cops away from the car. He had learned from experience to take such precautions, to always plan for the worst case scenario. That was what Horace had taught him at Raiford. All those nights together.

In the detective bureau of the Santa Monica Police Department, he was roughly but silently ushered into a small interview room. They sat him down on one of the gray steel chairs and took off one of the cuffs, which they then locked to an iron ring attached by a bolted clamp to the top center of the table. The detectives then walked out and he was left alone for more than an hour.

On the wall he faced there was a mirrored window and Gladden knew he was in a viewing room. He just couldn't figure out for sure whom they would have on the other side of the glass. He saw no way that he could have been tracked from Phoenix or Denver or anywhere else.

At one point he thought he could hear voices from the other side of the glass. They were in there, watching him, looking at him, whispering. He closed his eyes and turned his chin down to his chest so they couldn't see his face. Then suddenly he raised his face with a leering, maniacal grin and he yelled, 'You'll be fucking sorry!'

That ought to put a stutter in the mind of whoever the cops have in there, he thought. That fucking ticket taker, he thought again. He went back to his daydream of revenge against her.

In the ninetieth minute of his cloistering in the room, the door finally opened and the same two cops came in. They took chairs, the woman directly across from him and the man to his left side. The woman put a tape recorder on the table along with the duffel bag. This was nothing, he told himself over and over like a mantra. He'd be kicked loose before the sun was down.

'Sorry to make you wait,' the woman said cordially.

'No problem,' he said. 'Can I have my cigarettes?'

He nodded toward the duffel bag. He didn't really want a smoke, he just wanted to see if the camera was still in there. You couldn't trust the fucking cops. He didn't even need Horace to teach him that. The detective ignored his request and turned on the tape recorder. She then identified herself as Detective Constance Delpy and her partner as Detective Ron Sweetzer. Both were with the Exploited Child Unit.

Gladden was surprised that she seemed to be taking the lead here. She looked to be about five to eight years younger than Sweetzer. She had blond hair kept in an easily managed short style. She was maybe fifteen pounds overweight and that was mostly in her hips and upper arms. Gladden guessed she worked out on the pipes. He also thought she was a lesbian. He could tell these things. He had a sense.

Sweetzer had a washed-out face and a laconic demeanor. He had lost hair in a pattern that left him with a thin strip of growth down the center of his pate. Gladden decided to concentrate on Delpy. She was the one.

Delpy took a card from her pocket and read Gladden his constitutional rights.

'What do I need those for?' he asked when she was done. 'I didn't do anything wrong.'

'Do you understand those rights?'

'What I don't understand is why I'm here.'

'Mr Brisbane, do you under –?'

'Yes.'

'Good. By the way, your driver's license is from Alabama. What are you doing out here?'

'That's my business. I'd like to contact a lawyer now. I'm not answering any questions. Like I said, I do understand those rights you just read.'

He knew that what they wanted was his local address and the location of his car. What they had was nothing. But the fact that he had run would probably be enough for a local judge to find probable cause and give them a warrant to search his premises and car if they knew where those were. He couldn't allow that, no matter what.

'We'll talk about your lawyer in just a moment,' Delpy said. 'But I want to give you the chance to clear this up, maybe even walk out of here without wasting your money on a lawyer.'

She opened the duffel bag and pulled out the camera and the bag of Starburst candy the kids liked so much.

'What is all of this?' she asked.

'Looks pretty evident to me.'

She held the camera up and looked at it as if she had never seen one before.

'What is this used for?'

'Takes pictures.'

'Of children?'

'I'd like a lawyer now.'

'What about this candy? What do you do with that? Do you give that to children?'

'I'd *like* to speak to a lawyer.'

'Fuck the lawyer,' Sweetzer said angrily. 'We've got your ass, Brisbane. You were taking pictures of kids at the showers. Little naked kids with their mothers. You fucking disgust me.'

Gladden cleared his throat and looked at Delpy with dead eyes.

'I don't know anything about that. But I do have a question. I have to ask, where is the crime? You know? I'm not saying I did it, but if I did, I didn't know taking photos of children at the beach was against the law now.'

Gladden shook his head as if confused. Delpy shook her head as if disgusted.

'Detective Delpy, I can assure you that there are numerous legal precedents that have held that observation of acceptable public nudity – in this case, a mother cleaning up a young child at the beach – cannot be transcribed as prurient interest. You see, if the photographer who took such a picture committed a crime, then you'd have to prosecute the mother as well for providing the opportunity. But you probably know all of this. I'm sure one of you spent the last hour and a half consulting the city attorney.'

Sweetzer leaned close to him across the table. Gladden noted the smell of cigarettes and barbecued potato chips on his breath. He guessed Sweetzer had eaten the chips on purpose, just so his breath would be intolerable during the interrogation.

'Listen to me, asshole, we know exactly what you are and what you're doing. I've worked rape, homicide ... but you guys, you are the lowest form of life there is on the planet. You don't want to talk to us? Fine, no sweat. What we're going to do is take you down to Biscailuz tonight and put you in with the general population. I know some people in there, Brisbane. And I'm going to put out the word. Know what happens to pedophiles in there?'

Gladden turned his head slowly until he was staring calmly into Sweetzer's eyes for the first time.

'Detective, I'm not sure but I think your breath alone might constitute cruel and unusual punishment. If by chance

I am ever convicted of taking photographs at the beach, I might make it a point of appeal.'

Sweetzer swung his arm back.

'Ron!'

He froze, looked at Delpy and slowly lowered his arm. Gladden had not even flinched at the threat. He would have welcomed the blow. He knew it would have helped him in court.

'Cute,' Sweetzer said. 'What we've got here is a jailhouse lawyer thinks he knows all the angles. That's nice. Well, you're going to be filing some briefs tonight, if you know what I mean.'

'Can I call a lawyer now,' Gladden said in a bored voice.

He knew what they were doing. They had nothing and they were trying to scare him into making a mistake. But he wouldn't accommodate them because he was too smart for them. And he suspected that deep down they knew he was.

'Look, I'm not going to Biscailuz and we all know it. What have you got? You've got my camera, which, I don't know if you checked, has no pictures in it. And you've got some ticket taker or a lifeguard or somebody else who says I took some photos. But there is no evidence of that other than their word. And if you just had them looking through the mirror at me, then that identification is tainted as well. It wasn't by any stretch of the imagination an unbiased line up.'

He waited but they said nothing. He was in charge now.

'But the bottom line to this whole matter is that whoever you had behind that glass, she or he is a witness to something that wasn't even a crime. How that equates to a night in the county jail, I don't know. But maybe you can explain that to me, Detective Sweetzer, if it isn't too much of a strain on your intelligence.'

Sweetzer stood up, knocking his chair back into the wall. Delpy reached an arm over, this time physically restraining him.

'Take it easy, Ron,' she ordered. 'Sit down. Just sit down.'

Sweetzer did as instructed. Delpy then looked at Gladden.

'If you are going to continue this, I'll have to make that call,' he said. 'Where's the phone, please?'

'You'll get the phone. Right after you're booked. But you can forget the cigarettes. The county jail is a smoke-free facility. We care about your health.'

'Booked on what charge? You can't hold me.'

'Pollution of public waterways, vandalism of city property. Evading a police officer.'

Gladden's eyebrows went up in a questioning look. Delpy smiled at him.

'You forgot something,' she said. 'The trash can you threw into Santa Monica Bay.'

She nodded in victory and turned off the tape recorder.

In the holding cell of the police station Gladden was allowed to make his call. When he held the receiver to his ear he smelled the industrial-strength soap they had given him to wash the ink off his fingers. It served as a reminder to him that he had to get out before the prints went through the national computer. He dialed a number that he had committed to memory the first night he had made it to the coast. Krasner was on the network list.

At first the lawyer's secretary was going to put him off but Gladden said to tell Mr Krasner that the caller was referred by Mr Pederson, the name suggested on the network bulletin board. Krasner came on the line quickly after that.

'Yes, this is Arthur Krasner, what can I do for you?'

'Mr Krasner, my name is Harold Brisbane and I have a problem.'

Gladden then proceeded to tell Krasner in detail what had happened to him. He spoke low into the phone because he was not alone. There were two other men in the holding cell, waiting to be transferred to the county jail at Biscailuz Center. One was lying on the floor asleep, an addict on the nod. The other was sitting on the opposite side of the cell but he was watching Gladden and attempting to listen to him because there was nothing else to do. Gladden thought he might be a plant, a cop posing as a prisoner so he could eavesdrop on his call to the lawyer.

Gladden left nothing out save for his real name. When he was done Krasner was silent for a long time.

'What's that noise?' he finally asked.

'Guy sleeping on the floor in here. Snoring.'

'Harold, you shouldn't be amongst people like that,' Krasner lamented in a patronizing tone Gladden disliked. 'We've got to do something.'

'That's why I'm calling.'

'My fee for my work on this today and tomorrow will be one thousand dollars. That is a generous discount. I offer it to those referrals I receive from ... Mr Pederson. If my involvement goes further than tomorrow, then we'll have to discuss it. Will it be a problem for you to have the money?'

'No, no problem.'

'What about bail? After my fee, what can you do on bail? It sounds like pledging property is out of the question. Bondsmen need ten percent of the bail fixed by the judge. That amount is their fee. You won't get it back.'

'Yes, forget property. After taking care of your exorbitant fee I can probably go up to five more. That's immediately. I can get more but it might be difficult. I want to keep it to five max and I want to get out as soon as possible.'

Krasner ignored the remark about his fee.

'Is that five thousand?' he asked.

'Yes, of course. Five thousand. What can you do with it?'

Gladden figured Krasner was probably kicking himself over discounting his inflated fee.

'Okay, that means you can handle fifty thousand bail. I think we're in good shape. It's a felony arrest for now. But the fleeing and the pollution are wobblers, meaning they can be filed as either felonies or misdemeanors. I am sure that they will go low on them. It's a bullshit case trumped up by the cops. We just have to get you into court and out on bail.'

'Yes.'

'I think fifty thousand will be high for this matter but it will be part of the horse trading I do with the filing deputy. We'll see how it goes. I take it you do not want to provide an address.'

'That's correct. I need a new one.'

'Then we might have to go the whole fifty. But in the meantime I will see about an address. There may be additional expenses incurred from that. It won't be much. I can prom –'

'Fine. Just do it.'

Gladden looked back at the man on the other side of the cell.

'What about tonight?' he asked quietly. 'I told you, these cops are going to try to get me hurt.'

'I think they are bluffing but –'

'That's easy for you to –'

'*But* I am not taking any chances. Hear me out, Mr Brisbane. I can't get you out tonight but I am going to make some calls. You will be okay. I am going to get you in there with a K-9 jacket.'

'What's that?'

'It's keep-away status in the jail. It's usually reserved for informants or high-power cases. I'll make a call to the jail and inform them that you are an informant in a federal investigation out of Washington.'

'Won't they check?'

'Yes, but it will be too late today. They'll put you in a K-9 jacket and by the time they find out tomorrow it's bogus, you'll be in court and then hopefully free after that.'

'That's a nice scam, Krasner.'

'Yes, but I won't be able to use it again. I think I may have to raise the fee we just discussed a bit to cover the loss.'

'Fuck that. Look, this is the deal. I have access to six grand max. You get me out and whatever's left after the bondsman, you get. It's an incentive deal.'

'That's a deal. Now, one other thing. You also mentioned the need to beat the prints. I need to have an idea about this. So that in clear conscience I will not make any statements before the court that will –'

'I have a history, if that is what you're asking. But I don't think you and I have to go into that.'

'I understand.'

'When will my arraignment be?'

'Late morning. When I make my calls to the jail after we hang up, I'll see to it you are scheduled for the early bus to Santa Monica. It's better to wait in the court hold than Biscailuz.'

'I wouldn't know. My first time here.'

'Uh, Mr Brisbane, I need to bring up my fee and the bail money again. I'm afraid I'll need that in my possession before I go into court tomorrow.'

'You have a wire account?'

'Yes.'

'Give me the number. I'll have it wired in the morning. Will I be able to dial long distance in K-9?'

'No. You'll have to call my office. I'll tell Judy to expect the call. She'll then dial the number you give her on the other line and cross-connect you. It will be no problem. I've done it this way before.'

Krasner gave him his wire account number and Gladden used the memorizing technique Horace had taught him to commit it to memory.

'Mr Krasner, you would be doing yourself a great favor if you destroy the wire records of this transaction and simply carry the fee as paid in cash on your accounts.'

'I understand. Anything else on your mind?'

'Yes. You better put something on the PTL net, tell the others what happened, tell them to stay away from that carousel.'

'Will do.'

After he hung up, Gladden turned his back to the wall and slid down until he was sitting on the floor. He avoided looking at the man across the room. He noticed the snoring had stopped and guessed that maybe the man on the floor might be dead. OD'd. Then the man stirred slightly. For a moment Gladden considered reaching down and pulling the plastic bracelet off the man and replacing it with his own. He'd probably be released in the morning without the cost of a lawyer and $50,000 bail.

It was too risky, he decided. The man sitting across the cell might be a cop and, besides, the one on the floor might be a multiple repeat offender. You never knew when a judge was going to say enough was enough. Gladden decided to take his chances with Krasner. After all, he'd gotten his name off the network board. The lawyer must know what he was doing. Still, the six thousand bothered him. He was being extorted by the judicial system. Six thousand for what? What had he done wrong?

His hand went to his pocket for a cigarette but then he remembered they had been taken away. That brought the anger down on him even heavier. And the self-pity. He was being persecuted by society and for what? His instincts and desires were not of his choosing. Why couldn't they understand that?

Gladden wished he had his laptop with him. He wanted to sign on and talk to those on the network. Those of his kind. He felt lonely in the cell. He thought that he might even start to cry except that the man leaning against the other wall was watching him. He would not cry in front of him.

8
·········

I didn't sleep well after my day with the files. I kept thinking about the photos. First of Theresa, then of my brother. Both of them captured forever in horrible poses, stored away in envelopes. I wanted to go back and steal the photos and burn them. I didn't want anyone ever to see them.

In the morning, after I had made coffee, I turned on my computer and dialed into the Rocky's system to check messages. I ate handfuls of Cheerios from the box as I waited for the connection to be made and my password to be approved. I kept my laptop and printer set up on the dining room table because I most often ate while using them. It beat sitting at the table alone and thinking about how I'd been eating alone for more years than I cared to remember.

My home was small. I'd had the same one-bedroom apartment with the same furniture for nine years. It wasn't a bad place but it was nothing special. Other than Sean, I couldn't remember who the last visitor was. When I was with women, I didn't take them there. There hadn't been many of them, anyway.

I thought when I first moved in I'd only be staying a couple years, that maybe I'd eventually buy a house and get married or have a dog or something. But it hadn't happened and I'm not sure why. The job, I guess. At least that's what I told myself. I concentrated my energy on my work. In each room of the apartment there were stacks of newspapers with my stories in them. I liked to reread them and save them. If I died at home, I knew they'd come in there and find me and mistakenly think I was one of those pack rats I'd written about who die with newspapers stacked to the ceiling and their cash stuffed into the mattress. They wouldn't bother to pick up one of the papers and read my story.

On the computer I had only a couple of messages. The most recent was from Greg Glenn asking how it was going. It had been sent at six-thirty the night before. The timing annoyed me; the guy okayed the assignment Monday morning and on Monday night he wanted to know where I was going with it. 'How's it going?' was editor-speak for 'Where's the story?'

Fuck him, I thought. I sent back a brief reply saying I had spent Monday with the cops and was convinced of my brother's suicide. That out of the way, I would begin exploring the causes and frequency of police suicide.

The previous message on the tube was from Laurie Prine in the library. It had been sent at four-thirty Monday. All it said was, 'Interesting stuff on Nexis. It's on the counter.'

I sent a message back thanking her for the quick search and saying I had unexpectedly been tied up in Boulder but would pick up the search package right away. I thought she had an interest in me, though I had never responded to her on anything other than the professional level. You have to be careful and be sure. You make a wanted advance and you're cool. You make an unwanted advance and you get a personnel complaint. My view is that it's better just to avoid the whole thing.

Next I scrolled through the AP and UPI wires to see if there was anything interesting going on. There was a story about a doctor being shot outside a women's clinic in Colorado Springs. An anti-abortion activist was in custody, but the doctor had not died yet. I made an electronic copy of the story and transferred it to my personal storage basket, but I didn't think I'd ever do anything with it unless the doctor died.

There was a knock on my door and I looked through the peephole before opening it. It was Jane, who lived across the hall and down one. She'd been there about a year and I'd met her when she asked for help moving some furniture around when she was setting up her place. She was impressed when I told her I was a newspaper reporter, not knowing anything about what it was like. We'd gone to the movies twice and dinner once and spent a day skiing at Keystone but these outings were spread over the year she'd been in the building and nothing ever seemed to come of it. I think it was my hesitation, not hers. She was attractive in an outdoorsy sort of way and maybe that was it. I was outdoorsy myself – at least in my mind – and wanted something different from that.

'Hello, Jack. I saw your car in the garage last night so I knew you were back. How was the trip?'

'It was good. It was good to get away.'

'Did you ski?'

'A little bit. I went out to Telluride.'

'Sounds nice. You know, I was going to tell you but you already left, if you're ever going away again, I could take care of your plants or pick up the mail or whatever. Just ask.'

'Oh, thanks. But I don't really have any plants. I end up traveling a lot overnight for the job, so I don't keep any.'

I turned from the door and looked back into the apartment as if to make sure. I guess I should have invited her in for coffee but I didn't.

'You on your way to work?' I asked instead.

'Yeah.'

'Me, too. I better get going. But, listen, once I get settled in, let's do something. A movie or something.'

We both liked DeNiro movies. That was the one thing we had.

'Okay, call me.'

'I will.'

After closing the door I chastised myself again for not inviting her in. In the dining room I shut the computer down and my eyes caught on the inch-thick stack of paper next to the printer. My unfinished novel. I had started it more than a year earlier but it wasn't going anywhere. It was supposed to be about a writer who becomes a quadriplegic in a motorcycle accident. With the money from the legal settlement, he hires a beautiful young woman from the local university to type for him as he orally composes the sentences. But soon he realizes she is editing and rewriting what he tells her before she even types it in. And what dawns on him is that she is the better writer. Soon he sits mute in the room while she writes. He only watches. He wants to kill her, strangle her with his hands. But he can't move his hands to do it. He is in hell.

The stack of pages sat there on the table daring me to try again. I don't know why I didn't shove it into a drawer with the other one I had started and never finished years earlier. But I didn't. I guess I wanted it there where I could see it.

The *Rocky*'s newsroom was deserted when I got there. The morning editor and the early reporter were at the city desk but I didn't see anybody else. Most of the staffers didn't start coming in until nine or later. My first stop was the cafeteria for more coffee and then I swung by the library, where I took a thick computer printout with my name on it off the counter. I checked Laurie Prine's desk to thank her in person but she wasn't in yet, either.

Back at my desk I could see into Greg Glenn's office. He was there, on the phone as usual. I began my usual routine of reading the *Rocky* and the *Post* in tandem. I always enjoyed this, the daily judging of the Denver newspaper war. If you were keeping tabs, exclusive stories always scored the most points. But, generally, the papers covered the same stories and this was the trench war, where the real battle was. I would read our story and then I would read theirs, seeing who wrote it better, who had the best information. I didn't always pull for the *Rocky*. In fact, most times I didn't. I worked with some real assholes and didn't mind seeing their butts kicked by the *Post*. I would never admit this to anyone, though. It was the nature of the business and the competition. We competed with the other newspaper, we competed with each other. That was why I was sure some of them watched me whenever I walked through the newsroom. To some of the younger reporters I was almost a hero, with the kind of story clips, talent and beat to shoot for. To some of the others, I'm sure I was a pathetic hack with an undeservedly cushy beat. A dinosaur. They wanted to shoot at me. But that was okay. I understood this. I'd think the same thing if I were in their position.

The Denver papers were feeders for the bigger dailies in New York and L.A, and Chicago and Washington. I probably should have moved on long ago and had even turned down an offer with the *L.A. Times* a few years back. But not before I used it as leverage with Glenn to get my murder beat. He thought the offer was for a hot shot job covering the cops. I didn't tell him it was a job in a suburban section called the Valley Edition. He offered to create the murder beat for me if I stayed. Sometimes I thought I had made a mistake taking Glenn's offer. Maybe it would be good to start somewhere fresh.

We had done all right in the morning competition. I put the papers aside and picked up the library printout. Laurie Prine had found several stories in the eastern papers analyzing the pathology of police suicides and a handful of smaller spot news reports on specific suicides from around the country. She had the discretion not to print the *Denver Post* report on my brother.

Most of the longer reports examined suicide as a job risk that went with police work. Each started with a particular cop's suicide and then steered the story into a discussion among shrinks and police experts on what made cops eat their guns. All of the stories concluded that there was a causal relationship between police suicide and job stress and a traumatic event in the life of the victim.

The articles were valuable because what experts I would need for my story were named right there. And several pieces mentioned an ongoing FBI-sponsored study on police suicides at the Law Enforcement Foundation in Washington, D.C. I highlighted this, figuring that I could use updated statistics from the bureau or foundation to lend my story freshness and credibility.

The phone rang and it was my mother. We hadn't spoken since the funeral. After a few preliminary questions about my trip and how everybody was doing, she got to the point.

'Riley told me you are going to write about Sean.'

It wasn't a question but I answered as if it was.

'Yes, I am.'

'Why, John?'

She was the only one who called me John.

'Because I have to. I ... just can't go on now like it didn't happen. I have to at least try to understand.'

'You always took things apart when you were a boy. You remember? All the toys you ruined.'

'What are you talking about, Mom? This is –'

'What I am saying is that when you take things apart you can't always put them back together again. Then what have you got? Nothing, Johnny, you have nothing.'

'Mom, you're not making sense. Look, I have to do this.'

I did not understand why I was so quick to anger when I talked to her.

'Have you thought about anyone else besides yourself? Do you know how putting this in the paper can hurt people?'

'You mean Dad? It might also help him.'

There was a long silence and I imagined her in her kitchen at the table, eyes closed and holding the phone to her ear. My father was probably sitting there, too, afraid to talk to me about it.

'Did you have any idea?' I asked quietly. 'Did either of you?'

'Of course not,' she said sadly. 'No one knew.'

More silence and then she made her last plea.

'Think about it, John. It's better to heal in private.'

'Like with Sarah?'

'What do you mean?'

'You never talked about it ... you never talked to me.'

'I can't talk about that now.'

'You never can. It's only been twenty years.'

'Don't be sarcastic about something like that.'

'I'm sorry. Look, I'm not trying to be like this.'

'Just think about what I asked you.'

'I will,' I said. 'I'll let you know.'

She hung up as angry with me as I was with her. It

bothered me that she didn't want me to write about Sean. It was almost as if she was still protecting and favoring him. He was gone. I was still here.

I straightened up in my seat so I could look over the sound partitions of the pod my desk was in. I could see the newsroom was filling up now. Glenn was out of his office and at the city desk talking with the morning editor about the coverage plan for the abortion-doctor shooting. I slumped back down in my chair so they wouldn't see me and get the idea of assigning me to rewrite. I was always dodging rewrite. They'd send out a bunch of reporters to a crime scene or disaster and these people would call their info back to me. I then had to write up the story on deadline and decide which names went on the byline. It was the newspaper business at its most fast and furious, but I was burned out by it. I just wanted to write my stories about murder and be left alone.

I almost took the printout up to the cafeteria so I'd be out of sight but decided to take my chances. I went back to reading. The most impressive piece had run in the *New York Times* five months earlier. No surprise there. The *Times* was the Holy Grail of journalism. The best. I started reading the piece and then decided to put it down and save it for last. After I had scanned and read through the rest of the material, I went up for another cup of coffee, then started to reread the *Times* article, taking my time with it.

The news peg was the seemingly unrelated suicides of three of New York's finest within a six-week period. The victims didn't know each other but all succumbed to the police blues, as it was called in the article. Two with their guns at home; one hanged himself in a heroin shooting gallery while six stoned hypes watched in dazed horror. The article reported at length on the ongoing police suicide study being conducted jointly by the FBI's Behavioral Science Services in Quantico, Virginia, and the Law Enforcement Foundation. The article quoted the foundation's director, Nathan Ford, and I wrote the name down in my notebook before going on. Ford said the project had studied every reported police suicide in the last five years looking for similarities in causes. He said the bottom line was that it was impossible to determine who might be susceptible to the police blues. But once diagnosed, it could be properly treated if a suffering officer sought help. Ford said the goal of the project was to build a database that could be translated into a protocol that would help police managers spot officers with the police blues before it was too late.

The *Times* article included a sidebar story about a year-old Chicago case where the officer had come forward but still was not saved. As I read, my stomach tightened. The article said Chicago police detective John Brooks had begun therapy sessions with a psychiatrist after a particular homicide case he was assigned to began bothering him. The case was the kidnapping and murder of a twelve-year-old boy named Bobby Smathers. The boy was missing for two days before his remains were found in a snowbank near the Lincoln Park Zoo. He had been strangled. Eight of his fingers were missing.

An autopsy determined that the fingers had been severed before his death. That, and not being able to identify and catch the killer, apparently was too much for Brooks to take.

Mr Brooks, a highly regarded investigator, took the death of the precocious, brown-eyed boy unusually hard.

After supervisors and colleagues became aware that it was affecting his work, he took a four-week leave and began intensive therapy sessions with Dr Ronald Cantor, whom he was referred to by a Chicago Police Department psychologist.

At the start of these sessions, according to Dr Cantor, Brooks openly spoke of his suicidal feelings and said he was haunted by dreams of the young boy screaming in agony.

After twenty therapy sessions over a four-week period, Dr Cantor approved of the detective's return to his assignment in the homicide unit. Mr Brooks by all accounts functioned properly and continued to handle and solve several new homicide cases. He told friends that his nightmares were gone. Known as 'Jumpin' John' because of his frenetic, go get'em attitude, Mr Brooks even continued his ultimately unsuccessful pursuit of the killer of Bobby Smathers.

But sometime during the cold Chicago winter something apparently changed. On March 13 – which would have been the thirteenth birthday celebrated by the Smathers boy – Mr Brooks sat in his favorite chair in the den where he liked to write poems as a distraction from his job as a homicide detective. He'd taken at least two tablets of Percocet he had left over from treatment of a back injury the year before. He wrote a single line in his poetry notebook. Then he put the barrel of his .38 Special into his mouth and pulled the trigger. He was found by his wife when she came home from work.

The death of Mr Brooks left family and friends bereaved and full of questions. What could they have done? What were the signs they had missed? Cantor shook his head wistfully when asked during an interview if there were answers for these troubling questions.

'The mind is a funny, unpredictable and sometimes terrible thing,' the soft-spoken psychologist said in his office. 'I thought that John had come very far with me. But, obviously, we did not come far enough.'

Mr Brooks and whatever it was that haunted him remain an enigma. Even his last message is a puzzle. The line he wrote on the pad offered little in the way of insight into what caused him to turn his gun on himself.

'Through the pale door,' were his last written words. The line was not original. Mr Brooks borrowed it from Edgar Allan Poe. In his poem 'The Haunted Palace,' which originally appeared in one of Poe's best-known stories, 'The Fall of the House of Usher,' Poe wrote:

> While like a ghastly rapid river,
> Through the pale door
> A hideous throng rush out forever
> And laugh – but smile no more.

The meaning of those words to Mr Brooks is unclear

but they certainly carry the melancholy incumbent in his final act.

Meantime, the murder of Bobby Smathers remains an open case. In the homicide unit where Mr Brooks worked and his colleagues still pursue the case, the detectives now say they are seeking justice for two victims.

'Far as I'm concerned, this is a double murder,' said Lawrence Washington, a detective who grew up with Brooks and was partnered with him in the homicide unit. 'Whoever did the boy also did Jumpin' John. You can't convince me any different.'

I straightened up and glanced around the newsroom. No one was looking at me. I looked back down at the printout and read the end of the story again. I was stunned, almost to the same degree as the night Wexler and St. Louis had come for me. I could hear my heart beating, my guts being taken in a cold and crushing grip. I couldn't read anything else but the name of the story. Usher. I had read it in high school and again in college. I knew the story. And I knew the character of the title. Roderick Usher. I opened my notebook and looked at the few notes I had jotted down after leaving Wexler the day before. The name was there. Sean had written it in the chronological record. It was his last entry.

RUSHER

After dialing the editorial library I asked for Laurie Prine.

'Laurie, it's –'

'Jack. Yes, I know.'

'Look, I need an emergency search. I mean, I think it's a search. I'm not sure how to get –'

'What is it, Jack?'

'Edgar Allan Poe. Do we have anything on him?'

'Sure. I'm sure we have lots of biographical abstracts. I could –'

'I mean do we have any of his short stories or works? I'm looking for 'The Fall of the House of Usher.' And sorry to interrupt.'

'That's okay. Um, I don't know what we would have right here as far as his written works go. Like I said, it's mostly biographical. I can take a look. But, I mean, any bookstore around here is going to sell his stuff if we don't have it.'

'Okay, thanks. I'll just go over to the Tattered Cover.'

I was about to put the phone down when she said my name.

'Yes?'

'I just thought of something. Like if you want to quote a line or something, we have lots of quotations on CD-ROM. I could just plug it in real quick.'

'Okay. Do it.'

She put the phone down for an eternity. I reread the end of the *Times* story again. What I was thinking seemed like a long shot but the coincidences in the way my brother and Brooks had died and in the names of Roderick Usher and RUSHER could not be ignored.

'Okay, Jack,' Laurie said after picking back up. 'I just checked our indexes. We have no books containing Poe's works in whole. I've got the poetry disk in, so let's give it a whirl. What do you want?'

'There is a poem called 'The Haunted Palace' that is part of the story 'The Fall of the House of Usher.' Can you get that?'

She didn't answer. I heard her typing on the computer.

'Okay, yeah, there are selected quotes from the story and the poem. Three screens.'

'Okay, is there a line that goes "Out of space, out of time"?'

'Out of space. Out of time.'

'Right. I don't know the punctuation.'

'Doesn't matter.'

She was typing.

'Uh, no. It's not in –'

'Damn!'

I don't know why I made such an outburst. It immediately bothered me.

'But, Jack, it is a line from another poem.'

'What? By Poe?'

'Yes. It's in a poem called 'Dream-Land.' You want me to read it? The whole stanza's here.'

'Read it.'

'Okay, I'm not that great at reading poetry but here goes. 'By a route obscure and lonely, / Haunted by ill angels only, / Where an Eidolon, named NIGHT, / On a black throne reigns upright, / I have reached these lands but newly, / From an ultimate dim Thule – / From a wild weird clime that lieth, sublime, / Out of SPACE – out of TIME.' That's it. But there is an editor's note. It says an Eidolon means a phantom.'

I didn't say anything. I was frozen still.

'Jack?'

'Read it again. Slower, this time.'

I wrote the stanza in my notebook. I could have just asked her to print it out and then gone and picked it up but I didn't want to move. I wanted, for the short moment, to be totally alone with this. I had to be.

'Jack, what is it?' she asked when she was done reading. 'You seem so anxious about this.'

'I don't know yet. I've gotta go.'

I hung up.

In an instant I began to feel overly warm, claustrophobic. As large as the newsroom was, I felt like the walls were closing in. My heart pounded. A vision of my brother in the car flashed through my mind.

Glenn was on the phone when I walked into his office and sat down in front of him. He pointed to the door and nodded like he wanted me to wait outside until he was done. I didn't move. He pointed again and I shook my head.

'Listen, I've got something happening here,' he said into the phone. 'Can I call you back? Great. Yeah.'

He hung up.

'What's –'

'I need to go to Chicago,' I said. 'Today. And then probably to Washington, then maybe Quantico, Virginia. To the FBI.'

*

Glenn didn't buy it.

'Out of space? Out of time? I mean, come on, Jack, that has got to be a thought that goes through the minds of many people who contemplate or actually do commit suicide. The fact that it's mentioned in a poem written by some morbid guy a hundred and fifty years ago who also wrote another poem this other dead cop quoted, it's not the stuff conspiracies are made of.'

'What about Rusher and Roderick Usher? You think that's a coincidence, too? So now we have a triple coincidence and you say it's not worth checking out.'

'I didn't say it's not worth checking out.' His voice rose a notch to a level signaling indignation. 'Of course, you check it out. Get on the phones, check it out. But I'm not sending you off on a national tour on the basis of what you've got now.'

He swiveled in his chair so he could check his computer for pending messages. There were none. He turned to face me again.

'What's the motive?'

'What?'

'Who'd want to kill your brother and this guy in Chicago? It doesn't make – How come the cops missed this?'

'I don't know.'

'Well, you spent the day with them and the case, where's the hole in the suicide? How could someone have done this and just walked away? How come you came away yesterday convinced that it was suicide? I got your message, you said you were convinced. How come the cops are convinced?'

'I don't have any answers for that yet. That's why I want to go to Chicago and then to the bureau.'

'Look, Jack, you've got a cushy beat here. I can't tell you how many times reporters have come in here saying they wanted it. You –'

'Who?'

'What?'

'Who wants my beat?'

'Never mind. It's not what we're talking about. The point

is, you've got it good here and you get to go anywhere in the state you want to go. But for this kind of travel, I've got to be able to justify it with Neff and Neighbors. I also have a newsroom full of reporters who would like to travel every once in a while on a story. I would like them to travel. It helps keep them motivated. But we're in an economic downturn here and I can't okay every trip that gets proposed.'

I hated these sermons and I wondered if Neff and Neighbors, the managing editor and editor of the paper, even cared whom he sent where as long as they got good stories. This was a good story. Glenn was full of shit and he knew it.

'Okay, I'll just take vacation time and do it myself.'

'You used everything you had after the funeral. Besides you're not going to run around the country saying you're a *Rocky Mountain News* reporter if you're not on an assignment for the *Rocky Mountain News*.'

'What about unpaid leave? You said yesterday that if I wanted more time you'd work something out.'

'I meant time to grieve, not go running across the country. Anyway, you know the rules on unpaid leave. I can't protect your position. You take a leave and you might not have the beat when you come back.'

I wanted to quit right there but I wasn't brave enough and I knew I needed the paper. I needed the institution of the media as my access card to cops, researchers, everybody involved. Without my press card, I'd be just some suicide's brother who could be pushed aside.

'I need more than what you've got now to justify this, Jack,' Glenn said. 'We can't afford an expensive fishing expedition, we need facts. If you had more, I could maybe see going to Chicago. But this foundation and the FBI you could definitely do by phone. If you can't, then maybe I can get somebody from the Washington news bureau to go over there.'

'It's my brother, my fucking story. You're not giving it to anybody.'

He raised his hands in a calming manner. He knew his suggestion was way out of bounds.

'Then work the phones and come back to me with something.'

'Look, don't you see what you're saying? You're saying don't go without the proof. But I need to go to get the proof.'

Back at my desk, I opened up a new computer file and began typing in everything I knew about the deaths of Theresa Lofton and my brother. I put down every detail I could remember from the files. The phone rang but I didn't answer it. I only typed. I knew I needed to start with a base of information. Then I would use it to knock apart the case against my brother. Glenn had finally cut a deal with me. If I got the cops to reopen my brother's case, I'd go to Chicago. He said we'd still have to talk about D.C., but I knew that if I got to Chicago I would get to Washington.

As I typed, the picture of my brother kept coming back to me. Now that sterile, lifeless photo bothered me. For I had believed the impossible. I had let him down and now felt a keener sense of guilt. It was my brother in that car, my twin. It was me.

9

....

I ended up with four pages of notes which I then synthe-
sized after an hour of study and thought to six lines of
shorthand questions I had to find the answers to. I had found
that if I looked at the facts of the case from the opposite
perspective, believing Sean had been murdered and had not
taken his own life, I saw something the cops had possibly
missed. Their mistake had been their predisposition to believe
and therefore accept that Sean had killed himself. They knew
Sean and knew he was burdened by the Theresa Lofton case.
Or maybe it was something every cop could believe about
every other cop. Maybe they'd all seen too many corpses and
the only surprise was that most didn't kill themselves. But
when I sifted through the facts with a disbeliever's eye, I saw
what they did not see.

I studied the list I had written on a page in my notebook.

Pena: his hands?
after – how long?
Wexler/Scalari: the car?
heater?
lock?
Riley: gloves?

I realized I could handle Riley by phone. I dialed and was
about to hang up after six rings when she picked up.

'Riley? It's Jack. You okay? This a bad time?'

'When's a good time?'

It sounded like she had been drinking.

'You want me to come out, Riley? I'm coming out.'

'No, don't, Jack. I'm okay. Just, you know, one of those blue days. I keep thinking about him, you know?'

'Yes. I think about him, too.'

'Then how come you hadn't been around for so long before he went and ... I'm sorry, I shouldn't bring things up ...'

I was quiet a moment.

'I don't know, Riles. We sorta had a fight about something. I said some things I shouldn't have. He did, too, I guess. I think we were kind of in a cooling-off period ... He did it before I could get back with him.'

I realized I hadn't called her Riles in a long time. I wondered if she had noticed.

'What was the fight about, the girl that got cut in two?'

'Why do you say that? Did he tell you about it?'

'No. I just guessed. She had him wrapped around her finger, why not you? That's all I was thinking.'

'Riley, you've got – Look, this isn't good for you to be dwelling on. Try to think about the good things.'

I almost broke down and told her what I was pursuing. I would have liked to give her something to ease her pain. But it was too early.

'It's hard to do that.'

'I know, Riley. I'm sorry. I don't know what to tell you.'

There was a long silence on the line between us. I heard nothing in the background. No music. No TV. I wondered what she was doing in the house alone.

'Mom called me today. You told her what I was doing.'

'Yes. I thought she should know.'

I didn't say anything.

'What did you want, Jack?' she finally asked.

'Just a question. It's kind of out of left field but here it is. Did the cops show you or give you back Sean's gloves?'

'His gloves?'

'The ones he was wearing that day.'

'No. I haven't gotten them. Nobody asked me about them.'

'Well, then, what kind of gloves did Sean have?'

'Leather. Why?'

'Just something I'm playing with. I'll tell you about it later if it amounts to anything. What about the color, black?'

'Yes, black leather. I think they were fur-lined.'

Her description matched the gloves I had seen in the crime scene photographs. It didn't really mean anything one way or the other. Just a point to check, one duck put in the row.

We talked for a few minutes more and I asked if she wanted to have dinner that night because I was coming out to Boulder, but she said no. After that we hung up. I was worried about her and hoped the conversation – just the human contact – would raise her spirits. I contemplated dropping by her place anyway, after I was done with everything else.

As I passed through Boulder I could see snow clouds forming along the tops of the Flatirons. I knew from growing up out there how fast it could come down once the clouds moved in. I hoped the company Tempo I was driving had chains in the trunk but knew it was unlikely.

At Bear Lake I found Pena standing outside the ranger shack talking with a group of cross-country skiers who were passing through. While I waited I walked out to the lake. I saw a few spots where people had cleared away the snow down to the ice. I tentatively walked out on the frozen lake and looked down into one of these blue-black portals and imagined the depths below. I felt a slight tremor at my center. Twenty years earlier my sister had slipped through the ice and died in this lake. Now my brother had died in his car not fifty yards away. Looking down at the black ice I remembered hearing somewhere that some of the lake fish get frozen in the winter but when the thaw comes in spring they wake up and just snap out of it. I wondered if it was true and thought it was too bad people weren't the same way.

'It's you again.'

I turned around and saw Pena.

'Yes, I'm sorry to bother you. I have just a few more questions.'

'No bother. I wish I could have done something before, you

know? Maybe had seen him before, when he first pulled in, seen if he needed help. I don't know.'

We had started walking back toward the shack.

'I don't know what anybody could have done,' I said, just to be saying something.

'So, what are your questions?'

I took out my notebook.

'Uh, first off, when you ran to the car, did you see his hands? Like where they were?'

He walked without speaking. I think he was envisioning the incident in his mind.

'You know,' he finally said, 'I think I did look at his hands. Because when I ran up and saw it was just him, I immediately figured he had shot himself. So I'm pretty sure I looked at his hands to see if he was holding the gun.'

'Was he?'

'No. I saw it on the seat next to him. It fell on the seat.'

'Do you remember if he was wearing gloves when you looked in?'

'Gloves ... gloves,' he said, as if he was trying to prompt an answer from his memory banks. After another long pause he said, 'I don't know. I'm not getting a picture in my mind. What do the police say?'

'Well, I'm just trying to see if you remember.'

'Well, I'm not getting anything, sorry.'

'If the police wanted to, would you let them hypnotize you? To see if they could bring it out that way?'

'Hypnotize me? They do that sort of stuff?'

'Sometimes. If it's important.'

'Well, if it was important, I guess I'd do it.'

We were standing in front of the shack now. I was looking at the Tempo parked in the same place my brother had parked.

'The other thing I wanted to ask about was the timing. The police reports say that you had the car in sight within five seconds of hearing the shot. And with only five seconds there is no way anybody could make it from the car and into the woods without being seen.'

'Right. No way. Would've seen 'em.'

'Okay, then what about after?'

'After what?'

'After you ran to the car and saw the man was shot. You told me the other day you ran back to the shack here and made two calls. That right?'

'Yes, nine one one and my supe.'

'So you were inside the shack here and couldn't see the car, right?'

'Right.'

'How long?'

Pena nodded, seeing what I was getting at.

'But that doesn't matter because he was alone in the car.'

'I know but humor me. How long?'

He shrugged his shoulders as if to say what the hell and fell silent again. He walked into the shack and made a motion with his hand like lifting up the phone.

'I got through on nine one one right away. That was pretty quick. They took my name and stuff and that took some time. Then I called in and asked for Doug Paquin, that's my boss. I said it was an emergency and they put me through right away. He got on and I told him what happened and he told me to go out and watch the vehicle until the police came. That was it. I went back out.'

I considered all of that and figured that he had probably been out of sight of the Caprice for at least thirty seconds.

'On the car, when you first ran out, did you check all the doors to see if any were unlocked?'

'Just on the driver's side. But they were all locked.'

'How do you know?'

'When the cops got out here they tried them all and they were locked. They had to use one of those slim jim things to pop the lock.'

I nodded and said, 'What about the backseat? You said yesterday that the windows were fogged. Did you put your face up to the glass and look directly into the backseat? Down at the floor?'

Pena understood now what I was asking about. He thought for a moment and shook his head in the negative.

'No, I didn't look directly into the back. I just thought it was the one guy, is all.'

'Did the cops ask you these questions?'

'No, not really. I see what you're driving at, though.'

I nodded.

'One last thing. When you called it in, did you say it was a suicide or just that it was a shooting?'

'I . . . , Yeah, I said somebody up here went and shot hisself. Just like that. They got a tape, I 'spect.'

'Probably. Thanks a lot.'

I started back to my car as the first flurries started floating down. Pena called after me.

'What about the hypnotizing?'

'They'll call you if they want to do it.'

Before getting in the car I checked the trunk. There were no chains.

On my way back through Boulder I stopped at a bookstore called, appropriately enough, The Rue Morgue and picked up a thick volume containing the complete stories and poems of Edgar Allan Poe. My intention was to start reading it that night. As I drove back to Denver I worked on trying to put Pena's answers into the theory I was working on. And no matter how I moved his answers around, there was nothing that derailed my new belief.

When I got to the DPD, I was told up in the SIU office that Scalari was out of the building, so I went to homicide and found Wexler behind his desk. I didn't see St. Louis around.

'Shit,' Wexler said. 'You here to bust my chops again?'

'No,' I said. 'You going to bust mine?'

'Depends on what you're going to ask me.'

'Where's my brother's car? It back in service yet?'

'What is this, Jack? Can't you even conceive of the possibility that we know how to run an investigation?'

He angrily threw the pen he was holding into a trash can in the corner of the room. He then realized what he had done and went and picked it out.

'Look, I'm not trying to show you up or cause you any

problems,' I said in an even tone. 'I'm just trying to settle all my questions and the more I try the more questions I have.'

'Like what?'

I told him about my visit with Pena and I could see him getting angry. Blood rushed into his face and there was a slight tremor along his left jawline.

'Look, you guys closed the case,' I said. 'There is nothing wrong with me talking to Pena. Besides, you or Scalari or somebody missed something. The car was out of his sight for more than half a minute while he was calling it in.'

'So fucking what?'

'You guys were only concerned with the time prior to his seeing the car. Five seconds, so nobody could've run away. Case closed, suicide. But Pena told me the windows were fogged. They had to have been for someone to have written the note. Pena didn't look in the back, onto the floor. Then he leaves for at least thirty seconds. Somebody could've been lying down in the back, got out while he was making the calls and run into the woods. It could have happened easily.'

'Are you fucked in the head? What about the note? What about the GSR on the glove?'

'Anybody could have written on the windshield. And the glove with the residue could have been worn by the killer. Then he took it off and put it on Sean. Thirty seconds is a long time. It might've been longer. It probably was longer. He made two calls, Wex.'

'It's too iffy. The killer would be relying too much on Pena taking that much time.'

'Maybe not. Maybe he figured he'd either have enough time or he'd just take out Pena. The way you guys handled this thing, you would have just said Sean killed him and then himself.'

'That's bullshit, Jack. I loved your brother like he was my own fucking brother. You think I want to believe he swallowed the goddamn bullet?'

'Let me ask you something. Where were you when you found out about Sean?'

'Right here at the desk. Why?'

'Who told you? You get a call?'

'Yeah, I got a call. It was the captain. Parks called the watch captain. He called our captain.'

'What did he tell you? His exact words.'

Wexler hesitated a moment as he remembered.

'I don't remember. He just said that Mac was dead.'

'He said it like that or did he say Mac had killed himself?'

'I don't know what he said. He might've. What's the point?'

'The ranger out there who called it in said Sean shot himself. That started the whole thing rolling. You all went out there expecting a suicide and that's what you found. The parts of the puzzle fit into the picture you brought with you. Everybody around here knew what the Lofton case was doing to him. You see what I'm saying? You were all predisposed to believe it. You even got me believing it on the ride out to Boulder that night.'

'That's all bullshit, Jack. And I don't have the time. There's no proof of what you're saying and I don't have time for theories from somebody who can't face the facts.'

I was silent a moment, letting him cool down.

'Then where's the car, Wex? If you're so sure, show me the car. I know how I can prove it to you.'

Wexler paused himself. I guessed he was contemplating whether he should get involved. If he showed me the car, he was admitting that I had at least put a small doubt in his own mind.

'It's still in the yard,' he finally said. 'I see it every goddamn day when I come in.'

'Is it still in the same condition as the day it was found?'

'Yeah, yeah, still the same. It's sealed. Every day I come in I get to see his blood all over the window.'

'Let's go look at it, Wex. I think there's a way to convince you. One way or the other.'

The snow flurries had made it over from Boulder. In the police yard Wexler got the key from the fleet manager. He also checked an inventory list to see if anyone had taken the keys or been inside the car other than the investigators. No one had. The car would be in the same condition as it was when it was towed in.

'They've been waiting for a requisition from the chief's office to clean it up. They have to send it out. You know there are companies that specialize in cleaning houses and cars and stuff after somebody's been killed in them? Some fuckin' job.'

I think Wexler was talking so much because he was nervous now. We approached the car and stood there looking at it. The snow was swirling around us in a current. The blood sprayed on the inside back window had dried to a dark brown.

'It's going to stink when we open it,' Wexler said. 'Christ, I can't believe I'm doing this. This is going no further until you tell me what is going on.'

I nodded.

'Okay. There are two things I want to look at. I want to see if the heat switch is on high and if the security lock on the rear doors is on or off.'

'What for?'

'The windows were fogged and it was cold but it wasn't that cold. I saw in the pictures that Sean was dressed warmly. He had his jacket on. He wouldn't need the heat on high. How else do windows get fogged when you're parked with the engine off?'

'I don't –'

'Think about surveillances, Wex. What causes fogging? My brother once told me about the stakeout you two blew 'cause the windows fogged up and you missed the guy coming out of his house.'

'Talking. It was the week after the Super Bowl and we were talking about the fucking Broncos losing again and the hot air fogged everything up.'

'Yeah. And last I knew, my brother didn't talk to himself. So if the heat is on low and the windows are fogged enough to write on them, I think it means there was someone with him. They were talking.'

'That's a long shot that doesn't prove anything either way. What about the lock?'

I gave him the theory: 'Somebody is with Sean. Somehow he gets Sean's gun. Maybe he comes with his own gun and disarms Sean. He also tells him to hand over his gloves. Sean does. The guy puts the gloves on and then kills Sean with his own gun. He then jumps over the seat into the back where he hides down on the floor. He waits until Pena comes and goes, then he leans back over the seat, writes the note on the windshield and puts the gloves back on Sean's hands – now you've got the GSR on Sean. Then the doer gets out the back door, locks it and splits into the cover of the trees. No footprints, 'cause the lot's been plowed. He's gone by the time Pena comes back out to watch the car like he's told to do by his supervisor.'

Wexler was silent a long time while catching up.

'Okay, it's a theory,' he finally said. 'Now prove it.'

'You know my brother. You worked with him. What was the routine with the security lock? Always keep it on. Right? That way no mistakes with prisoners. No slip-ups. If you take a nonprisoner you can always disengage it for them. Like you did on the night you came for me. When I got sick, the lock was on. Remember? You had to switch it off so I could open the door to puke.'

Wexler said nothing but in his face I saw that I'd struck home. If the security lock was off in the Caprice it wouldn't be rock-solid proof of anything. But he would know in the way he knew my brother that Sean hadn't been alone in the car.

He finally said, 'You can't tell by looking at it. It's just a button. Somebody will have to get in the back and see if they can get out.'

'Open it. I'll get in.'

Wexler unlocked the door, flipped the electric locks and I opened the rear passenger side door. The sickly sweet smell of dried blood hit me. I stepped into the car and closed the door.

For a long moment I didn't move. I had seen the photos but they didn't prepare me for being in the car. The sickly smell, the dried blood sprayed over the window, the roof and the driver's headrest. My brother's blood. I felt the cloying grip of nausea in my throat. I quickly looked over the seat to the dashboard and the heater control panel. Then, through the right window, I looked out at Wexler. For a moment our eyes met and I wondered if I really wanted the security lock to be off. The thought occurred to me that it might be easier to just let it go, but I quickly ran it from my mind. I knew if I let this go I would be haunted for the rest of my life.

I reached over and hit the passenger lock switch for my door. I pulled the door handle and the door swung open. I stepped out and looked at Wexler. Snow was starting to stick to his hair and shoulders.

'And the heater's off. It couldn't have fogged the windows. I think Sean had somebody in the car with him. They were talking. Then whoever the bastard was killed him.'

Wexler looked as if he had seen a ghost. It was all clicking in his mind. It was more than just a theory now and he knew it. It looked as though he might start to cry.

'Goddamnit,' he said.

'Look, we all missed it.'

'No, it's different. A cop never lets his partner down like that. What good are we if we can't watch out for our own? A fucking reporter . . .'

He didn't finish but I think I knew what he was feeling. He felt as though he had somehow betrayed Sean. I knew that was how he felt because it was the same for me.

'It's not done with yet,' I said. 'We can still make up for believing the wrong thing.'

He still looked forlorn. I wasn't the one who could comfort him. That would have to come from within.

'All that's lost is a little time, Wex,' I said anyway. 'Let's go back inside. It's getting cold out here.'

My brother's house was dark when I went there to tell Riley. I paused before knocking, wondering at how absurd it was that I believed the news I was bringing might in some way cheer her. Good news, Riley, Sean didn't kill himself like we all thought, he was murdered by some nut who has probably done it before and probably will again.

I knocked anyway. It wasn't late. I imagined that she was sitting in there in the dark, or maybe in one of the back bedrooms which emitted no light. The lantern light came on above me and she opened up before I had to knock a second time.

'Jack.'

'Riley. I was wondering if I could come in and talk to you.'

I knew she didn't know yet. I had made a deal with Wexler. I would tell her in person. He didn't care. He was too busy reopening the investigation, drawing up lists of likely suspects, getting Sean's car inspected again for prints and other evidence. I hadn't told him anything about Chicago. I'd kept that to myself and I wasn't sure why. Was it the story? Did I want the story just for myself? That was the easy answer and I used it to soothe my uneasiness at not telling him everything. But in the deeper folds of my mind I believed it was something else. Something maybe I didn't want to bring out into the light to view.

'Come in,' Riley said. 'Is something wrong?'

'Not really.'

I walked in behind her and she led the way to the kitchen, where she turned on the light over the table. She was wearing blue jeans, heavy wool socks and a Colorado Buffaloes sweatshirt.

'There's just been some new developments about Sean and I wanted to tell you. You know, instead of on the phone.'

We both took chairs at the table. The circles under her eyes hadn't disappeared and she had done nothing with makeup to hide them. I felt her gloom descending on me and I looked away from her face. I thought I had escaped but it was impossible here. Her pain invaded every space in the house and was contagious.

'Were you asleep?'

'No, I was reading. What is it, Jack?'

I told her. But unlike Wexler, I told her everything. About

Chicago, about the poems, about what I wanted to do now. She nodded occasionally during the story but showed nothing else. No tears, no questions. All of that would come when I was done.

'So that's the story,' I said. 'I came to tell you. I'm going to Chicago as soon as I can.'

After a long silence she spoke.

'It's funny, I feel so guilty.'

I could see tears in her eyes but they didn't fall. She probably didn't have enough left for that.

'Guilty? About what?'

'All of this time. I've been so angry at him. You know, for what he'd done. Like he had done it to me, not himself. I started hating him, hating his memory. Now, you ... now this.'

'We were all like that. It was the only way to live with it.'

'Have you told Millie and Tom?'

My parents. She never felt comfortable addressing them any other way.

'Not yet. I will, though.'

'Why didn't you tell Wexler about Chicago?'

'I don't know. I wanted a head start, I guess. They'll find out about it tomorrow.'

'Jack, if what you're saying is true, they should know everything. I don't want whoever did this to get away just so you can pursue a story.'

'Look, Riley,' I said, trying to keep calm, 'whoever did this had already gotten away until I came along. I just want to get to the cops in Chicago before Wexler. One day.'

We were silent a moment before I spoke again.

'And make no mistake. I want the story, that's true. But it's about more than just the story. It's about me and Sean.'

She nodded and I let the silence hang between us. I didn't know how to explain to her my motives. My skill in life was putting words together in a coherent and interesting narrative but inside I had no words for this. Not yet. I knew she needed to hear more from me and I tried to give her what she needed, an explanation I didn't quite understand myself.

'I remember when we graduated from high school we both pretty much knew what we wanted to do. I was going to write books and be famous or rich or both. Sean was going to be chief of detectives at DPD and solve all of the mysteries of the city ... Neither of us quite made it. Sean was closest, though.'

She tried a smile at my memory but it didn't quite go with the rest of her face and so she put it aside.

'Anyway,' I continued, 'at the end of that summer I was leaving for Paris to go write the great American novel. And he was waiting to go into the service. We made this deal when we said good-bye. It was pretty corny. The deal was that when I got rich I would buy him a Porsche with ski racks. Like Redford had in *Downhill Racer*. That's it. That's all he wanted. He'd get to choose the model. But I'd have to pay. I told him it was a bad deal for me because he had nothing to trade. But then he said he did. He said that if anything ever happened to me – you know, like I got killed or hurt or robbed or anything – he'd find out who did it. He'd make sure nobody got away with it. And, you know, even back then I believed it. I believed he could do it. And something about it was a comfort.'

The story didn't seem to make much sense the way I had told it. I wasn't sure what the point was.

'But that was his promise, not yours,' Riley said.

'Yes, I know.' I was quiet for a few moments while she watched me. 'It's just that ... I don't know, I just can't sit back and watch and wait. I've got to be out there. I've got to ...'

There were no words to explain it.

'Do something?'

'I guess. I don't know. I can't really talk about it, Riley. I just have to do it. I'm going to Chicago.'

10

....

Gladden and five other men were ushered into a glass-enclosed seating area in the corner of the huge court-room. There was a foot-wide slot that ran the length of the glass enclosure at face height through which the arraignment proceedings in the courtroom could be heard and the defendants could answer questions from their attorneys or the judge.

Gladden was disheveled from a night of no sleep. He had been in a single cell but the noise of the jail kept him awake and reminded him too much of Raiford. He looked around the courtroom and didn't see anyone he recognized. This included the cops, Delpy and Sweetzer. He also didn't see any television or still cameras. He took this as a sign that his true identity had not yet been discovered. He was encouraged by this. A man with curly red hair and thick glasses made his way around the attorneys' tables to the glass booth. He was short and had to raise his chin as if standing in tall water for his mouth to reach the slot in the glass.

'Mr Brisbane?' he asked, looking expectantly at the men who had just been ushered in.

Gladden walked over and looked down through the opening.

'Krasner?'

'Yes, how are you?'

He reached his hand up and through the slot. Gladden shook it reluctantly. He didn't like being touched by anyone, unless it was a child. He didn't answer Krasner's question. It was the wrong thing to ask someone who had spent the night in county jail.

'You talk to the prosecutor yet?' he asked instead.

'Yes, I did. We had quite a conversation. Your bad luck is continuing in that the deputy DA assigned the case is a woman who I have had some dealings with before. She is a ballbuster and the arresting officers have informed her of the, uh, situation as they saw it at the pier.'

'So she's going to go balls to the wall against me.'

'Right. However, this judge is okay. We're all right there. He's the only one in the building, I think, who wasn't a prosecutor before being elected.'

'Well, hurray for me. Did you get the money?'

'Yes, that happened just as you said. So we're set. One question, do you want to enter a plea today or continue it?'

'What does it matter?'

'Not a great deal. In arguing for bail it might just move the judge an inch or so our way if, you know, psychologically he knows you've already denied the charges and are readying for a fight.'

'Okay, not guilty. Just get me out of here.'

Santa Monica municipal judge Harold Nyberg called the name Harold Brisbane and Gladden went back to the slot. Krasner came back around the tables and stood by the slot so he could confer, if needed, with his client. Krasner announced himself as did deputy district attorney Tamara Feinstock. After Krasner waived a lengthy reading of the charges, he told the judge that his client pleaded not guilty. Judge Nyberg hesitated a moment. It was apparent that entering a plea so early in a case was unusual.

'Are you sure that Mr Brisbane wishes to enter a plea today?'

'Yes, Your Honor. He wants to move quickly because he is absolutely one hundred percent not guilty of these allegations.'

'I see . . .' The judge hesitated while he read something in front of him. So far, he had not even looked over in Gladden's direction. 'Well, then I take it you do not wish to waive your ten days.'

'A moment, Your Honor,' Krasner said, then he turned to Gladden and whispered. 'You have a right to a preliminary hearing on the charges within ten court days. You can waive and he'll schedule a hearing to then set the prelim. If you don't waive, he'll set the prelim now. Ten days from now. If you don't waive, it's another sign that you're going to fight, that you aren't looking for a handout from the DA. It might help on the bail.'

'Don't waive.'

Krasner turned back to the judge.

'Thank you, Your Honor. We don't waive. My client does not believe these charges will survive a preliminary hearing and, therefore, urges the court to schedule it as soon as possible so he can put this –'

'Mr Krasner, Ms Feinstock may not object to your added comments, but I do. This is an arraignment court. You're not arguing your case here.'

'Yes, Your Honor.'

The judge turned and studied a calendar hanging on the far wall, above one of the clerk's desks. He chose the date ten court days away and ordered a preliminary hearing in Division 110. Krasner opened an appointment book and wrote it down. Gladden saw the prosecutor doing the same. She was young but unattractive. So far, she had said nothing during the three-minute hearing.

'Okay,' the judge said. 'Anything on bail?'

'Yes, Your Honor,' Feinstock said, standing for the first time. 'The people urge the court to depart from the bail schedule and set an amount of two hundred and fifty thousand dollars.'

Judge Nyberg looked up from his papers at Feinstock and then over at Gladden for the first time. It was as if he was trying to determine upon physical inspection of the defendant why he was worth such a high bail for what seemed like so lowly a set of charges.

'Why is that, Ms Feinstock?' he asked. 'I don't have anything before me that suggests a deviation.'

'We believe the defendant is a flight risk, Your Honor. He

refused to provide the arresting officers with a local address or even a license plate number of a car. His driver's license was issued in Alabama and we have not verified it as a legitimate issuance. So, basically, we don't know if Harold Brisbane is even his real name. We don't know who he is or where he lives, if he has a job or family, and until we do, he is considered a flight risk.'

'Your Honor.' Krasner jumped in. 'Ms Feinstock is misstating the facts. My client's name is known to police. He provided a legitimate Alabama driver's license of which there was no mention of a problem. Mr Brisbane has just arrived in the area from Mobile seeking work and does not yet have a permanent address. When he does, he will be glad to provide it to authorities. In the meantime, he can be contacted if needed through my office and has agreed to check in twice daily with me or any representative of the court Your Honor chooses. As Your Honor knows, a deviation from the bail schedule should be based on a defendant's propensity for flight. Not having a permanent address is in no way an acknowledgment of flight. To the contrary, Mr Brisbane has entered a plea and waived any delays in this case. He clearly wishes to attack these charges and clear his name as soon as possible.'

'Calling your office is fine, but what about the address?' the judge asked. 'Where's he going to be? You seem to have left out of your dissertation any mention of the apparent fact that this man already fled from police prior to his arrest.'

'Your Honor, we challenge that charge. These officers were in plainclothes and at no time identified themselves as police officers. My client was carrying a rather expensive piece of camera equipment – with which, by the way, he earns his living – and feared he was about to become the victim of a robbery. That is why he ran from those people.'

'That's all very interesting,' the judge said. 'What about an address?'

'Mr Brisbane has a room at the Holiday Inn on Pico Boulevard. From there he is endeavoring to find work. He is a freelance photographer and graphic arts designer and is confident of his prospects. He isn't going anywhere. As I said before, he is going to fight these –'

'Yes, Mr Krasner, as you said before. What kind of bail are you looking for here?'

'Well, sir, a quarter million dollars for a charge of throwing a trash can into the ocean is utterly incomprehensible. I think a modest bail of five to ten thousand dollars is more in line with the charges. My client has limited funds. If he uses them all to make bail, he will not have the money on which to live or pay counsel.'

'You left out the evading and vandalism.'

'Your Honor, as I said, he ran from them but he had no earthly idea that they were police officers. He thought –'

'Again, Mr Krasner, save your arguments for the proper venue.'

'I'm sorry, Your Honor, but look at the charges. It is clear this is going to be a misdemeanor case, and the bail should be set accordingly.'

'Anything else?'

'Submitted.'

'Ms Feinstock.'

'Yes, Your Honor. Again, the people urge the court to consider a departure from the bail schedule. The two main charges against Mr Brisbane are felonies and will remain as such. Despite Mr Krasner's assurances, the people still are not convinced the defendant is not a flight risk or that his name is even Harold Brisbane. My detectives tell me that the defendant has dyed hair and that it was dyed at the time the photograph for this driver's license was issued. This is consistent with an attempt to hide identity. We are hoping to borrow the Los Angeles Police Department's fingerprint identification computer today and see if we can get a –'

'Your Honor,' Krasner interjected. 'I have to object here on the basis that –'

'Mr Krasner,' the judge intoned, 'you had your turn.'

'In addition,' Feinstock said, 'Mr Brisbane's arrest came as a result of other suspicious activities which he was involved in. Namely –'

'Objection!'

' – the photographing of young children – some of them unclothed – without their knowledge or the knowledge or consent of their parents. The incident for which –'

'Your Honor!'

' – the charges before you have arisen occurred when Mr Brisbane attempted to elude the officers investigating a complaint against him.'

'Your Honor,' Krasner said loudly. 'There are no outstanding charges against my client. All the district attorney is trying to do is prejudice this man before the court. It is highly improper and unethical. If Mr Brisbane did these things, then where are the charges?'

Silence filled the cavernous courtroom. Krasner's outburst had even served to make the other attorneys whispering to their clients hold their tongues. The gaze of the judge slowly moved from Feinstock to Krasner to Gladden before he finally looked back at the prosecutor and continued.

'Ms Feinstock, are there currently any other charges against this man being considered by your office at this time? And I mean *right* at this time.'

Feinstock hesitated and then grudgingly said, 'No other information has been presented for filing but the police, as I said, are continuing their investigation into the defendant's true identity and activities.'

The judge looked down at the papers in front of him again and began to write. Krasner opened his mouth to add something but then reconsidered. It was clear by the judge's demeanor that he had already made the decision.

'The bail schedule calls for bail to be set at ten thousand dollars,' Judge Nyberg said. 'I am going to make a slight departure and set bail at fifty thousand dollars. Mr Krasner, I will be glad to reconsider this at a later date if at that time your client has assuaged the district attorney's concerns about identity and address, etcetera.'

'Yes, Your Honor. Thank you.'

The judge called the next case. Feinstock closed the file she had in front of her, put it on the stack to her right, and took

another off the stack to her left and opened it. Krasner turned
to Gladden with a slight smile on his face.

'Sorry, I thought he might go twenty-five. The beauty of it
is she's probably happy. She asked for a quarter probably
hoping for a dime or a nickel. She got the nickel.'

'Never mind that. Just how long until I'm out of here?'

'Sit tight. I'll have you out in an hour.'

I I

·········

The edge of Lake Michigan was frozen, the ice left jagged and treacherous and beautiful after a storm. The upper floors of the Sears Tower were gone, swallowed whole by the grayish white shroud that hung over the city. I saw all of this while coming in on the Stevenson Expressway. It was late morning and I guessed it would be snowing again before day's end. I had thought it was cold in Denver until I landed at Midway.

It was three years since I had been back to Chicago. And despite the cold, I missed the place. I had gone to J-school at Medill in the early eighties and learned to truly love the city. After, I had hoped to stay and get on with one of the local papers but the *Tribune* and *Sun-Times* both took passes, the interview editors telling me to go out and get some experience and then come back with my clips. It was a bitter disappointment. Not the rejection as much as having to leave the city. Of course, I could've stayed on at the City News Bureau, where I worked during school, but that wasn't the kind of experience those editors were looking for, and I didn't like the idea of working for a wire service that paid you like you were a student needing clips more than money. So I went home and got the job at the *Rocky*. A lot of years went by. At first I went to Chicago at least twice a year to see friends and visit favorite bars but that tapered off over the years. The last time had been three years ago. My friend Larry Bernard had just landed at the *Tribune* after going out and getting the same experience they had told me to get. I went up to see him and I hadn't been back since. I guess I had the clips now for a paper like the *Tribune,* but I had never gotten around to sending them to Chicago.

The cab dropped me at the Hyatt across the river from the *Tribune*. I couldn't check in until three, so I left my bag with the bellman and went to the pay phones. After fumbling with the phone book I called the number for CPD's Area Three Violent Crimes and asked for Detective Lawrence Washington. When he answered, I hung up. I just wanted to locate him, make sure he was there. My experience with cops as a reporter had always been not to make appointments. If you did, all you were doing was giving them a specific place to avoid and the exact time to avoid it. Most didn't like talking to reporters, the majority didn't like even being seen with reporters. And the few that did you had to be cautious of. So you had to sneak up on them. It was a game.

I checked my watch after hanging up. Almost noon. I had twenty hours left. My flight to Dulles left at eight the next morning.

Outside the hotel I grabbed a cab and told the driver to turn up the heat and take me to Belmont and Western by way of Lincoln Park. On the way I'd take in the spot where the Smathers boy had been found. It was a year since his body had been discovered. My thought was that the spot, if I could find it, would look almost exactly as it did on that day.

I opened my satchel, booted the computer and pulled up the *Tribune* clips I'd downloaded the night before in the *Rocky*'s library. I scrolled through the stories on the Smathers case until I found the paragraph describing the discovery of the body by a zoo docent cutting through the park on the way from his girlfriend's apartment. The boy had been found in a snow-covered clearing where the Italian-American League's bocce tournaments were held in the summer. The story said the clearing off Clark near Wisconsin was within sight of the red barn, which was part of the city's farm in the zoo.

Traffic was light and we were in the park within ten minutes. I told the driver to cut over to Clark and to pull to the side when we got to Wisconsin.

The snow on the field was fresh and there were only a few tracks across it. It also stood about three inches high on the boards of the benches along the walkway. This area of the park seemed completely deserted. I got out of the cab and walked into the clearing, not expecting anything but in a way expecting something. I didn't know exactly what. Maybe just a feeling. Halfway across I came upon a grouping of tracks in the snow that cut across my intended path from left to right. I crossed these and came upon another grouping heading right to left, the party having headed back the way it had come. Kids, I thought. Maybe going to the zoo. If it was open. I looked toward the red barn and that was when I noticed the flowers at the base of a towering oak twenty yards away.

I walked toward the tree and instinctively knew what I was seeing. A one-year anniversary noted with flowers. When I got to the tree I saw that the flowers — bright red roses splashed like blood on the snow — were fake, made of wood shavings. In the cleft made by the first branching of the tree's trunk I saw that someone had propped a small studio photo of a smiling boy, his elbows on a table and his hands propped against his cheeks. He wore a red jacket and white shirt with a very small blue bow tie. The family had been here, I guessed. I wondered why they hadn't placed their memorial at the boy's grave.

I looked around. The lagoons near the barn were iced over and there were a couple of skaters. No one else. I looked over to Clark Street and saw the cab waiting. Across the street from it a brick tower rose. I saw that the sign on the awning out front said HEMINGWAY HOUSE. It was the place the zoo docent had come from before finding the small boy's body.

I looked back at the photo propped in the tree's cleft and without any hesitation reached up and took it down. It was sealed in plastic like a driver's license to protect it from the elements. On the back of it was written the boy's name but nothing else. I slid the photo into the pocket of my long coat. I knew that someday I might need it to run with the story.

The cab felt as welcome and warm to me as a living room with a fireplace. I began scrolling through the *Tribune* stories while we drove on to Area Three.

The major facts of the case were as horrifying as those in

the Theresa Lofton killing. The boy had been lured from a fenced recreation center at a Division Street elementary school. He and two others had gone out to make snowballs. When the teacher noticed they were missing from the classroom, she went out and rounded the boys up. But by then Bobby Smathers was gone. The two twelve-year-old witnesses proved unable to tell police investigators what happened. According to them, Bobby Smathers simply disappeared. They looked up from their work in the snow and didn't see him. They suspected he was hiding and waiting to ambush them, so they didn't go looking.

Bobby was found a day later in the snowbank near the bocce clearing in Lincoln Park. Weeks of full-time investigation headed by Detective John Brooks, who caught the case as lead investigator, never got any closer than the explanation of the two twelve-year-olds: Bobby Smathers had simply disappeared that day at the school.

As I reviewed the stories I looked for similarities to Lofton. There were few. She was a white female adult and he a black male child. As far different in terms of prey as would seem possible. But both were missing for more than twenty-four hours before being found and the mutilated bodies of both victims were found in city parks. Lastly, both had been at children's centers on their last day. The boy at his school, the woman at the day care center where she worked. I didn't know the significance of these connections but they were all I had.

The Area Three headquarters was an orange-brick fortress. It was a two-story sprawling building that also housed the Cook County First Municipal District Court. There was a steady stream of citizens going in and out of the smoked-glass doors. I pushed through the doors to a lobby where the floor was wet with melted snow. The front counter was made of matching brick. Somebody could drive a car through the glass doors and they still wouldn't get to the cops behind the counter. The citizens standing in front of it were another matter.

I looked at the stairs to my right. I knew from memory that they led to the detective bureau and was tempted to ignore procedure and head up. But I decided against it. You break even the mundane rules with the cops and they can get testy. I stepped up to one of the cops behind the counter. He eyed the computer bag slung over my shoulder.

'You moving in with us, are you?'

'No, this is just a computer,' I said. 'Detective Lawrence Washington. I'd like to speak with him.'

'And you are?'

'My name's Jack McEvoy. He doesn't know me.'

'You have an appointment?'

'No. It's about the Smathers case. You can tell him that.'

The cop's eyebrows climbed an inch up his forehead.

'Tell you what, open up the bag and let's check the computer while I make the call.'

I did what he asked, opening up the computer the way they used to make me do at airports. I turned it on, turned it off and put it away. The cop watched with the phone to his ear while talking to someone I assumed was a secretary. I figured that mentioning Smathers would at least get me through the preliminary round.

'Got a citizen down here to see Larry Legs about the kid.'

He listened a few moments and then hung up.

'Second floor. Up the stairs, to your left, go down the hall, last door. Says Homicide. He's the black guy.'

'Thanks.'

As I headed up the stairs I thought about how the cop had simply referred to Smathers as 'the kid' and whoever he had spoken to had understood what he meant. It told me a lot about the case, more than what had been in the newspapers. Cops try their best to depersonalize their cases. They are like serial killers in that way. If the victim is not a person who lived and breathed and hurt, he can't haunt you. Calling a victim 'the kid' is the opposite of that practice. It told me that a year later the case still had a strong hold on Area Three.

The homicide squad room was about the size of half a tennis court and had dark green industrial carpet. There were three work pods consisting of five desks each. Two pairs of desks faced each other and the fifth, the sergeant's desk, was pushed in at the end. Along the wall to my left were row after row of file cabinets with locking bars running through the pull handles. Along the far wall, behind the work pods, were two offices with glass windows looking out on the squad room. One was the lieutenant's office. The other looked like an interview room. There was a table in there and I could see a man and a woman in the room eating sandwiches off deli paper unwrapped and used as place mats. Besides those two there were three others at desks in the room and a secretary sat behind a desk near the door.

'You want to see Larry?' she said to me.

I nodded and she pointed to the man sitting at a desk on the far side of the room. He was alone in the pod. I headed over. He didn't look up from his paperwork, even when I got to him.

'It snowing out there yet?' he asked.

'Not yet. But it's going to.'

'It always does. I'm Washington, whaddaya need?'

I looked at the two detectives in the other pods. Nobody even glanced at me.

'Well, I wanted to talk to you alone, if I could. It's about the Smathers kid. I have some information on it.'

I could tell without looking at them that this made the others look over at me. Washington, too, finally put down his pen and looked up at me. He looked like he was in his thirties but already there was a dusting of gray in his shortcropped hair. Still, he was in good shape. I could tell that before he even stood up. He also looked sharp. He wore a dark brown suit with a white shirt and striped tie. The suit jacket could barely contain his massive chest.

'You want to talk to me alone? Whaddaya got?'

'Well, that's what I want to talk to you alone about.'

'You're not one of these guys wants to confess, are you?'

I smiled.

'What if I was? Maybe I'd be the real thing.'

'That'd be the day. All right, let's go in the room. But I

hope you're not going to waste my time – what'd you say your name was?'

'Jack McEvoy.'

'Okay, Jack, if I kick those people outta there and you waste my time, they and me aren't going to be too happy about it.'

'I don't think it will be a problem.'

He stood up now and I could see that he was shorter than I had thought. He had the lower half of another man's body. Short, stubby legs beneath a wide and strong upper torso. Thus the name the desk cop had used, Larry Legs. No matter how sharply he dressed this oddness in his physique would always betray him.

'Something wrong?' he asked when he came around to me.

'Uh, no. I was . . . Jack McEvoy.'

I put down the laptop and held out my hand but Washington didn't take it.

'Let's go into the room, Jack.'

'Sure.'

He had traded the snub of my stare for one of his own. It was okay. I walked behind him over to the door of the room where the man and woman were eating their lunch. He glanced back once, looking down at the satchel I carried.

'Whaddaya got in there?'

'Computer. A couple things to show you if you're interested.'

He opened the door and the man and woman looked up.

'Sorry, folks, picnic's over,' Washington said.

'Can you give us ten, Legs?' the man asked before getting up.

'Can't do it. Got a customer here.'

They rewrapped what was left of their sandwiches and left the room without a further word. The man gave me a stare that I interpreted to be annoyance. I didn't care. Washington signaled me in and I put my computer case down on the table next to a folded cardboard sign with the no-smoking symbol on it. We sat down on opposite sides of the table. The room smelled like stale smoke and Italian salad dressing.

'Now, what can I do for you?' Washington asked.

I gathered my thoughts and tried to appear calm. I was never comfortable dealing with cops, even though their world fascinated me. I always felt that they might suspect something about me. Something bad. Some telling flaw in me.

'I'm not sure where to begin. I'm from Denver. I just got in this morning. I'm a reporter and I came across –'

'Wait a minute, wait a minute. You're a reporter? What kind of reporter?'

I could see a slight pulse of anger beneath the dark skin of his upper left jaw. I was prepared for this.

'Newspaper reporter. I work for the *Rocky Mountain News*. Just hear me out and then if you want to throw me out, that's fine. But I don't think you will.'

'Look, man, I've heard about every pitch in the world from guys like you. I don't have the time. I don't –'

'What if John Brooks was murdered?'

I watched his face for any sign that he might already believe this. There was nothing. He gave nothing away.

'Your partner,' I said. 'I think he might have been murdered.'

Washington shook his head.

'Now, I've heard everything. By who? Who killed him?'

'By the same person who killed my brother.' I stalled a moment and looked at him until I had his full attention. 'He was a homicide cop. He worked in Denver. He was killed about a month ago. They thought at first it was a suicide, too. I started looking into it and I ended up here. I'm a reporter but this isn't really about that. It's about my brother. And it's about your partner.'

Washington creased his brow into a dark V and just stared at me for a long moment. I waited him out. He was at the cliff. He either went over with me or he threw me out. He broke the stare and leaned back. Out of his inside coat pocket he took a pack of cigarettes and lit one. He pulled a steel trash can over from the corner so he could use it for ashes. I wondered how many times he had heard people tell him that smoking would stunt his growth. He cocked his head when he exhaled so that the blue smoke went up and hovered against the ceiling. He leaned forward across the table.

'I don't know if you are some nut or not. Let me see some ID.'

We were going over the cliff. I took out my wallet and gave him my driver's license, press card and DPD police pass. He eyed them all closely but I knew he had already decided to listen to the story. There was something about Brooks's death that made Washington want to listen to a story from a reporter he didn't even know.

'Okay,' he said as he handed the IDs back. 'So you're legit. It still doesn't mean I have to believe a word you say.'

'No. But I think you believe it already.'

'Look, you going to tell your story or not? Don't you think if there was something not right that I'd be on the fucking thing like . . . like – What do you know about it, anyway?'

'Not much. Just what was in the papers.'

Washington stubbed the cigarette out on the side of the trash can and then dropped the butt in.

'Hey, Jack, tell your story. Otherwise, do me a big favor and just get the fuck out of here.'

I didn't need my notes. I told the story with every detail because I knew each one of them. It took a half hour during which Washington smoked two more cigarettes but never asked a question. Each time he kept the cigarette in his mouth, so the smoke curled up and hid his eyes. But I knew. Just like with Wexler. I was confirming something that he had felt inside his guts all along.

'You want Wexler's number?' I asked at the end. 'He'll tell you everything I just said is legit.'

'No, I'll get it if I need it.'

'You have any questions?'

'No, not at the moment.'

He just stared at me.

'Then what's next?'

'I'm going to check this out. Where you going to be?'

'The Hyatt down by the river.'

'Okay, I'll call you.'

'Detective Washington, that's not good enough.'

'How do you mean?'

'I mean, I came here to get information, not just to give it and then go back to my room. I want to ask you about Brooks.'

'Look, kid, we didn't have any kind of deal like that. You came here, you told the story. There was no –'

'Look, don't patronize me by calling me "kid" like I'm some kind of hick from the sticks. I've given you something and I want something back. That's why I came.'

'I don't have anything for you now, Jack.'

'That's bullshit. You can sit there and lie, Larry Legs, but I know you've got something. I need it.'

'What, to make a big story that'll bring the rest of the jackals like you out?'

I was the one who leaned forward this time.

'I told you, this isn't about a story.'

I leaned back and we both looked at each other. I wanted a cigarette but didn't have any and I didn't want to ask him for one. The silence was punctuated when one of the detectives I had seen in the homicide room opened the door and looked in.

'Everything okay?' he asked.

'Get the fuck out of here, Rezzo,' Washington said. After the door was closed, he said, 'Nosy prick. You know what they're thinking, don't you? They're thinking maybe you're in here coppin' to doin' the kid. It's the year anniversary, you know. Weird things happen. Wait till they hear this story.'

I thought of the photo of the boy in my pocket.

'I went by there on the way over,' I said. 'There's flowers.'

'They're always there,' Washington said. 'The family goes by there all the time.'

I nodded and for the first time felt guilty about taking the photo. I didn't say anything. I just waited for Washington. He seemed to ease up some. His face became softer, relaxed.

'Look, Jack, I gotta do some checking. And some thinking. If I tell you I'll call you, I'm gonna call you. Go back to the hotel, get a massage, whatever. I'll call you one way or the other in a couple hours.'

I nodded reluctantly and he stood up. He held his arm across the table, his right hand out. I shook it.

'Pretty good work. For a reporter, I mean.'

I picked up my computer and left. The squad room was more crowded now and a lot of them watched me go. I guess I had been in there long enough for them to know I wasn't a crackpot. Outside it was colder and the snow was beginning to come down hard. It took me fifteen minutes to flag down a cab.

On the ride back I asked the driver to swing by Wisconsin and Clark and I jumped out and ran across the snow to the tree. I put the photo of Bobby Smathers back where I'd found it.

12

·········

Larry Legs kept me twisting in the wind the rest of the afternoon. At five I tried calling him but couldn't locate him at Area Three or Eleven-Twenty-One, as the department's headquarters was known. The secretary in the homicide office refused to disclose his whereabouts or to page him. At six I was resigned to being blown off when there was a knock on my door. It was him.

'Hey, Jack,' he said without stepping in. 'Let's take a ride.'

Washington had his car parked in the valet lane in the hotel drive-up. On the dash he had placed a Police Business card so there was no problem. We got in and pulled out. He crossed the river and started north on Michigan Avenue. The snow had not abated as far as I could tell and there were drifts along both sides of the road. Many of the cars on the road had a three-inch frosting on their horizontal surfaces. I could see my breath in Washington's car and the heater was on high.

'Guess you get a lot of snow where you come from, Jack.'

'Yeah.'

He was just making conversation. I was anxious to see what he really had to say but thought it better to wait, to let him tell me at his speed. I could always pull the reporter act and ask questions later.

He turned west on Division and headed away from the lake. The sparkle of the Miracle Mile and the Gold Coast soon disappeared and the buildings began to get a little more seedy and in need of repair and upkeep. I thought maybe we were heading toward the school Bobby Smathers had disappeared from but Washington didn't say.

It was completely dark now. We went under the El and soon passed a school. Washington pointed at it.

'That's where the kid went. There's the yard. Just like that, he was gone.' He snapped his fingers. 'I staked it all day yesterday. You know, a year since the disappearance. Just in case something happened or the guy, the doer, came back by.'

'Anything?'

Washington shook his head and dropped into a brooding silence.

But we didn't stop. If Washington wanted me to see the school, the view had been quick. We kept heading west and eventually came upon a series of brick towers that somehow looked abandoned in some way. I knew what they were. The projects. They were dimly lit monoliths against the blue-black sky. They had assuredly taken on the appearance of those that were housed within. They were cold and despairing, the have-nots of the city skyline.

'What are we doing?' I asked.

'You know what this place is?'

'Yeah. I went to school here – I mean in Chicago. Everybody knows Cabrini-Green. What about it?'

'I grew up here. So did Jumpin' John Brooks.'

Immediately, I thought of the odds. First of just surviving in such a place, next of surviving and *then* becoming a cop.

'Vertical ghettos, each one of them. Me and John used to say it was the only time when you had to take the elevator up when you were going to hell.'

I just nodded. This was out of my realm completely.

'And that's only if the elevators were working,' he added.

I realized that I never considered that Brooks might be a black man. There was no photo in the computer printouts and no reason to mention race in the stories. I had just assumed he was white and it was an assumption I would have to analyze later. At the moment, I was trying to figure out what Washington was trying to tell me by taking me here.

Washington pulled into a lot next to one of the buildings. There were a couple of dumpsters coated with decades of graffiti slogans. There was a rusted basketball backboard but the rim was long gone. He put the car in park but left it running. I didn't know if that was to keep the heat flowing or to allow us a quick getaway if needed. I saw a small group of teenagers in long coats, their faces as dark as the sky, scurry from the building closest to us, then cross a frozen courtyard and hustle into one of the other buildings.

'At this point you're wondering what the hell you're doing here,' Washington said then. 'That's okay, I understand. A white boy like you.'

Again I said nothing. I was letting him run out his line.

'See that one, third on the right. That was our building. I was on fourteen with my grand-auntie and John lived with his mother on twelve, one below us. They didn't have no thirteen, already enough bad luck 'round here. Neither of us had fathers. At least ones that showed up.'

I thought he wanted me to say something but I didn't know what. I had no earthly idea what kind of struggle the two friends must have had to make it out of the tombstone of a building he had pointed at. I remained mute.

'We were friends for life. Hell, he ended up marrying my first girlfriend, Edna. Then on the department, after we both made homicide and trained with senior detectives for a few years, we asked to be partnered. And damn, it got approved. Story about us in the *Sun-Times* once. They stuck us in Three because it included this place. They figured it was part of our expertise. A lot of our cases come outta here. But it's still on rotation. So we just happened to be the ones catching on the day that boy turned up without no fingers. Shit, the call came in right at eight. Ten minutes before and it would've gone to night shift.'

He was silent for a while, probably thinking about what kind of difference it would have made if the call had gone to somebody else.

'Sometimes at night when we'd been workin' a case or on a stake or something, me'n John would drive out here after shift, park right where we are now and just look the place over.'

It occurred to me then what the message was. Larry Legs

knew Jumpin' John hadn't pulled the trigger on himself because he had known the exact struggle Brooks had experienced coming out of a place like this. Brooks had fought his way out of hell and he wasn't about to go back by his own hand. That was the message.

'This is how you knew, isn't it?'

Washington looked across the seat at me and nodded once.

'It was just one of those things you know, that's all. He didn't do it. I told them that in MIU but they just wanted to get it the fuck away from them.'

'So all you had was your gut. There was nothing out of line anywhere else?'

'There was one thing but it wasn't enough for them. I mean they had the handwriting, his history with the shrink, all that in place. It fit too nicely for them. He was a suicide before they zipped up the bag and took him away. Cut and dried.'

'What was the one thing?'

'The two shots.'

'What do you mean?'

'Let's get out of here. Let's get some food.'

He put the car in drive and made a large circle in the lot and then out onto the street. We headed north on streets I had never been on. I had an idea where we were going, though. After five minutes of this I was tired of waiting for the next part of the story.

'What about the two shots?'

'He fired two shots, right?'

'Did he? It wasn't in the papers.'

'They never put out all the details on anything. But I was there at the house. Edna called me after she found him. I got there ahead of MIU. There was one shot in the floor and one shot in the mouth. The official explanation was that the first shot was supposed to be him seeing if he could do it or something, like a practice. Gettin' the courage up. Then the second time was when he went ahead and did it. It didn't make sense. Not to me.'

'Why not? What did you think the two shots were for?'

'I think the first one went in the mouth. The second one was for gunshot residue. The perp wrapped John's hand around the gun and fired it into the floor. John's hand gets GSR on it. The case goes suicide. End of story.'

'But nobody agreed with you.'

'Not until today. Not until you turn up with this Edgar Allan Poe thing. I went to Major Investigations to tell them what you've got. I reminded them of the problems with the suicide. My problems. They are going to reopen it and take another look. Tomorrow A.M. we've got a start-up meeting over at Eleven-Twenty-One. The MIU chief is going to get me detached and put on the squad.'

'That's great.'

I watched out the window and was silent for a while. I was excited. Things were falling into place. I now had the presumed self-inflicted deaths of two cops in two different cities being reinvestigated as possible murders and possibly connected. That was a story. A damn good one. And it was something I could use as a wedge in Washington to get into the foundation records and even the FBI. That is, if I got there first. If Chicago or Denver went to the bureau first, I'd likely be squeezed out because they wouldn't need me anymore.

'Why?' I said out loud.

'Why what?'

'Why is somebody doing this? *What* exactly are they doing?'

Washington didn't answer. He just drove through the cold night.

We had dinner in a booth in the back of the Slammer, a cop bar near Area Three. Both of us ordered the special, roast turkey and gravy, good cold-weather food. As we ate, Washington gave me a rundown on the MIU plan. He told me everything was off the record and that if I wanted to write anything, I had to get it from the lieutenant who would eventually head up the squad. I had no problem with that. The squad was going to exist because of me. The lieutenant would have to talk to me.

Washington kept both elbows on the table while he ate. It looked like he was guarding his food. He spoke with his mouth full at times but that was because he was excited. So was I. I was also wary of protecting my place in the investigation, in the story.

'We'll start off with Denver,' Washington said. 'We'll work together, get our ducks lined up and then see what happens. Hey, did you talk to Wexler? He was mad at you, boy.'

'How come?'

'Why you think? You didn't tell him about Poe, Brooks, Chicago. I think you lost a source there, Jack.'

'Maybe. They got anything new there?'

'Yeah, the ranger.'

'What about him?'

'They did the hypnosis thing. Took him back to that day. He said your brother was wearing only one glove when he looked in the window of the car for the gun. Then that glove, with the GSR, somehow gets back on the hand. Wexler said they've got no doubts about it now.'

I nodded more to myself than to Washington.

'You and Denver, you'll have to go to the FBI, won't you? You're talking about crimes connected across state lines.'

'We'll see. You gotta remember, the locals here never get much excited about working with the G. We go to them and we get bigfooted. Every time, right up the ass. But you're right, it's probably the only way. If this is what I think it is, and what you think it is, the bureau will eventually have to run the show.'

I didn't tell Washington I was going to the FBI myself. I knew I had to get there first. I pushed my plate aside, looked at Washington and shook my head. This story was incredible.

'What's your feeling on this? What are we talking about?'

'Only a few possibilities,' Washington said. 'One, we're talking about one guy, somebody out there killing people, then doubling back and taking out the lead cop working the case.'

I nodded. I was with him.

'Second, the first killings are unrelated and our doer just comes into town, waits for a case he likes or sees on the TV and goes after the cop who heads up the investigation.'

'Yeah.'

'And third is we have two killers. In both cities one does the first killing and the second comes in and does the second, takes out the cop. Of the three, I don't like this one. Too many questions. Do they know each other? Are they working together? It gets pretty far out there.'

'They would have to know each other. How else would the second guy know where the first one has been?'

'Exactly. So we are concentrating on possibilities one and two. We haven't decided whether Denver is coming here and we'll send some people there but we've got to look at the boy and the college kid. Look for any connection and if we find one we go from there.'

I nodded. I was thinking of the first possibility. One person, one killer doing all of this.

'If it is just one guy, who is the real target?' I asked, more to myself than Washington. 'Is it the first victim or the cop?'

Washington put the V back in his brow.

'Maybe,' I said, 'we've got somebody who wants to kill cops. That's his objective, okay? So he uses the first killing – Smathers, Lofton – to draw out his prey. The cop.'

I looked around the table. Saying it out loud, though I had been thinking it since I was on the plane, sent a chill through me.

'Spooky, huh?' Washington asked.

'Yeah. Real spooky.'

'And you know why? Because if this is the case, there's got to be others. Every time a cop supposedly kills himself the investigation is quick and quiet. No department wants that kind of story. So they go through the motions quick and then that's it. So there's gotta be more of them out there. If the first possibility is the correct one, then this guy didn't begin with Brooks and end with your brother. There's more. I'd bet on it.'

He pushed his plate away. He was finished.

A half hour later he dropped me at the front of the Hyatt. The wind off the lake was chilling. I didn't want to stand outside but Washington said he wasn't coming up to the room. He gave me a business card.

'I got my home and beeper on there. Call me.'

'I will.'

'Okay then, Jack.' He put his hand out and I took it. 'And thanks, man.'

'For what?'

'For making believers out of them. I owe you one for that. So does Jumpin' John.'

13
....

Gladden stared at the bright blue screen for several seconds before starting. It was an exercise he routinely followed to help clear his mind of the pressures and the hatred. But this time it was hard. He was full of rage.

He shook it off and pulled the computer onto his lap. He cleared the screen and rolled the ball with his thumb until the arrow moved from window to window on the screen and stopped on the TERMINAL icon. He clicked the ENTER button and then chose the program he wanted. He clicked on DIAL and then waited while listening to the harsh screech of the computer's uplink. It was like birth, he thought, every time. The horrible screech of the newly born. After the connection was complete, the welcome template appeared on the screen.

WELCOME TO THE PTL CLUB

After a few seconds the screen moved up and there was a coded prompt for Gladden's first password. He entered the letters, waited while they were acknowledged, then entered the second password when he got the prompt. In a moment his entry was approved and the warning template appeared on the screen.

PRAISE THE LORD!

RULES OF THE ROAD

1. NEVER EVER USE A REAL NAME
2. NEVER PROVIDE SYSTEMS NUMBERS TO ACQUAINTANCES

3. NEVER AGREE TO MEET ANOTHER USER
4. BE AWARE THAT OTHER USERS MAY BE FOREIGN BODIES
5. SYSOP RESERVES THE RIGHT TO DELETE ANY USER
6. MESSAGE BOARDS MAY NOT BE USED FOR DISCUSSION OF ANY ILLEGAL ACTIVITIES — THIS IS FORBIDDEN!
7. PTL NETWORK IS NOT RESPONSIBLE FOR CONTENT
8. PRESS ANY KEY TO CONTINUE

Gladden pressed ENTER and the computer informed him he had a private message waiting to be read. He lightly touched the appropriate keys and the message from the systems operator filled the top half of the laptop's screen.

THANKS FOR THE WARNING. HOPE ALL IS WELL AND MOST SORRY TO HEAR OF YOU IN HARM'S WAY. ALL IS WELL ON THIS END. IF YOU ARE READING THIS THEN I ASSUME YOU ARE OUT AND ABOUT. BRAVO! GOOD LUCK AND STAY IN TOUCH WITH YOURSELF AND OTHERS. (HEH, HEH)

PTL

Gladden typed in an R and hit ENTER and a reply message template appeared on the screen. He typed out a message to the sender of the first message.

NOT TO WORRY ABOUT ME. ALL IS TAKEN CARE OF. YOURS TRULY IS NOW OUT AND ABOUT..........PTL

That done, Gladden typed in commands so that he could move to the main bulletin board directory. Finally, the screen filled with the directory of message boards. Each board was listed with the number of active messages available to be read.

He quickly typed in the necessary commands to move to the Musings & Whinings board. It was one of the most popular boards. He'd already read through most of the files and had contributed a few himself. The writers were all ranting about how unfair life was to them. How maybe in a different time their tastes and instincts would be accepted as normal. It was more whining than musing, Gladden had always thought. He called up the file marked Eidolon and began reading it again.

I think they will know about me soon. My time in the light of public fascination and fear is near. I am ready. Each one of my kind eventually assumes the mantle. Anonymity will be lost. I will be given a name, a designation not reflective of who I am nor of my many skills, but simply determined by its ability to fit nicely into a tabloid newspaper headline and stimulate the masses to thoughts of fear. We study what we fear. Fear sells newspapers and television shows. Soon it will be my turn to sell.

I will be hunted soon and I will be notorious. But they won't find me. Never. That's what they won't realize. That I have always been ready for them.

I have decided it is time to tell my story. I want to tell it. I will input all that I have, all that I am. Through these windows you will see me live and die. My laptop Boswell makes no judgments, cringes not at a single word. Who better to hear my confession than Laptop Boswell? Who more accurate a biographer than Laptop Boswell? I will begin to tell you all now. Turn on your flashlights. I will live and die here in the dark.

Man is sometimes extraordinarily, passionately, in love with suffering

I didn't write that first but I wish that I had. But it doesn't matter because I believe it. My suffering is my passion, my religion. It never leaves me. It guides me. It is me. I can see that now. I think what is meant by those words is that our pain is the pathway upon which we make our life's travels and choices. It paves the way, so to speak, for all that we do and become. Therefore, we embrace it. We study it and, for all its harshness, we love it. We have no choice.

I have a great feeling of clarity about this, of complete understanding. I can turn and look back on my path and see how the pain made all my choices. I look forward and can see where it will take me. I don't really walk along the path any more. It moves beneath me, carrying me, like a great ribbon through time. It carried me here.

My pain is the rock upon which I make my stand. I am the perpetrator. The Eidolon. True identity is pain. My pain. Until death do we part.

Drive safely, dear friends.

He read it again and felt deeply moved by it. It touched his true heart.

He went back to the main menu and switched into the Barter Board to see if there were any new customers. There weren't. He typed the G command for good-bye. He then turned off the computer and folded it closed.

Gladden wished the cops hadn't taken his camera. He couldn't risk going to claim it and he could barely afford to buy another one with the money he had left. But he knew that without a camera he could not fill orders and there would be no more money. The anger building inside him felt like razors moving through his blood, cutting him from inside. He decided to wire more money out from Florida, then go shopping for another camera.

He went to the window and looked out at the cars slowly

moving along Sunset. It was an endless moving parking lot. All that smoking steel, he thought. All that flesh. Where was it going? He wondered how many of them in those cars were like himself. How many had the urges and how many felt the razors? How many had the courage to follow through? Again the anger pushed through his thoughts. It was something palpable inside him now, a black flower spreading its petals in his throat, choking him.

He went to the phone and dialed the number Krasner had given him. Sweetzer picked up after four rings.

'Busy, Sweetzer?'

'Who's this?'

'It's me. How are the kids?'

'What – who is this?'

His instincts told Gladden to hang up right then. Don't deal with their kind. But he was so curious.

'You have my camera,' he said.

There was a short moment of silence.

'Mr Brisbane, and how are you?'

'Fine, Detective, thank you.'

'Yes, we have your camera and you are entitled to have that back since you require it to make a living. Do you want to make an appointment to pick it up?'

Gladden closed his eyes and squeezed the phone until he thought he would crush it. They knew. If they didn't they would have told him to forget the camera. But they knew something. And they wanted him to come in. The question was how much did they know? Gladden wanted to scream but a higher thought was to keep cool with Sweetzer. No false moves, he told himself.

'I'll have to think about that.'

'Well, it looks like a nice camera. I'm not sure how it works but I wouldn't mind having it. It's here if you want –'

'Fuck you, Sweetzer.'

The anger overtook him. Gladden spoke the words through a clenched jaw.

'Look, Brisbane, I was doing my job. If you got a problem with that come see me and we'll do something about that. If you want your fucking camera then you can come and get that, too. But I'm not going to stay on the line while you –'

'You got kids, Sweetzer?'

The line was silent for a long moment but Gladden knew the detective was there.

'What did you say?'

'You heard me.'

'Are you threatening my family, you motherfucking son of a bitch?'

Now Gladden was silent for a moment. Then a low sound started deep in his throat and grew into a maniacal laugh. He let it out uncontrolled until it was all he could hear and think about. Then, suddenly, he slammed the receiver down on the phone and cut the laughter off like a knife in the throat. He had an ugly grimace across his face and he shouted to the empty room through clenched teeth.

'Fuck you!'

Gladden opened his laptop again and accessed the photo directory. The computer's screen was state of the art for a laptop model but the graphics chip still wasn't nearly the quality he'd have on a stationary PC. But the images were clear enough and he was able to make do. He went through the file photo by photo. It was a macabre collection of the dead and the living. Somehow, he was able to find solace in the photos, a sense that he had control over things in his life.

Still, he was saddened by what he saw before him and what he had done. These little sacrifices. Offered up so that he could salve his wounds. He knew how selfish it was, how grotesquely warped it was. And the fact that he turned these sacrifices into money tore away his comfort, turned it into the self-loathing and disgust that always came. Sweetzer and the others were right. He deserved to be hunted.

He rolled onto his back and looked at the water-stained ceiling. Tears filled his eyes. He closed them and tried to sleep, tried to forget. But his Best Pal was there in the darkness behind his eyelids. As always, he was there. His face set, a horrible slash for lips.

Gladden opened his eyes and looked at the door. There had

been a knock. He quickly sat up as he heard the metal scrape of a key going into the outside knob. He realized his mistake. Sweetzer had had a trace on the line. They knew he would call!

The door to the room swung open. A small black woman in a white uniform stood in the doorway with two towels draped over her arm.

'Housekeeping,' she said. 'I am sorry I'm so late today but it's been a busy day. Tomorrow I'll do your room first.'

Gladden exhaled and noticed that he had neglected to put the DO NOT DISTURB sign on the outside knob.

'It's okay,' he said, quickly getting up to stop her entrance into the room. 'Just the towels today, anyway.'

As he took the towels he noticed embroidered on her uniform the name Evangeline. She had a lovely face and he immediately felt sorry that this was her job, cleaning up after others.

'Thank you, Evangeline.'

He noticed her eyes go past him into the room and fall down to the bed. It was still made. He hadn't pulled the covers down the night before. Then she looked back at him and nodded with what he guessed was a smile.

'That'd be all you need?'

'Yes, Evangeline.'

'Have a nice day.'

Gladden closed the door and turned around. There on the bed was the open laptop computer. On the screen was one of the photographs. He moved to the bed and studied it without moving the computer. Then he moved back to the door, opened it and stood under the door frame where she had been. He looked at the computer. He could tell. The boy on the ground and what else could that be against the perfect white canvas of snow but blood.

He quickly went to the computer and hit the emergency kill button he had programmed himself. The door was still open. Gladden tried to think. Jesus, he thought, what a mistake.

He walked to the door and stepped out. Evangeline was

down the walkway standing next to a housekeeping cart. She looked back at him, her face revealing nothing. But Gladden knew he had to be sure. He could not risk everything on reading this woman's face.

'Evangeline,' he said. 'I changed my mind. The room could probably use a going-over. I need toilet paper and soap, anyway.'

She put down the clipboard she had been writing on and stooped to get toilet paper and soap out of the cart. As Gladden watched he put his hands in his pockets. He noticed she was chewing gum and clicking it. An insulting thing to do in front of someone else. It was like he was invisible. He was nothing.

When Evangeline approached him with the items from the cart, he made no move to take his hands from his pockets. He took a step back to allow her to go into the room. After she stepped in, Gladden walked down to the cart and looked at the clipboard she had placed on top. After room 112 was the notation 'Just Towels.'

Gladden looked around as he headed back to the room. The motel was a courtyard design with two floors of about twenty-four rooms each. He saw another housekeeping cart on the upper floor across the way. It was parked in front of an open door but there was no sign of the maid. The pool at the center of the courtyard was empty of guests. Too cold. He saw no one else anywhere.

He stepped into the room and closed the door as Evangeline came out of the bathroom holding the bag from the trash can.

'Sir, we have to keep the door open when we're working inside a room. Those are the rules.'

He blocked her way to the door.

'Did you see the photograph?'

'What? Sir, I have to open the –'

'Did you see the photo on the computer? On the bed?'

He pointed to the laptop and watched her eyes. She looked confused but didn't turn.

'What photo?'

She turned to look at the sagging bed and then back to him with a look of confusion and growing annoyance on her face.

'I didn't take anything. You call Mr Barrs right now if you think I took somethin'. I'm an honest lady. He can have one of the other girls search me. I don't got your photo. I don't even know what picture you mean.'

Gladden looked at her a moment and then smiled.

'You know, Evangeline, I think maybe you are an honest lady. But I have to be sure. You understand.'

14

·······

The Law Enforcement Foundation was on Ninth Street in Washington, D.C., a few blocks from the Justice Department and FBI headquarters. It was a large building and I assumed other agencies and foundations funded from the public trough were housed here as well. Once I was in through the heavy doors I checked the directory and took the elevator to the third floor.

It looked like the LEF had the entire third floor. From the elevator I was greeted by a large reception desk behind which sat a large woman. In the news business we call them deception desks because the women they hire to sit behind them rarely let you go where you want to go or see whom you want to see. I told her I wanted to speak to Dr Ford, the foundation director quoted in the *New York Times* article about police suicides. Ford was the keeper of the database to which I had to get access.

'He's at lunch. Do you have an appointment?'

I told her I had no appointment and put one of my cards down in front of her. I looked at my watch. Quarter to one.

'Oh, well, a reporter,' she said as if the profession were synonymous with convict. 'That's entirely different. You have to go through the public affairs office before it is even decided that you may speak to Dr Ford.'

'I see. You think there's anybody in public affairs or are they out to lunch, too?'

She picked up the phone and made a call.

'Michael? Are you there or are you on lunch? I have a man here who says he is from the *Rocky Mountain News* in – No, he first asked to see Dr Ford.'

She listened a few moments and then said okay and hung up.

'Michael Warren will see you. He says he has a one-thirty appointment so you'd better hurry.'

'Hurry where?'

'Room three oh three. Go down the hall behind me, take your first right and then it's the first door on the right.'

As I made the trek I kept thinking that the name Michael Warren was familiar but couldn't place it. The door to 303 opened as I was reaching for it. A man of about forty was about to step out when he saw me and stopped.

'Are you the one from the *Rocky*?'

'Yes.'

'I was beginning to wonder if you took a wrong turn. Come on in. I only have a few minutes. I'm Mike Warren. Michael if you use my name in print, though I prefer you don't use it and talk to the staff here instead. Hopefully I can help you with that.'

Once he was behind his cluttered desk I introduced myself and we shook hands. He told me to take a seat. There were newspapers stacked on one side of the desk. On the other side were photos of a wife and two children, angled so that Warren could see them as well as his visitors. There was a computer on a low table to his left and a photo of Warren shaking the president's hand on the wall above it. Warren was clean shaven and wore a white shirt with a maroon tie. The collar was frayed a bit where his afternoon whiskers rubbed against it. His jacket was draped over the back of his chair. His skin was very pale and set off by dark sharp eyes and straight black hair.

'So what's up? Are you in the Scripps D.C. bureau?'

He was talking about the parent company. It maintained a bureau of reporters that fed Washington stories to all papers in the chain. It was the office Greg Glenn had suggested I go through earlier in the week.

'No, I'm out from Denver.'

'Well, what can I do you for?'

'I need to talk to Nathan Ford or maybe whoever is directly handling the police suicide study.'

'Police suicide. That's an FBI project. Oline Fredrick's the researcher handling that with them.'

'Yes, I know the FBI is involved.'

'Let's see.' He picked up the desk phone but then put it back down. 'You know, you didn't call ahead on this, did you? I don't recognize the name.'

'No, I just got into town. It's a breaking story, you could say.'

'Breaking story? Police suicide? That doesn't sound like deadline stuff. Why the hurry?'

Then it struck me who he was.

'Did you used to work for the *L.A. Times*? The Washington bureau? You that Michael Warren?'

He smiled because he, or his name, had been recognized.

'Yes, how'd you know?'

'The *Post-Times* wire. I've been scrolling it for years. I recognized the name. You covered Justice, right? Did good stuff.'

'Until a year ago. I quit and came here.'

I nodded. There was always a moment of uneasy silence when I crossed paths with somebody who had left the life and was now on the other side of the line. Usually, they were burnouts, reporters who grew tired of the always-on-deadline and always-need-to-produce life. I once read a book about a reporter written by a reporter who described the life as always running in front of a thresher. I thought it was the most accurate description I'd read. Sometimes people got tired of running in front of the machine, sometimes they got pulled in and were left shredded. Sometimes they managed to get out from in front of it. They used their expertise in the business to seek the steadiness of a job as a person who handled the media rather than was part of it. This is what Warren had done and somehow I felt sorry for him. He had been damn good. I hoped he didn't feel the same regret.

'You miss it?'

I had to ask him, just to be polite.

'Not yet. Every now and then a good story comes along and I wish I was in there with everybody else, looking for the odd angle. But it can run you ragged.'

He was lying and I think he knew I knew it. He wanted to go back.

'Yeah, I'm beginning to feel it some myself.'

I returned the lie, just to make him feel better, if that was possible.

'So what about police suicides? What's your angle?'

He looked at his watch.

'Well, it wasn't a breaking story until a couple days ago. Now it is. I know you only have a few minutes but I can explain it pretty quickly. I just ... I don't want to be insulting but I'd like for you to promise me what I say here is in confidence. It's my story and when it's ready, I'm going to break it.'

He nodded.

'Don't worry, I understand completely. I won't discuss whatever it is you are going to tell me with any other journalist unless that other journalist specifically asks about the same thing. I may *have* to talk about it with other people here at the foundation or in law enforcement, for that matter. I can't make any promise in that regard until I know what we are talking about.'

'That's fair.'

I felt myself trusting him. Maybe because it is always easy to trust somebody who has done what you have done. I also think I liked telling what I'd learned to somebody who would know its value as a story. It was a form of bragging and I wasn't above it. I started.

'At the start of this week I began working on a story about police suicide. I know, it's been done before. But I had a new angle. My brother was a cop and a month ago he supposedly committed suicide. I –'

'Oh, Jesus, I am sorry.'

'Thank you, but I didn't bring it up for that reason. I decided to write about it because I wanted to understand what he had done, what the police in Denver said he had done. I went through the routine, pulled clips on a Nexis search and, naturally, I came up with a couple references to the foundation's study.'

He tried to surreptitiously look at his watch and I decided to get his attention.

'To make a long story short, in trying to find out why he killed himself I found out he didn't.'

I looked at him. I had his attention.

'What do you mean, he didn't?'

'My investigation has so far determined that my brother's suicide was a carefully disguised murder. Someone killed him. The case has been reopened. I have also linked it to a supposed cop suicide last year in Chicago. That one also has been reopened. I just came in from there this morning. The cops in Chicago and Denver and I think that somebody might be moving around the country killing cops and making it look like suicide. The key to finding the other cases may be in the information collected for the foundation's study. Don't you have all the records on cop suicides for the whole country over the last five years?'

We sat in silence for a few moments. Warren just stared at me.

'I think you better tell me the long story,' he finally said. 'No, wait.'

He held up his hand like a crossing guard signaling stop, picked up the phone with the other and pushed a speed-dial number.

'Drex? Mike. Listen, I know this is late but I'm not going to make it. Something's come up over here ... No ... We'll have to reschedule. I'll talk to you tomorrow. Thanks, bye.'

He put down the phone and looked at me.

'It was just a lunch. Now tell me this story of yours.'

A half hour later, after he had made some calls to set up a meeting, Warren led me through the labyrinth of the foundation's hallways to a room marked 383. It was a conference room and already seated there were Dr Nathan Ford and

Oline Fredrick. The introductions were quick and Warren and I sat down.

Fredrick looked like she was in her mid-twenties with curly blond hair and an uninterested air about her. I immediately paid more attention to Ford. Warren had prepped me. He said any decisions would be made by Ford. The foundation director was a small man in a dark suit but he had a presence that commanded the room. He wore glasses with thick black frames and rose-tinted lenses. He had a full beard of uniform gray that perfectly matched his hair. He didn't moved his head as much as he did his eyes when he followed our movements as we entered and took seats around the large oval table. He had his elbows on the table and his hands clasped together in front of him.

'Why don't we get started,' he said once the introductions were over.

'What I'd like to do is just have Jack tell you both what he told me a little while ago,' Warren said. 'And then we'll go from there. Jack, you mind going over it again?'

'Not at all.'

'I'm going to take some notes this time.'

I told the story in pretty much the same detail as I had with Warren. Every now and then I would remember something new and not necessarily significant but I would throw that in anyway. I knew I needed to impress Ford because he would be the one to decide whether or not I got Oline Fredrick's help.

The only interruption during the telling came from Fredrick. When I spoke of my brother's death, she mentioned that the protocol from the DPD on the case had been received the week before. I told her she could now toss it in the trash can. When I was finished reciting the story, I looked at Warren and raised my hands.

'Anything I missed?'

'I don't think so.'

We both looked at Ford then and waited. He hadn't moved much during the telling. Now he raised his clasped hands and gently bumped them repeatedly against his chin as he thought. I wondered what kind of doctor he was. What do you have to be to run a foundation? More politician than doctor, I thought.

'It's a very interesting story,' he said quietly. 'I can see why you are excited. I can see why Mr Warren is excited. He was a reporter for most of his adult life and I think the excitement of the story remains in his blood sometimes, possibly to the detriment of his current profession.'

He didn't look at Warren as he delivered this blow. His eyes stayed on me.

'What I don't understand, and therefore the reason I don't seem to share the same excitement as you two, is what this has to do with the foundation. I'm not clear on that, Mr McEvoy.'

'Well, Dr Ford,' Warren began, 'Jack has to –'

'No,' Ford cut him off. 'Let Mr McEvoy tell me.'

I tried to think in precise terms. Ford didn't want a lot of bullshit. He just wanted to know how he would benefit from this.

'I assume the suicide project is on a computer.'

'That is correct,' Ford said. 'Most of our studies are collated on computer. We rely on the great number of police departments out there for our field research. Reports come in – the protocol Ms Fredrick mentioned earlier. They are entered on the computer. But that means nothing. It is the skilled researcher who must digest these facts and tell us what they mean. On this study, the researcher is joined by FBI experts in reviewing the raw data.'

'I understand all of that,' I said. 'What I am saying is that you have a huge databank of incidents of police suicide.'

'Going back five, six years, I believe. The work was started before Oline came on board.'

'I need to go into your computer.'

'Why?'

'If we're right – and I'm not just talking about me. The detectives in Chicago and in Denver are thinking this way, too. We've got two cases that are connected. The –'

'Seemingly connected.'

'Right, seemingly connected. If they are, then the chances

are that there are others. We're talking about a serial killer. Maybe there's a lot, maybe a few and maybe none. But I want to check and you've got the data right here. All the reported suicides in the last six years. I want to get inside your computer and look for the ones that might be the fakes, that might be our guy.'

'How do you propose doing that?' Fredrick said. 'We've got several hundred cases on file.'

'The protocol that police departments fill out and send in, does it include the victim's rank and position in the department?'

'Yes.'

'Then we first look at all homicide detectives who killed themselves. The theory I'm working with is that this person is killing homicide cops. Maybe it's a hunted-turns-on-the-hunter sort of thing. I don't know the psychology of it, but that's where I'd start. With homicide cops. Once we have that breakout, we look at each case. We need the notes. The suicide notes. From –'

'That's not on computer,' Fredrick said. 'In each incidence, if we even have a copy of the note, it's in the hard-copy protocols in file storage. The notes themselves aren't part of the study unless they have some allusion to the pathology of the victim.'

'But you've kept the hard copies?'

'Yes, all of them. In file storage.'

'Then we go to them,' Warren chimed in excitedly.

His intrusion brought silence. Eventually, everyone's eyes were drawn to Ford's.

'One question,' the director finally said. 'Does the FBI know about this?'

'At the moment, I can't say for sure,' I said. 'I know it is the intention of the Chicago and Denver police to retrace my steps and then, once they are satisfied that I am on the right path, they are going to call in the bureau. It will go from there.'

Ford nodded and said, 'Mr McEvoy, could you step out and wait in the reception area for me? I want to talk to Ms

Fredrick and Mr Warren privately before making any decision on this matter.'

'No problem.' I stood up and headed to the door, where I hesitated and looked at Ford. 'I hope ... I mean ... I hope we can do this. Anyway, thanks.'

Michael Warren's face told the story before he said anything. I was sitting on a lumpy vinyl-covered couch in the reception area when he came down the hallway with downcast eyes. When he saw me he just shook his head.

'Let's go back to my office,' he said.

I followed silently behind him and took the same seat I had before. He looked as dejected as I felt.

'Why?' I asked.

'Because he's an asshole,' he whispered. 'Because the Justice Department punches our ticket and the FBI is the Justice Department. It's their study – they commissioned it. He's not going to let you walk through it without telling them first. He's not ever going to do anything that might knock the gravy train off the tracks. You said the wrong thing in there, Jack. You should have said the FBI was made aware of this and took a pass.'

'He wouldn't have believed that.'

'The point is, he could've said he did. If it ever blew up on him that he was helping a reporter to information before the bureau, he could have just put it on you and said he thought the bureau passed.'

'So what now? I can't just drop this.'

I wasn't really asking him. I was asking myself.

'You got any sources in the bureau? Because I guarantee he's in his office calling the bureau right now. Probably going right to Bob Backus.'

'Who's that?'

'One of the big shots down there. The suicide project belongs to his team.'

'I think I know that name.'

'You probably know Bob Backus Sr. His father. He was

some kind of supercop the bureau brought in years ago to help set up the Behavioral Science Services and the Violent Criminal Apprehension Program. I guess Bobby Jr. is trying to fill his shoes. The point is, as soon as Ford's off the phone with him, Backus will shut this thing down. Your only way in will be through the bureau.'

I couldn't think. I was totally backed into a corner. I stood up and started pacing in the small office.

'Jesus Christ, I can't believe this. This is my story ... and I'm getting pushed out of it by some dopey guy in a beard who thinks he's J. Edgar Hoover.'

'Nah, Nat Ford doesn't wear dresses.'

'It's not really that damn funny.'

'I know. I'm sorry.'

I sat back down. He made no move to dismiss me, even though our business was done. It finally occurred to me what it was he expected me to do. I just wasn't sure about how to ask. I'd never worked in Washington and didn't know how it worked. I decided to do it the Denver way. To be blunt.

'You can get into the computer anyway, right?'

I nodded at the terminal to his left. He looked over at me for a moment before responding.

'No fucking way. I'm no Deep Throat, Jack. This isn't about anything other than a crime story. That's the bottom line. You just want to get there ahead of the FBI.'

'You're a reporter.'

'Former reporter. I work here now and I'm not going to jeopardize my –'

'You know it's a story that has to be told. If Ford's in there on the phone with the FBI, they'll be out here by tomorrow and the story will be gone. You know how hard it was to get stuff from them. You were there. This ends completely right here or is published as some half-assed story in a year or maybe longer with more conjecture than facts. That's if you don't get me on that computer.'

'I said no.'

'Look, you're right. All it is is a story that I want. The big scoop. But I deserve it. You know I do. The FBI wouldn't be coming around if it wasn't for me. But I'm getting shut out ... Think about it. Think if it was you. Think if it was your brother that this happened to.'

'I have and I just said no.'

I stood up.

'Well, if you change your –'

'I won't.'

'Look, when I leave here, I'm going to check in at the Hilton. The one where Reagan got shot.'

That's all I said as I left him there and he didn't say another word.

15
· · · · · · · ·

Passing the time in my room at the Hilton I updated my computer files on what little I had learned at the foundation and then called Greg Glenn to fill him in on everything that had transpired in Chicago and Washington. When I was done, he whistled loudly and I pictured him leaning back in the chair, thinking of the possibilities.

It was a fact that I already had a good story, but I was unhappy. I wanted to stay on the leading edge of it. I didn't want to have to rely on the FBI and other investigators to tell me what they felt like telling me. I wanted to investigate. I had written countless stories about murder investigations but each time I was always an outsider looking in. This time I was inside and wanted to stay there. I was riding the front of the wave. I realized that my excitement must be the same as Sean felt when he was on a case. In the hunt, as he called it.

'You there, Jack?'

'What? Yeah, I was just thinking of something else.'

'When can we do the story?'

'Depends. Tomorrow's Friday. Give me till tomorrow. I have this feeling about the foundation guy. But if I don't hear anything by mid-morning tomorrow I'll try the FBI. I've got a name of a guy. If that doesn't get me anywhere I'll come back and write the story Saturday for Sunday.'

Sunday was the biggest circulation day. I knew Glenn would want to go big with it on a Sunday.

'Well,' he said, 'even if we have to settle for that, what you've got is a hell of a lot. You've got a nationwide investigation of a serial killer of cops who's been operating with impunity for who knows how long. This will –'

'It's not that strong. Nothing is confirmed. Right now it's a two-*state* investigation into the *possibility* of a cop killer.'

'It's still damn good. And once the FBI is in, it's nation-wide. We'll have the *New York Times*, the *Post*, all of them following our ass.'

Following *my* ass, I felt like saying but didn't. Glenn's words revealed the real truth behind most journalism. There wasn't much that was altruistic about it anymore. It wasn't about public service and the people's right to know. It was about competition, kicking ass and taking names, what paper had the story and which one was left behind. And which one got the Pulitzer at the end of the year. It was a dim view but after as many years as I had been at it, my view pretty much wasn't anything else but cynical.

Still, I'd be lying if I said I didn't savor the idea of busting out a national story and watching everybody follow. I just didn't like talking about it out loud like Glenn. And there was Sean, too. I was not losing sight of that. I wanted the man who did this to him. I wanted that more than anything.

I promised Glenn I'd call if anything developed and hung up. I paced around the room for a while and I have to admit I was thinking about the possibilities, too. I was thinking about the profile this story could give me. It could definitely get me out of Denver if I wanted it to. Maybe to one of the big three. L.A., New York, Washington. To Chicago or Miami, at the least. Then beyond that, I even began to think about a publishing deal. True crime was a major market.

I shook it off, embarrassed. It's lucky no one else knows what our most secret thoughts are. We'd all be seen for the cunning, self-aggrandizing fools we are.

I needed to get out of the room but couldn't leave because of the phone. I turned on the TV and it was just a bunch of competing talk shows serving up the usual daily selection of white trash stories. Children of strippers on one channel, porno stars whose spouses were jealous on another and men who thought women should be kept in line with occasional beatings on a third. I turned it off and thought of an idea. All I had to do was leave the room, I decided. It would guarantee that Warren would call because I wouldn't be there to take the call. It worked every time. I just hoped he would leave a message.

The hotel was on Connecticut Avenue near Dupont Circle. I walked toward the circle and stopped into Mystery Books to buy a book called *Multiple Wounds* by Alan Russell. I'd read a good review of it somewhere and figured reading would take my mind off things.

Before going back into the Hilton I spent a few minutes walking around the outside of the hotel looking for the spot where Hinckley had waited with a gun for Reagan. I remembered the pictures of the chaos vividly but I couldn't find the spot. It made me think the hotel had made some renovations, maybe so that the spot didn't become a tourist destination.

As a police reporter I was a tourist of the macabre. I moved from murder to murder, horror to horror without blinking an eye. Supposedly. As I walked back in through the lobby toward the bank of elevators I thought about what this said about me. Maybe something was wrong with me. Why was the spot where Hinckley waited important to me?

'Jack?'

I turned around at the elevators. It was Michael Warren.

'Hey.'

'I called your room . . . I thought you might be around.'

'I was just taking a walk. I was beginning to give up on you.'

I said it with a smile and a lot of hope. This moment would determine a lot of things for me. He was no longer in the suit he had on at his office. It was blue jeans and a sweater. He had a long tweed coat over his arm. He was following the pattern of a confidential source, coming in person rather than leaving a possible phone record.

'You want to go up to the room or talk down here?'

He moved toward the elevator saying, 'Your room.'.

We didn't speak in the elevator of anything of consequence. I looked at his clothes again and said, 'You've already been home.'

'I live off Connecticut on the other side of the beltway. Maryland. Wasn't that far.'

I knew that was a toll call and that was why he hadn't called first. I also figured that the hotel was on the way from his house to the foundation. I was beginning to feel the small tick of excitement in my chest. Warren was going to turn.

There was a damp smell in the hallway that seemed to be the same in every hotel I had ever been in. I got out my card key and let him into my room. My computer was still open on the little desk and my long coat and the one tie I had brought with me were thrown across the bed. Otherwise, the room was neat. He threw his coat on the bed and we took the only chairs in the room.

'So what's going on?' I asked.

'I did a search.'

He started to take a folded paper out of his back pocket.

'I have access to main computer files,' he said. 'Before I left for the day, I went in and searched the field reports for victims who were homicide detectives. There were only thirteen. I have names, departments and dates of death here on a printout.'

He offered me the unfolded page and I took it from him as gently as if it were a sheet of gold.

'Thank you,' I said. 'Will there be a record of your search?'

'I don't really know. But I don't think so. It's a pretty wide-open system. I don't know if there's a security trace option or not.'

'Thank you,' I said again. I didn't know what else to say.

'Anyway, that was the easy part,' he said. 'Going through the protocols in file storage, that's going to take some time ... I wanted to know if you'd want to help. You'd probably know better than me which ones were important.'

'When?'

'Tonight. It's the only time. The place will be closed up but I have a key to file storage because sometimes I have to dig out old things for media requests. If we don't do it tonight the hard-copy files may be gone tomorrow. I have a feeling the FBI isn't going to like them sitting up here, especially knowing you asked for them. They'll come and grab them first thing tomorrow.'

'Is that what Ford said?'

'Not exactly. I heard it through Oline. He talked to Rachel Walling, not Backus. He said she's –'

'Wait a minute. Rachel Walling?'

I knew the name. It took a moment but then I remembered she was the profiler who had signed the VICAP survey Sean had submitted on Theresa Lofton.

'Yes, Rachel Walling. She's a profiler down there. Why?'

'Nothing. The name's familiar.'

'She works for Backus. Sort of the liaison between the center and the foundation on the suicide project. Anyway, Oline says she told Ford she's going to take a look at all of this. She might even want to talk to you.'

'If I don't talk to her first.' I stood up. 'Let's go.'

'Listen, one thing.' He stood up. 'I didn't do this, okay? You use these files as an investigative tool only. You never publish a story that says you had access to foundation files. You never admit that you even saw a file. It could be my job. Do you agree?'

'Absolutely.'

'Then say it.'

'I agree. To all of it.'

We headed toward the door.

'It's funny,' he said. 'All those years procuring sources. I never really realized what they were risking for me. Now I do. It's kind of scary.'

I just looked at him and nodded. I was afraid if I said anything he'd change his mind and go home.

On the way to the foundation in his car, he added a few more ground rules.

'I am not to be a named source in your story, okay?'

'Okay.'

'And any information from me cannot be attributed to a "foundation source," either. Just a "source familiar with the investigation," okay? That gives me some cover.'

'Okay.'

'What you're looking for here are names that might be connected to your guy. If you find them, fine, but later on you don't have to report on how you got them. Do you understand?'

'Yeah, we've been over this. You're safe, Mike. I don't give up sources. Ever. All I'll do is use what we get here to get other confirmation. It'll be the blueprint. It's no problem.'

He was quiet for a few moments before doubts must have crept into his mind.

'He's going to know it's me, anyway.'

'Then why don't we stop? I don't want to jeopardize your job. I'll just wait for the bureau.'

I didn't want to do that but I had to give him the option. I wasn't that far gone yet that I'd talk a guy into losing his job just to get information for a story. I didn't want that on my conscience. There was enough there already.

'You can forget the FBI as long as it's Walling's case.'

'You know her? She tough?'

'Yeah, one of those as hard as nails with fingernail polish on. I tried shooting the shit with her once. She just shut me down. From what I hear from Oline, she got divorced or something a while back. I guess she's still in her "men are pigs" mode and it's looking permanent to me.'

I held up saying anything. Warren had to make a decision and I couldn't help.

'Don't worry about Ford,' he finally said. 'He may think it's me but he won't be able to do anything about it. I'll deny. So, unless you break the agreement, he'll have nothing but his suspicions.'

'You've got nothing to worry about with me.'

He found a spot on Constitution a half block from the foundation and parked. Our breath was coming out in thick clouds when we got out. I was nervous, whether or not he thought his job was in danger. I think we both were.

There was no guard to be fooled. No staff members working overtime to surprise us. We got in the front door with Warren's key and he knew right where we were going.

The file storage room was about the size of a double-wide garage and was taken up by rows of eight-foot steel shelves stacked with manila files with different-colored tabs.

'How're we going to do this?' I whispered.

He took the folded printout from his pocket.

'There's a section on the suicide study. We look up these names, take the protocols to my office and copy the pages we need. I left the copier on when I left. Won't even have to warm it up. And you don't have to whisper. There's nobody here.'

I noticed he said 'we' one too many times but I didn't say anything about it. He led me down one of the aisles, his finger out and pointing as he read the program headings printed on the shelves. Eventually, he found the heading for the suicide study. The files had red tabs on them.

'These here,' Warren said, raising his hand to point.

The files were thin, yet they took up three complete shelves. Oline Fredrick had been right, there were hundreds. Each red tag protruding from a file was a death. There was a lot of misery on the shelves. Now I had to hope that a few of them didn't belong there. Warren handed me the printout and I scanned the thirteen names.

'Out of all of these files only thirteen were homicide cops?'

'Yeah. The project has accumulated data on over sixteen hundred suicides. About three hundred a year. But most are street cops. Homicide dicks see the bodies but I guess for them the misery is over by the time they get there. They're usually the best and the brightest and the toughest. Seems like less of them eat the gun than the cops out on the beat. So I only came up with thirteen. Your brother and Brooks in Chicago also came up but I figured you have that stuff.'

I just nodded.

'They should be alphabetical,' he said. 'Read me the names on the list and I'll pull the files. And give me your notebook.'

It took less than five minutes to pull the files. Warren tore blank pages from my notebook and marked the spots in the stacks so they could be slipped back in quickly when we were done. It was intense work. It wasn't meeting a source like Deep Throat in a parking garage to help take down a president but my adrenaline was flowing anyway.

Still, the same rules applied. A source, no matter what his information is, has a reason, a motive, for putting himself on the line for you. I looked at Warren and couldn't see the true motive. It was a good story but it wasn't his story. He got nothing from helping other than knowing he had helped. Was that enough? I didn't know but I decided that at the same time that we were entering this sacred bond of reporter and secret source, I had to keep him at arm's length. Until I knew the true motive.

Files in hand, we walked quickly down two hallways until we got to room 303. Warren suddenly stopped and I almost rammed into him from behind. The door to his office was open two inches. He pointed to it and shook his head, signaling that he hadn't left it that way. I raised and dropped my shoulders, signaling back that it was his call. He leaned an ear toward the crack and listened. I heard something, too. It sounded like the crunching of papers, then a swishing sound. I felt a cold finger moving over my scalp. Warren turned back to me with a curious look on his face when suddenly the door swung inward and open.

It was like dominoes. Warren made a startled move, followed by me and then the small Asian man who stood there in the doorway with a feather duster in one hand and a trash bag in the other. We all took a moment to get our normal breathing going again.

'Sorry, mister,' the Asian man said. 'I clean your office.'

'Oh, yeah,' Warren said, smiling. 'That's fine. That's good.'

'You leff copy machine on.'

With that, he carried his goods down the hallway and used a key attached by a chain to his belt to get into the next office down. I looked at Warren and smiled.

'You're right, you're no Deep Throat.'

'You're no Robert Redford. Let's go.'

He told me to close the door, then turned the compact photocopy machine back on and moved around behind his desk, files in hand. I sat in the same chair I had been in earlier in the day.

'Okay,' he said. 'Let's start going through them. There should be a synopsis section in each protocol. Any kind of note or other significant detail should be there. If you think it fits, copy it.'

We started going through the files. As much as I liked him, I didn't like the idea of letting him decide in half of the cases if they fit into my theory. I wanted to look at all of them.

'Remember,' I said, 'we're looking for any kind of flowery language that might sound like literature or a poem or whatever.'

He closed the file he was looking at and dropped it on the stack.

'What?'

'You don't trust me to do this.'

'No. I just . . . I want to make sure we're both on the same wavelength about this, that's all.'

'Look, this is ridiculous,' he said. 'Let's just copy them all and get out of here. You can take them to your hotel and go through them there. It's quicker and safer. You don't need me.'

I nodded and realized it was the way we should have done it all along. For the next fifteen minutes he operated the copier while I took the protocols from the files and replaced them after they were copied. It was a slow machine, not made for heavy use.

When we were done he turned off the machine and told me to wait in the office.

'I forgot about the cleaners. It might be better if I just take these back to storage, then come get you.'

'Okay.'

I started looking through the copied protocols while he was gone but was too nervous to concentrate on them. I felt like running out the door with the copies and getting away before anything could go wrong. I looked around his office to try to pass the time. I picked up the photo of Warren's family. A pretty, petite wife and two kids, a boy and a girl. Both of preschool age in the photo. The door opened while the frame was still in my hand. It was Warren and I felt embarrassed. He paid no notice.

'Okay, we're ready.'

And like two spies we snuck out under cover of darkness.

Warren was silent almost all the way back to the hotel. I think it was because his involvement was over and he knew it. I was the reporter. He was the source. It was my story. I felt his jealousy and desire. For the story. For the job. For what he'd once been and had.

'Why'd you really quit, man?' I asked.

This time he dropped the bullshit.

'My wife, family. I was never home. One crisis after another, you know. I had to cover them all. Finally, I had to make a choice. Some days I think I made the right one. Some days I don't. This is one of those that I don't. This is a hell of a story, Jack.'

Now I was silent for a while. Warren drove into the hotel's main entrance and headed around the circle to the doors. He pointed through the windshield to the right side of the hotel.

'See down there? That's where Reagan got it. I was there. Fuckin' five feet from Hinckley while we were waiting. He even asked me what time it was. Almost no other reporters were out there. Back then, most of them didn't bother staking his exits. But they did after that.'

'Wow.'

'Yeah, that was a highlight.'

I looked over at him and nodded seriously and then we both laughed. We both knew the secret. Only in a reporter's world would it be a highlight. We both knew that probably the only thing better than witnessing a presidential assassination attempt as a reporter was witnessing a successful assassination. Just as long as you didn't catch a bullet in the crossfire.

He pulled over at the door and I got out and leaned my head back into the car.

'You're showing your true identity there, pal.'

He smiled.

'Maybe.'

16

....

Each of the thirteen files was thin, containing the five-page protocol questionnaire supplied by the FBI and the foundation, and usually just a few more pages of ancillary notes or testimonials to the pressures of the job from colleagues of the deceased.

Most of the stories were the same. Job stress, alcohol, marital difficulty, depression. A basic formula for the police blues. But depression was the key ingredient. In almost all of the files depression of one sort or another was reported as attacking the victim from inside the job. However, only a handful mentioned that the victims were troubled by any specific case, unsolved or otherwise, that they had been assigned to investigate.

I did a quick read-through of the conclusion segment of each of the protocols and quickly eliminated several of the cases from my investigation because of varying factors ranging from the suicides being witnessed by others to their taking place under circumstances precluding a setup.

The remaining eight cases were going to be more difficult to whittle down because each, at least in the summary remarks, seemed to fit. In each of these cases there was some mention of specific cases burdening the victim. The burden of an unsolved case and the quotes from Poe were really all I had as far as a pattern went. So I stayed with it and made it the standard by which I judged whether these eight remaining cases could be part of a series of false suicides.

Following this as my own protocol led to the dropping of two more cases when I found references to the suicide notes. In each, the victim wrote to a specific person, a mother in one, a wife in the other, and asked for forgiveness and understanding. The notes contained nothing resembling a line of poetry or, actually, any kind of literature. I dropped them and then I had six.

Reading one of the remaining files I came across the victim's suicide note – one line, like those left by my brother and Brooks – in an addendum containing the investigator's report. Reading the words sent a chilling, electric surge through me. For I knew them.

I am haunted by ill angels

I quickly opened my notebook to the page where I had written the stanza from 'Dream-Land' that Laurie Prine had read to me from the CD-ROM.

> By a route obscure and lonely,
> Haunted by ill angels only,
> Where an Eidolon, named NIGHT,
> On a black throne reins upright,
> I have reached these lands but newly,
> From an ultimate dim Thule –
> From a wild weird clime that lieth, sublime,
> Out of SPACE – out of TIME,

I had it cold. My brother and Morris Kotite, an Albuquerque detective who supposedly killed himself with a shot to the chest and another to the temple, left suicide notes that quoted the same stanza of poetry. It was a lock.

But these feelings of vindication and excitement quickly gave way to a deep, growing rage. I was angry at what had happened to my brother and to these other men. I was angry at the living cops for not seeing this sooner and my mind flashed to what Wexler had said when I had convinced him of my brother's murder. A fucking reporter, he had said. Now I knew his anger. But most of all, I realized, my anger was for the one who had done this and for how little I knew about him. In his own words, the killer was an Eidolon. I was chasing a phantom.

It took me an hour to get through the remaining five cases. I took notes on three of them and dropped the other two. One was rejected when I noticed the death occurred on the same day John Brooks was killed in Chicago. It seemed unlikely, given the planning each of the killings must have involved, that two could be carried out on one day.

The other case was rejected because the victim's suicide had been attributed, among other things, to his despair over a heinous kidnap-murder of a young girl on Long Island, New York. It initially appeared, though the victim had left no note, that the suicide would generally fit my pattern and require further scrutiny, but I learned when I read the report to the end that this detective had actually cleared the kidnap-murder with the arrest of a suspect. This was outside the pattern and, of course, didn't fit with the theory that Larry Washington had floated in Chicago and that I subscribed to, that the same person was killing both the first victim and the homicide cop.

The final three that held my interest – in addition to the Kotite case – included Garland Petry, a Dallas detective who put one shot into his chest and then another into his face. He left a note that read, 'Sadly, I know I am shorn of my strength.' Of course, I hadn't known Petry. But I had never heard a cop use the word 'shorn' before. The line he had supposedly written had a literary feel to it. I just didn't think it would have come from the hand and mind of a suicidal cop.

The second of the cases was also a one-liner. Clifford Beltran, a detective with the Sarasota County Sheriff's Department in Florida, had supposedly killed himself three years earlier – it was the oldest of the cases – leaving behind a note that said simply, 'Lord help my poor soul.' Again, it was a conglomeration of words that sounded odd to me in the mouth of a cop, any cop. It was just a hunch but I included Beltran on my list.

Lastly, the third case was included on my list even though there was no mention of a note in the suicide of John P. McCafferty, homicide detective with the Baltimore police. I put McCafferty on the list because his death eerily resembled the death of John Brooks. McCafferty had supposedly fired one shot into the floor of his apartment before firing the second and fatal shot into his throat. I remembered Lawrence Washington's belief that this was a way of getting gunshot residue on the victim's hands.

Four names. I studied them and the rest of the notes I had taken for a while and then pulled the book on Poe I had bought in Boulder out of my flight bag.

It was a thick book with everything that Poe had supposedly ever written. I checked the contents page and noted there were seventy-six pages containing his poetry. I realized that my long night was going to get longer. I ordered an eight-cup pot of coffee from room service and asked them to bring some aspirin as well for the headache I felt sure I would get from the caffeine binge. I then started reading.

I'm not one who has ever been afraid of aloneness or the dark. I've lived by myself for ten years, I've even camped alone in the national parks and I've walked through deserted, burned-out buildings to get to a story. I've sat in dark cars on darker streets waiting to confront candidates and mobsters, or to meet timid sources. While the mobsters certainly put fear in me, the fact that I was out there by myself in the dark never did. But I have to say that Poe's words put a chill in me that night. Maybe it was being alone in a hotel room in a city I didn't know. Maybe it was being surrounded by the documents of death and murder, or that I felt the presence of my dead brother somehow near. And maybe also it was just the knowledge of how some of the words I was reading were now being used. Whatever it was, I put a scare on myself that didn't lift as I read, even when I turned the television on to provide the comforting hum of background noise.

Propped against the pillows on the bed, I read with the lights on either side of me turned on and bright. But, still, I bolted upright when a sudden sharp sound of laughter shot down the hallway outside my room. I had just settled back into the comfort of the shell my body had formed in the pillows and was reading a poem titled 'An Enigma' when the

phone rang and jolted me again with its double ring so foreign to the sound of my phone at home. It was half past
midnight and I assumed it was Greg Glenn in Denver, two
hours behind.

But as I reached for the phone I knew I was wrong. I
hadn't told Glenn where I had checked in.

The caller was Michael Warren.

'Just wanted to check in – I figured you'd be up – and see
what you came up with.'

Again I felt uneasy about his self-involvement, his many
questions. It was unlike any other source that had ever provided me with information on the sly. But I couldn't just get
rid of him, given the risk he had taken.

'I'm still going through it all,' I said. 'Sitting here reading
the poetry of Edgar Allan Poe. I'm scaring myself shitless.'

He laughed politely.

'But does any of it look good – as far as the suicides go?'

Just then I realized something.

'Hey, where are you calling from?'

'Home. Why?'

'Didn't you say you live up in Maryland?'

'Yeah. Why?'

'Then this is a toll call, right? It will be a record on your
bill that you called me here, man. Didn't you think about
that?'

I couldn't believe his carelessness, especially in light of his
own warnings about the FBI and Agent Walling.

'Oh, shit, I ... I don't really think I care. Nobody's going
to pull my records. It's not like I passed on defense secrets,
for crying out loud.'

'I don't know. You know'em better than me.'

'So never mind that, what have you got?'

'I told you I'm still looking. I've got a couple names that
might be good. A few names.'

'Well, then, good. I'm glad it was worth the risk.'

I nodded but realized he couldn't see me do this.

'Yeah, well, like I said before, thanks. I gotta get back to it
now. I'm fading and want to get it done.'

'Then I'll leave you to it. Maybe tomorrow, when you get a chance, give me a call to let me know what's going on.'

'I don't know if that will be a good idea, Michael. I think we better lay low.'

'Well, whatever you think. I guess I'll be reading all about it, eventually, anyway. You have a deadline yet?'

'Nope. Haven't even talked about it.'

'Nice editor. Anyway, go back to it. Happy hunting.'

Soon I was back in the embrace of the words of the poet. Dead a hundred and fifty years but reaching from the grave to grip me. Poe was a master of mood and pace. The mood was gloom and the pace often frenetic. I found myself identifying the words and phrases with my own life. 'I dwelt alone / In a world of moan,' Poe wrote. 'And my soul was a stagnant tide.' Cutting words that seemed, at least at that moment, to fit me.

I read on and soon felt myself gripped by an empathic hold of the poet's own melancholy when I read the stanzas of 'The Lake.'

> But when the Night had thrown her pall
> Upon that spot, as upon all,
> And the mystic wind went by
> Murmuring in melody –
> Then – ah then I would awake
> To the terror of the lone lake

Poe had captured my own dread and fitful memory. My nightmare. He had reached across a century and a half to me and put a cold finger on my chest.

> Death was in that poisonous wave,
> And in its gulf a fitting grave

I finished reading the last poem at three o'clock in the morning. I had found only one more correlation between the poetry and the suicide notes. The line attributed in the reports to Dallas detective Garland Petry – 'Sadly, I know I am shorn of my strength' – was taken from a poem entitled 'For Annie.'

But I found no match of the last words attributed to Beltran, the Sarasota detective, with any poem that Edgar Allan Poe had written. I began to wonder if through my fatigue I had simply missed it but knew that I had read too carefully, despite the lateness of the hour. There simply wasn't a match. 'Lord help my poor soul.' That was the line. I now thought that it had been the last true prayer of a suicidal man. I scratched Beltran from the list, thinking that his words of misery were truly his.

I studied my notes while fending off sleep and decided that the McCafferty case of Baltimore and the Brooks case of Chicago were too similar to be ignored. I knew then what I would do in the morning. I would go to Baltimore to find out more.

That night my dream came back. The only recurring nightmare of my entire life. As always, I dreamed I was walking across a vast frozen lake, the ice blue-black beneath my feet. In all directions I was equal distances from nowhere, all horizons were a blinding, burning white. I put my head down and walked. I hesitated when I heard a girl's voice, a call for help. I looked around but she was not there. I turned and headed on. A step. Two. Then the hand came up through the ice and gripped me. It pulled me toward the growing hole. Was it pulling me down or trying to pull its way out? I never knew. In all the times I'd had the dream I never knew.

All I saw was the hand and slender arm, reaching up from the black water. I knew the hand was death. I woke up.

The lights and the television were still on. I sat up and looked around, not comprehending at first and then remembering where I was and what I was doing. I waited for the chill to pass and then got up. I flicked the TV off and went to the minibar, broke the seal and opened the door. I selected a small bottle of Amaretto and sipped it without a glass. I checked it off on the little list they give you. Six dollars. I studied the list and the exorbitant prices just to give myself something to do.

Eventually, I felt the liquor start to warm me. I sat on the bed and checked the clock. It was quarter to five. I needed to go back. I needed sleep. I got under the covers and pulled the book off the bed table. I turned to 'The Lake' and read it again. My eyes kept returning to the two lines.

> Death was in that poisonous wave,
> And in its gulf a fitting grave

Eventually, troubled thoughts gave way to exhaustion. I put the book down and collapsed back into my bed's shell. I slept the sleep of the dead after that.

17
....

It was against Gladden's instincts to stay in the city but he couldn't leave just yet. There were things he had to do. The wired-funds transfer would land at the Wells Fargo branch in a few hours and he had to get a replacement camera. That was a priority and that couldn't be done if he was on the road, running to Fresno or someplace. So he had to stay in L.A.

He looked up at the mirror over the bed and studied his image. He had black hair now. He hadn't shaved since Wednesday and already the whiskers were coming in thick. He reached to the bed table for the glasses and put them on. He had dumped the colored contacts in the trash can at the In N Out where he'd eaten dinner the night before. He looked back up at the mirror and smiled at his new image. He was a new man.

He glanced over at the television. A woman was performing fellatio on one man while another was having sex with her in the position instinctively favored by dogs. The sound was turned down but he knew what the sound would be if it wasn't. The TV had been on all night. The porno movies that came with the price of the room did little in the way of arousing him because the performers were all too old and looked world-weary. They were disgusting. But he kept the TV on. It helped him remember that everyone had unholy desires.

He looked back to his book and began to read the poem by Poe again. He knew it by heart after so many years and so many readings. But, still, he liked to see the words on the page and hold the book in his hands. He somehow found it comforting.

In visions of the dark night
I have dreamed of joy departed –
But a waking dream of life and light
Hath left me broken-hearted

Gladden sat up and put the book down when he heard a car pull to a stop outside his room. He walked to the curtains and peeked through at the parking lot. The sun hurt his eyes. The car was just somebody checking in. A man and a woman, they both looked drunk already and it wasn't yet noon.

Gladden knew it was time to go out. He first needed to get a newspaper to see if there was a story about Evangeline. About himself. Then to the bank. Then to find the camera. Maybe, if there was time, he'd go searching after that.

He knew that the more he stayed inside, the better his chances were of avoiding detection. But he also felt confident that he had covered his tracks sufficiently. He had changed motels twice since leaving the Hollywood Star Motel. The first room, in Culver City, he used only to dye his hair. He cleaned up, wiped the place down and left. He then drove to the Valley and checked into the dump in which he sat now, the Bon Soir Motel on Ventura Boulevard in Studio City. Forty bucks a night, three channels of adult films included.

He was registered under the name Richard Kidwell. It was the name on his last ID. He'd have to get on the net and trade for a few more. And he realized that would require him to set up a mail drop to receive the IDs and that was another reason to stay in L.A. At least for a while. He added the mail drop to his list of things to do.

As he pulled on his pants he glanced at the television. A woman with a rubber penis held to her abdomen with straps that went around her pelvis was having sex with another woman. Gladden tied his shoes, turned the TV off and left the room.

Gladden cringed at the sight of the sun. He strode across the parking lot to the motel office. He wore a white T-shirt with a picture of Pluto on it. The dog was his favorite cartoon animal. In the past, wearing the shirt had helped soothe the fears of the children. It always seemed to work.

Behind the glass window of the office sat a frumpy-looking woman with a tattoo on what had been at one time the upper curve of her left breast. Her skin was sagging now and the tattoo was so old and misshapen it was hard to tell it wasn't a bruise. She had on a large blond wig, bright pink lipstick and enough makeup on her cheeks to frost a cupcake or pass for a TV evangelist. She was the one who had checked him in the day before. He put a dollar bill in the pass-through slot and asked for three quarters, two dimes and a nickel. He didn't know how much the papers cost in L.A. In the other cities they had ranged from a quarter to fifty cents.

'Sorry, babe, I don't have change,' she said in a voice that begged for another cigarette.

'Ah shit,' Gladden said angrily. He shook his head. There was no service in this world anymore. 'What about in your purse? I don't want to have to walk down the fuckin' street for a paper.'

'Let me check. And watch that mouth. You don't have to get so testy.'

He watched her get up. She wore a short black tube skirt that embarrassingly displayed a network of varicose veins running down the back of her thighs. He realized he had no idea how old she was, a used-up thirty or an over-the-hill forty-five. It seemed that when she bent over to get her purse out of a lower file drawer, she was intentionally giving him the view. She came up with the purse and dug around in it for change. While the large black bag swallowed her hand like an animal she looked at him through the glass with appraising eyes.

'See anything you like?' she asked.

'No, not really,' Gladden replied. 'You got the change?'

She pulled her hand out of the maw of the bag and looked at the change.

'You don't have to be so rude. Besides, I only got seventy-one cents.'

'I'll take it.'

He shoved the dollar through.

'You sure? Six of it is pennies.'

'Yes, I'm sure. There's the money.'

She dropped the change into the slot and he had a difficult time getting it all up because his fingernails were bitten away to nothing.

'You're in room six, right?' she said, looking at an occupancy list. 'Checked in a single. Still by yourself?'

'What, now is this twenty questions?'

'Just checking. What are you doin' in there alone, anyhow? I hope you're not jerkin' off on the bedspread.'

She smirked. She had gotten him back. His anger boiled up and he lost it. He knew he should keep calm, not leave an impression, but he couldn't hold back.

'Now who's being rude, hmmm? You know what you are, you are fucking disgusting. Those veins running up your ass look like the road map to hell, lady.'

'Hey! You watch your –'

'Or what? You kicking me out?'

'Just watch what you say.'

Gladden got the last coin up, a dime, and turned to walk away without replying. Out on the street, he went to the newspaper box and bought the morning edition.

Safely back inside the dark confines of his room, Gladden dug through the newspaper until he found the Metro section. The story would be here, he knew. He quickly scanned through the eight pages of the section and found nothing about the motel murder case. Disappointed, he guessed that maybe the death of a black maid wasn't news in this town.

He tossed the paper down on the bed. But as soon as it landed a photograph on the front page of the section caught his attention. It was a shot of a young boy on his way down a sliding board. He picked the section back up and read the caption that went with the photo. It said that swing sets and other children's amusements had finally been replaced at MacArthur Park following the long period of their removal while a subway station construction project caused the closure of most of the park.

Gladden looked at the photo again. The boy on the slide

was identified as seven-year-old Miguel Arax. Gladden wasn't familiar with the area where the new park was located but he assumed that a subway station would be approved only for a low-income area. That meant most of the children would be poor and with dark brown skin like the boy in the photo. He decided that he would go to the park later, after taking care of his chores and getting situated. It was always easier with the poor ones. They needed and wanted so much.

Situated, Gladden thought. He knew then that getting situated was his real priority. He couldn't stay in this motel or any other, no matter how well he had covered his tracks. It wasn't safe. The stakes were constantly rising and they would be looking for him soon. It was a feeling not based on anything other than his gut instinct. They would be looking soon and he needed to find a safe place.

He put the paper aside and went to the phone. The smoke-cured voice that answered after he dialed zero was unmistakable.

'This is, uh, Richard . . . in six. I just wanted to say I'm sorry about what happened earlier. I was rude and I apologize.'

She didn't say anything and he pressed on.

'Anyway, you were right, it's getting pretty lonely in here and I was wondering if that offer you sort of made before was still out there.'

'What offer?'

She was going to make it difficult.

'You know, you asked if I saw anything I liked. Well, I did, actually.'

'I don't know. You were pretty testy. I don't like testy. Whatcha got in mind?'

'I don't know. But I've got a hundred bucks to make sure it's a good time.'

She was silent a moment.

'Well, I get outta this dump at four. Then I got the whole weekend. I could come over.'

Gladden smiled but kept it out of his voice.

'Can't wait.'

'Then I'm sorry, too. About being rude and the things I said.'

'That's nice to hear. See you soon – oh, you still there?'

'Sure, baby.'

'What's your name?'

'Darlene.'

'Well, Darlene, I can't wait till four.'

She laughed and hung up. Gladden wasn't laughing.

18

·········

In the morning I had to wait until ten before Laurie Prine was at her desk in Denver. By then I was anxious to get on with the day but hers was just starting and I had to go through the greeting and questions about where I was and what I was doing before finally getting to the point.

'When you did that run on police suicides for me, would that have included the *Baltimore Sun*?'

'Yep.'

I assumed it would have but had to check. I also knew that computer searches sometimes missed things.

'Okay, then can you run a search of the *Sun* using just the name John McCafferty.'

I spelled it for her.

'Sure. How far back?'

'I don't know, five years would be good.'

'When do you need it by?'

'Last night.'

'I guess that means you're going to hold.'

'It does.'

I listened to the tapping of keys as she conducted the search. I pulled the Poe book onto my lap and reread some of the poems while I waited. With daylight coming through the curtains, the words did not have the same hold on me as the night before.

'Okay – whoa – we've got a lot of hits here, Jack. Twenty-eight. Anything in particular you're looking for?'

'Uh, no. What's the most recent?'

I knew that she could scan the hits by having just the headlines print out on her screen.

'Okay, last one. "Detective fired for part in former partner's death."'

'That's weird,' I said. 'This should have come up in the first search you did. Can you read me some of that?'

I heard her tap a few keys and then wait for the story to be printed on her screen.

'Okay, here goes. "A Baltimore police detective was fired Monday for altering a crime scene and attempting to make it appear that his longtime partner had not killed himself last spring. The action was taken by a departmental Board of Rights panel against Detective Daniel Bledsoe after a two-day closed hearing. Bledsoe could not be reached for comment but a fellow officer who represented him during the hearing said that the highly decorated detective was being treated with undue harshness by a department he had served well for twenty-two years. According to police officials, Bledsoe's partner, Detective John McCafferty, died of a self-inflicted gunshot wound on May 8. His body was found by his wife, Susan, who first called Bledsoe. Bledsoe, officials said, went to his partner's apartment, destroyed a note he found in the dead detective's shirt pocket and altered other aspects of the crime scene to make it appear that McCafferty had been killed by an intruder who had grabbed the detective's gun. Police said" – Do you want me to keep reading, Jack?'

'Yeah, go ahead.'

'"Police said Bledsoe went so far as to fire an additional shot into McCafferty's body, striking him in the upper leg. Bledsoe then told Susan McCafferty to call 911 and he left the apartment, feigning surprise when he was later informed that his partner was dead. In killing himself, McCafferty had apparently already fired one shot into the floor of his home before placing the gun in his mouth and firing the fatal shot. Investigators contend that Bledsoe attempted to make the death appear to be a murder because Susan McCafferty stood to receive a higher amount of death, health and pension benefits if it could be proved her husband had not killed himself. However, the scheme unraveled when suspicious investigators interviewed Susan McCafferty at length on the day her husband died. She eventually admitted to what she had watched Bledsoe do." Am I reading too fast? Are you taking notes?'

'No, it's fine. Keep going.'

'Okay. "Bledsoe refused to acknowledge any part in the scheme during the investigation and declined to testify in his behalf during the Board of Rights hearing. Jerry Liebling, Bledsoe's fellow detective and defense representative during the hearing, said Bledsoe did what any loyal partner would do for a fallen comrade. 'All he did was try to make things a little better for the widow,' Liebling said. 'But the department has gone too far. He tried to do the good thing and now he's lost his job, his career, his livelihood. What kind of message does this send to the rank and file?' Other officers contacted Monday expressed similar feelings. But ranking officials said that Bledsoe had been treated fairly and cited the department's decision not to file criminal charges against Bledsoe or Susan McCafferty as a sign of compassion for the two. McCafferty and Bledsoe had been partners for seven years and handled some of the higher-profile murders in the city during that time. One of those killings was attributed in part to McCafferty's death. Police said that McCafferty's depression over the unsolved killing of Polly Amherst, a first-grade teacher who was abducted from campus at the private Hopkins School, sexually mutilated and strangled, led him to thoughts of killing himself. McCafferty was also struggling with a drinking problem. 'So now the department hasn't lost one fine investigator,' Liebling said after Monday's hearing, 'it has lost two. They'll never find two guys that were as good as Bledsoe and McCafferty. The department really blew it today.'" That's it, Jack.'

'Okay. Uh, I'm going to need you to send that to my computer basket. I have my laptop. I can get it.'

'Okay. What about the other stories?'

'Can you go back to the headlines? Are any of them about McCafferty's death or are they all stories on cases?'

She took a half minute to scroll through the headlines.

'It looks like they are all about cases. There are quite a few on the schoolteacher. Nothing else on the suicide. And you know what, the reason that story I just read didn't come up on my search on Monday was because the word "suicide" was never in it. That was the keyword I plugged in.'

I'd already figured that out. I asked her to ship the stories on the teacher to my computer basket, thanked her and hung up.

I called the main detective bureau of the Baltimore Police Department and asked for Jerry Liebling.

'Liebling, autos.'

'Detective Liebling, my name is Jack McEvoy and I'm wondering if you can help me. I'm trying to reach Dan Bledsoe.'

'That would be in regard to what?'

'I'd rather talk to him about it.'

'I'm sorry I can't help you and I've got another call.'

'Look, I know what he tried to do for McCafferty. I want to tell him something that I think will help him. That's really all I can say. But if you don't help me, you are missing a chance to help him. I can give you my number. Why don't you call him and give it to him. Let him decide.'

There was a long silence and I suddenly thought I had been talking to a dead line.

'Hello?'

'Yeah, I'm here. Look, if Dan wants to talk to you he'll talk to you. You call him. He's in the book.'

'What, the phone book?'

'That's right. I gotta go.'

He hung up. I felt foolish. I never even considered the phone book because I never knew a cop who put his name in it. I dialed information for Baltimore again and gave the former detective's name.

'I have no listing for a Daniel Bledsoe,' the operator said. 'I have Bledsoe Insurance and Bledsoe Investigations.'

'Okay, give me those and can I get the addresses, please?'

'Actually, they are separate listings and numbers but the same address in Fells Point.'

He gave me the information and I called the investigations number. A woman answered, 'Bledsoe Investigations.'

'Yes, can I speak to Dan?'

'I'm sorry, he's unavailable.'

'Do you know if he'll be in later today?'

'He's in now. He's just on the line. This is his service. When he's out or on his line it rings through. But I know he's there. He checked for messages not ten minutes ago. But I don't know for how long. I don't keep his schedule.'

Fells Point is a spit of land east of Baltimore's Inner Harbor. The tourist shops and hotels give way to funkier pubs and shops and then old brick factories and Little Italy. On some streets the asphalt has worn off the underlying brick and when the wind is right there is the damp tang of the sea or the smell of the sugar factory just across the inlet. Bledsoe Investigations and Insurance was in a one-story brick building at Caroline and Fleet.

It was a few minutes after one. On the door of his small street-front office was a plastic clock face with adjustable hands and the words BE BACK AT. The clock was set at one. I looked around, saw no one making a run for the door to beat the deadline and decided to wait for him anyway. I had nowhere else to go.

I walked down to the market on Fleet, bought a Coke and went back to my car. From the driver's seat I could see the door to Bledsoe's office. I watched it for twenty minutes until I saw a man with jet-black hair, a middle-age paunch peeking through his jacket and a slight limp walk up, unlock the door and go in. I got out with my computer satchel and headed for him.

Bledsoe's office looked as though it had once been a doctor's office, though I could not figure out why a doctor would have hung a shingle out in this working district. There was a little entry room with a sliding window and counter behind which I imagined a receptionist at one time sat. The window, glazed like a shower door, was closed. I had heard a buzz when I had opened the door but no one responded to it. I stood there a few moments looking around. There was an old couch and a coffee table. Not much room for anything else. A variety of magazines were fanned across the table, none of them fresher than six months old. I was about to call out a hello or knock on the door to the inner sanctum when I heard a toilet flush somewhere on the other side of the sliding window. Then I saw a blurred figure move behind the glass and the door to the left opened. The man with the black hair stood there. I noticed now that he had a mustache as thin as a freeway on a map traveling over his lip.

'Yes, can I help you?'

'Daniel Bledsoe?'

'That's right.'

'My name's Jack McEvoy. I'd like to ask you about John McCafferty. I think we both might be able to help each other.'

'John McCafferty was a long time ago.'

He was eyeing the computer satchel.

'It's just a computer,' I said. 'Can we sit down someplace?'

'Uh, sure. Why not?'

I followed through the door and down a short hallway that had three more doors lined along the right side. He opened the first one and we stepped into an office of cheap faux maple paneling. His state license was framed on the wall as well as some photos from his days as a cop. The whole thing seemed about as cheesy as his mustache but I was determined to play it out. The thing I know about cops, and I guessed that it extended to former cops, was that looks were deceiving. I knew some in Colorado who would still be wearing pale blue polyester leisure suits if they made them anymore. But nevertheless they were some of the best and brightest and toughest of their departments. I suspected it was that way with Bledsoe. He took a seat behind a desk with a black Formica top. It had been a poor choice when he'd bought it at the secondhand office furniture store. I could plainly see the dust buildup on the shiny surface. I sat across from Bledsoe in the only other chair. He accurately registered my impressions.

'Place used to be an abortion clinic. Guy went away for

doing third-trimester jobs. I took it over and don't care about the dust and looks. I get a lot of my work over the phone, selling policies to cops. And I usually go to clients, the ones that want an investigation. They don't come to me. The people that do come here usually just leave flowers out by the door. Memorials, I guess. I figure they must be working off old phone books or something. Why don't you tell me what you're looking for here.'

I told him about my brother and then about John Brooks in Chicago. I watched his face fill with skepticism as I talked. It told me I was maybe ten seconds from being thrown out the door.

'What is this?' he said. 'Who sent you here?'

'Nobody. But it's my guess that I'm maybe a day or so ahead of the FBI. But they'll be coming. I just thought you'd maybe talk to me first. I know what it's like, you see. My brother and me, we were twins. I've always heard that long-time partners, especially on homicide, become like brothers. Like twins.'

I held up for a few moments. I had played everything but my ace and I had to wait for the right moment. Bledsoe seemed to cool down a little. His anger was maybe giving way to confusion.

'So what do you want from me?'

'The note. I want to know what McCafferty said in the note.'

'There was no note. I never said there was a note.'

'But his wife said there was.'

'Then go talk to her.'

'No, I think I'd rather talk to you. Let me tell you something. The doer on these cases somehow gets the victims to write out a line or two as a suicide note. I don't know how he does it or why they oblige him, but they do. And every time the line is from a poem. A poem by the same writer. Edgar Allan Poe.'

I reached down to my computer satchel and unzipped it. I pulled out the thick book of Poe's works. I put it on the desk so that he could see it.

'I think your partner was murdered. You came in and it looked like a suicide because that was how it was supposed to look. That note you destroyed, I'd bet you your partner's pension that it's a line from a poem that's in that book.'

Bledsoe looked from me to the book and then back at me again.

'You apparently thought you owed him enough to risk your job to make his widow's life a little easier.'

'Yeah, look what it got me. A piece-of-shit office with a piece-of-shit license on the wall. I sit in a room where they used to cut babies out of women. It's not very noble.'

'Look, everybody on the force knew there was something noble about what you did, else you wouldn't be selling any insurance. You did what you did for your partner. You should follow through, now.'

Bledsoe turned his head and looked at one of the photos on the wall. It was him and another man, arms around each other's neck, smiling with abandon. It looked like it had been taken in a bar somewhere during the good days.

'"The fever called living is conquered at last,"' he said, without looking away from the photo.

I slapped my hand down on the book. The sound scared us both.

'Got it,' I said and picked up the book. I had bent the pages of the poems where the killer's quotes had been taken. I found the page with the poem 'For Annie' on it, scanned until I knew I was right, then put the book on the desk and turned it so he could read it.

'First stanza,' I said.

Bledsoe leaned over to read the poem.

Thank Heaven! the crisis –
The danger is past,
And the lingering illness
Is over at last –
And the fever called 'Living'
Is conquered at last.

19
·······

As I hurried through the lobby of the Hilton at four, I envisioned Greg Glenn slowly making his way out from behind his desk and heading toward the daily news meeting in the metro conference room. I needed to talk to him and I knew that if I didn't snag him first he'd be holed up in that meeting and the weekend meeting that followed for the next two hours.

As I approached the elevators I saw a woman stepping through the open doors of the one available car and quickly followed her in. She had already pushed the 12 button. I moved to the rear of the car and checked my watch again. I thought I was going to make it. The editors' meetings never seemed to get off on time.

The woman had moved to the right side of the car and we had settled into the slightly uncomfortable silence that always comes when strangers are enclosed in an elevator. In the polished-brass trim on the door I could see her face. Her eyes watched the lights over the doors that marked our ascent. She was very attractive and I found it hard to turn away from the reflection, even though I feared she would turn her eyes and catch me. I imagined that she knew I was watching her. I've always believed that beautiful women know and understand they are always being watched.

When the elevator opened on twelve I waited for her to step out first. She turned to the left and headed down the hall. I turned right and headed to my room, stopping myself from taking a backward glance at her. As I approached my door, pulling the card key out of my shirt pocket, I heard light steps on the hallway carpet. I turned and it was her. She smiled.

'Wrong way.'

'Yeah,' I said and smiled. 'After a while it's all a maze.'

Dumb thing to say, I thought as I opened the door and she passed behind me. As I entered the room, I felt a hand suddenly grip the back of my jacket collar and I was shoved into the room. As this happened another hand went up under my jacket and grabbed onto my belt. I was slammed facedown onto the bed. I managed to hold on to the computer bag, not wanting to drop a two-thousand-dollar piece of equipment, but then it was roughly yanked out of my grasp.

'FBI! You're under arrest. Don't move!'

While one hand stayed on the back of my neck and held me facedown, the other then patted my body in a search.

'What the fuck is this?' I managed to say in a voice muffled by the mattress.

Just as suddenly as they had gripped me, the hands were gone.

'Okay, up. Let's go.'

I turned and raised myself until I was seated on the bed. I looked up. It was the woman from the elevator. My mouth dropped open a little. Something about being handled so easily by her, and her alone, burned me deeply and anger flushed my cheeks.

'Don't worry. I've done it to bigger and badder men than you.'

'You better have an ID or you're going to need a lawyer.'

She pulled a wallet out of her coat pocket and flipped it open in front of my face.

'You're the one who needs the lawyer. Now, I want you to take the chair from the desk, put it in the corner and sit there while I go through this place. It won't take long.'

She had what looked like a legitimate FBI badge and ID. It said Special Agent Rachel Walling. Once I read that I began to get an idea of what was going on.

'C'mon, chop, chop. In the corner you go.'

'Let's see the search warrant.'

'You have a choice,' she said sternly. 'Go to the corner or I take you into the bathroom and cuff you to the drain trap under the sink. Make it.'

I stood up and dragged the chair into the corner and sat down.

'I still want to see the fuckin' warrant.'

'Are you aware that your use of coarse language is a rather lame attempt to reestablish your sense of male superiority?'

'Jesus. Are you aware that you are full of shit? Where's the warrant?'

'I don't need a warrant. You invited me in and allowed me to search, then I arrested you after I found the stolen property.'

She stepped back to the door, her eyes on me, and closed it.

'I didn't invite you anywhere. You try that shit and you'll crash and burn. Do you believe any judge is going to believe I was stupid enough to invite a search *if* I had stolen property in here?'

She looked at me and smiled sweetly.

'Mr McEvoy, I am five feet five and weigh one hundred and fifteen pounds. That's with my gun on. Do you think a judge will believe your version of what happened? Would you even want to reveal what I just did to you in open court?'

I looked away from her and out the window. The maid had opened the curtains. The sky was beginning to lose the light.

'I didn't think so,' she said. 'Now, you want to save me some time? Where are the protocols you copied?'

'In the computer bag. I committed no crime in getting them and just having them is not a crime.'

I had to be careful of what I said. I didn't know if Michael Warren had already been found out or not. She was going through the satchel. She pulled out the Poe book, looked at it quizzically and threw it on the bed. She then pulled out my notebook and the sheaf of copies of the protocols. Warren had been right. She was a beautiful woman. A hard shell but beautiful just the same. About my age, maybe a year or two older, her hair was brown and falling to just above her shoulders. Sharp green eyes and the strong aura of confidence.

That was what was most attractive about her. Though at the moment I think I hated her, the attraction was not lost on me.

'Breaking and entering is a crime,' she said. 'It came under my jurisdiction when it was determined that the documents stolen belonged to the bureau.'

'I didn't break into anything and I didn't steal anything. What this is is harassment. I've always heard that you bureau people get upset when somebody else does your job for you.'

She was leaning over the bed looking through the papers. She straightened up, reached into her pocket and pulled out a clear plastic evidence bag with a single sheet of paper in it. She held it up for me to look at. I recognized it as having been torn from a reporter's notebook. There were six lines written on it in black ink.

> Pena: his hands?
> after – how long?
> Wexler/Scalari: the car?
> heater?
> lock?
> Riley: gloves?

I recognized my own handwriting and then it all tumbled together. Warren had torn sheets from my notebook to mark the spots of the files we had pulled. He had torn a page with old notes on it and somehow had left it behind when he returned the files. Walling must have seen the recognition in my face.

'Sloppy work. After we get the handwriting analyzed and compared, I think it'll be a slam dunk. What do you think?'

I couldn't even manage a *fuck you* this time.

'I'm seizing your computer, this book and your notebooks as possible evidence. If we don't need any of it, you'll get it back. Okay, we're going to go now. My car's right out front. The one thing I'm willing to do for you to show I'm not such a mean girl is take you down without the cuffs. We've got a long ride down to Virginia, though we might beat some of the traffic if we get going now. Are you going to behave? One false move, as they say, and I'll put you in the back with the cuffs on as tight as a wedding ring.'

I just nodded and stood up. I was in a daze. I couldn't meet her eyes. I walked toward the door with my head down.

'Hey, what do you say?' she said to me.

I mumbled my thanks and I heard her soft laughter behind me.

She was wrong. We didn't beat the traffic. It was Friday evening. More people were trying to get out of the city than most nights and we crawled along with them as we crossed the city to get to a freeway. For a half hour neither of us spoke, except when she cursed at a traffic snarl or a red light. I was in the front seat, thinking the whole time. I had to make a call to Glenn as soon as possible. They had to get me a lawyer. A good one. I saw that the only way out was to reveal a source I had promised I would never reveal. I considered the possibility that if I called Warren he would come forward and confirm that I hadn't broken into the foundation. But I discarded it. I had made a covenant with him. I had to honor it.

When we finally made it south of Georgetown the traffic opened up a little bit and she seemed to relax, or at least remember I was in the car with her. I saw her reach into the ashtray and pull out a white card. She put the dome light on and held the card on the top of the steering wheel so she could read it while she drove.

'You have a pen?'

'What?'

'A pen. I thought all reporters carried pens.'

'Yes. I have a pen.'

'Good. I'm going to read you your constitutional rights.'

'What rights? You've already violated most of them.'

She proceeded to read from the card and then asked if I understood them. I mumbled that I did and she handed me the card.

'Okay, good. I want you to take your pen and sign and date the back of that.'

I did as instructed and handed the card back. She blew on the ink until it dried and then put the card in her pocket.

'There,' she said. 'Now we can talk. Unless you want to call your lawyer. How'd you get into the foundation?'

'I didn't break in. That's all I can say till I talk to a lawyer.'

'You saw the evidence. Are you going to say that's not yours?'

'It can be explained ... Look, all I'm saying is I did nothing illegal to get those copies. I can't say anything more without revealing ...'

I didn't finish. I'd said enough.

'The old can't-reveal-my-sources trick. Where were you all day today, Mr McEvoy? I've been waiting since noon.'

'I was in Baltimore.'

'Doing what?'

'That's my business. You have the originals on those protocols, you can figure it out.'

'The McCafferty case. You know, interfering with a federal investigation can get you charged with additional crimes.'

I gave her my best fake laugh.

'Yeah, right,' I said sarcastically. 'What federal investigation? You'd still be down there in your office counting suicides if I hadn't talked to Ford yesterday. But that's the bureau's way, right? If it's a good idea, oh that's *our* idea. If it's a good case, yeah, *we* made that case. Meantime, it's hear no evil, see no evil and a lot of shit goes by unnoticed.'

'Jesus, who died and made you the expert?'

'My brother.'

She didn't see that coming and it shut her down for a few minutes. It also seemed to have the effect of breaking through the shell she surrounded herself with.

'I'm sorry about that,' she finally said.

'So am I.'

All the anger about what had happened to Sean welled up inside of me but I swallowed it back. She was a stranger and I couldn't share something so profoundly personal with her. I shoved it back and thought of something else to say.

'You know, you might've known him. You signed the

VICAP survey and the profile he got from the bureau on his case.'

'Yes, I know. But we never spoke.'

'How about if you answer a question now?'

'Maybe. Go ahead.'

'How did you find me?'

I was wondering if Warren had somehow put her on to me. If I could determine that he had, then all bets were off and I wasn't going to go to jail protecting the person who had set me up in the first place.

'That was the easy part,' she said. 'I had your name and pedigree from Dr Ford at the foundation. He called me after your little meeting yesterday and I came up this morning. I thought it might be wise to safeguard those files and sure enough I was right. Just a little late. You do quick work. Once I found the page from a reporter's notebook, it was pretty easy to figure out you'd been there.'

'I didn't break in there.'

'Well, everyone associated with the project denies talking to you. In fact, Dr Ford specifically remembers telling you that you could not have access to the files until the bureau signed off on it. And funny thing, here you are with the files.'

'And how'd you know I was at the Hilton? Was that written on a piece of paper for you, too?'

'Bluffed your city editor like he was a copy boy. I told him I had important information for you and he told me where you were.'

I smiled but turned and looked out the window so she wouldn't see it. She had just made a mistake that was as telling as if she had said outright that Warren had revealed where I was.

'They don't call them copy boys anymore,' I said. 'It's politically incorrect.'

'Copy person?'

'Close enough.'

With a straight face I looked over at her for the first time while in the car. I felt myself making a comeback. The confidence she had so expertly stomped into the bedspread in the hotel room was getting a second life. Now I was playing her.

'I thought you people always worked in twos,' I said.

We were stopping at another red light. I could see the freeway entrance up ahead. I had to make my move.

'Usually,' she said. 'But today was busy, a lot of people out, and, actually, when I left Quantico, I thought I was just going up to the foundation to talk to Oline and Dr Ford and to pull the records. I wasn't counting on a custody arrest.'

Her show was falling apart quickly. I was seeing it now. No cuffs. No partner. Me in the front seat. And I knew that Greg Glenn didn't know where I was staying in D.C. I hadn't told him and I hadn't made the reservation through the *Rocky*'s travel office because there hadn't been time.

My computer satchel was on the seat between us. On top of it she had stacked the copies of the protocol files, the Poe book and my notebook. I reached over and pulled it all onto my lap.

'What are you doing?' she asked.

'I'm getting out of here.' I tossed the protocols onto her lap. 'You can keep those. I've got all the information I need.'

I pulled the door handle and opened the door.

'Don't you fucking move!'

I looked at her and smiled.

'Are you aware that your use of coarse language is a lame attempt to reestablish your superiority? Look, it was a nice play but you ran out of the right answers. I'll just catch a cab back to the hotel. I've got a story to write.'

I got out of the car with my things and stepped onto the sidewalk. I looked around and saw a convenience store with a phone out front and started walking that way. Next I saw her car cut into the parking lot and park in my path. She jerked it to a stop and jumped out.

'You're making a mistake,' she said, coming quickly toward me.

'What mistake? You made the mistake. What was that charade all about?'

She just looked at me. She was speechless.

'Okay, I'll tell you what it was,' I said. 'It was a scam.'

'Scam? Why would I scam you?'

'Information. You wanted to know what I had. Let me guess, once you had what you wanted, you were going to come in and say, "Oh gee, sorry, your source just copped. Never mind, you're free to go and sorry about the little mis-understanding." Well, you better go back down to Quantico and practice your act.'

I walked around her and headed to the pay phone. I picked the receiver off the hook and the phone was dead. I didn't let on, though. She was watching me. I dialed information.

'I need a cab company,' I said to a nonexistent operator.

I dropped a quarter in the slot and dialed a number. I then read the address off the phone and asked for a cab. When I hung up and turned around, Agent Walling was standing there very close. She reached past me and picked up the phone. After holding it to her ear for a second she smiled slightly and hung it back up. She pointed to the side of the box to where the receiver cable was attached. It was severed, the wires tied together in a knot.

'Your act could use some polish, too.'

'Fine. Just leave me alone.'

I turned away and started looking through the store windows to see if there was another phone inside. There wasn't.

'Look, what did you want me to do?' she asked my back. 'I need to know what you know.'

I whipped around on her.

'Then why didn't you just ask? Why'd you have to ... try to humiliate me?'

'You are a reporter, Jack. Are you going to tell me you were just going to open up your files and share with me?'

'Maybe.'

'Yeah, right. That'll be the day, when one of you people do that. Look at Warren. He's not even a reporter anymore and he was acting like one. It's in the blood.'

'Hey, you know, speaking of blood, there's more at stake

here than a story, okay? You don't know what I would have done if you had approached me like a human being.'

'Okay,' she said softly. 'Maybe I don't. I'll grant you that.'

We did a little pacing in opposite directions until she spoke.

'So what do we do? Here we are, you found me out, and now you have a choice. I need to know what you know. Are you going to tell me or are you going take your ball and go home? You do that and we both lose out. So does your brother.'

She had skillfully backed me into a corner and I knew it. On principle I should have walked off. But I couldn't. Despite everything, I liked her. I silently walked to the car, got in and then looked at her through the windshield. She nodded once and came around to the driver's side. After getting in she turned to me and held out her hand.

'Rachel Walling.'

I took it and shook it.

'Jack McEvoy.'

'I know. Nice to meet you.'

'Likewise.'

20

. . . .

As a show of good faith Rachel Walling went first – after
extracting a promise from me that the conversation was
off the record until her team supervisor decided how much
cooperation, if any, the bureau would give me. I didn't mind
making the promise because I knew I was holding the high
hand. I already had a story and the bureau would likely not
want a story published yet. I figured that gave me a lot of
leverage, whether Agent Walling realized it yet or not.

For a half hour while we moved slowly south on the
freeway toward Quantico she told me what the bureau had
been doing for the last twenty-eight hours. Nathan Ford of
the Law Enforcement Foundation had called her at three
o'clock Thursday to inform her of my visit to the foundation,
the findings of my own investigation to that point and my
request to see the suicide files. Walling concurred with his
decision to rebuff me and then consulted with Bob Backus,
her immediate supervisor. Backus gave her the go-ahead to
drop the profiling work she had been assigned and proceed
with a priority investigation of the claims I had made in my
meeting with Ford. At this time, the bureau had not yet heard
from anyone from the Denver or Chicago police departments.
Walling started her work on the Behavioral Science Services
computer, which had a direct tie to the foundation computer.

'Basically, I did the same search Michael Warren did for
you,' she said. 'In fact, I was on-line in Quantico when he
went in and did it. I just ID'ed the user and literally watched
him do it on my laptop. I guessed right then that you had
turned him as a source and he was doing the search for you.
This became a problem of containment, as you can imagine. I

didn't need to go up to the city today because we have hard copies of all the protocols at Quantico. But I had to see what you were doing. I got a second confirmation that Warren was leaking to you and that you had copies of the protocols when I found your notebook page left in the files.'

I shook my head.

'What's going to happen to Warren?'

'After I told Ford, we confronted him this morning. He admitted what he had done, even told me what hotel you were at. Ford asked for his resignation and Warren gave it.'

'Shit.'

I felt a pang of guilt, yet I was not overwrought by what had happened. For I wasn't sure if Warren hadn't somehow engineered his own dismissal. Maybe it was a self-derailment. At least, that's what I told myself. It was easier to handle that way.

'By the way,' she said, 'where did I go wrong with my act?'

'My editor didn't know where I was staying. Only Warren knew.'

She was quiet for a few moments until I prompted her to continue the chronology of her investigation. She told me that on Thursday afternoon when she ran the computer search she'd come up with the same thirteen names of dead homicide detectives that Warren had gotten for me, plus my brother and John Brooks of Chicago. She then pulled the hard copies of the protocols and looked for ties, keying on the suicide notes as I had told Ford I wanted to do. She had the aid of a bureau cryptologist and the FBI cipher computer, which had a database that made the *Rocky*'s look like a comic book.

'Including your brother and Brooks, we came up with a total of five direct connections through the notes,' she said.

'So in about three hours you did what it took me all week to do. How'd you get McCafferty without the note in the file?'

She took her foot off the gas and looked over at me. Only for a moment, then she took the car back up to speed.

'We didn't count McCafferty. There are agents from the Baltimore field office on that now.'

This was puzzling because I had five cases, including McCafferty.

'Then what five have you got?'

'Uh, let me think . . .'

'Okay, my brother and Brooks, that's two.'

I was opening my notebook as I said this.

'Right.'

Reading my notes, I said, 'You got Kotite in Albuquerque? "Haunted by ill angels"?'

'Right. We have him. There was one in –'

'Dallas. Garland Petry. "Sadly, I know I am shorn of my strength." From "For Annie."'

'Yeah, got that.'

'And then I had McCafferty. Who'd you have?'

'Uh, something or other from Florida. It was an old one. He was a sheriff's deputy. I need my notes.'

'Wait a minute.' I flipped through a few pages of my notebook and found it. 'Clifford Beltran, Sarasota County Sheriff's Department. He –'

'That's it.'

'But wait a minute. I've got his note as "Lord help my poor soul." I read all the poems. That wasn't in any of them.'

'You're right. We found it somewhere else.'

'Where? One of the short stories?'

'No. They were his last words. Poe's last words. "Lord help my poor soul."'

I nodded. It wasn't a poem but it fit. So now there were six. I was quiet a moment, almost in respect to the new man added to the list. I looked down at my notes. Beltran had been dead three years. A long time for a murder to go unnoticed.

'Was Poe a suicide?'

'No, though I suppose his lifestyle might be considered a long suicide. He was a womanizer and a heavy drinker. He died at forty, apparently after a lengthy drinking bout in Baltimore.'

I nodded, thinking about the killer, the phantom, and wondering if he drew corollaries to Poe's life.

'Jack, what about McCafferty?' she asked. 'We had him as a possible but no note according to the protocol. What did you get?'

Now I had another problem. Bledsoe. He had revealed something to me that he had not revealed to anyone before. I didn't feel I could just turn around and give it to the FBI.

'I've gotta make a call first before I can tell you.'

'Oh, Jesus, Jack. You're going to pull that shit after all I just told you? I thought we had a deal.'

'We do. I just have to make a call first and clear something with a source. Get me to a phone and I'll do it right then. I don't think it will be a problem. Anyway, the bottom line is McCafferty is on the list. There was a note.'

I looked through my notebook again and then read from it.

' "The fever called living is conquered at last." That was the note. It's from "For Annie." Just like Petry in Dallas.'

I looked over at her and could tell she was still upset.

'Look, Rachel – can I call you that? – I'm not going to hold back on you. I'll make the call. Your agents from the field office probably already got this anyway.'

'Probably,' she said, in a voice that seemed to say, *Anything you can get we can get better.*

'Okay, so go on, then. What happened after you came up with the list of five?'

She told me that at six o'clock Thursday evening she and Backus had convened a meeting of BSS and Critical Incident Unit agents to discuss her preliminary findings. After she trotted out the five names she had and explained the connections, her boss, Backus, became agitated and ordered a full-scale priority investigation. Waller was named lead agent, reporting to him. Other BSS and CIU agents were assigned to victimology and profiling tasks, and VICAP liaison agents from local field offices in the five cities where the deaths occurred were scrambled to immediately begin gathering and shipping data on the deaths involved. The team had literally worked through the night.

'The Poet.'

'What?'

'We're calling him the Poet. Every task force investigation gets a code name.'

'Jesus,' I said. 'The tabloids are going to love that. I can see the headlines. "The Poet Kills without Rhyme or Reason." You guys are asking for it.'

'The tabs will never know about it. Backus is determined to get this guy before he's spooked by any press leaks.'

There was silence while I thought of how to answer that.

'Aren't you forgetting something?' I finally asked.

'Jack, I know you're a reporter and you're the one who started this whole thing. But you've got to understand, if you start a media firestorm about this guy, we'll never get him. He'll get spooked and go back underneath his rock. We'll lose our chance.'

'Well, I'm not on the public payroll. What I am, though, is paid to report and write stories ... The FBI *cannot* tell me what and when to write.'

'You can't use anything I just told you.'

'I know it. I agreed and I'll keep my word. I don't need to use it. I already had it. Most of it. All except for Beltran and all I have to do is read the bio section of this book and I'll find his last words ... I don't need the FBI's information or permission for this story.'

That brought the silence back. I could tell she was steaming but I had to stand my ground. I had to play my cards as shrewdly as I could. In this kind of game you don't get a second deal. After a few minutes of this I started seeing the freeway signs for Quantico. We were close.

'Look,' I said. 'We will talk about the story later. I'm not going to run off and start writing. My editor and I will calmly talk about it and I will let you know what we are going to do. Is that okay?'

'That's fine, Jack. I hope you're thinking about your brother when you have that discussion. I'm sure your editor won't be.'

'Look, do me a favor. Don't talk to me about my brother

and my motives. Because you don't know a thing about me or him or what I'm thinking about.'

'Fine.'

We drove a few miles in solid silence. My anger wore off a bit and I began wondering if I'd been too harsh. Her goal was to capture this person they now called the Poet. It was mine, too.

'Look, I'm sorry about the speech,' I said. 'I still think we can help each other. We can cooperate and maybe catch this guy.'

'I don't know,' she replied. 'I don't see the point in cooperating when what I say is just going to show up in the newspapers and then the TV and then the tabloids. You're right, I don't know what you're thinking. I don't know you and I don't think I can trust you.'

She didn't say another word until we got to the gatehouse at Quantico.

21
·········

It was dark and I couldn't see the grounds well as we drove in. The FBI Academy and the research center were located in the heart of a U.S. Marine base. It consisted of three sprawling brick buildings connected by glassed walkways and atriums. Agent Walling pulled into a lot marked for FBI agents only and parked.

She continued her silence as we got out. It was getting to me. I did not want her unhappy with me or thinking of me as self-serving.

'Look, my main priority is obviously to get this guy,' I tried. 'Let me just use a phone. I'll call my source and my editor and we'll work something out. Okay?'

'Sure,' she said grudgingly.

One word and I was happy just to have finally leveraged something out of her. We went into the center building and took a series of hallways to a set of stairs which we took down to the National Center for the Analysis of Violent Crime. It was the basement. She led me past a reception area into a large room that didn't look much different from a newsroom. There were two rows of desks and work spaces with sound partitions between them and a row of private offices running down the right side. She stepped back and pointed me into one of the private offices. I assumed it was hers, though it was austere and impersonal. The only photo I saw anywhere was the one of the president on the rear wall.

'Why don't you sit there and use the phone,' she said. 'I'm going to find out where Bob is and see what's been going on. And don't worry, the phone's not tapped.'

As I noted the sarcasm in her voice I saw her eyes scan the

desk, making sure I would not be left alone with any important documents lying about. Satisfied there was nothing, she left. I sat behind the desk and opened my notebook to the numbers Dan Bledsoe had given me. I got him at home.

'It's Jack McEvoy. From today.'

'Right, yeah.'

'Listen, I got picked up by the FBI after I got back into D.C. They're doing a major deal on this guy and they've connected up five cases. But they don't have McCafferty yet because of no note. I can give it to them and they'll go from there. But I wanted to check with you first about it. They'll probably come talk to you if I tell them. They'll probably come even if I don't.'

While he thought about this my eyes scanned the desk as Walling had done. It was very clean, taken up mostly by a monthly calendar that also served as a blotter. I noted that she had just come back from a vacation, the date blocks for the prior week having 'vac' written in each one. There were abbreviated notations in the blocks for other dates of the month but they were indecipherable to me.

'Give it to 'em,' Bledsoe said.

'You sure?'

'Sure. If the bureau comes out and says Johnny Mac was murdered, then his wife gets the bread. That's all I wanted in the first place, so tell 'em. They're not going to do anything to me. They can't. What's done is done. I already heard from a friend that they were up here going through records today.'

'Okay, man, thanks.'

'You going to get a piece of it?'

'I don't know. I'm working on it.'

'It's your case. Hang in there. But don't trust the G, Jack. They'll use you and what you got and then leave you on the sidewalk like dog shit.'

I thanked him for the advice and as I hung up a man in the standard-issue gray FBI suit walked by the open door of the office, noticed me behind the desk and stopped. He stepped in, a curious look on his face.

'Excuse me, what are you doing in here?'

'Waiting for Agent Walling.'

He was a large man with a sharp and ruddy face and short, black hair.

'And you are?'

'My name is Jack McEvoy. She –'

'Just don't sit behind the desk.'

He made a twirling motion with his hand, indicating I should come around to the front of the desk and take one of the chairs there. Rather than argue the point I followed his instructions. He thanked me and left the office. The episode served as a reminder to me of why I never liked dealing with FBI agents. In general, they all carried anal-retentive genes. More than most.

After I was sure he was gone I reached across the desk to Walling's phone and punched in Greg Glenn's direct number. It was shortly after five in Denver and I knew he would be busy supervising deadline, but I had no choice of when I could call.

'Jack, can you call back?'

'No. I've got to talk to you.'

'Okay, hurry. We had another clinic shooting and we're bending deadline.'

I quickly brought him up to date on what I had and what had happened with the FBI. He seemed to forget all about the clinic shooting and the deadline, repeatedly saying that what I had was fantastic and was going to be a fantastic story. I left out the part about Warren losing his job and Walling's attempt to scam me. I told him where I was and what I wanted to do. He approved it.

'We're probably going to need the whole news hole for this clinic stuff anyway,' he said. 'At least the next couple of days. It's going crazy here. I could use you on rewrite.'

'Sorry.'

'Yeah. Well, you go ahead and play it out and see what you get, then let me know. This is going to be great, Jack.'

'I hope so.'

Glenn started talking about the possibilities again in terms of journalism awards and kicking the competition's ass, breaking a national story. While I listened, Walling stepped into the office with a man I assumed was Bob Backus. He also wore a gray suit but had the air of the man in charge. He looked like he was in his mid- to late thirties and was still in good shape. He had a pleasant look on his face, short-cropped brown hair and piercing blue eyes. I held one finger up to signal I was almost done. I cut in on Glenn.

'Greg, I gotta go.'

'Okay, well let me know. And one thing, Jack.'

'What?'

'Get me some art.'

'Right.'

As I hung up, I thought that might be a little too hopeful on his part. Getting a photographer in on this would be a long shot. I had to worry about getting myself in first.

'Jack, this is Bob Backus, assistant special agent in charge. He leads my team. Bob, Jack McEvoy of the *Rocky Mountain News*.'

We shook hands and Backus had a vise for a grip. That was as standard FBI macho as the suit. As he spoke he reached down absentmindedly to the desk and straightened the calendar.

'Always glad to meet one of our friends in the Fourth Estate. Especially one that doesn't come from inside the beltway.'

I just nodded. It was bullshit and everybody there knew it.

'Jack, why don't we go over to the Boardroom and get a cup of coffee,' Backus said. 'It's been a long day. I'll show you around a little on the way.'

As we went upstairs Backus said nothing of consequence other than to express condolences about my brother. After the three of us were seated with our coffee at one of the tables in the cafeteria called the Boardroom, he got down to business.

'Jack, we are off the record,' Backus said. 'Everything that you see or hear while in Quantico is off the record. Are we clear on that?'

'Yes. For the time being.'

'Okay. If you want to talk about changing that agreement, talk to me or Rachel and we'll hash it out. Would you be willing to sign an agreement to that effect?'

'Sure. But I'm going to be the one who writes it.'

Backus nodded as if I had scored a point in a debate final.

'Fair enough.' He moved his coffee cup to the side, brushed some unseen impurity off his palms and leaned across the table toward me. 'Jack, we've got a status meeting in fifteen minutes. As I am sure Rachel has told you, we are going full speed. We'd be criminally negligent, in my opinion, if we proceeded with this investigation in any other way. I've got my entire team on it, eight other BSS agents on loan, two techs assigned full-time and six field offices involved. I can't remember when we've had that kind of commitment to an investigation before.'

'I'm glad to hear that ... Bob.'

He didn't seem to flinch at my use of his first name. It had been a small test. He was seemingly treating me as an equal, calling me by my first name often. I decided to see what would happen if I did the same. So far, so good.

'You have done some very fine work,' Backus continued. 'What you have done has given us a solid blueprint. It's a start and I want to tell you we're already more than twenty-four solid hours into it.'

Behind Backus I saw the agent who had spoken to me in Walling's office sit down at another table with a cup of coffee and a sandwich. He watched us as he began to eat.

'We are talking about a tremendous amount of resources being committed to the investigation,' Backus said. 'But right now our number one priority is one of containment.'

It was going exactly the way I had expected and I had to struggle to keep a look on my face that did not give away that I knew I held sway over the FBI and the investigation. I had leverage. I was an insider.

'You don't want me to write about it,' I said quietly.

'Yes, that's exactly right. Not yet, at least. We know that you have enough, even without what you've learned from us, to write a hell of a story. It's an explosive story, Jack. If you write about it out there in Denver it is going to attract attention. Overnight it will be on the network and in every newspaper. Then "Hard Copy" and the rest of the TV tabloids. Anybody who doesn't have his head in the sand is going to know about it. And, Jack, plain and simple, we can't have that. Once the offender knows we know about him, he could disappear. If he is smart, and we already know he is damn smart, he will disappear. We'll never get him then. You don't want that. We're talking about the person who killed your brother. You don't want that, do you?'

I nodded that I understood the dilemma and was silent a moment as I composed my reply. I looked from Backus to Walling and then back to Backus.

'My paper has already invested a lot of time and money,' I said. 'I've got the story down cold. Just so you understand, I could write a story tonight that says authorities are conducting a nationwide investigation into the likelihood that a serial killer of cops has been operating for as long as three years without detection.'

'As I said, you've done very good work and nobody's arguing what kind of story this is.'

'So then what are you proposing? I just kill it and walk away, wait for you to hold a press conference one day when, and *if*, you get this guy?'

Backus cleared his throat and leaned back. I glanced over at Walling but her face showed nothing.

'I won't sugarcoat it,' Backus said. 'But, yes, I want you to sit on the story for a little while.'

'Until when? What's "a little while"?'

Backus looked around the cafeteria as if he had never been there. He answered without looking at me.

'Until we get this person.'

I whistled low.

'And what would I get for sitting on the story? What would the *Rocky Mountain News* get?'

'First and foremost, you'd be helping us catch your brother's killer. If that is not enough for you, I'm sure we could work out some sort of exclusivity agreement on the arrest of the suspect.'

No one spoke for a long moment because it was clear the ball was in my court. I weighed my words carefully before finally leaning forward across the table and speaking.

'Well, Bob, as I think you know, this is one of those rare occasions when you guys don't hold all the cards and can't call all of the shots. This is my investigation, you see? I started it and I'm not just going to drop out. I'm not going to go back to Denver and sit behind my desk and wait for the phone to ring. I'm in and if you don't keep me in, then I go back to write the story. It will be in the paper Sunday morning. It's our best circulation day.'

'You'd do that to your own brother?' Walling said, the words tight with anger. 'Don't you give a shit?'

'Rachel, please,' Backus said. 'It's a good point. What we –'

'I give a shit,' I said. 'I was the only one who did. So don't try to lay any guilt on me. My brother stays dead whether you find this guy or not and whether I write the story or not.'

'Okay, Jack, we're not questioning your motives here,' Backus said, his hands raised in a calming gesture. 'We seem to have gotten into an adversarial stance and I don't want that. Why don't you clearly tell me what you want. I'm sure we are going to work this out right here. Before the coffee even gets cold.'

'It's simple,' I said quickly. 'Put me on the investigation. Complete access as an observer. I won't write a word until we either get the son of a bitch or give up.'

'That's blackmail,' Walling said.

'No, it's the agreement I'm offering to make,' I responded. 'It's actually a concession because I have the story now. Having to sit on it is against my instincts and against what I do.'

I looked at Backus. Walling was angry but I knew it didn't matter. Backus would make the call.

'I don't think we can do that, Jack,' he finally said. 'It's against bureau regulations to bring somebody in like that. It could be dangerous to you as well.'

'I don't care about that. Any of it. That's the deal. Take it or leave it. Call whoever you've got to call. But that's the deal.'

Backus pulled his cup in front of him and looked down into the still steaming blackness. He hadn't even sipped it.

'This proposal is well above my level of authority,' he said. 'I'll have to get back to you.'

'When?'

'I'll make the call right now.'

'What about the status conference?'

'They can't start without me. Why don't both of you wait here. This shouldn't take long.'

Backus stood up and carefully slid his chair into the table.

'Just so we're clear,' I said before he turned away, 'if allowed into this as an observer, with two exceptions I will not write about the case until we have an arrest or you determine it is fruitless and focus your primary efforts on other cases.'

'What are the exceptions?' Backus asked.

'One is if you ask me to write about it. There may come a time that you'll want to flush this guy out with a story. I'll write it then. The other exception is if the story leaks. If this shows up in any other paper or on TV, all bets are off. Immediately. If I even get wind that somebody else is about to break it, I'll break it myself first. This is my goddamn story.'

Backus looked at me and nodded.

'I won't be long.'

After he had left, Walling looked at me and quietly said, 'If that had been me, I would have called your bluff.'

'That was no bluff,' I said. 'That was for real.'

'If that's true, that you'd trade catching the guy who killed your brother for a story, then that makes me feel very sad for you. I'm going to get more coffee.'

She got up then and left me. As I watched her walk back to the concession counter my mind wandered over what she had said and then came to rest on the lines by Poe that I had read the night before and that would not leave my memory.

> I dwelt alone
> In a world of moan
> And my soul was a stagnant tide

22
....

When I entered the conference room with Backus and Walling, there were few seats in the room without agents in them. The status meeting was set up with agents sitting around the long table and then an outside layer of sitters on chairs lining the walls. Backus pointed to a chair on the outer rim and signaled me to sit. He and Walling then went to the two remaining slots at the center of the table. The chairs had apparently been exclusively reserved for them. I felt a lot of eyes on me as the stranger but I reached down to the floor and fiddled with my computer satchel, acting like I was looking for something so I did not have to meet any of their stares.

Backus had taken the deal. Or rather, whoever he had called had taken the deal. I was along for the ride, with Agent Walling assigned to baby-sit – as she called it. I had written out and signed an agreement stating that I would not write about the investigation until its fruition or disbanding, or in the event of the occurrence of either of the exceptions I had mentioned earlier. I had asked Backus about a photographer joining me and he said that wasn't part of the deal. But he did agree to consider specific requests for photography. It was the best I could do for Glenn.

After Backus and Walling were settled in their seats and interest in me lagged, I looked about. There were a dozen other men and three women in the room, including Walling. Most of the men were in shirtsleeves and appeared to have been at whatever they were doing for a while. There were a lot of Styrofoam cups, a lot of paperwork on laps and on the table. A woman was making her way around the room handing out a sheaf of papers to each agent. I noticed one of the agents was the sharp-faced man I had encountered in Walling's office and then had seen again in the cafeteria. When Walling had gone to refill her coffee cup, I had seen him get up from his meal and go to the food counters to talk to her. I couldn't hear what was said but I could tell she had dismissed him and he didn't seem too happy about it.

'Okay, people,' Backus said. 'Let's get this going if we can. It's been a long day and they're probably only going to get longer from here.'

The murmur of conversation abruptly halted. As smoothly as possible I reached down to my computer bag and slid out a notebook. I opened it to a fresh page and got ready to take notes.

'First of all, a short announcement,' Backus said. 'The new man you see seated against the wall is Jack McEvoy. He is a reporter for the *Rocky Mountain News* and he plans to be with us until this is over. It is his fine work that resulted in this task force being formed. He discovered our Poet. He has agreed not to write about our investigation until we have the offender in custody. I want all of you to extend him every courtesy. He has the special agent in charge's blessing to be here.'

I felt the eyes on me again and I sat frozen with my notebook and pen in hand, as if I had been caught at a crime scene with blood on my hands.

'If he's not going to write, how come he's got the notebook out?'

I looked toward the familiar voice and saw it was the sharp-faced man from Walling's office who had asked the question.

'He needs to take notes, so that when he does write he has the facts,' Walling said, unexpectedly coming to my defense.

'That'll be the day one of them reports the facts,' the agent threw back at her.

'Gordon, let's not make Mr McEvoy uncomfortable,' Backus said, smiling. 'I trust he will do a good job. The special agent in charge trusts that he will. And, in fact, he has done an excellent job up until now so we are going to give him both the benefit of the doubt and our cooperation.'

I watched the one called Gordon shake his head in dismay,

his face darkening. At least I was getting clues right away about whom to steer clear of. The next came when the woman with the handouts passed by me without giving me anything.

'This will be our last group meeting,' Backus said. 'Tomorrow most of us separate and the OC for this investigation will move to Denver, site of the latest case. Rachel will remain case agent and coordinator. Brass and Brad will stay here to do the collating and all that good stuff. I want hard-copy reports from all agents by eighteen hundred eastern to Denver and Quantico every day. For now use the fax of the Denver field office. The number should be on the printout you just received. We'll set up our own lines and we'll get those numbers to you as soon as we do. Now, let's go over what we've got. It's very important that we're all on the same wavelength. I don't want anything to slip through the cracks on this one. We've had enough of that already.'

'We better not screw up,' Gordon said sarcastically. 'We've also got the press watching us.'

A few people laughed but Backus cut it off.

'All right, all right, Gordon, you've made your disagreement loud and clear. I'm going to yield to Brass for a few minutes and she'll go over what we've got so far.'

A woman across the table from Backus cleared her throat. She spread three pages of what looked like computer printouts in front of her on the table and stood up.

'Okay,' she said. 'We have six dead detectives in six states. We also have six unsolved homicides that the detectives had been working individually at the time of their own death. The bottom line is we don't feel comfortable yet making a firm commitment to whether we have one or two offenders out there – or possibly even more, though this seems unlikely. Our hunch, however, is that we are dealing with one but at the moment I don't have a lot backing that up. What we do feel comfortable with is that the deaths of the six detectives are certainly linked and therefore most likely the work of one hand. For the moment our emphasis is on this offender. The one we are calling the Poet. Beyond that, we only have the theory of linkage to the other cases. We'll talk about them later. First, let's start with the detectives. Take a look at the first PVR in your package for a few seconds and then I'll point out some things.'

I looked at everyone studying the handout and felt annoyed at being left out. I decided that after the meeting I would talk to Backus about it. I looked over at Gordon and saw him looking at me. He winked at me and then turned his face to the reports in front of him. I then saw Walling get up and come around the table to my side of the room. She handed me a copy of the printout. I nodded my thanks but she had already headed back to her spot. I noticed that as she walked back she glanced at Gordon and their eyes locked in a long stare.

I looked at the pages in my hands. The first sheet was just an organizational structure with the names of the agents involved and their assignments. There were also the phone and fax numbers for the field offices in Denver, Baltimore, Tampa, Chicago, Dallas and Albuquerque. I ran my eyes down the list of agents and found only one Gordon. Gordon Thorson. I saw that his assignment simply read 'Quantico – Go.'

Next I looked for Brass on the list and guessed easily enough that she was Brasilia Doran, assigned on the sheet as 'victim coordinator/ profiling.' Other assignments to agents were listed. There were handwriting and cryptology assignments but most were just noted as cities of assignment followed by a victim's name. Apparently two BSS agents would go to each city where the Poet had been to coordinate investigations of those cases with agents from the city's field office and local police.

I turned the page to the next sheet, which was the one everybody else was reading.

PRELIMINARY VICTIMOLOGY REPORT
– THE POET, BSS95-17

Vict#
1. Clifford Beltran, Sarasota County Sheriff's Dept., homicide.
   WM, DOB 3-14-34, DOD 4-1-92
   Weapon: S&W 12 gauge shotgun

one shot – head
POD : residence. No witness

2. John Brooks, Chicago Police Dept., homicide, Area 3.
   BM, DOB 7-21-54, DOD 10-30-93
   Weapon: service, Glock 19
   two shots, one impact – head
   POD : residence. No witness

3. Garland Petry, Dallas Police Dept., homicide.
   WM, DOB 11-11-51, DOD 3-28-94
   Weapon: service, Beretta 38
   two shots, two impacts – chest and head
   POD : residence. No witness

4. Morris Kotite, Albuquerque Police Dept., homicide.
   HM, DOB 9-14-56, DOD 9-24-94
   Weapon: service, S&W 38
   two shots, one impact – head
   POD : car. No witness

5. Sean McEvoy, Denver Police Dept., homicide.
   WM, DOB 5-21-61, DOD 2-10-95
   Weapon: service, S&W 38
   one shot – head
   POD : car. No witness

The first thing I noticed was that they didn't have McCafferty on the list yet. He'd be number two. I then realized that the eyes of many of those in the room were falling on me again as people read to the last name and apparently realized who I was. I kept my eyes on the page in front of me, staring at the notes under my brother's name. His life had been reduced to short descriptions and dates. Brasilia Doran finally rescued me from the moment.

'Okay, FYI, these were printed up before the sixth case was confirmed,' she said. 'If you want to put it on your sheet now, it will be between Beltran and Brooks. The name is John McCafferty, a homicide detective with the Baltimore Police Department. We'll get more details later. Anyway, as you can see, not a lot of things are consistent through these cases. The weapons used differ, places of death differ, and we have three whites, one black and one Hispanic as victims ... The additional case, McCafferty, is a white male, forty-seven years old.

'But there are limited common denominators to the physical scene and evidence. Each victim was a male homicide detective who was killed by a fatal head shot and there were no eyewitnesses to these shootings. From there we get into the two key commonalities that we want to exploit. We have a reference to Edgar Allan Poe in each case. That's one. The second key is that each victim was believed by his colleagues to have been obsessive about a particular homicide case – two of them to the point that they had sought counseling.

'If you turn to the next page ...'

The sound of pages turning whispered through the room. I could feel a grim fascination settling over everyone. It was a surreal moment for me. I felt like maybe a screenwriter does when he finally sees his movie on the screen. Before, all of this was something hidden in my notebooks and computer and head as part of the far realm of possibility. But here was a room crowded with investigators openly talking about it, looking at printouts, confirming the existence of this horror.

The next page contained the suicide notes, all the quotes from Poe's poems that I had found and written down the night before.

'This is where the cases irrefutably come together,' Doran said. 'Our Poet likes Edgar Allan Poe. We don't know why yet, but it's something we'll be working on here at Quantico while you people go traveling. I am going to defer to Brad for a moment to have him tell you a little about this.'

The agent sitting directly next to Doran stood up and took up the lead. I flipped to the front page of the package and found an Agent Bradley Hazelton listed. Brass and Brad. What a team, I thought. Hazelton, a gangly man with acne-scarred cheeks, poked his glasses back on his nose before speaking.

'Um, what we've got here are that the six quotes in these cases – that's including the Baltimore case – come from three of Poe's poems as well as his own last reported words. We are looking at these to determine if we can get some kind of common fix on what the poems were about and how they may relate to this offender. We're looking for anything there. It seems pretty clear that this is where the offender's playing with us and where he is taking the most risk. I don't think we'd be here today or Mr McEvoy would have found a connection among these cases if our guy didn't decide to quote Edgar Allan Poe. So, then, these poems are his signature. We'll be trying to find out why he chose Poe as opposed to, say, Walt Whitman but I –'

'I'll tell you why,' said an agent sitting at the far end of the table. 'Poe was a morbid asshole and so is our guy.'

A few people laughed.

'Uh, yes, probably that's correct in a general sense,' Hazelton said, oblivious that the comment was made to lighten everyone up. 'Nevertheless, Brass and I will be working on this and if you have any ideas, I'd like to hear them. As for right now, a couple things to throw out. Poe is credited with being the father of detective fiction with the publication of *The Murders in the Rue Morgue,* which is basically a mystery story. So we may have an offender out there who is looking at this as some kind of mystery puzzle. He simply likes to taunt us with his own sort of mystery, by using Poe's words as clues. Also, I've started reading through some of the established criticism and analysis of Poe's work and found something interesting. One of the poems that our guy used is called "The Haunted Palace." This poem was contained within a short story called "The Fall of the House of Usher." I'm sure you've all heard of it or read it. Anyway, the standard analysis of this poem is that while at face value it serves as a description of the house of Usher, it is also a disguised or subconscious description of the story's focal character, Roderick Usher. And that name, you know if you were at last night's briefing, came up in the death of victim number six. I'm sorry, that's Sean McEvoy. He's not just a number.'

He looked over at me and nodded and I nodded back.

'The description in the poem ... hold on.' Hazelton was

looking through his notes, then found what he needed, pushed his glasses back again and continued. 'Okay, we've got, "Banners yellow, glorious, golden; / On its roof did float and flow," and then later on we have, "Along the ramparts plumed and pallid." Okay, and then a few lines later we have mention of "two luminous windows" blah, blah, blah. Anyway, what this translates to as far as a description goes is that of a reclusive white male with blond hair, perhaps long or curly blond hair, and eyeglasses. There's your start on the physical profile.'

There was a roll of laughter through the room and Hazelton seemed to take it personally.

'It's in the books,' he protested. 'I'm serious and I think it's a place to start.'

'Wait a minute, wait a minute,' said a voice from the outer rim. A man stood up so he'd have the attention of the whole room. He was older than most of the other agents and carried the no-nonsense air of a veteran. 'What are we talking about here? Yellow banners flowing – what is this shit? This Poe stuff is great, it'll probably help that kid over there sell a lot of papers, but nothing's convinced me in the last twenty hours that I've been here that there's some mope out there on the street who somehow some way got the drop on five, six veteran dicks and put their own weapons in their mouths. I'm having a hard time seeing it, is what I'm saying. Whaddaya got on that?'

There was the hum of agreeing comments and nods in the room. I heard someone call the agent who had started the ball rolling 'Smitty' and I saw a Chuck Smith listed on the front page of the packet. He was heading to Dallas.

Brass Doran stood up to address the issue.

'We know that's the rub,' she said. 'Methodology is what we are least prepared to discuss at this point. But the Poe correlation is definitive in my judgment and Bob agrees. So what's our alternative? Do we say this is impossible and drop it? No, we act as if other lives may be at stake because they may very well be. The questions you have will, hopefully, be answered as we go. But I agree it is something we need to be considering and it is always healthy to be skeptical. It's a question of control. How does the Poet get control of these men?'

She turned her head and scanned the room. Smitty was silent now.

'Brass,' Backus said. 'Let's go on to the first victims.'

'Okay, folks, next page.'

The page we turned to contained information on the murders that had obsessed the detectives the Poet killed. These were called secondary victims on the report, even though in each city they had actually died first. I noticed that once again the sheet was not up to date. Polly Amherst, the woman whose murder had obsessed John McCafferty in Baltimore, had not yet made the list.

SECONDARY VICTIMOLOGY — PRELIMINARY

1. Gabriel Ortiz, Sarasota, FL
   student
   HM, DOB 6-1-82, DOD 2-14-92
   Ligature strangulation, molestation
   (kapok fiber)
2. Robert Smathers, Chicago
   student
   BM, DOB 8-11-81, DOD 8-15-93
   Manual strangulation, mutilation antemortem
3. Althea Granadine, Dallas
   student
   BF, DOB 10-10-84, DOD 1-4-94
   Multiple stabbing, chest, mutilation antemortem
4. Manuela Cortez, Albuquerque, NM
   housekeeper
   HF, DOB 4-11-46, DOD 8-16-94
   Multiple blunt force, mutilation postmortem
   (kapok fiber)
5. Theresa Lofton, Denver, CO
   student, day care employee
   WF, DOB 7-4-75, DOD 12-16-94
   Ligature strangulation, mutilation postmortem
   (kapok fiber)

'Okay, once again we are missing one,' Doran said. 'Balti-more. I understand the case was not a child, but a teacher. Polly Amherst. Ligature strangulation and postmortem mutilation.'

She waited a beat in case people were writing notes.

'We are still in the process of having files and data faxed in on these cases,' she continued. 'This was just put together for the meeting. But, preliminarily, what we are looking at as far as these secondary cases go is a commonality involving children. Three victims were children, two worked directly with children and the last one, Manuela Cortez, was a housekeeper who was abducted and murdered at some point while going to the school her employer's children attended to walk them home. The extrapolation is that the intended targets in this chain were children but in half the cases perhaps something went wrong, the stalking pattern was somehow interrupted by the adult victims, and they were eliminated.'

'What is to be made from the mutilation?' an agent on the outer rim asked. 'Some of it's post and with the kids . . . it wasn't.'

'We're not sure, but a guess at this time is that it might be part of his cloaking. By using differing methodology and pa-thology he has been able to camouflage himself. On this page these cases may look similar but the more complete the anal-ysis the more different they are. It is as if six different men with differing pathologies killed these victims. In fact, all the cases were submitted on VICAP questionnaires by the local agencies but none drew matches to the others. Remember, the questionnaire is now up to eighteen pages.

'Bottom line, I think this offender's read up on us. I think he knew how to do things differently enough with each of these victims so that our trusty computer never scored a match. The only mistake he made was the kapok fibers. That is how we have him.'

An agent on the outer rim raised his hand and Doran nodded at him.

'If there were three incidents of kapok fiber being recov-ered, why didn't we get a match on the VICAP computer if all cases were entered like you said?'

'Human error. In the first case, the Ortiz boy, kapok was indigenous to the area and dismissed. It wasn't put on the questionnaire. In the Albuquerque case, the fibers were not identified until after a VICAP survey was submitted. Once they were identified as kapok, the survey was not updated. An oversight. We missed the match. We only got that from the field office today. Only in the Denver case was the kapok seen as significant enough to include on the VICAP request.'

There was a groan from several of the agents and I felt my own heart sink a bit. The possibility of confirming that there was a serial killer at work as early as the Albuquerque case had been missed. What if it hadn't been missed, I wondered. Maybe Sean would be alive.

'That brings us to the big question,' Doran said. 'How many killers have we got? One who does the first string and another who does the detectives? Or just one? One who does them all. For the moment, based primarily on the logistical improbabilities associated with two killers, we are pursuing a theory of linkage. Our assumption is that in each city the two deaths are linked.'

'What's the pathology?' Smitty asked.

'We're only guessing now. The obvious one is that he sees killing the detective as a way of covering his tracks, ensuring his escape. But we have another theory as well. That is that the first homicide was committed by the offender in order to draw a homicide detective into the frame. In other words, the first kill is bait, presented in such a horrific fashion as to attract a homicide detective's obsession. We are assuming that the Poet then stalked each one of these officers and learned their habits and routines. That enabled him to get close and carry out the eventual murder without detection.'

This silenced the room. I got the feeling that many of the agents, though surely veterans of numerous investigations of serial killings, had never before encountered a predator like the one they were calling the Poet.

'Of course,' Brass said, 'all we have is theory for the time being ...'

Backus stood up.

'Thank you, Brass,' he said, then addressing the room added, 'Quickly now, because I want to do some profiling and get this wrapped up, Gordon, you had something for us.'

'Yes, real quick,' Thorson said, standing up and moving to an easel with a large drawing pad on it. 'The map in your package is outdated because of the Baltimore connection. So if I can have your attention up here for a moment.'

He quickly drew the outline of the United States with a thick black marker. Then, with a red marker, he began to draw the Poet's trail. Starting in Florida, which he had drawn proportionately small compared to the rest of the country, the line went up to Baltimore then over to Chicago then down to Dallas then up to Albuquerque and finally up further to Denver. He picked up the black marker again and wrote the dates of the killings in each of the cities.

'It's pretty self-explanatory,' Thorson said. 'Our man is heading west and he's obviously pissed off at homicide cops about something.'

He raised his hand and waved it over the western half of the country he had drawn.

'We'll look for the next hits out here unless we get lucky and get him first.'

Looking at the terminus of the red line Thorson had drawn gave me a strange feeling about what was ahead. Where was the Poet? Who was next?

'Why don't we just let him get to California, so he can be among his own kind? End of problem.'

Everyone laughed at the joke from one of the agents seated in the outer rim. The humor emboldened Hazelton.

'Hey, Gordo,' he said, reaching back to the easel and tapping a pencil on the small rendering of Florida. 'I hope this map wasn't some kind of Freudian slip on your part.'

That brought the loudest laughter of the meeting and Thorson's face reddened, though he smiled at the joke at his expense. I saw Rachel Walling's face light up with delight.

'Very funny, Hazel,' Thorson loudly retorted. 'Why don't you go back to analyzing the poems. You're good at that.'

The laughter dried up quickly and I suspected that

Thorson had taunted Hazelton with a barb that was more personal than witty.

'Okay, if I can continue,' Thorson said, 'FYI, tonight we'll be alerting all the FOs, particularly in the West, to be on watch for something like this. It would help us a lot if we could get an early notice on the next one and get our lab into one of the scenes. We'll have a go team ready. But right now we are relying on the locals for everything. Bob?'

Backus cleared his throat to continue the discussion.

'If nobody has anything else, we come to profiling. What can we say about this offender? I would like to put something on the alert Gordon sends out.'

Then came a procession of thrown-out observations, a lot of them free-form non sequiturs, some of them even bringing laughter. I could see there was a lot of camaraderie among the agents. There was also some strife, as exhibited by the play between Thorson and Walling and then Thorson and Hazelton. Nevertheless, I got the feeling that these people had sat around the table in this room doing this before. Sadly, many times before.

The profile that emerged would be of small use in catching the Poet. The generalities the agents threw into the ring were primarily interior descriptions. Anger. Isolation. Above-average education and intelligence. How do you identify these things among the masses, I thought. No chance.

Occasionally, Backus would step in and throw out a question to get the discussion back on course.

'If you subscribe to Brass's last theory, why homicide cops?'

'You answer that and you've got him in a box. That's the mystery. This poetry stuff is the diversion.'

'Rich or poor?'

'He's got money. He has to. Wherever he goes, he's not staying long. No job – killing is his job.'

'He's gotta have a bank account or rich parents, something. And he's got wheels and he needs money to put gas in the tank.'

The session went on for another twenty minutes with

Doran taking notes for the preliminary profile. Then Backus ended it and told everyone to take the rest of the night off before traveling in the morning.

As the meeting broke up, a few people came up to me and introduced themselves, expressed condolences for my brother and admiration for my investigation. But it was only a few and they included Hazelton and Doran. After a few minutes of this I was left alone and was looking about for Walling when Gordon Thorson approached. He held his hand out and after hesitating, I shook it.

'Didn't mean to give you a hard time,' he said smiling warmly.

'That's okay. It was fine.'

He had a tight grip and after the standard two-second shake I tried to pull away but he wouldn't let go. Instead, he pulled my hand toward him and leaned forward so that only I would hear what he had to say next.

'It's good that your brother isn't around to see this,' he whispered. 'If I did what you did to get on this case, I'd be ashamed. I couldn't live with myself.'

He straightened up, always continuing the smile. I just looked at him and inexplicably nodded. He dropped my hand and stepped away. I felt humiliated in that I had not defended myself. I had stupidly just nodded my head.

'What was that about?'

I turned. It was Rachel Walling.

'Uh, nothing. He just . . . nothing.'

'Whatever he said, forget it. He can be an asshole.'

I nodded.

'Yeah, I was getting that idea.'

'C'mon, let's go back to the Boardroom. I'm starved.'

In the hallway she told me the travel plans.

'We're leaving early tomorrow. It's better if you stay here tonight instead of going all the way back to the Hilton. The visitor dorms mostly clear out on Fridays. We can put you in one of those and have the Hilton just clear your room and send your stuff to Denver. Will that be a problem?'

'Uh, no. I guess . . .'

I was still thinking about Thorson.

'Fuck him.'

'What?'

'That guy, Thorson, he *is* an asshole.'

'Forget about him. We're leaving tomorrow and he's staying here. What about the Hilton?'

'Yeah, fine. I've got my computer and everything else that's important already with me.'

'I'll see about getting you a fresh shirt in the morning.'

'Oh, my car. I've got a rental in the Hilton's garage.'

'Where are the keys?'

I pulled them out of my pocket.

'Give them to me. We'll take care of it.'

23
....

In the early hours, when dawn was still only a hint around the curtains, Gladden moved about Darlene's apartment, too nervous to sleep, too excited to want to. He paced through the small rooms, thinking, planning, waiting. He looked in on Darlene in the bedroom, watched her on the bed for a few moments and then returned to the living room.

Unframed posters from old porno movies were taped to the walls and the place was filled with bric-a-brac souvenirs of a worthless life. There was a nicotine veneer on everything. Gladden was a smoker but still found it disgusting. The place was a mess.

He paused in front of one of the posters, from a film called *Inside Darlene*. She had told him she'd been a star in the early eighties before video revolutionized the business and she started looking old, the wear and tear of the life showing around her eyes and mouth. She'd pointed with a wistful smile to the posters where the air-brushed photos showed her body and face smooth and unlined. She was billed simply as Darlene. No last name needed. He wondered what it was like living in a place where the images of your former glorious self mocked your present self from the walls.

He turned away and noticed her purse on the card table in the dining room and looked through it. It was full of makeup, mostly, and empty cigarette packages and matchbooks. There was a small spray can for repelling attackers and her wallet. She had seven dollars. He looked at her license and discovered for the first time what her full name was.

'Darlene Kugel,' he said out loud. 'Pleased to meet you.'

He took the money and put everything else back in the

purse. Seven dollars wasn't much but it was seven dollars. The man at the digiTime dealership had made him pay in advance to order the camera. Gladden was now down to a few hundred dollars and he figured seven more couldn't hurt.

He put his money worries aside and began to pace again. He had a problem of timing. The camera had to be shipped from New York. It wouldn't be in until Wednesday. Five more days. He knew that to be safe he'd have to wait it out right here in Darlene's apartment. And he knew he could do it.

He decided to make a list for the store. Darlene's shelves were almost empty except for tuna fish and he hated that shit. He'd have to go out, get supplies, and then dig in until Wednesday. He wouldn't need much. Spring water – Darlene apparently drank tap water. Also Fruit Loops, maybe some Chef Boyardee.

He heard a car drive by outside. He moved toward the door to listen and finally he heard the sound he had been waiting for. The newspaper hitting the ground. Darlene had told him the tenant in the apartment next door got the paper. Gladden was proud of himself for having thought to ask. He went to the window now and peered through the blinds to the street. Dawn was coming up gray and misty. He saw no activity outside.

After turning the two locks, Gladden opened the door and stepped out into the crisp morning air. He looked around and saw the folded newspaper on the sidewalk in front of the apartment next door. No lights were on behind the apartment's doors. Gladden quickly walked to the newspaper, picked it up and returned to the apartment he had come from.

On the couch he quickly went to the Metro section of the paper and flipped through the eight pages. There was no story. Nothing on the maid. He tossed the section aside and picked up the front section.

He turned the section over and there it was at last, his own photo at the bottom right corner of the front page. It was the mug shot from the Santa Monica arrest. He pulled his eyes away from his own image and started reading the story. He was overjoyed. He had made the front page again. After so many years. His face flushed as he read.

MOTEL MURDER SUSPECT ESCAPED THE LAW IN FLORIDA
By Keisha Russell, Times Staff Writer

A Florida man who authorities said escaped justice as a child molester in Florida has been identified as the suspect in the brutal mutilation murder of a Hollywood motel maid, Los Angeles police said Friday.

William Gladden, 29, is being sought in the death of Evangeline Crowder, whose body was found in Gladden's room at the Hollywood Star Motel. The 19-year-old victim's body had been cut into pieces and placed in three drawers of a bureau in the room.

The body was discovered after Gladden checked out of the motel. A motel employee who was looking for the missing maid entered the room and saw blood seeping from the bureau, police said. Crowder was the mother of an infant boy.

Gladden was registered at the hotel under the name Bryce Kidder. But police said that analysis of a fingerprint found in the room identified the suspect as Gladden.

Gladden was sentenced to 70 years in prison after a highly publicized child molestation trial in Tampa, Fla., seven years ago.

However, after serving only two years in prison, he was released when his conviction was overturned on appeal. Key evidence – photos of nude children – was ruled illegally obtained by authorities. After the legal setback, prosecutors allowed Gladden to plead guilty to lesser charges. He was released on probation for time already served in prison.

In another irony, police have also learned that Gladden was arrested in Santa Monica three days before the motel murder was discovered. He was taken into custody on a variety of minor charges stemming from a complaint that he was taking photos of children being washed at beach showers and at the carousel on the pier. However, he was arraigned and released on bail before his true identity was learned.

–Continued, page 14A

Gladden had to open the section and follow the story to an inside page. There he saw another photograph of himself staring out at the reader. This was of the thin-faced and red-haired twenty-one-year-old he had been before the persecution had begun in Florida. And there was another story about him as well. He quickly finished reading the first story.

–Continued from 1A

Police said they have not determined a motive for Crowder's slaying. Though the motel room where Gladden had stayed for nearly a week had been meticulously wiped clean of fingerprints, LAPD detective Ed Thomas said Gladden made one mistake that led to his identification. That was leaving a single fingerprint behind on the underside of the toilet's flush handle.

'It was a lucky break,' Thomas said. 'That one print was all we needed.'

The print was fed into the department's Automated Fingerprint Identification System, part of a nationwide computer network of fingerprint data. A match was found to Gladden's fingerprints, which were on file with the Florida Department of Law Enforcement computer.

According to Thomas, Gladden has been wanted on probation violation for nearly four years. The violation was filed when he stopped regular visits to a probation officer in Florida and disappeared.

In the Santa Monica case, detectives arrested Gladden on Sunday after a chase from the carousel at the pier where they observed him watching young children on the popular ride.

While attempting to run from police, he threw a trash

can off the pier into the bay. He was finally captured in a restaurant on the Third Street Promenade.

Gladden, who had used the name Harold Brisbane when arrested, was charged with pollution of public waterways, vandalism of city property and evading a police officer. However, the district attorney's office declined to file any charges relating to his alleged photographing of children, citing insufficient evidence of a crime.

SMPD detective Constance Delpy said she and her partner began watching the carousel ride after receiving a complaint from an employee who had described Gladden as loitering near children and taking pictures out on the beach of nude children being washed at the showers by their parents.

Though Gladden was fingerprinted upon his arrest, Santa Monica does not have its own fingerprint computer and relies on use of a Department of Justice computer and other departments, including the LAPD, to run prints on the AFIS network. The process usually takes days because departments run their own prints as priorities.

In this case, the Santa Monica prints taken of the man originally identified as Brisbane were not run by the LAPD until Tuesday. By then, Gladden – who had spent Sunday night in the county jail – had bailed out by posting a $50,000 bond.

The LAPD then also identified Gladden late Thursday through the print taken from the motel room.

Detectives involved in the two cases were left to wonder about the sequence of events and how they allegedly took a murderous turn.

'There is always second-guessing when things like this happen,' said Delpy of the SMPD Exploited Child Unit. 'What could we have done better to keep him locked up? I don't know. Sometimes you win and sometimes you lose.'

Thomas said the real crime was in Florida where Gladden was allowed to go free.

'Here you have a man, an obvious pedophile, and the system lets him go,' Thomas said. 'When the system doesn't work, it always seems to be a case like this, where somebody innocent pays the price.'

Gladden quickly went on to the other story. He felt a weird sense of elation as he read about himself. He reveled in the glory of it.

SUSPECT DID AN 'END RUN AROUND JUSTICE' IN FLORIDA
By Keisha Russell, Times Staff Writer

A gifted jailhouse lawyer, according to authorities, William Gladden used his prison-learned wiles to subvert the justice system and then disappear – until this week.

Gladden worked at the Little Ducks Childcare Center in Tampa eight years ago when he was arrested and charged with molesting as many as 11 children over a three-year period.

The arrest spawned a highly publicized trial resulting in his conviction on twenty-eight of the charges two years later. By all accounts, the key evidence leading to the convictions was a cache of Polaroid pictures of nine of the young victims. In the photos, the children were seen in various stages of undress in a closet at the now defunct childcare center.

The telling thing about the pictures, however, was not that some of the children were nude, but the looks on their faces, according to Charles Hounchell, the former Hillsborough County prosecutor who was assigned to the case.

'All the kids were scared,' Hounchell said Friday in a telephone interview from Tampa where he is now in private practice. 'These kids didn't like what was being done and it showed. It really went to the truth of the case. What their faces said in the photos matched the things they told the counselors.'

But at trial, the photos were more important than the counselors and what the children had told them. Despite objections from Gladden that the photos had been discovered during an illegal search of his apartment by a police officer whose son was one of the alleged molestation victims, the judge allowed the photos into evidence.

Jurors said afterward that they relied almost exclusively on the photos to convict Gladden because the two counselors who dealt with the children had been discredited by the attorney representing Gladden for their alleged methods of leading the children into voicing accusations against Gladden.

After his conviction, Gladden was sentenced to 70 years' imprisonment to be served at the Union Correctional Institute at Raiford.

In the prison, Gladden, who already had a degree in English literature, studied poetry, psychology and the law. It appears that it is in the law that he excelled. The convicted molester quickly learned the skills of a jailhouse lawyer, according to Hounchell, and helped other inmates with appellate briefs while composing his own.

Among his more celebrated 'clients' in the prison's sexual offender ward were Donel Forks, the so-called pillowcase rapist of Orlando, former Miami surfing champion Alan Jannine and Las Vegas stage hypnotist Horace Gomble. All three are serving time for multiple rape convictions and Gladden was unsuccessful in his attempts to win them freedom or new trials with appeals he wrote while serving time with them.

But within a year of his imprisonment, Hounchell said, Gladden filed a thoroughly researched appeal of his own conviction which challenged once again the search that led to the discovery of the incriminating photos.

Hounchell explained that Raymond Gomez, the officer who found the photos, had gone to Gladden's home in a rage after his five-year-old son revealed that he had been molested by a man who worked at the boy's childcare center.

Receiving no answer after knocking, the off-duty officer said he found the door unlocked and entered. Gomez later testified in a hearing on the matter that he found the photos spread out on a bedspread. He quickly extricated himself from the house and reported his knowledge to detectives who then obtained a search warrant.

Gladden was arrested after the detectives went back later that day with the warrant and found the photos hidden in a closet. Gladden maintained at trial that the door was not unlocked when he had left his apartment and the photos were not on display. Regardless of whether the door was unlocked and the photos left out, he argued, the search by Gomez was a clear breach of his constitutional rights to protection from unlawful search and seizure.

However, the trial judge ruled that Gomez was acting as a father, not a police officer, when he entered the apartment. The accidental discovery of the key evidence was therefore not a breach of the Constitution.

An appeals court later sided with Gladden, saying that Gomez had knowledge through his police training of search and seizure laws and should have known better than to enter the premises without authority. The Florida Supreme Court later refused to reverse the appeals court, clearing the way for a new trial without the use of the photos as evidence.

Faced with the difficult task of winning a case without key evidence the first jury said was vital, authorities allowed Gladden to plead guilty to one count of lewd behavior with a child.

The maximum sentence for such a crime is five years in prison and five years of consecutive probation. By that point, Gladden had served 33 months in prison and had earned an equal amount in good-behavior gain time. At his sentencing, he received the maximum penalty but still walked out of court a free man on probation.

'It was an end run around justice,' Hounchell, the

prosecutor, recalled. 'We knew he did it but we couldn't use the evidence we had in our hands. After that sentencing, it was hard for me to look at those parents and their children. Because I knew this guy would be out there and that he'd probably want to do it again.'

Within a year of his release, Gladden disappeared and a warrant was issued for probation violation. He resurfaced this week in southern California with what authorities here called deadly consequences.

Gladden read the story completely through a second time. He was fascinated by its thoroughness and the credit it gave him. He also liked how, if you read between the lines, it questioned the story of the cop Gomez. That liar, Gladden thought. He broke in and he ruined the case. Served him right. He was almost tempted to pick up the phone and call the reporter to thank her for the story but decided against it. Too risky. He thought of Hounchell, the young prosecutor.

'End run,' he said aloud. Then he yelled it out, 'End run!'

His mind raced and filled with joy. There was so much they didn't know and already he was on the front page. They would certainly learn soon. They would know. His moment of glory was coming. Soon now.

Gladden got up and went into the bedroom to prepare to go to the store. He thought it would be best to go early. He looked at Darlene again. Bending over the bed he touched her wrist and tried to lift her arm. Full rigor mortis had set in. He looked at her face. The jaw muscles were already contracting, pulling her lips back into an ugly grin. Her eyes appeared to be staring at their own reflection in the mirror over the bed.

He reached over and pulled the wig off her head. Her real hair was reddish brown and short, unattractive. He noticed some of the blood had gotten on the lower fringe of blond curls and he took the wig into the bathroom to wash it off and to get himself ready. Afterward, he returned to the bedroom and gathered the things from the closet he would need to go to the store. Glancing back at the body as he was leaving the room, Gladden realized he had never asked her what the tattoo was supposed to be. Now it was too late.

Before closing the door and leaving the room he turned the air conditioner on high. In the living room, as he changed clothes, he made a mental note to pick up some more incense at the store. He decided he would use the seven dollars he had taken from her purse. She was creating the problem, he thought, she should pay to fix it.

24

· · · · · · · ·

Saturday morning we took a helicopter from Quantico to National and boarded a small bureau jet bound for Colorado. It was where my brother had died. It was where the freshest trail was. It was me, Backus, Walling and a forensic specialist named Thompson I recognized from the meeting the evening before.

Beneath my jacket I was wearing a light blue pullover shirt with the FBI seal on the left breast. Walling had knocked on the door of my dorm that morning and presented it to me with a smile. It was a nice gesture but I couldn't wait to get to Denver so I could change into my own clothes. Still, it beat wearing the same shirt I had already worn for two days.

The ride was smooth. I sat in the back, three rows behind Backus and Walling. Thompson sat behind them. I passed the time by reading the biographical note on Poe in the book I had bought and typing notes into my laptop.

About halfway across the country, Rachel got up from her spot and came back to visit me. She'd dressed in jeans, a green corduroy shirt and black hiking boots. As she moved into the seat next to me she hooked her hair back behind her ear and it helped frame her face. She was beautiful and I realized that in less than twenty-four hours I had gone from hating her to wanting her.

'What're you thinking about all alone back here?'

'Nothing much. My brother, I guess. If we get this guy I guess maybe I'll find out how it happened. It's still hard to believe.'

'Were you close to him?'

'Most of the time.' I didn't have to think about it. 'But in the last few months, no ... It had happened before. It was kind of cyclical. We'd get along and then we'd get sick of each other.'

'Was he older or younger?'

'Older.'

'How much older?'

'Three minutes. We were twins.'

'I didn't know.'

I nodded and she frowned as if the thought that we had been twins made the loss all the more hurtful. Maybe it had.

'I didn't catch that in the reports.'

'Probably not important.'

'Well, it helps explains why you ... I've always wondered about twins.'

'You mean like did I get a psychic message from him the night he was killed? The answer is no. That kind of stuff never happened with us. Or, if it did, I never recognized it and he never said anything about it.'

She nodded and I looked back out the window for a few seconds. I felt good being with her, despite the rocky start of the day before. But I was beginning to suspect that Rachel Walling could put her worst enemy at ease.

I tried asking her questions about herself to turn it around. She mentioned the marriage I already knew about from Warren but she didn't say much about her former husband. She said she had gone to Georgetown to study psychology and was recruited in her last year by the bureau. After becoming an agent in the New York field office, she had gone back to school at night at Columbia for a law degree. She freely admitted that being a woman plus having a law degree put her on the bureau's fast track. The BSS was a plum assignment.

'Your folks must be very proud of you,' I said.

She shook her head.

'No?'

'My mother left when I was young. I haven't seen her in a long time. She doesn't know anything about me.'

'Your father?'

'My dad died when I was very young.'

I knew I had strayed beyond the bounds of routine conversation. But my instinct as a journalist was always to ask the next question, the one they don't expect. I also sensed that she wanted to say more but wouldn't unless I asked.

'What happened?'

'He was a policeman. We lived in Baltimore. He killed himself.'

'Oh, man. Rachel, I'm sorry. I shouldn't have –'

'No, it's okay. I wanted you to know that. I think it has everything to do with what I am and what I'm doing. Maybe it's that way with your brother and this story. That's why I wanted to tell you that if I was harsh with you yesterday, I'm sorry.'

'Don't worry about it.'

'Thanks.'

We were silent for a few moments but I sensed the subject wasn't closed yet.

'The suicide study with the foundation, is that … ?'

'Yes, that's why I started it.'

Another void of silence followed but I was not uncomfortable and I don't think she was either. Eventually she got up and went to a storage area at the back of the cabin and got everybody sodas. When Backus was through joking about what a fine stewardess she made she sat down with me again. As the conversation began again I tried to move the subject away from the memory of her father.

'Do you ever regret not being a practicing shrink?' I asked. 'Isn't that what you first went to school for?'

'Not at all. This is more satisfying. I've probably had more firsthand experience with sociopaths than most shrinks have in a lifetime.'

'And that's only the agents you work with.'

Her laugh came easily.

'Boy, if you only knew.'

Maybe it was only the fact that she was a woman, but I sensed she was different from the other agents I had known and dealt with over the years. She wasn't as sharp around the edges. She was a listener, not a teller, a thinker, not a reactor. I was beginning to feel I could tell her what I was thinking at any given time and not worry about the consequences.

'Like Thorson,' I said. 'He seems like he's got his top screwed on a little too tight.'

'Definitely,' she said and then an uneasy smile and shake of the head followed.

'What's with him, anyway?'

'He's angry.'

'At what?'

'A lot of things. He's got a lot of baggage. Including me. He was my husband.'

It didn't really surprise me. There had been the visible tension between them. My initial impression of Thorson was that he could be poster boy for the Men Are Pigs Society. No wonder Walling had a dim view of the other side.

'Sorry I brought him up, then,' I said. 'I'm batting a thousand here.'

She smiled.

'That's okay. He leaves that impression on a lot of people.'

'Must be hard to have to work with him. How come you're both in the same unit?'

'We're not exactly. He's in Critical Incident Response. I float between Behavioral Science and CIR. We only have to work together at times like these. We used to be partners before we married. We both worked on the VICAP program and spent a lot of time on the road together. Then we just came apart.'

She drank some of her Coke and I didn't ask any more questions. I couldn't ask any of the right ones so I decided to cool it for a while. But she continued on unbidden.

'When we divorced I left the VICAP team, started handling mostly BSS research projects, profiles and an occasional case. He switched over to Critical Response. But we still have our little meetings in the cafeteria and on cases like this.'

'Then why don't you transfer all the way out?'

'Because, like I said, assignment to the national center is a plum. I don't want to leave and neither does he. It's either that or he just stays around to spite me. Bob Backus talked to us once and said he thought it would be better if one of us transferred out, but neither of us will blink. They can't move Gordon because he's got seniority. He's been there since the center started. If they move me the unit loses one of only three females and they know I'll make a beef about it.'

'What could you do?'

'Just say I'm being moved because I'm the woman. Maybe talk to the *Post*. The center is one of the bureau's bright spots. When we come to town to help the local cops we're heroes, Jack. The media laps it up and the bureau doesn't want to dim that. So Gordon and I get to keep making dirty faces at each other across the table.'

The plane pushed over into a descent and through the window I could look up ahead. On the far west horizon were the familiar Rockies. We were almost there.

'Were you involved in the interviews of Bundy and Manson, people like that?'

I had heard or read somewhere about the BSS project to interview all known serial rapists and killers in prisons across the country. From the interviews came the psychological data bank the BSS used to create profiles of other killers. The interview project had taken years and I remembered something about it having taken its toll on the agents who faced these men.

'That was a trip,' she said. 'Me, Gordon, Bob, we were all part of that. I still get a letter from Charlie every now and then. Usually around Christmas. As a criminal he was most effective in manipulation of his female followers. So I think he thinks that if he is going to get anybody to sympathize with him at the bureau, it will be a woman. Me.'

I saw the logic and nodded.

'And the rapists,' she said. 'A lot of the same pathology as the killers. They were some sweet guys, I tell you. I could just feel them sizing me up when I'd go in. I could tell they were trying to figure out how much time they'd have before the guard could get in. You know, whether they could take me before help came in. It really showed their pathology. They only thought in terms of help coming to save me, not that I might be able to defend myself. Save myself. They simply looked at all women as victims. As prey.'

'You mean you talked to these people alone? No separation?'

'The interviews were informal, usually in a lawyer room. No separation but usually a hack hole. The protocol –'

'Hack hole?'

'A window one of the guards could watch through. The protocol called for two agents in all the interviews but in practice there were just too many of these guys. So most of the time, we'd go to a prison and split up. It was quicker that way. The interview rooms were always monitored but every now and then I'd get this creepy chill from some of those guys. Like I was alone. But I couldn't look up to see if the hack was watching because then the subject would look up and if he saw the hack wasn't looking, then ... you know.'

'Shit.'

'Well, for some of the more violent offenders, my partner and I would do it together. Gordon or Bob or whoever was with me. But it was always faster when we split up and did separate interviews.'

I imagined that if you spent a couple years doing those interviews you'd come away with some psychological baggage of your own. I wondered if that was what she had meant when she had talked about her marriage to Thorson.

'Did you wear the same clothes?' she asked.

'What?'

'You and your brother. You know, like you see some twins do.'

'Oh, the matching stuff. No, thank God. My parents never pulled any of that with us.'

'So who was the black sheep of the family? You or him?'

'Me, definitely. Sean was the saint and I was the sinner.'

'And what are your sins?'

I looked at her.

'Too many to recount here.'

'Really? Then what was the most saintly thing he ever did?'

As the smile dropped off my face at the memory that would be her answer, the plane banked sharply to the left, came out of it and started to climb. Rachel immediately forgot her question and leaned into the aisle so she could look toward the front. Presently I saw Backus coming down the aisle, his hands grabbing the bulkhead for balance. He signaled to Thompson to follow him and they both made their way back to us.

'What is it?' Rachel asked.

'We're diverting,' Backus said. 'I just got a call from Quantico. This morning the field office in Phoenix responded to our alert. One week ago a homicide detective was found dead in his home. It was supposed to be a suicide but something was wrong. They've ruled it a homicide. Looks like the Poet made a mistake.'

'Phoenix?'

'Yes, the freshest trail.' He looked at his watch. 'And we have to hurry. He's to be buried in four hours and I want to have a look at the body first.'

25
· · · · · · · ·

Two government cars and four agents from the field office met us after the jet landed at Sky Harbor International in Phoenix. It was a warm day, compared to where we had come from, and we took our jackets off and carried them with our computer bags and overnighters. Thompson also carried a toolbox which contained his equipment. I rode with Walling and two agents named Matuzak and Mize, white guys who looked like they had less than ten years' experience combined. It was clear by their deferential treatment of Walling that they held the BSS unit in high esteem. They had either been briefed on the fact that I was a reporter or judged by my beard and hair that I was not an agent despite the FBI seal on my shirt. They paid little attention to me.

'Where are we going?' Walling asked as our gray nondescript Ford followed the gray nondescript Ford carrying Backus and Thompson out of the airport.

'Scottsdale Funeral Home,' Mize said. He was in the front passenger seat while Matuzak drove. He looked at his watch. 'Funeral is at two. Your man is probably going to have less than a half hour with the body before they'll have to suit him up and put him in the box for the show.'

'Was it open casket?'

'Yeah, last night,' Matuzak said. 'He's already been embalmed and made up. I don't know what you're expecting.'

'We're not expecting anything. We just want to look. I assume Agent Backus is being briefed up ahead of us. Do you two care to fill us in?'

'*That's* Robert Backus?' Mize said. 'He looks so young.'

'Robert Backus Junior.'

'Oh.' Mize made a face that seemed to show that he understood why such a young man was running the show. 'Figures.'

'You don't know what you're talking about,' Rachel said. 'He's got the name but he's also the hardest-working and most thorough agent I've ever worked with. He earned the position he has. It probably would have been easier for him, in fact, if he had a name like Mize. Now can one of you fill us in on what's going on?'

I saw Matuzak study her in the mirror. He then looked over at me and Rachel registered this.

'He's fine,' she said. 'He's got approval from the top to be here. He knows everything we do. You have a problem with that?'

'Not if you don't,' Matuzak said. 'John, you tell it.'

Mize cleared his throat.

'Not a lot to fill in. We don't have a lot because we weren't invited in. But what we do know is they found this guy, name's William Orsulak, they found him in his house on Monday. Homicide cop. They figured he'd been dead at least three days. He was off Friday 'cause of comp time and the last anybody remembered seeing him was Thursday night at a bar they all go to.'

'Who found him?'

'Somebody from the squad when he didn't show Monday. He was divorced, lived alone. Anyway, they apparently spent all week on the fence. You know, suicide or murder? Eventually, they went with murder. That was yesterday. Apparently there were too many problems with the suicide.'

'What do you know about the scene?'

'I hate to tell you this Agent Walling, but you'd learn just as much as me by picking up one of the local papers. Like I said, Phoenix police didn't invite us to the dance so we don't know what they have. After we got the wire from Quantico this morning, Jamie Fox, he's up in the lead car with Agent Backus, took a look at it while working a little OT doing paperwork. It seemed to fit with what you people were working on and he made the call. Then me and Bob got called out, but like I said, we don't know what's what for sure.'

'Fine.' She sounded put out. I knew she wanted to be up in the lead car. 'I'm sure we'll get it at the funeral home. What about the locals?'

'They're meeting us.'

We parked in the back of the Scottsdale Funeral Home on Camelback Road. The lot was already crowded, though the funeral was still two hours away. There were several men milling about or leaning on cars. Detectives. I could tell. Probably waiting to hear what the FBI had to say. I saw one TV truck with the dish on top parked at the far end of the lot.

Walling and I got out and joined Backus and Thompson and we were led to a rear door of the mortuary. Inside we stepped into a large room with white tile running up to the ceiling. There were two stainless-steel tables for bodies in the center with overhead spray hoses, and stainless-steel counters and equipment against three walls. A group of five men were in the room and as they moved to greet us I could see the body on the far table. I assumed it to be Orsulak, though there was no obvious sign of damage from a gunshot to the head. The body was naked and someone had taken a yard-long length of paper towel from the roll on the counter and placed it across the dead cop's waist to cover the genitals. The suit Orsulak would wear to the grave was on a hanger on a hook on the far wall.

Handshakes were passed all around between us and the living cops. Thompson was directed to the body and he carried his case over and went to work examining it.

'I don't think you'll get anything we don't already have,' said the one called Grayson, who was in charge of the investigation for the locals. He was a stocky man with an assured and good-natured demeanor. He was deeply tanned, as were the other locals.

'We don't, either,' said Walling, quick with the politically correct response. 'You've been over him. Now he's been washed and readied.'

'But we need to go through the motions,' Backus said.

'Why don't you folks tell us what you're working?' Grayson asked. 'Maybe we can make some sense out of this.'

'Fair enough,' Backus said.

As Backus gave an abbreviated report on the Poet investigation, I watched Thompson do his work. He was at home with the body, not timid about touching, probing, squeezing. He spent a good amount of time running gloved fingers through the dead man's gray-white hair and then carefully brushed it back in place with a comb from his own pocket. He then made a careful study of the mouth and throat, using a lighted magnifying glass. At one point he put the magnifier aside and pulled a camera from the toolbox. He took a photo of the throat, the flash drawing the attention of the cops assembled in the room.

'Just documentary photos, gentlemen,' Thompson said, not even looking up from his work.

Next he began studying the extremities of the body, first the right arm and hand, then the left. He used the magnifier again when he studied the left palm and fingers. Then he took two photos of the palm and two of the index finger. The cops in the room didn't seem to make much of this, seemingly accepting his earlier statement that the photos were routine. But because I had noticed that he had not taken photos of the right hand, I knew he had found something of possible significance on the left. Thompson returned the camera to the box after placing the four new Polaroids it had spit out on the counter. He then continued his search of the body but took no more photos. He interrupted Backus to ask for help in turning the body over, then the head-to-foot search began again. I could see a patch of a dark, waxy material in the back of the dead man's head and I assumed this to be where the exit wound was. Thompson didn't bother taking a Polaroid of this.

Thompson finished with the body at about the same time Backus finished his briefing and I wondered if it hadn't been planned that way.

'Anything?' Backus asked.

'Nothing of note, I don't think,' Thompson said. 'I'd like

to review the autopsy if I could. Was the report brought along?'

'As requested,' Grayson said. 'Here's a copy of everything.'

He handed a file to him and Thompson stepped back with it to a counter where he opened it and began scanning pages.

'So, I've told you what I know, gentlemen,' Backus said. 'Now I'd like to hear what it was about this case that dissuaded you from calling it suicide.'

'Well, I don't think I was entirely dissuaded until I heard your story,' Grayson said. 'Now I think this Poet fucker – excuse me, Agent Walling – is our guy. Anyway, we raised the question and then decided to go with a classification of homicide because of three reasons. One, when we found Bill, his hair was parted the wrong way. For twenty years he's been coming in the office, his part is on the left. We find him dead and the part's on the right. That was a little thing but there were two others and they add up. Next was the forensics. We had a guy swab the mouth for GSR so we could make a determination if the gun was in his mouth or held a few inches outside or what. We got the GSR but we also got some gun oil and a third substance that we haven't been able to identify properly. Until we could explain it I wasn't comfortable going suicide on this.'

'What can you tell me about the substance?' Thompson asked.

'Some kind of animal-fat extract. There's pulverized silicon in it, too. It's in the forensic report that you've got in that file, too.'

I thought I saw Thompson glance at Backus and then away, a tacit admission of knowledge.

'You know it?' Grayson asked, seeming to catch the same impression.

'Not offhand,' Thompson said. 'I'll get the specifics from the report and have the lab in Quantico run it on the computer. I'll let you know.'

'What was the third reason?' Backus asked, quickly leaving the subject.

'The third reason came from Jim Beam, Orsulak's old partner. He's retired now.'

'That's his name, Jim Beam?' Walling asked.

'Yeah, the Beamer. He called me up from Tucson after he heard about Bill and asked if we'd recovered the slug. I said sure, we dug it out of the wall behind his head. Then he asked me if it was gold.'

'Gold?' Backus asked. 'Real gold?'

'Yes. A golden bullet. I told him no, it was a lead slug like all the others in his clip. Like the one we dug out of the floor, too. We'd figured that the floor shot was the first one, a get-up-the-courage shot. But then Beamer told me it was no suicide, that it was murder.'

'And how did he know this?'

'He and Orsulak went back a lot of years and he knew that Orsulak occasionally ... hell, there probably isn't a single cop who hasn't thought about it at one time or another.'

'Killing himself,' Walling said, a statement, not a question.

'Right. And Jim Beam tells me that one time Orsulak showed him this golden bullet that he got from somewhere, he didn't know, a mail-order catalog or something. And he says to Beamer, "This is my golden parachute. When I can't take it no more, this one's for me." So what Beam was saying was no golden bullet, no suicide.'

'Did you find the golden bullet?' Walling asked.

'Yeah, we found it. After we talked to Beam we found it. It was in the drawer right next to his bed. Like it was kept nearby in case he ever needed it.'

'So that convinced you.'

'In totality, all three things leaned it way over toward homicide. Murder. But like I said, I wasn't convinced of anything until you walked in here and told your story. Now I got a hard-on for this Poet the size of – sorry for the offense, Agent Walling.'

'None taken. We all have a hard-on for him. Was there a suicide note?'

'Yes, and that's the thing that made it so hard for us to call it a homicide. There was a note and damn if it wasn't in Bill's writing.'

Walling nodded that what he had just said was no surprise.

'What did the note say?'

'It didn't make a whole lot of sense. It was like a poem. It said – well, hold on here. Agent Thomas, let me borrow that file a sec.'

'Thompson,' Thompson said as he handed it over.

'Sorry.'

Grayson looked through some pages until he found what he wanted. He read out loud.

'"Mountains toppling evermore / Into seas without a shore." That was it.'

Walling and Backus looked at me. I opened the book and started paging through the poems.

'I remember the line but I'm not sure where.'

I went to the poems that the Poet had already used and started reading quickly. I found it in 'Dream-Land,' the poem used twice before, including the note left on my brother's windshield.

'I got it,' I said.

I held the book out so Rachel could read the poem. The others crowded around her as well.

'Son of a bitch,' Grayson muttered.

'Can you give us a rundown on how you think it happened?' Rachel asked him.

'Uh, sure. Our theory is whoever this doer was, he came in and surprised Bill in his sleep. With Bill's own gun. He made him get up and get dressed. That's when Bill parted his hair wrong. I mean, he didn't know what was going to happen or maybe he did. Either way, he leaves us a little sign. From there he's taken out into the living room, put in the chair and the doer makes him write out that note on a piece of paper torn outta his own notebook he keeps in his coat pocket. Then he pops him. One in the mouth. Puts the gun in Bill's hand, puts the slug into the floor and you've got gunshot residue on the hand. The doer's outta there and we don't find poor Bill for three days.'

Grayson looked over his shoulder at the body, noticed it was being unattended and looked at his watch.

'Hey, where's the guy?' he said. 'Somebody go get him and tell him we're through. You're through with the body, right?'

'Yes,' Thompson said.

'We have to get him ready.'

'Detective Grayson,' Walling said. 'Was there a specific case that Detective Orsulak was currently pursuing?'

'Oh, yeah, there was a case. The Little Joaquin case. Eight-year-old kid abducted last month. All they found of him was his head.'

Mention of the case and its brutality brought a moment of silence in the room where the dead were prepared. Before that moment I had no doubt that Orsulak's death was related to the others, but after hearing of the crime against the boy I felt an unwavering certainty and the anger that was becoming so familiar to me foaming in my guts.

'I assume everyone is going to the funeral?' Backus said.

'That's right.'

'Can we arrange a time to meet again? We would like to see the reports on the boy, Joaquin, as well.'

They set the meeting for nine o'clock Sunday morning at the Phoenix Police Department. Grayson apparently felt that if it was on his turf he might be better able to hang on to a piece of it. But I had a feeling that the Big G was about to move in and sweep him aside like a tidal wave hitting a lifeguard stand.

'One last thing, the press,' Walling said. 'I saw a TV truck outside.'

'Yeah, they've been all over this, especially when they . . .'

He didn't finish.

'When they what?'

'Well, somebody sort of put it out on the police frequency that we were meeting the FBI here.'

Rachel groaned and Grayson nodded as if he expected it.

'Look, this absolutely has to be contained,' Rachel said. 'If any of what we just told you men gets out, the Poet will go under. We'll never catch the man who did that.'

She nodded at the corpse and a few of the cops turned to make sure it was still there. The undertaker had just stepped into the room and was lifting the hanger containing Orsulak's last suit. He was looking at the assemblage of investigators, waiting for them to leave so that he could be alone with the body.

'We're about out of here, George,' Grayson said. 'You can start.'

Backus said, 'Tell the media that the FBI's interest was purely routine and that you will continue to handle the investigation as a suspected homicide. Don't act like you are sure of anything.'

As we were walking back through the lot to the government cars, a young woman with bleached-blond hair and a grim look on her face came up to us with a microphone, a cameraman in tow. Holding the mike to her own mouth she asked, 'Why is the FBI here today?'

She turned the microphone and pointed it directly under my chin for the response. I opened my mouth but nothing came out. I had no idea why I was chosen but then realized it was the shirt I wore. The FBI seal on the breast pocket apparently assured her that she was talking to the bureau.

'I'll answer that,' Backus said quickly and the microphone went to his chin. 'We came at the request of the Phoenix Police Department to make a routine examination of the body and to hear details of the case. It is expected that our involvement ends here and further questions should go to the police. We have no further comment, thank you.'

'But are you convinced that Detective Orsulak was the victim of foul play?' the reporter persisted.

'I'm sorry,' Backus said. 'You'll have to refer your questions to the Phoenix police.'

'And your name is?'

'I'd rather keep my name out of it, thank you.'

He brushed by her and got into one of the cars. I followed

Walling to the other. In a few minutes we were out of there and driving back toward Phoenix.

'Are you worried?' Rachel asked.

'About what?'

'The exclusivity of your story.'

'I'm getting there. But I'm hoping she's like most TV reporters.'

'And how are they?'

'Sourceless and senseless. If she is, then I'll be okay.'

26

· · · · · · · ·

The field office was in the federal courthouse on Washington Street, just a few blocks from the police department where we would meet with the locals the next day. As we followed Mize and Matuzak down a polished corridor to a conference room, I sensed anxiety in Rachel and I thought I knew what it was. By traveling with me, she had been unable to be in the other car when Thompson filled Backus in on what he had learned from the body.

The conference room was far smaller than the one we had used in Quantico. When we entered, Backus and Thompson were already seated at the table and Backus held a phone to his ear. He covered the mouthpiece when we entered and said, 'Guys, I'm going to need to talk to my people alone for a few minutes. Uh, what you could do is get us some cars if you can. We'll also need to reserve rooms somewhere. Six rooms, it looks like.'

Matuzak and Mize looked like they had just gotten word that they were demoted. They nodded glumly and left the room. I didn't know where that left me, if I was invited or excluded, since I really wasn't one of Backus's people.

'Jack, Rachel, have a seat,' Backus said. 'Let me finish up and I'll have James bring you up to date.'

We took seats and watched and listened to the one-sided phone conversation. It was clear Backus was listening to messages and responding to them. Not all seemed to have something to do with the Poet investigation.

'Okay, what about Gordon and Carter?' he said after the messages were apparently finished with. 'What's the ETA? That late? Damn. Okay, listen, three things. Call Denver and have them go to the evidence in the McEvoy case. Tell them to check the insides of the gloves for blood. If they find blood, tell them to start exhumation proceedings ... Right, right. If it's a problem call me right away. Also, tell them to see if the police took GSR swabs from the mouth of the victim and if they did, have it all sent to Quantico. That goes for all the cases. The third thing is James Thompson will be FedExing to the lab from out here. We need substance identification ASAP. Same with Denver, if it comes. What else? When's the conference call with Brass? Okay, we'll talk then.'

He hung up and looked at us. I wanted to ask what he meant by exhumation but Rachel spoke first.

'Six rooms? Is Gordon coming out here?'

'He and Carter are coming here.'

'Bob, why? You know –'

'We need them, Rachel. We are hitting critical mass on this investigation and things are moving. At the most, we are now ten days behind this offender. We need more bodies to make the moves we're going to have to make. It's that simple and that's more than enough said about it. Now, Jack, did you have something to say?'

'That exhumation you are talking about ...'

'We'll talk about that in a few minutes. It will become clear. James, tell them what you found on the body.'

From his pocket Thompson pulled four Polaroid photos and spread them on the table in front of Rachel and me.

'This is the left palm and index finger. The two on the left were taken with the one-to-one. The other two are ten times magnified.'

'Perforations,' Rachel said.

'Right.'

I didn't see them until she had said it, but then I recognized the tiny punch holes in the lines of the skin. Three in the palm, two in the tip of the index finger.

'What is it?' I asked.

'On the surface it looks like nothing more than pinpricks,' Thompson said. 'But there is no scabbing or closing of the wounds. They occurred close to time of death. Shortly before or possibly after, though there wouldn't be much of a point to it after.'

'Point to what?'

'Jack, we're looking for ways this could have been done,' Backus said. 'How could veteran, tough cops be taken like this? Control is what we are talking about. It's one of the keys.'

I waved a hand toward the photos.

'And what does this tell you?'

'That and other things may indicate hypnosis was involved.'

'You're saying this guy hypnotized my brother and these others into putting a gun in their mouths and pulling the trigger?'

'No, I don't think it's that simple. You have to remember that it is quite difficult to use hypnotic suggestion to override the self-preservation instinct in an individual's mind. Most experts say it's flatly impossible. But if a person is susceptible to hypnotism, that person can be controlled to varying extents. He can be made docile, manageable. It's only a possibility at this point. But we have five perforations on this victim's hand. A standard method of testing for hypnotic trance would be to prick the skin with a pin after placing the suggestion that there will be no pain. If the patient reacts, the hypnosis is not working. If he shows no signs of feeling the pain, he is under trance conditions.'

'And controllable,' Thompson added.

'You want to look at my brother's hand.'

'Yes, Jack,' Backus said. 'We'll need an exhumation order. I believe the files said he was married. Will his widow allow this?'

'I don't know.'

'We may need your help on that.'

I just nodded. Things were getting stranger all the time.

'What were the other things? You said the perforations and other things may indicate hypnosis was involved.'

'The autopsies,' Rachel answered. 'None of the victims' blood screens came out totally clean. Each one had something in his blood. Your brother –'

'Cough syrup,' I said defensively. 'From the car's glove box.'

'Right. It ranges from over-the-counter things like cough syrup to prescription drugs. One of them had Percocet, which had been prescribed for a back injury eighteen months earlier. I think that was the Chicago case. Another one – I think it was Petry in Dallas – had codeine in his blood. It came from prescription Tylenol with codeine. The prescription bottle was in his medicine cabinet.'

'Okay, so what's it mean?'

'Well, individually it meant nothing at the time of each of these deaths. Whatever came up on the blood screen in each case was explained by the victim's access to it. I mean, it's reasonable to believe that if someone was going to kill himself, he might take a couple of the Percocets from the old prescription bottle to calm himself. So these things were dismissed.'

'But now they mean something.'

'Possibly,' she said. 'The finding of the perforations suggests hypnosis. If you add to that the introduction of some chemical suppressor into the blood, then you begin to see how these men may have been controlled.'

'Cough syrup?'

'It could possibly enhance a subject's susceptibility to hypnosis. Codeine is a tested enhancer. Over-the-counter cough medications don't have codeine in them anymore but some of the replacement ingredients could still act as similar enhancers.'

'Have you known this all along?'

'No, it was just something that had no context until now.'

'Has it come up before? How do you know so much?'

'Hypnosis is used fairly often as a law enforcement tool,' Backus said. 'It's also come up on the other side before.'

'There was one case several years ago,' Rachel said. 'There was a man, a Las Vegas nightclub kind of guy who did hypnotism as his act. He was also a pedophile. And what he'd do is, when he'd do shows at county fairs and so forth, he'd get close to kids. He had a children's act, a matinee, and he'd tell the audience he needed a young volunteer. The parents would practically throw their kids at him. He'd pick the lucky one and say he had to go backstage to prepare the child while some other act was going on. He'd hypnotize the kid back there, rape her and then through hypnotic suggestion, wipe the memory. Then he'd trot the kid onstage, do his act and then take her out of the trance. He used codeine as an enhancer. Put it in their Cokes.'

'I remember,' Thompson said, nodding. 'Harry the Hypnotic.'

'No, it was Horace the Hypnotist,' Rachel said. 'He was one of our interviews on the rape project. At Raiford down in Florida.'

'Wait a minute,' I said. 'Could he –'

'No, this is not him. He'd still be in prison in Florida. He got something like a twenty-five-year bid. This was only six, seven years ago. He's still inside. He's got to be.'

'I'll have it checked anyway,' Backus said. 'To be sure. But, regardless, you see the possibility we're looking at here, Jack? I'd like you to call your sister-in-law. It would be better if she heard it from you. Tell her how important it is.'

I nodded.

'Okay, Jack, we appreciate it. Now, why don't we take a break here and see what there is to eat in this town? We've got the conference call with the other FOs in an hour and twenty minutes.'

'What about the other thing?' I said.

'What thing?' Backus asked.

'The substance in that detective's mouth. It looked like you guys knew what that was.'

'No. I just made arrangements to send the swab they took back east and then, hopefully, we'll know.'

He was lying and I knew it but I let it go. Everybody stood up and headed into the hallway. I told them I wasn't hungry and needed to find a place to buy some clothes. I said I'd find a cab if there were no stores within walking distance.

'I think I'll go with Jack,' Rachel said.

I didn't know if she really wanted to or her job was just to watch me, make sure I didn't run off and write a story. I raised my hand in an I-don't-care attitude.

With directions from Matuzak we started walking toward a mall called Arizona Center. It was a beautiful day and the walk was a nice break from the intensity of recent days. Rachel and I talked about Phoenix – it was her first visit, too – and eventually I steered the conversation back to my last question to Backus.

'He was lying, so was Thompson.'

'You mean about the oral swabs.'

'Right.'

'I think Bob just doesn't want you to know more than you need to. I'm not talking about as a reporter. I mean, as a brother.'

'If there is something new, I want to know it. The deal was I'd be on the inside. Not on the inside sometimes and then on the outside – like with this hypnosis crap – other times.'

She stopped and turned to me.

'I will tell you, if you want to know, Jack. If it's what we think and all the killings follow a pattern, then it's not going to be very pleasant for you to dwell on.'

I looked in the direction we were headed. The mall was in sight. A sandstone-colored edifice with welcoming open-air walkways.

'Tell me,' I said.

'Nothing is for sure until the swab is analyzed. But it sounds like the substance Grayson described was something we've seen before. You see, some repeat offenders are smart. They know about leaving evidence behind. Evidence like semen. So they use condoms. But if it's a lubricated condom the lubricant can be left behind. Detected. Sometimes it's accidental . . . and sometimes they want us to know what they did.'

I looked at her and almost released an audible groan.

'You're saying the Poet . . . had sex with him?'

'Possibly. But to be frank, we've suspected it from the start.

Serial killers ... Jack, it's almost always about sexual gratification. It's about power and control and these are components of sexual gratification.'

'There wouldn't have been time.'

'What do you mean?'

'With my brother. The ranger was right there. There couldn't have...' I stopped, realizing that there only wasn't time afterward. 'Jesus ... Oh, man.'

'That was what Bob had hoped not to have to tell you.'

I turned away and looked up at the blue sky. The only imperfection was the slash of the twin contrails of a jet long out of the picture.

'I don't get it. Why is this guy doing this?'

'We may never know that, Jack.' She put a comforting hand on my shoulder. 'These people that we hunt ... sometimes there is no explanation. That's the very hardest part, coming up with the motivation, understanding what drives them to do what they do. We have a saying about it. We say these people are from the moon. Sometimes it is the only way to describe it when we don't have the answers. Trying to figure these people out is like putting a shattered mirror back together. There is no way to explain the behavior of some humans, so we simply say they are not humans. We say they are from the moon. And on the particular moon where the Poet comes from, these instincts that he is following are normal and natural. He is following those instincts, creating scenes that give him satisfaction. It's our job to chart the Poet's moon and then we'll be better able to find him and send him back.'

All I could do was take it all in and nod. There was no comfort in her words. All I knew was that, if given the chance, I wanted to send the Poet back to the moon. I wanted to do it myself.

'C'mon,' she said. 'Try to forget about that for now. Let's go get you some new things. We can't have those reporters thinking you're one of us anymore.'

She smiled and I returned it weakly and let her push me toward the mall.

27
....

We met back in the conference room of the field office at
six-thirty. Backus was there, trying to work out the logis-
tics with the phone, along with Thompson, Matuzak, Mize
and three agents I hadn't been introduced to. I put my shopping bag under the conference table. It contained two new
shirts, a pair of pants and a package of underwear and socks. I
immediately wished I had changed into one of the new shirts
because the unintroduced agents studied me and my FBI
shirt with grim looks that suggested I had committed some
kind of sacrilege by trying to impersonate an agent. Backus
told whoever he was talking with to call him back when it was
set up and then hung up.

'Okay,' he said. 'We start the full meeting as soon as they
have the phones set up. Meantime, let's talk about Phoenix.
Beginning tomorrow I want to start a ground-zero investigation of both the detective and the boy. Both cases, from the
top. What I'd like – Oh, I'm sorry. Rachel, Jack, this is Vince
Pool, SAC Phoenix. He's going to give us whatever we need.'

Pool, who looked like he had twenty-five years on the job,
the most of anyone in the room, nodded at us and said nothing. Backus didn't bother to introduce the other men.

'We have the meeting with the locals tomorrow at oh nine
hundred,' Backus said.

'I think we'll be able to brush them aside gently,' Pool said.

'Well, we don't want any animosity. These are the fellows
who knew Orsulak the best. They'll be good sources. I think
we have to bring them into this but remain firmly in control.'

'No problem.'

'This one may be our best chance. It's fresh. We've got to

hope the offender made a mistake and between these two deaths, the boy and the detective, we can find it. I'd like to see –'

The phone on the table buzzed and Backus picked up the receiver and said hello.

'Hold on.'

He pushed a button on the phone and hung up the receiver.

'Brass, you there?'

'Here, boss.'

'Okay, let's run down the list, see who've we got.'

Agents from six cities announced their presence on the speaker.

'Okay, good. I want this to be as informal as possible. Why don't we go round-robin to see what people have. Brass, I'd like to finish up with you. So Florida. Is that you, Ted?'

'Uh, yes sir, with Steve, here. We are just getting our feet wet in this and hope to have more by tomorrow. But there are some anomalies here that we think are already worth noting.'

'Go ahead.'

'Uh, this is the first, or believed to be the first, of the Poet's stops. Clifford Beltran. The second incident – in Baltimore – did not take place until nearly ten months later. That is the longest interval we have as well. This leads us to possibly question the randomness of this first kill.'

'You think the Poet knew Beltran?' Rachel asked.

'It's possible. At the moment, though, it's just a hunch we are working. There are a few other things that when thrown into the stew are worth taking a look at in support, however. First, this is the only one with a shotgun. We checked the autopsy file today and they weren't pretty pictures. Total obliteration with both barrels. We all know the symbolic pathology of that.'

'Overkill,' Backus said. 'Suggesting knowledge or acquaintance of the victim.'

'Right. Next we have the weapon itself. According to reports, it was an old Smith and Wesson that Beltran kept in a closet, on a top shelf out of sight. This information is attributed in the reports to his sister. Beltran had never married and lived in the house he grew up in. We haven't talked to the sister ourselves. The point is, if this was a suicide, yeah, fine, he went to the closet and got out the shotgun. But now we come along and say this was no suicide.'

'How did the Poet know the shotgun was up there on the shelf?' Rachel said.

'Riiiiiight . . . How did he know?'

'Good one, Ted, Steve,' Backus said. 'I like it. What else?'

'The last thing is kind of sticky. Is the reporter there?'

Everyone in the room looked at me.

'Yes,' Backus said. 'But we are still off the record. You can say what you were going to say. Right, Jack?'

I nodded and then realized they wouldn't see this in all the other cities.

'That's right,' I said. 'We're off the record.'

'Okay, well, this is more speculation at this time and we're not sure how it fits but we have this. On the autopsy of the first victim, the boy, Gabriel Ortiz, the coroner concluded, based on examination of the anal glands and muscles, that the boy was the victim of long-term molestation. If the boy's killer was also his abuser over a period of time, then this does not fit with our pattern of random selection and acquisition of victims. So that seems unlikely to us.

'However, looking at it from Beltran's point of view three years ago of not having the benefit of our knowledge, something here doesn't fit. He had this one case, knew nothing about the others we know about now. When the autopsy came back concluding the boy was the victim of long-term molestation, it stands to reason that Beltran should have jumped all over that and looked for the abuser as suspect numero uno.'

'He didn't?'

'No. He headed a team of three detectives and he directed almost all investigative work toward the park where the boy had been abducted after school. I got this off the record from one of the guys on the team. He said he suggested a wider focus looking into the boy's background but Beltran turned him down.

'Now the good stuff. My source at the sheriff's tells me Beltran specifically asked for the investigation. He wanted it. After he supposedly offed himself, my source did some checking and it turns out Beltran had known the kid through a local social services program called Best Pals, which puts fatherless boys with adults. Like a Big Brother program. Beltran was a cop, so he had no trouble going through the screening process. He was the boy's Best Pal. I'm sure you can all take it from there.'

'You think perhaps Beltran was the boy's molester?' Backus asked.

'It's possible. I think that's what my source was driving at but he won't put it on the line. Everybody's dead. It was written off. They're not going to go public with a story like that. Not with one of their own and sheriff being an elective office.'

I watched Backus nod his head.

'That's to be expected.'

There was silence for a few moments.

'Ted, Steve, this is all very interesting,' Backus said. 'But how does it fit? Is it just an interesting offshoot or are you seeing something there?'

'We're not sure ourselves. But if you say Beltran was a molester, a pedophile no less, and add that he was put down with a shotgun that somebody knew was on the top shelf of the closet because he knew Beltran, then we are getting into an area I think we should explore further.'

'I agree. Tell us, what else did your source know about Beltran and Best Pals?'

'He said he was told that Beltran had been with Best Pals for a long time. He'd been with a lot of boys, we assume.'

'And that is where you will pursue this, correct?'

'We'll hit it hard in the morning. Nothing we can do with it tonight.'

Backus nodded and put a finger to his mouth in a contemplative gesture.

'Brass?' Backus said. 'What do you think of all of this? How would that play with the psychopathology?'

'Children are a string all through this. So are homicide cops. We just don't have a handle yet on what this guy is all about. I think this is something that should be pursued vigorously.'

'Ted, Steve, do you need more bodies?' Backus asked.

'I think we're set. We've got everybody in the Tampa FO wanting in on this. So what we need, we can take from there.'

'Excellent. By the way, have you talked to the boy's mother about her son's relationship with Beltran?'

'We are still trying to track her as well as Beltran's sister. Remember, it's been three years. Hopefully, we'll get to them tomorrow after Best Pals.'

'Okay, then, how about Baltimore? Sheila?'

'Yes, sir. We spent most of the day re-covering the ground of the locals. We talked to Bledsoe. The theory he had on the Polly Amherst case from the start was that they were looking for a molester. Amherst was a teacher. Bledsoe said he and McCafferty always thought that she might've stumbled onto a molester on the school grounds, was abducted, strangled and then butchered as a means of disguising the true motivation of the crime.'

'Why did it have to be a molester?' Rachel asked. 'Could she have stumbled onto a burglar, a drug deal, anything else?'

'Polly Amherst had third-period recess watch on the day she disappeared. The locals interviewed every child who had been in the yard. A lot of conflicting stories but a handful of the kids remember a man at the fence. He had stringy blond hair and glasses. He was white. Sounds like Brad wasn't too far off with his description of Roderick Usher. They also said this man had a camera. That was about the extent of the description.'

'Okay, Sheila, what else?' Backus asked.

'The one piece of physical evidence recovered with the body was a strand of hair. Bleached blond. Natural color is reddish brown. That's about it for now. We are going to work with Bledsoe again tomorrow.'

'Okay. Chicago's next.'

The rest of the reports contained nothing noteworthy in

terms of identifying or adding to the growing database on the Poet. The agents were mostly covering ground the locals had already trod and they were finding nothing new. Even the report from Denver contained mostly old information. But at the end, the agent on the line said that an examination of the gloves worn by my brother was conducted and a single blood spot was found in the fur lining of the right-hand glove. The agent asked whether I was still willing to call Riley and ask her to allow an exhumation. I didn't answer because I was in a daze thinking about what the indication of hypnotism meant my brother's last moments were like. Asked again, I said I would call in the morning.

As an afterthought the agent concluded his report by saying he had shipped the GSR swabs from my brother's mouth to the lab in Quantico.

'They run a pretty good ship here, boss, and I don't think we'll get more than what they found.'

'Which was?' Backus asked, careful not to look at me.

'Just the GSR. Nothing else.'

I didn't know what I felt when I heard those words. I guess there was relief but it was no proof that anything did or did not happen. Sean was still dead and I was still haunted by thoughts of what his last moments and thoughts had been. I tried to shove it aside and concentrate on the conference call. Backus had asked Brass to update everyone on the victimology and I had missed most of the report.

'So we are discounting any correlation,' she was saying. 'Aside from the possibilities mentioned earlier in Florida, I'm saying they are picked at random. They didn't know each other, they never worked together and the paths of all six never crossed. We've found out that four of them went to some kind of bureau-sponsored homicide seminar at Quantico four years ago, but the other two didn't and we don't know if the four who did go ever even met or talked to each other at the seminar. All of this doesn't include Orsulak in Phoenix. We haven't had time yet to do a track on him.'

'So if there is no correlation, we are to assume they are

chosen by the offender simply because they take the bait?' Rachel asked.

'I think that's correct.'

'So he must stand by and watch and see his prey for the first time after the bait kill.'

'Again, correct. All of these bait cases received heavy local media attention. He could've seen each of the detectives for the first time on TV or in a newspaper photo.'

'No physically archetypal attraction involved?'

'No. He simply takes whoever gets the case. The lead detective becomes the prey. Now, that is not to say that after that selection, he may not find that one or more of these subjects were more attractive or fulfilling to his fantasy. That can always happen.'

'What fantasy?' I asked, struggling just to keep up with what Brass was saying.

'Is that Jack? Well, Jack, we don't know what fantasy. That's the point. We are coming at it from the wrong direction. We don't know the fantasy that motivates this killer and what we are seeing and guessing about are the parts. We may never know what rocks his world. He's down from the moon, Jack. The only way we'll really ever know is if he decides to tell us someday.'

I nodded and thought of another question. I waited until it was clear no one else had anything.

'Uh, Agent Brass – I mean, Doran?'

'Yes?'

'You might've already said this, but what about the poems? Do you have any more of an idea how they fit?'

'Well, they are obviously being used in exhibition. We noted this yesterday. This is his signature, and though he obviously wants to elude capture, at the same time his psychology is such that he just has to leave a little something that says, *Hey, I was here.* This is where the poems come in. As for the poems themselves the correlation is that they all are or can be read as being about death. There is also the theme that death is a portal to other things, other places. "Through the pale door," I believe, is one of the quotes he used. What it may be is that the Poet may believe he is sending these men he has killed to a better world. He is transforming them. It's something to think about when we consider the pathology of this individual. But once again, we come back to the instability of all our conjectures. It's kind of like we are looking through a full trash can to try to find out what somebody ate for dinner last night. We don't know what this man is doing and we won't until we have him.'

'Brass? Bob again. What are you reading on the planning of these crimes?'

'I'll let Brad answer that.'

'This is Brad. Uh, we're calling this guy a modified traveler. Yes, he is using the whole country as his canvas but he is staying put for weeks and sometimes months at a time. This is unusual in our prior profiling. The Poet is not a hit-and-run killer. He hits and then he stays around for a while. We are to expect that during this period the hunter watches the hunted. He must come to know his victim's routines and nuances. Possibly, he even strikes up a passing acquaintance. That's something to look for. A new friend or acquaintance in each detective's life. Maybe a new neighbor or guy at the local bar. The situation in Denver also suggests that he may come at them as a source, someone with information. He may be using a combination of these approaches.'

'Which leads to the next step,' Backus said. 'After contact.'

'Power,' Hazelton said. 'After he gets close enough to these victims, how does he take control? Well, we assume he has some kind of weapon that initially allows him to take theirs, but there is something more. How does he get six, now seven, homicide detectives to write out lines of poetry? How does he avoid a struggle in every one of these cases? At the moment, we are exploring the possibility of hypnosis combined with chemical enhancers taken from the victims themselves. All but one of these incidents occurred in the victim's home. The McEvoy case is the anomaly. Setting it aside and looking at the others, there is probably no one among us who has an empty medicine cabinet. And there probably isn't a cabinet among the bunch that doesn't have some prescription or store-bought medication that wouldn't serve as an enhancer. Obviously some things work better than others. But the point is, if this scenario is correct, the Poet is using the things made available to him by the victims. We are looking at this hard. That's it, for now.'

'Okay, then,' Backus said. 'Any other questions?'

The room and phone speaker remained silent.

'Okay, people,' he said, leaning forward, his hands on the table and his mouth close to the phone speaker. 'Your best work. We really need it this time.'

Rachel and I followed Backus and Thompson to the Hyatt where Matuzak had reserved rooms. I had to check in and pay for my room while Backus checked in and got keys for the other five, which the government would pay for. Still, I got the discount the hotel regularly gave the FBI. It must have been the shirt.

Rachel and Thompson were waiting in the lobby lounge where we had decided on a drink before dinner. When Backus gave her one of the keys, I heard him say that she was in room 321 and I committed it to memory. I was four doors away in room 317 and I was already thinking about the night ahead, about closing that gap.

After a half hour of small talk Backus stood up and said he was going to his room to review the day's reports before heading out to the airport to pick up Thorson and Carter. He turned down an offer to join us for dinner and headed toward the elevator. A few minutes later, Thompson split, too, saying he wanted to read through the autopsy report on Orsulak in detail.

'Just you and me, Jack,' Rachel said when Thompson was out of earshot. 'What do you feel like eating?'

'I'm not sure. What about you?'

'Haven't thought about it. I know what I want to do first though . . . That's take a hot bath.'

We agreed to meet in an hour for dinner. We rode the elevator up to our floor in a silence couched in sexual tension.

In my room, I tried to take my mind off Rachel by connecting my computer to the phone line and checking my messages in Denver. There was only one, from Greg Glenn asking where I was. I answered it but doubted that he would see it until he came back into work on Monday. I then sent a message to Laurie Prine asking her to search for any stories on Horace the Hypnotist that might have run in the Florida newspapers in the last seven years. I asked her to ship any hits she got to my computer basket but said it was no hurry.

After that I showered and changed into my new clothes for my dinner with Rachel. I was ready twenty minutes early and I thought about going down and seeing if there was a drugstore nearby. But then I thought about the impression it would give Rachel if things worked out and I came to her bed, a condom already in my pocket. I decided against the drugstore. I decided to play things as they came.

'Did you see CNN?'

'No,' I said. I was standing in the doorway of her room. She went back to the bed and sat down to put her shoes on. She looked refreshed and was wearing a cream-colored shirt with black jeans. The TV was still on but it was a story about the clinic shootings in Colorado. I didn't think that was what she was talking about.

'What did it say?'

'We were on. You, me and Bob coming out of the funeral home. Somehow they got Bob's name and put it on the screen.'

'Did it say he was BSS?'

'No, just FBI. But it doesn't matter. CNN must've taken the feed off the local channel. Wherever he is, if our guy saw it, we could have a problem.'

'How come? It's not that unusual for the FBI to take a look at cases like this. The bureau's always sticking its nose in.'

'The problem is it plays to the Poet. We see it in almost all of the cases. One concept of the gratification these kinds of killers seek is seeing their work on TV and in the papers. In a way it allows them to relive the fantasy of the incident. Part of that infatuation with the media extends to the pursuers. I get the feeling that this guy, the Poet, knows more about us than we do about him. If I'm right, then he's probably read books on serial killers. The commercial dreck and even some of the more serious work. He may know names. Bob's father is in many of them. Bob himself is in some. So am I. Our names, photos, our words. If he saw that on CNN and recognized us, then he'll assume we are right behind him. We may lose him now. He might go under.'

Ambivalence won the night. Unable to decide what or where we wanted to eat, we settled for the hotel's restaurant. The food was okay but we shared a bottle of Buehler cabernet that was perfect. I told her not to worry about the government per diem because the newspaper was paying. She ordered cherries jubilee for dessert after I told her that.

'I get the feeling that you'd be happy if there were no free media in the world,' I told her when we were slowing down on the dessert. The implications of the CNN report had dominated the conversation during dinner.

'Not at all. I respect the media as a necessity in a free society. I don't respect the irresponsibility that you see more often than you don't.'

'What was irresponsible about that report?'

'That one was marginal but it bothers me that they used our images without bothering to ask what the ramifications could be. I just wish that sometimes the media would concentrate on the larger picture or story, rather than go for the immediate gratification every time.'

'Not every time. I didn't blow you people off and say I'm writing my story. I went long-term. I went for the larger story.'

'Oh, very noble, coming from somebody who extorted his way into the investigation.'

She was smiling and so was I.

'Hey,' I protested.

'Can we talk about something else? I'm tired of all of this. God, I'd love to just be able to lie back and forget about it for a while.'

There it was again. Her choice of words, the way she looked at me as she said them. Was I reading it correctly or only reading what I wanted to read?

'Okay, forget about the Poet,' I said. 'Let's talk about you.'

'Me? What about me?'

'This stuff going on with Thorson is like a TV sitcom.'

'That's private.'

'Not when you guys are staring daggers across the room all the time and you're trying to get Backus to take him off the case.'

'I don't want him off the case. I just want him off my back and I don't want him out here. He always finds a way to sneak in and try to take over. You watch.'

'How long were you married?'

'Fifteen glorious months.'

'When did it end?'

'Long time ago, three years.'

'That's a long time for hostilities to linger.'

'I don't want to talk about this.'

But I sensed she did. I let a little time go by. The waiter came and refilled our coffee cups.

'What happened?' I asked softly. 'You don't deserve to be unhappy like that.'

She reached up and tugged gently on my beard, the first time she had touched me since ramming my face into the bed back in Washington.

'You're sweet.' She shook her head. 'It was just the wrong thing for both of us. Sometimes, I don't even know what we saw in each other. It just didn't work.'

'How come?'

'Just because. It was a just-because type of thing. Like I said, we both had a lot of baggage. His was heavier. He'd worn a mask and I didn't see all the rage behind it until it was too late. I got out as soon as I could.'

'What was he angry about?'

'A lot of things. He carries a lot of anger. From other women, relationships. I was his second failed marriage. The job. Sometimes it came out like a blowtorch.'

'Did he ever hurt you?'

'No. I didn't stay long enough for him to try. Of course, all men deny the woman's intuition, but I think if I stayed it would have come to that. It was the natural course of things. I still try to stay away from him.'

'And he still has something for you.'

'You're crazy if you think that.'

'There's something there.'

'The only thing he has for me is a desire to see me unhappy. He wants to get back at me for being the cause of his bad marriage, his bad life, everything.'

'How's a guy like that keep his job?'

'Like I said, he's got a mask. He's good at hiding it. You saw him at the meeting. He was contained. You also have to understand something about the FBI. They don't go looking to bust their agents. As long as he did the work, it didn't matter what I felt or said.'

'You complained about him?'

'Not directly. That would've been cutting my own throat. I've got an enviable position in the BSS but make no mistake, the bureau's a man's world. And you don't go to the boss to complain about things you *think* your ex-husband might do. I'd probably end up on the bank squad in Salt Lake City if I tried that.'

'So what can you do?'

'Not much. Indirectly, I've dropped enough hints on Backus for him to know what's going on. As you can tell by what you heard today, he's not going to do anything about it. I have to assume that Gordon's dropping hints in his other ear. If I were Bob, I'd just sit back like he's doing and wait for one of us to fuck up. The first one to do it gets shipped out.'

'And what would constitute a fuck-up?'

'I don't know. With the bureau you never know. But he's got to be more careful with me than him. Prevailing factors, you know. He's got to have his shit together if he's going to try to move a woman out of the unit. So, that's my edge.'

I nodded. We had come to a natural end to that branch of the conversation. But I didn't want her to go back to her room. I wanted to be with her.

'You're a pretty good interviewer, Jack. Pretty sly.'

'What?'

'We've spent the whole time talking about me and the bureau. What about you?'

'What about me? Never married, never divorced. I don't even have plants at home. I sit behind a computer all day. It's not in the same league as you and Thorson.'

She smiled and then giggled a bit girlishly.

'Yes, we are a pair. Were. Do you feel any better after the meeting today, about what they found in Denver?'

'You mean what they didn't find? I don't know. I guess it's better that it looks like he didn't have to go through that. There still is nothing to feel better about, though.'

'Did you call your sister-in-law?'

'No, not yet. I'll do it in the morning. Seems like something that should be discussed in daylight.'

'I've never spent a lot of time with the families of the victims,' she said. 'The bureau always gets called in later.'

'I have . . . I'm the master of interviewing the fresh widow, the now childless mother, father of the dead bride. You name it, I've interviewed it.'

We were quiet a long moment. The waiter came by with his coffeepot but we both passed. I asked for the check. I knew it wasn't going to happen with her tonight. I had lost the nerve to pursue it because I didn't want to risk her rejection. My pattern had always been the same. When I didn't care whether a woman rejected me, I always took the chance. When I did care and knew rejection would cut me, I always held back.

'What are you thinking about?' she asked.

'Nothing,' I lied. 'My brother, I guess.'

'Why don't you tell that story?'

'What story?'

'The other day. You were about to tell me something good about him. The nicest thing he ever did for you. What made him a saint.'

I looked across the table at her. I knew the story instantly but thought about it before speaking. I could've easily lied and told her the nicest thing he did was just love me but I trusted her. We trust the things we find beautiful, the things we want. And maybe I wanted to confess to somebody after so many years.

'The nicest thing he ever did was not blame me.'

'For what?'

'Our sister died when we were kids. It was my fault. He knew. He was the only one who really knew. And her. But he never blamed me and he never told anyone. In fact, he took on half the guilt. That was the nicest thing.'

She leaned forward across the table with a pained look on her face. I think she would have made a good, sympathetic psychologist if she had followed that path.

'What happened, Jack?'

'She fell through the ice at the lake. The same place where Sean's body was found. She was bigger than me, older. We'd gone out there with our parents. We had a camper and my folks were making lunch or something. Me and Sean were outside and Sarah was watching us. I ran out on the frozen lake. Sarah ran out after me to stop me from going too far out, to where the ice was thin. Only she was older and bigger and heavier and she fell through. I started screaming. Sean started screaming. My father and some other people there tried but they couldn't get to her in time . . .'

I drank from my coffee cup but it was empty. I looked at her and continued.

'Anyway, everybody was asking what happened, you know, and I couldn't . . . I couldn't talk. And he – Sean – said we had both been out on the ice and then when Sarah came out it cracked and she fell through. It was a lie and I don't know if my parents ever believed it. I don't think they did. But he did it for me. It was like he was willing to share the guilt with me, make it easier by half.'

262

I stared into my empty cup. Rachel said nothing.

'You might've made it big as a shrink. That's a story I've never told anyone.'

'Well, I think telling it might've just been something you felt you owed your brother. Maybe a way of thanking him.'

The waiter placed a check on our table and thanked us. I opened my wallet and put a credit card down on top of it. I can think of a better way to thank him, I thought.

After we stepped off the elevator I became nearly paralyzed with fear. I couldn't bring myself to act on my desire. We moved to her door first. She pulled the card key from her pocket and looked up at me. I hesitated, said nothing.

'Well,' she said after a long moment. 'I guess we start early tomorrow. Do you eat breakfast?'

'Just coffee, usually.'

'Okay, well, I'll call you and maybe if there's time we can grab a cup.'

I nodded, too overrun with the embarrassment of my failure and cowardice to say anything.

'Good night, Jack.'

''Night,' I managed to say before walking off down the hall.

I sat on the edge of the bed watching CNN for a half hour, hoping to see the report she had mentioned or anything to take my mind off the disastrous end of the night. Why is it, I wondered, that it is the ones who mean so much that are the hardest to reach out to? Some deep instinct told me that the moment in the hall had been the time, the right moment. And I had ignored it. I had run from it. And now I feared that my failure would haunt me forever. Because that instinct might never come back.

I don't think I heard the first knock. Because the one that raised me from my dark reverie was very loud and surely not the first effort. It had the urgency of a third or fourth knock. Jarred by the intrusion, I quickly turned off the TV and went to the door, opening it without looking through the peephole. It was her.

'Rachel.'

'Hi.'

'Hi.'

'I, uh, thought I'd give you a chance to redeem yourself. That is, if you wanted to.'

I looked at her and a dozen responses went through my mind, all engineered to neatly put the ball back in her court and make her make the move. But the instinct came back and I knew what she wanted and what I needed to do.

I stepped toward her and put an arm behind her back and kissed her. Then I pulled her into the room and closed the door.

'Thank you,' I whispered.

Almost nothing was said after that. She hit the light switch, then led me to the bed. She put her arms around my neck and pulled me down into a long, deep kiss. We fumbled with each other's clothes and then decided wordlessly to just take off our own. It was faster.

'Do you have something?' she whispered. 'You know, to use?'

Crestfallen by the consequences of my inaction earlier, I shook my head no and was about to offer to go to the drugstore, a trip that I knew would destroy the moment.

'I think I might,' she said.

She pulled her purse onto the bed and I heard the zipper of an interior pocket opening. She then pressed the plastic condom package into my palm.

'Always keep one for emergencies,' she said with a smile in her voice.

We made love after that. Slowly, smiling in the shadows of the room. I think of it now as a wonderful moment, perhaps the most erotic and passionate hour of my life. In reality, though, when I strip the gauze from the memory, I know it was a nervous hour with both of us seemingly too eager and willing to please the other and perhaps thereby robbing ourselves of some of the true enjoyment of the moment. My sense of Rachel was that she was craving the intimacy of the act, not as much the sensual pleasure as the closeness with another human being. It was that way for me as well, but I also found a deep carnal desire for her body. She had wide and dark areolas on small breasts, a lovely rounded stomach with soft hair below it. As we found each other's rhythm her face flushed and became warm. She was beautiful and I told her so. But this seemed only to embarrass her and she pulled me down into an embrace so that I could not see her face. My face in her hair, I smelled the scent of apples.

Afterward, she rolled onto her stomach and I lightly rubbed her back.

'I want to be with you after this,' I said.

She didn't answer but that was okay. I knew that what we had just shared was genuine. She slowly pulled herself up into a sitting position.

'What is it?'

'I can't stay. I want to but I can't. I should be in my own room in the morning in case Bob calls. He'll want to talk before the meeting with the locals and he said he'd call.'

Disappointed, I wordlessly watched her dress. She moved about in the darkness skillfully, knowing her way. When she was finished, she bent down and lightly kissed me on the lips.

'Go to sleep.'

'I will. You, too.'

But after she was gone I couldn't sleep. I felt too good. I felt reaffirmed and filled with an unexplainable joy. Every day you fight death with life and what is more vital in life than the physical act of love? My brother and all that had happened seemed far away.

I rolled to the side of the bed and picked up the phone. Full of myself, I wanted to tell her these thoughts. But after eight rings she didn't pick up and the operator answered.

'Are you sure that was Rachel Walling's room?'

'Yes, sir. Three twenty-one. Would you like to leave a message?'

'No, thanks.'

I sat up and turned on the light. I turned on the television with the remote and flipped back and forth for a few minutes, not really watching. I tried her number again and still no answer.

Getting dressed, I told myself I wanted a Coke. I took change off the bureau and my key and went down the hall to the alcove where the vending machines were. On my way back I stopped by 321 and listened at the door. I heard nothing. I lightly knocked and waited, knocked again. She didn't answer.

At my door I fumbled to use the key and turn the knob while holding the can of Coke. Finally, I put the can down on the rug and was opening the door when I heard footsteps and turned to see a man coming down the hallway toward me. The hall lights were dimmed because of the hour and the bright lights from the elevator alcove cast the approaching man in silhouette. He was a large man and in his hand I saw he carried something. A bag maybe. He was ten feet away.

'Hiya, sport.'

Thorson. His voice, though recognizable, spooked me and I think he saw it in my face. I heard him chuckle as he passed by me.

'Pleasant dreams.'

I said nothing. I picked up the can and moved into my room slowly, continuing to watch Thorson move down the hall. He passed by 321 without hesitation and stopped at a room further down the hallway. As he was opening it with a key he looked back down the hall at me. Our eyes locked for a moment, then I slipped wordlessly into my room.

28

....

Gladden wished he had asked Darlene where the remote control was before he had killed her. It annoyed him to have to get up to switch channels. Every one of the Los Angeles television channels had picked up on the *Times* story. He'd had to sit right in front of the box, though, and manually change the channel to try to catch all the reports. He had seen what Detective Thomas looked like. He had been interviewed by all of the channels.

He lay on the couch, now too excited to sleep. He wanted to change the channel to CNN but didn't want to get up again. He was on some cable channel on the nether reaches of the list. A woman with a French accent was preparing crêpes filled with yogurt. Gladden didn't know whether it was a dessert or a breakfast but it was making him hungry and he considered opening another can of ravioli. He decided against it. He knew he had to conserve his supplies. Still four days to go.

'Where's the fucking remote, Darlene?' he called out.

He got up and switched the channel, then turned out the lights and returned to the couch. With the monologue of the CNN anchors as a calming background, he thought about the work ahead, his plans. They knew about him now and he had to be more careful than ever.

He fell into a doze, his eyes drooping and the TV noise lulling him finally to sleep. But just as he was about to drop off, his ears picked up on a report from Phoenix about the murder of a police detective. Gladden opened his eyes.

29
·······

In the morning Rachel called me before I was out of bed. I squinted at the clock and saw it was seven-thirty. I didn't ask why she hadn't answered either the phone or her door the night before. I'd already spent a good part of the night brooding about it and decided she had probably been taking a shower during the times I phoned or knocked.

'You up?'

'I am now.'

'Good. Call your sister-in-law.'

'Right. I will.'

'You want to get coffee? How long till you're ready?'

'I have to make the call and get a shower. An hour?'

'You're on your own then, Jack.'

'Okay, a half hour. You've already been up?'

'No.'

'Well, don't you have to take a shower?'

'I don't take an hour to get ready, even on a day off.'

'Okay, okay. A half hour.'

As I got up I found the torn condom package on the floor. I picked it up and committed the brand to memory since it obviously was the one she preferred, then threw it in the bathroom trash can.

I was almost hoping Riley wouldn't be home because I didn't know exactly how to ask her to let people dig up her husband's body or how she would react. But I knew that at five till nine on a Sunday morning there wasn't much chance that she would be anywhere else. As far as I knew, her only appearances in church in recent years were at Sean's funeral and her wedding before that.

She answered on the second ring with a voice that seemed more cheerful than I'd heard in the last month. At first I wasn't even sure it was her.

'Riles?'

'Jack, where are you? I was worried.'

'I'm in Phoenix. Why are you worried?'

'Well, you know, I didn't know what was going on.'

'I'm sorry I didn't call. Everything's okay. I'm with the FBI. I can't say a lot but they are looking into Sean's death. His and some others.'

I looked out the window and saw the lines of a mountain on the horizon. The tourist pamphlet that came with the room said it was called Camelback Mountain and the name fit. I didn't know if I was saying too much. But it wasn't like Riley was going to go sell the story to the *National Enquirer*.

'Uh, something's come up on the case. They think there might've been some evidence missed on Sean ... Uh, they want to ... Riley, they need to take him out of the ground to look at him again.'

There was no response. I waited a long time.

'Riley?'

'Jack, why?'

'It will help the case. The investigation.'

'But what do they want? Are ... are they going to cut him open again?'

She said the last part in a desperate whisper and I realized how I had bungled the job of telling her.

'Oh, no. Not at all. Uh, all they want to do is look at his hands. Nothing else. You have to give them permission. Otherwise, they have to go through courts and it's a long mess.'

'His hands? Why Jack?'

'It's a long story. I'm not really supposed to tell you but I'll tell you this. They think the guy ... whoever did this, he tried to hypnotize Sean. They want to look at his hands to see if there are pinpricks, you know. That's the test somebody might have given to see if Sean was really hypnotized.'

There was more silence.

'There was something else,' I said. 'Did Sean have a cough or a cold? You know, back on the day it happened.'

'Yes,' she said after a moment's hesitation. 'He was sick and I told him not to go in that day. I was sick, too, and I told him to stay home with me. Jack, you know what?'

'What?'

'I must've felt sick because I was pregnant. I found out Wednesday.'

It caught me off guard. I hesitated.

'Oh, Riley,' I finally said. 'That's wonderful. Did you tell the folks?'

'Yes, they know. They're very happy. It's like a miracle child because I didn't know and we hadn't really been trying.'

'It's great news.'

I didn't know how to get back to the other conversation we had been having. Finally, I just bull-rushed her to the point.

'I've got to go now, Riles. What can I tell them?'

Rachel was in the lobby when I stepped out of the elevator. She had both her computer bag and her overnighter with her.

'You checked out?' I asked, not understanding.

'FBI rules of the road. Never leave anything in the room because you never know when you'll have to fly. We get a break today, I'm not going to have time to come back and pack my things.'

I nodded. It was too late for me to pack and I had almost nothing to pack anyway.

'Did you call her?'

'Yes. She said fine. She said do it. For what it's worth, she also said he was sick. The cough syrup was his. And I figured out why Sean was killed in his car and not at home like the others.'

'Why?'

'His wife, Riley, was home because she was sick, too. My brother would have done everything he could not to take this guy back to his house. Not with her there.'

I nodded sadly at my brother's last and maybe bravest act.

'I think you're right, Jack. It fits. But listen, there's been a development. Bob's just got word and called me from the FO. He's delaying the meeting with the locals. We got a fax from the Poet.'

The mood of the conference room was decidedly somber. Only the agents from Quantico were taking part. Backus, Thompson, Thorson and an agent named Carter who had been at the first status meeting I had attended back at Quantico. I noticed Rachel and Thorson exchange contemptuous looks as we entered. I focused on Backus. He seemed lost in thought. He had his portable computer open on the table in front of him but he wasn't looking at it. He looked fresh in a different gray suit. A bemused smile spread on his face and he looked at me.

'Jack, you get to see firsthand now why we were concerned about containing this story. A five-second video bite was all it took and the offender knows we are on his trail.'

I nodded.

'I don't think he should be here for this,' Thorson said.

'A deal is a deal, Gordon. He certainly had nothing to do with the CNN story.'

'Still, I think it's not —'

'Can it, Gordon,' Rachel said. 'It doesn't matter what you think.'

'Okay, let's halt hostilities and concentrate on the problem,' Backus said. 'I've got copies here.'

He opened a file and passed copies of the fax across the table. I got my own copy. There was silence in the room as we all read.

Dear Bob Backus, FBI agent,
And hello to you, sir. I caught the news and saw you in Phoenix, you sly one. No comments to dim bulb reporters do not fool me. I know your face, Bob. You are coming for me and I anxiously await your arrival. But be

careful, my friend Bob! Not so close! After all, look what happened to poor Orsulak and those others. They put Orsulak in the ground today, the end of a good job. But an FBI man of such stature as yours, now that would be a noble hunt. Heh, heh.

Not to worry, Bob. You are safe. My next intended has been anointed. I've made my choice and I have him in sight, even as you read these words.

Are you huddled with your masses now? Wondering what makes your opponent tick? It's a terrible mystery, isn't it? Bothers like a pinprick in the palm I suspect. I offer you one clue. (What are friends for?) I am the rotten apple of my Best Pal's eye, who am I? When you know the answer, Bob, say it over and over again. Then you'll get it. You'll know. You're a pro and I'm sure you are up to the challenge. I'm counting on you, Bob!

I dwell alone in the world of moan, Bob, and my work has just begun. And Bob? May the best man win.

I cannot sign my correspondence for you haven't given me my name yet. What is it, Bob? I'll watch for you on television and I'll wait to hear my name. Until then I will close with this: Short and Tall – I killed them all!

Drive carefully!

I read the fax twice and each time it gave me the same chill. I knew what they meant now. About the moon. The letter was the voice of a man from someplace else. Not here. Not this planet.

'Everybody in agreement on authenticity?' Backus asked.

'There are several authenticators,' Rachel said. 'The pin-prick. The quote from Poe. What about the reference to Best Pal? Has Florida been informed about this?'

'Yes. The Best Pals angle obviously becomes the priority. They're dropping everything else for the time being.'

'What does Brass say?'

'That it obviously confirms the linkage theory. There are references here to both strings, the detectives and the others.

She and Brad were right. One offender. She's now going with the Florida killings as our model. Everything that follows is just a repetition of the initial crime sequence. He's repeating the ritual.'

'In other words, find out why he killed Beltran and you know why he killed the rest.'

'Right. Brass and Brad have been talking to Florida all morning. Hopefully, it won't take long to get some answers and put the model together.'

Everybody seemed to brood over this for a few moments.

'We're going to stay here?' Rachel asked.

'I think it's best,' Backus said. 'The answers may be in Florida but it's static. History. We're still closest to him here.'

'It says he's already chosen his next intended,' I said. 'Is that the next cop, you think?'

'That's exactly what I think,' Backus said somberly. 'So we've run out of time. As we sit here talking, he is watching another man, another cop, somewhere. And if we don't find out where that is, we're going to have another dead man on our hands.'

He pounded a fist on the table.

'We've got to make a break, people, we've got to do something. We have to find that man before it is too late!'

He said it with force and conviction. He was marshaling his troops. He had asked for their best work before. He needed it to be even better now.

'Bob,' Rachel said. 'The fax makes reference to Orsulak's funeral being *today*. When did this come in and where did it go to?'

'Gordon has that.'

Thorson cleared his throat and spoke without looking at Rachel or me.

'It came to a fax line at Quantico that is assigned to academy business,' Thorson said. 'Needless to say, its sender used a masking option on the sender ID. Nothing there. It arrived at three thirty-eight this morning. That's eastern time. I had Hazelton chase down the sequence. A fax call came into the general Quantico number, the operator recognized the fax beep and switched the call to the wire room. She couldn't tell where or who it was going to because all she had was the beep. So she took a guess and switched it to an academy fax and it was there in the basket until this morning when it was finally noticed and brought down to the center.'

'We're lucky it's not still sitting there unnoticed,' Backus added.

'Right,' Thorson said. 'Anyway, Hazelton took the original to the lab and came up with something. Their take is that it wasn't a fax-to-fax transmission. It came from an inboard fax.'

'A computer,' I said.

'With a fax modem. And since we know this guy is a traveler, it's not likely that he's lugging around an Apple Mac on his back. The speculation is he has a laptop computer with a fax modem. Most likely a cellular modem. It would give him the most freedom.'

Everyone digested this for a few moments. I wasn't sure of its significance. It seemed to me that a lot of the information they had amassed during the investigation was useless until they had a suspect in custody. Then it might be used to build a case against him for trial. But until then, it wasn't much help in catching him.

'All right, so he has state-of-the-art computer equipment,' Rachel finally said. 'What do we have in place for the next fax?'

'We'll be standing by to trace any fax calls to the general line,' Thorson said. 'At best we'll get the originating cell. No closer.'

'What's that mean?' I asked.

Thorson seemed reluctant to answer any question from me. Rachel stepped in when he didn't.

'It means if he's on a cellular we can't make a trace to a direct number or location. We'll get the city and the originating cell where the call came from. Probably at best that will knock it down to a search area of more than a hundred thousand people.'

'But we'll have the city,' Backus said. 'We'll be able to go to

274

the locals and look for cases that may serve as bait cases. It would only have to be a homicide committed in the last week. Just since Orsulak.'

He looked at Thorson.

'Gordon, I want another flag sent to all FOs. Tell them to check with the locals on any recent homicides. We're talking about all the whodunits in general, but child cases in particular and anything with unusual MO or violent assault on the corpse, before or after death. Get that out by this afternoon. Request acknowledgment from SACs by eighteen hundred tomorrow. I don't want it to fall through the cracks.'

'Got it.'

'Also, FYI, Brass suggested one other thing as well,' Backus added. 'And that's that the bit in the fax about his next target being selected could be a bluff. A design to make us react and scramble while the offender is actually slipping away, going under. Remember, it was the chief fear that we had about publicity.'

'I disagree,' Rachel said. 'Reading this, I see a braggart, someone who thinks he's better than us and wants to toy with us. I take him at his word. There's a cop out there somewhere and he's in the sights.'

'I tend to think that way, too,' Backus said. 'I think Brass does as well but felt the need to put the other possibility on the table.'

'So, then, what's our strategy now?'

'Simple,' Backus said. 'We find this guy and arrest him before he hurts anybody else.'

Backus smiled and everyone but Thorson followed suit.

'Actually, I think that until something else breaks, we stay put and redouble our efforts here. And let's keep this fax to ourselves. Meantime, we're ready to move if something develops. We hope for another fax from our guy and Brass is working up another alert for the field offices. I'll tell her to stress its importance to the FOs in the Pacific time zone.'

He scanned the room and nodded. He was finished.

'Need I say it again?' he asked. 'Your best work. We really need it now more than ever.'

30

· · · · · · · ·

The meeting with the locals didn't get under way until almost eleven. It was short and sweet. It was the kind of situation where the suitor asks the bride-to-be's father for approval of the marriage. Most of the time it doesn't really matter what the old man says. It's going to happen. In carefully chosen, friendly words Backus told the locals that the Big G was in town and was now running the show. There was a little bit of posturing and disagreement on some particulars but they rolled over with the empty promises Backus made.

During this meeting, I continued to avoid eye contact with Thorson. While driving over from the federal building Rachel had explained to me the reason for the morning's tensions between her and Thorson. The night before she had run into her former husband in the hotel hallway while leaving my room. Her disheveled appearance probably told him all he needed to know. I groaned when I heard, thinking about how it complicated things. She seemed to be unconcerned and viewed the situation as amusing.

At the end of the meeting with the locals, Backus divided assignments. Rachel and Thompson were given the Orsulak crime scene. I was to ride with them. Mize and Matuzak were to start backtracking on the interviews the locals had conducted of Orsulak's friends and to try to reconstruct the dead detective's movements on his last day. Thorson and Carter were given the Little Joaquin case and assigned to re-cover the ground trod by the locals. Grayson would act as liaison to the Phoenix cops, and Backus, of course, would run the show from the field office, maintaining contact on other developments in the case in Quantico and the other cities.

Orsulak had lived in a small yellow ranch house with stucco walls in South Phoenix. It was a marginal neighborhood. I counted three junk cars parked on gravel lawns and two Sunday morning garage sales in full swing on the block.

Rachel used the key she had gotten from Grayson to cut through an evidence sticker spread across the front doorjamb and then unlocked the door. Before pushing it open she turned to me.

'Remember, they didn't find him for three and a half days. Are you up to this?'

'Course.'

For some reason I was embarrassed that she had asked me this in front of Thompson, who smiled as if I were a rookie. That annoyed me, too, even though in actuality I was less than a rookie.

We were three steps in before the odor engulfed me. As a reporter I had seen plenty of bodies, but I'd never had the pleasure of entering a closed structure where a body had rotted for three days before discovery. The putrid odor was almost palpable. It was like the ghost of William Orsulak, haunting the place and all who dared enter. Rachel left the front door open to help air the place out some.

'What are you looking for?' I asked once I was reasonably assured that I had control of my throat.

'Inside, I don't know,' Rachel replied. 'It's already been gone over by the locals, his friends . . .'

She went to the dining room table in the room to the right of the door and put down and opened a file she had been carrying. She began leafing through the pages. It was part of the package the local cops had turned over to the agents.

'Have a look around,' she said. 'It looks like they were pretty thorough, but you might come up with something. Just don't touch anything.'

'Right.'

I left her there and started slowly to look about. My eyes first caught on the easy chair in the living room. It was a dark green but the headrest was stained darker with blood. It had flowed down the back into the seat of the chair. Orsulak's blood.

On the floor in front of the chair and near the wall behind it, chalk circles outlined two holes where bullets had been retrieved. Thompson knelt here and opened his toolbox. He began probing the bullet holes with a thin steel pick. I left him there and walked further into the house.

There were two bedrooms, Orsulak's and an extra that seemed dusty and unused. There were photos of two teen-aged boys on the bureau in the bedroom the detective had used, but I guessed his kids never used the other, they never came to visit. I moved slowly through these rooms and the hallway bathroom but I saw nothing that I thought mattered to the investigation. I secretly hoped I would come upon something that would help and that would impress Rachel, but I came up empty.

When I stepped back into the living room I saw neither Rachel nor Thompson.

'Rachel?'

No answer.

I walked through the dining room to the kitchen but it was empty. I went through the laundry room, opened a door and glanced into the dark garage but saw no one there either. Coming back into the kitchen I saw the door ajar and glanced through the window over the sink. I saw movement in the tall brush at the rear of the backyard. Rachel was walking, with her head down, through the brush, Thompson behind her.

The yard was cleared for maybe twenty yards going back. A seven-foot-high plank fence ran down both sides. But at the back there was no fence line and the dirt yard dropped down into a dry creek bed where there was a lot of brush. Rachel and Thompson were on a trail moving through the brush away from the house.

'Thanks for waiting,' I said when I caught up. 'What are you doing?'

'What do you think, Jack?' Rachel said. 'Did the Poet just park in the driveway, knock on the door and pop Orsulak after being invited in?'

'I don't know. I doubt it.'

'I do, too. No, he watched him. Maybe for days. But the locals canvassed the neighborhood and no neighbor saw a car that didn't belong. Nobody saw anything out of the routine.'

'So you think he came in through here?'

'It's a possibility.'

She studied the ground as we walked. She was looking for anything. A footprint in the mud, a broken twig. She stopped a few times to bend and look at pieces of debris alongside the trail. A cigarette box, an empty soft drink bottle. She didn't touch any of it. It could be collected later if necessary.

The trail took us under a stanchion holding up high-tension power lines and into a stand of heavy brush at the back end of a trailer park. We reached a high point and looked down into the park. It was not well kept and many of the units had crudely fashioned add-ons like porches and toolsheds. On some of the units the porches had been en-closed with plastic sheeting and were being used as additional bedrooms and living spaces. An aura of crowded poverty ema-nated from the thirty or so dwellings jammed together on the lot like toothpicks in a box.

'Well, shall we?' Rachel asked, as if we were going for high tea.

'Ladies first,' Thompson said.

Several of the inhabitants of the park were sitting on door stoops and old couches set in front of their units. They were mostly Latinos and a few blacks. Maybe some Indians. They watched us emerge from the brush with no real interest, which showed they recognized us as cops. We showed the same lack of interest in them as we started walking along the narrow lane between rows of trailers.

'What are we doing?' I asked.

'Just having a look,' Rachel answered. 'We can ask ques-tions later. If we take it slow and calm, they'll know we're not here to kick ass. It might help.'

Her eyes never stopped scanning the park and every trailer we passed as we walked. I realized that it was the first time I had seen her at work in the field. This wasn't sitting around a table trying to interpret facts. This was the gathering time. I found myself watching her more than anything else.

'He watched Orsulak,' Rachel said, more to herself than to either Thompson or me. 'And once he knew where he lived, he started planning. How to get in and how to get out. He had to have a getaway route and a getaway car, and it would not have been smart to park it anywhere on Orsulak's street.'

We were coming down the main street, as narrow as it was, to the front of the park and the entrance off a city street.

'So he parked somewhere over here and walked through.'

The first trailer at the entrance had a sign on the door that said OF CE. A larger sign, attached to an iron framework on top of the trailer, said SUNSHINE ACRES MOBILE HOME PARK.

'Sunshine Acres?' Thompson asked. 'More like Sunshine Half Acre.'

'Not much of a park, either,' I added.

Rachel was off on her own, not listening. She walked past the steps to the office door and out to the city street. It was four lanes and we were in an industrial area. Directly across from the trailer park was a U-Store-It and on either side of that were warehouses. I watched Rachel look around and take in the surroundings. Her eyes held on the one streetlight, which was a half block away. I knew what she was thinking. That it would be dark here at night.

She walked alongside the curb, her eyes scanning the asphalt, looking for something, anything, maybe a cigarette butt or a piece of luck. Thompson stood with me, kicking at the ground with one foot. I couldn't take my eyes off Rachel. I saw her stop and look down and bite her lip for a moment. I walked over.

Glimmering like a cache of diamonds against the curb was a pile of shattered safety glass. She toed her shoe through the glass stones.

The trailer park's manager was already about three shots into the day when we opened the door and stepped into the cramped space advertised outside as an office. It was clear the place was also the man's home. He was sitting in a green corduroy La-Z-Boy chair with the feet extension up. Its sides were scarred by cat scratches but it was still the nicest piece of furniture he had. Other than the television. That was a new-looking Panasonic with a built-in VCR. He was watching a home-shopping show and it took him a long time to pull his eyes off the tube to have a look at us. The device being sold sliced and chopped vegetables without all the mess and setup time of a food processor.

'You the manager?' Rachel asked.

'That should be obvious, shouldn't it, Officer?'

A wise guy, I thought. He was about sixty and he wore green fatigues and a white sleeveless T-shirt with burn holes on the chest through which a crop of gray chest hair protruded. He was balding and had a drinker's red face. He was white, the only white person I had seen so far in the park.

'It's Agent,' she said, showing him the inside of her badge wallet.

'FBI? What's the G care about a little car break-in? See, I read a lot. I know you people call yourselves the G. I like that.'

Rachel looked at me and Thompson and then back at the man. I felt the small tingling of anxiousness.

'How do you know about the car break-in?' Rachel asked.

'I seen you out there. I got eyes. You was lookin' at the glass. I swept it up into a pile. Street cleaners only come 'round here maybe once a month. More in the summer when it's dusty out.'

'No. I mean, how did you even know there was a car burglary?'

''Cause I sleep back there in the back room. I heard 'em break the window. I saw them messing about inside that car.'

'When was this?'

'Let's see, that'd be Thursday last. I was wondering when the guy'd report it. But I didn't think no FBI agent would be coming out. How 'bout you two, you with the G, too?'

'Never mind that, Mr – what is your name, sir?'

'Adkins.'

'Okay, Mr Adkins, do you know whose car got broken into?'

'Nope, never saw him. I just heard the window and saw the kids.'

'What about a plate?'

'Nope.'

'You didn't call the police?'

'Don't have no phone. I could use Thibedoux's over to lot three but it was the middle of the night and I knew those cops wouldn't come running on a car rob'ry. Not here. They got too much to do.'

'So you never at any point saw the owner of the car and he never knocked on the door to see if maybe you heard the break-in or saw anybody?'

'That's right.'

'What about the kids who broke in?' Thompson asked, robbing Rachel of the payoff question. 'You know them, Mr Atkins?'

'Adkins. With a D, no T, Mr G.'

Adkins laughed at his command of the alphabet.

'Mr Adkins,' Thompson said, correcting himself. 'Well, do you?'

'Do I what?'

'Know who the kids were.'

'No, I don't know who they were.'

His eyes strayed past us to the television. On the program they were now selling a glove with small rubber bristles on the palm for grooming pets.

'I know what else you could use that for,' Adkins said. He made a masturbation motion with his hand and winked and smiled at Thompson. 'That's what they're really selling that for, you know.'

Rachel stepped over to the TV and turned it off. Adkins didn't protest. She straightened up and looked at him.

'We're investigating the murder of a police officer. We'd like your attention. We have reason to believe the car you saw burglarized belonged to a suspect. We are not interested in prosecuting the boys who broke into the car, but we need to speak to them. You were lying just then, Mr Adkins. I saw it in your eyes. The boys came from this park.'

'No, I –'

'Let me finish. Yes, you were lying to us. But we're going to give you another chance. You can tell us the truth now or we'll go back and get more agents and police and we'll go through this dump you call a trailer park like an army laying siege. You think we'll find any stolen property in those tin cans? You think we might run across some people wanted on warrant? How about some illegals? What about safety code violations? We passed one back there, I saw the extension cord going out the door into the shed. They've got somebody living in there, don't they? And I bet you and your employer charge extra for that. Or maybe just you do. What's your employer going to say when he finds out? What's he going to say when the receivables go down because the people who are supposed to be paying you rent cannot because they've been deported or they're in lock-up on warrant holds for not paying child support? What about you, Mr *Ad*-kins? You want me to run the serial number off that television on the computer?'

'The TV's mine. Bought it fair and square. Know what you are, FBI lady? Fucking Bitch Investigator.'

Rachel ignored the comment, though I thought Thompson turned away to hide a smile.

'Fair and square from who?'

'Never mind. It was those Tyrell brothers, okay? They're the ones what robbed that car. Now if they come in here and beat the shit outta me, I'm suing you. Got that?'

With directions from Adkins we arrived at a trailer four units in from the main entrance. Word had spread that the law was in the park. There were more people on stoops and sitting on the outdoor couches. When we got to Number 4, the Tyrell brothers were waiting for us.

They were sitting on an old glider beneath a blue canvas

awning extending from the side of a double-wide trailer. Next to the door of the trailer were a washer and dryer set beneath a blue canvas cover to keep the rain off. The two brothers were teenagers, maybe a year apart and of mixed race, black and white. Rachel stepped to the edge of the shade provided by the awning. Thompson took a spot about five feet to her left.

'Guys,' Rachel said and got no response. 'Your mother home?'

'Nah, she not, Officer,' the older one said.

He looked at the brother with slow eyes. The brother started rocking the glider back and forth with his leg.

'You know,' Rachel said, 'we know you're smart. We don't want any trouble with you. Don't want to give you any trouble. We promised Mr Adkins that when we went in there to ask where your trailer was.'

'Adkins, shit,' the younger one said.

'We're here about the car that was parked out on the road last week.'

'Didn't see it.'

'No, we didn't see it.'

Rachel walked over close to the older one and bent down to talk directly into his ear.

'Come on now,' she said softly. 'This is one of those times your mother told you about. Think now. Use your head. Remember what she told you. You don't want trouble for her or for yourselves. You want us to go away and leave you alone. And there's only one way we're going to do that.'

When Rachel walked into the squad room at the field office, she carried the plastic bag like a trophy. She set it down on Matuzak's desk and a handful of agents gathered around to look. Backus came in and looked down at it as if he were looking at the Holy Grail. Then he looked up at Rachel with excitement plain in his eyes.

'Grayson checked with the PD,' he said. 'No record of any break-in reported at that spot. Not on that day, not on that week. You'd think a legal citizen who gets his car broken into would make a report.'

Rachel nodded.

'You'd think.'

Backus nodded to Matuzak, who picked the evidence bag up off the table.

'You know what to do?'

'Yes.'

'Bring us back some luck. We need it.'

What the bag contained was a car stereo stolen from a late-model Ford Mustang, white or yellow depending on which of the Tyrell brothers had better eyesight in the dark.

It was all we got from them but the feeling, the hope, was that it was enough. Rachel and Thompson had interviewed them separately and then switched sides and interviewed them again, but the radio was all the Tyrell brothers could give. They said they never saw the driver who left the Mustang at the curb in front of Sunshine Acres and they took nothing but the stereo in a quick smash-and-grab. They never bothered to open the trunk. They never looked at the plate to see if the car was even registered in Arizona.

While Rachel spent the rest of the afternoon doing paperwork and preparing an addendum on the car to be transmitted to all field offices, Matuzak fed the serial number of the stereo to the Automotive ID unit at Washington, D.C., headquarters, then gave the stereo itself to a lab tech for processing. Thompson had taken prints of the Tyrell brothers for elimination purposes.

The lab got no usable prints off the stereo other than those left by the Tyrells. But the serial number was not a dead end. It came back to a 1994 pale yellow Mustang registered to Hertz Corporation. Matuzak and Mize then headed to Sky Harbor International to continue tracing the car.

The mood of the agents in the field office was upbeat. Rachel had delivered. There was no guarantee that the Mustang had been driven by the Poet. But the time of its being parked outside Sunshine Acres matched the time period in which Orsulak had been killed. And there was the fact that the break-in by the brothers had never been reported to the police. It added up to a viable lead and, more so, it gave them a little more knowledge about how the Poet operated. It was an important gain. They felt like I felt. That the Poet was an enigma, a phantom somewhere out there in the darkness. Coming up with a lead like the car stereo seemed to make the possibility of catching him more believable. We were closer and we were coming.

For most of the afternoon I stayed out of the way and simply watched Rachel work. I was fascinated by her skill, amazed at how she had come up with the stereo and how she had talked to Adkins and the Tyrells. At one point in the office she noticed my gaze and asked what I was doing.

'Nothing, just watching.'

'You like watching me?'

'You are good at what you do. It's always interesting to watch somebody like that.'

'Thank you. I just got lucky.'

'I have a feeling you get lucky a lot.'

'I think in this business you make your own luck.'

At the end of the day, after Backus had picked up and read a copy of the alert she had transmitted, I watched his eyes narrow into two black marbles.

'I wonder if that choice of car was intentional?' he asked. 'A pale yellow Mustang.'

'Why's that?' I asked.

I saw Rachel nodding. She knew the answer.

'The Bible,' Backus said. '"Behold a pale horse: and his name that sat on him was Death."'

'"And Hell followed with him,"' Rachel finished.

We made love again Sunday night and she seemed even more giving and needing of the intimacy. In the end, if either of us was holding back, it was me. While I wanted nothing more in the world at that moment than to surrender to the feelings I had for her, a low whisper in the back of my mind found just enough volume to question her motives. Perhaps it was a testament to my own precarious self-confidence, but I couldn't help but listen to the voice when it suggested that perhaps her aim was just as much to hurt her ex-husband as to please me and herself. The thought made me feel guilty and insincere.

When we held each other afterward, she whispered that this time she was going to stay until dawn.

31

·········

The phone pulled me out of a sound sleep. I looked around the strange confines of the room, getting my bearings, and my eyes fell on Rachel's.

'You better get it,' she said calmly. 'It's your room.'

She didn't seem to have nearly the same difficulty I had coming awake. In fact, for a moment I had the feeling she had already been awake and was watching me when the phone rang. I lifted the receiver on what I guessed was the ninth or tenth ring. At the same time I saw that the clock on the bed table said it was seven-fifteen.

'Yes?'

'Put Walling on the line.'

I froze. There was something reminiscent about the voice but I didn't place it in my jumbled mind. Then a thought occurred to me that Rachel shouldn't be in my room.

'You got the wrong room. She's in –'

'Don't fuck with me, reporter. Put her on.'

I covered the phone with my hand and turned to Rachel.

'It's Thorson. He says he knows you're there – here.'

'Give it to me,' she said angrily and jerked the phone out of my hand.

'What do you want?'

There was a period of silence. He must've said two or three sentences to her.

'Where did it come from?'

More silence.

'Why are you calling me?' she asked, the anger back in her voice. 'Go ahead and tell him, if that's what you want. If you want him to know. It says as much about you as me. I'm sure he'd like to know that you're some kind of Peeping Tom.'

She handed me the phone and I hung it up. She pulled a pillow over her face and moaned. I pulled it off her face.

'What is it?'

'I've got bad news for you, Jack.'

'What?'

'In this morning's edition of the *Los Angeles Times* there was a story about the Poet. I'm sorry. I've got to bring you into the FO for a meeting with Bob.'

I was silent for a moment, confused.

'How'd they . . .'

'We don't know. That's what we're going to talk about.'

'How much did they have, did he say?'

'No. But apparently it was enough.'

'I knew I should have written this yesterday. Damn it! Once it was clear that this guy knew about you people, there was no reason not to write it.'

'You made a deal and stuck to it. You had to, Jack. Look, let's wait on this until we get to the office and talk about what they had.'

'I've got to call my editor.'

'You can do that later. Bob's apparently already in and waiting for us. I guess he doesn't sleep.'

The phone rang again. She jerked the phone out of the cradle.

'What is it?' she said in a voice painted with annoyance. Then in a softer tone, she said, 'Hold on.'

She smiled sheepishly and handed me the phone. She then lightly kissed me on the cheek, whispered that she was going to her room to get ready and started to get dressed. I put the phone to my ear.

'Hello?'

'It's Greg Glenn. Who was that?'

'Uh, that was an FBI agent. We've got a meeting. I guess you've heard about the *L.A. Times*.'

'You're damn right I have.'

The sinking sensation in my chest was growing. Glenn went on.

'They've got a story on the killer in the paper. *Our* killer, Jack. They're calling him the Poet. You told me we had the exclusive on this and we were protected.'

'We were.'

It was all I could manage to say. As Rachel finished throwing her clothes on she watched me with sympathetic eyes.

'Not anymore. You've got to come back this morning and write ours for tomorrow. Whatever you've got. And you better have more than they've got. We could've had this in the paper, Jack, but you convinced me. Now we're playing catch-up on our own story, goddamnit.'

'All right!' I said sharply just to shut him up.

'And I hope I don't find out that you've extended your stay in Phoenix just because you found some babe to bang down there.'

'Fuck you, Greg. Do you have the story there or not?'

'Of course I do. It's a great story. A great read. But it's in the wrong paper!'

'Just read it to me. No, wait a minute. I gotta go to this meeting. Have somebody in the library –'

'Don't you listen, Jack? You aren't going to any meeting. I want you on the next plane back here to write this for tomorrow.'

I watched Rachel blow a kiss at me and then go out the door.

'I understand. You'll have it for tomorrow. But I can write it here and ship it.'

'No. This is a hands-on story. I want to work this one right here with you.'

'Let me go to this meeting and call you back.'

'Why?'

'There's a new development,' I lied. 'I don't know what it is and I have to go to find out. Let me go and I'll call you. Meantime, have the library take the *Times* story off their wire and ship it to my basket. I'll call it up here. I gotta go.'

I hung up before he could protest. I quickly got dressed and headed out the door with my computer bag. I was in a daze. I didn't know how this could have happened. But a thought was pushing through.

Thorson.

We each grabbed two cups to go from a hospitality stand in the lobby and then headed to the federal building. She had packed all her things again. I had forgotten.

We didn't talk until we had finished our first cups. I imagined we had completely different dilemmas and different thoughts going through our minds.

'Are you going back to Denver?' she asked.

'I don't know yet.'

'How bad was it?'

'It was bad. Last time he'll ever listen to one of my promises.'

'I don't understand how it could've happened. They would have had to call Bob Backus for comment.'

'Maybe they did.'

'No, he would have told you. He would have kept his deal. He's second-generation bureau. I've never seen anyone toe the line like that man.'

'Well, I hope he keeps the deal now. Because I'm writing today.'

'What did the story say?'

'I don't know. I should have it as soon as I can hook up to a phone.'

We were at the courthouse. She pulled into the garage for federal employees.

Only Backus and Thorson were in the conference room.

The meeting began with Backus expressing his regret that the story had leaked before I could write it. It seemed legitimate to me and I regretted impugning his integrity with my comment earlier to Rachel.

'Do you have it? I can get it on my computer if I can use the phone line.'

'By all means. I've been waiting for someone from the L.A. field office to fax it. The only reason I know about it is because Brass tells me we're already getting calls from other media into Quantico.'

I plugged in and turned on my computer and dialed into the *Rocky* system. I didn't bother to read any of my messages. I went right to my personal basket and looked at the files. I noticed there were two new ones: POETCOPY and HYP-STORIES. I remembered then that I had asked Laurie Prine for stories on hypnosis and Horace the Hypnotist but I'd have to look at those files later. I called up POETCOPY and got a shock that I should have seen coming before I had even read the first line of the story.

'Damn it!'

'What?' Rachel asked.

'It was written by Warren. He resigns from the Law Enforcement Foundation and then turns around and uses *my* story to get back with the *Times*.'

'Reporters,' Thorson said with unhidden joy. 'Just can't trust them.'

I ignored him but it was hard. I was angry about what had happened. At Warren and at myself. I should have seen it coming.

'Read it, Jack,' Backus said.

I did.

FBI, POLICE SEEK SERIAL COP KILLER
The Hunted Turns on the Hunters
By Michael Warren, Special to the Times

The FBI has begun a manhunt for a serial killer who has claimed as many as seven homicide detectives as his victims in a nationwide rampage begun as long as three years ago.

Dubbed the 'Poet' because he has left notes containing lines of poetry from the work of Edgar Allan Poe at each murder scene, the suspect has attempted to disguise the deaths of his victims as suicides.

And for as long as three years his victims were counted as such until the similarities of the crimes, including the quotes from Poe, were discovered last week, according to a source close to the investigation.

That discovery prompted the FBI to act quickly in its efforts to identify and capture the Poet. Dozens of FBI agents and police in seven cities are carrying out the investigation under the direction of the FBI's Behavioral Science Services. The investigation currently has its most intense focus on Phoenix, where the latest death attributed to the Poet occurred, the source said.

The source, who talked to the *Times* on the condition of anonymity, declined to disclose how the activities of the Poet were discovered but said that a joint study by the FBI and the Law Enforcement Foundation of police suicides in the last six years provided key information.

The story went on to list the names of the victims and some of the details of each case. It then included a few paragraphs on the BSS unit as filler and ended with a wrap-up quote from the unnamed source saying that the FBI had little to go on in terms of knowing who or where the Poet was.

By the time I was done reading it, my cheeks were hot with anger. There is nothing worse than living by the letter of an agreement when one of the people you made the deal with doesn't. The story was weak, in my opinion, a lot of words around a few facts and all attributed to an anonymous source. Warren didn't even mention the fax or, more importantly, the bait murders. I knew that what I would write that day would be the definitive piece on the Poet. But that didn't move the anger back in my throat much. For whatever the shortcomings of the story were, it was still clear that Warren had talked to somebody in the bureau. And I couldn't help but think that that person was sitting at the conference room table with me.

'We had a deal,' I said, looking up from the computer. 'Somebody gave this to this guy. He knew what I had when I came in to him on Thursday, but he went to somebody in the

293

bureau for the rest. Probably someone on the task force. Probably somebody –'

'That may be true, Jack, but –'

'He already had this because of you,' Thorson interrupted. 'You only have yourself to blame.'

'Wrong,' I said, glaring back at him. 'I gave him most of it but not the Poet. The offender wasn't even called that when I was with Warren. That came from the task force. And that blows our deal. Somebody's talking who shouldn't be talking. The story's out. I have to go write what I know today for tomorrow.'

A small measure of silence passed through the room.

'Jack,' Backus said, 'I know this won't do you much good now but I want you to know that when I get some time and space on this thing, I am going to find out who the leak was and that person won't be working for me anymore, and maybe not even the bureau.'

'You're right. It doesn't do me much good.'

'I need to ask a favor, nonetheless.'

I looked at Backus, wondering if he was actually foolish enough to try again to persuade me to hold off on writing a story every TV station and paper in the country would be running anyway that night and the next day.

'What is it?'

'When you write this . . . I want you to please keep in mind that we still need to get this man. You have information that could irreparably harm our chances of doing that. I'm talking about specific things. Details of the profile. Details about the possible hypnosis, the condoms. If you print those, Jack, and they are repeated on TV or in a newspaper he has access to, then he will change his routine. See what I'm saying? It will only make it harder for us.'

I nodded but then looked at him with a hard stare.

'You're not going to tell me what to write.'

'I know that. I'm asking you to think about your brother, about us, and be *careful* of what you write. I trust you, Jack. Implicitly.'

I thought about that for a long moment and then nodded again.

'Bob, I made a deal with you and came out on the short end. If you want me to protect you now, there's got to be a new deal. You're going to have reporters coming out of the woodwork today. But I want you to refer all calls to public affairs in Quantico. I talk to and quote from you exclusively. Also, I get the fax from the Poet exclusively. You give me that and I won't mention the details of the profile or the hypnosis in my story.'

'That's a deal,' Backus said.

He said it so quickly that I started to think he knew exactly what I had been going to say, that he had known all along that I was going to suggest the new deal.

'But one thing, Jack,' Backus said. 'Let's agree on holding back one line from the fax. If we start getting confessions, we'll be able to use the hold-back line to weed out the phonies.'

'No problem,' I said.

'I'll be here. I'll tell the front that your calls can come through. No one else from the press.'

'There will be a lot of those calls.'

'My intention was to let public affairs handle it anyway.'

'If the statement they put out includes the origination of the case, tell them not to use my name. Just say inquiries from the *Rocky Mountain News* started it rolling.'

Backus nodded.

'One last thing,' I said and then paused a moment. 'I'm still concerned about the leak. If I find out the *L.A. Times* or any other media outlet also got the Poet fax today, then I'll put everything I know into the next story. The profile, everything. Okay?'

'Understood.'

'You weasel,' Thorson said angrily. 'You think you can just come in here and dictate what –'

'Fuck you, Thorson,' I said. 'I've been wanting to say that to you since Quantico. Fuck you, okay? If I was betting, I'd say you were the leak, so don't tell me anything about being a weas –'

'FUCK YOU!' Thorson roared as he stood up to challenge me.

But quickly Backus was up and putting a hand on his shoulder. He gently pushed him back down into his seat. Rachel watched the whole thing, a small, thin smile on her face.

'Easy, Gordon,' Backus soothed. 'Easy. Nobody's accusing anyone of anything. Let's keep things cool. Everybody's a little hot and bothered today but it's no reason why we can't cool down. Jack, that's a dangerous accusation. If you have something to back it up, let's hear it. If not, you'd best leave things like that unsaid.'

I said nothing. I only had my gut instinct that Thorson had leaked the story to fuck me over because of some paranoia about reporters in general and my relationship with Rachel in particular. It wasn't the kind of thing to bring up for discussion. Everybody eventually took their seats and just stared at each other.

'That was entertaining as hell, fellas, but I'd like to do some work today,' Rachel finally said.

'And I have to go,' I said. 'What line do you want to hold back on the fax?'

'The riddle,' Backus answered. 'Don't mention Best Pals.'

I thought a moment. It was one of the better lines.

'Fine. No problem.'

I stood up and so did Rachel.

'I'll give you a ride back to the hotel.'

'Is it that bad, getting scooped like that?' she asked as we were headed back to the hotel.

'It's bad. I guess it's like with you guys, the ones that get away. I hope Backus busts Thorson for this. The asshole.'

'It will be hard for him to prove anything. It's just going to be suspicion.'

'If you told Backus about us and told him that Thorson knew, then he'd believe it.'

'I can't. If I told Backus about us I'd be the one who'd go down.'

After some silence she changed the subject back to the story.

'You'll have so much more than he had.'

'What? Who?'

'I'm talking about Warren. You'll have the better story.'

'First with the story, first with the glory. That's an old newspaper saying. But it's true. In most stories, the one that's there first is always the one who gets the credit, even if the first story is full of holes and bullshit. Even if it's a stolen story.'

'Is that what it's about? Getting credit? Just being first, even if you don't have it right?'

I looked over at her and tried to smile.

'Yeah, sometimes. Most times. Pretty noble job, huh?'

She didn't answer. We drove in silence for a while. I wished that she would say something about us and what we had or didn't have but she didn't. We were getting close to the hotel now.

'What if I can't convince him to let me stay here and I have to go back to Denver? What happens to us?'

She didn't answer for a while.

'I don't know, Jack. What do you want to happen?'

'I don't know but I don't want it to just end like this. I thought . . .'

I didn't know how to say what I wanted to tell her.

'I don't want it to end like this, either.'

She drove to the front of the hotel to drop me off. She said she had to get back. A guy in a red jacket with gold braid on the shoulders opened the door for me, robbing us of any privacy. I wanted to kiss her but something about the situation and being in the G car made it seem inappropriate and awkward.

'I'll see you when I can,' I said. 'As soon as I can.'

'Good,' she said, smiling. 'Good-bye, Jack. Good luck with the story. Call me at the field office and let me know if you are writing from here. Maybe we can get together tonight.'

That was a better reason than any I had come up with for staying in Phoenix. She reached over and touched my beard like she had done once before. And just before I got out of the car she told me to wait. She took a card out of her purse and wrote a number on the back of it, then she gave it to me.

'That's my pager number in case something happens. It's on the satellite, so you can beep me wherever I am.'

'In the whole world?'

'The whole world. Until the satellite falls.'

32
········

Gladden looked at the words on the screen. They were beautiful, as if written by the unseen hand of God. So right. So knowledgeable. He read them again.

They know about me now and I am ready. I await them. I am prepared to take my place in the pantheon of faces. I feel as I did as a child when I waited for the closet door to be opened so that I could receive him. The line of light at the bottom. My beacon. I watched the light and the shadows each of his footfalls made. Then I knew he was there and that I would have his love. The apple of his eye.

We are what they make us and yet they turn from us. We are cast off. We become nomads in the world of the moan. My rejection is my pain and motivation. I carry with me the vengeance of all the children. I am the Eidolon. I am called the predator, the one to watch for in your midst. I am the cucoloris, the blur of light and dark. My story is not one of deprivation and abuse. I welcomed the touch. I can admit it. Can you? I wanted, craved, welcomed the touch. It was only the rejection — when my bones grew too large — that cut me so deeply and forced on me the life of a wanderer. I am the cast off. And the children must stay forever young.

He looked up when the phone rang. It was on the counter in the kitchen and he stared at it as it rang. It was the first call she had gotten. The machine picked up after three rings and her taped message played. Gladden had written it out on a piece of paper and made her read it three times before it was recorded on the fourth. Stupid woman, he thought as he listened now. She wasn't much of an actress – at least with her clothes on.

'Hello, this is Darlene, I . . . I can't take your call right now. I've had to go out of town because of an emergency. I will be checking messages – uh, messages and will call you as soon as I can.'

She sounded nervous and Gladden worried that because of the repeat of the one word that a caller would know she was reading. He listened as a male voice left an angry message after the beep.

'Darlene, goddamnit! You better call me as soon as you get this. You left me in a big lurch over here. You shoulda called and you just might not have a job to come back to, girl, goddamnit!'

Gladden thought it had worked. He got up and erased the message. Her boss, he assumed. But he wouldn't be getting a callback from Darlene.

He noticed the smell as he stood in the kitchen doorway. He grabbed his matches off his cigarettes on the living room coffee table and went into the bedroom. He studied the body for a few moments. The face was a pale green but darker since the last time he had checked. Bloody fluid was draining from the mouth and nose, as the body purged itself of decomposition fluids. He had read about these purges in one of the books he had successfully petitioned to receive before the warden at Raiford. *Forensic Pathology.* Gladden wished he had the camera so he could document the changes in Darlene.

He lit four more sticks of jasmine incense, placing them in ashtrays at the four corners of the bed.

This time, after he had left and closed the bedroom door, he laid a wet towel along the threshold, hoping it would prevent the odor from spreading into the area of the apartment where he was living. He still had two days to go.

33

········

I talked Greg Glenn into letting me write from Phoenix. For
the rest of the morning I stayed in my room making calls,
gathering comments from players in the story ranging from
Wexler in Denver to Bledsoe in Baltimore. I wrote for five
straight hours after that and the only disturbances I had all
day were calls from Glenn himself, nervously asking how I
was doing. An hour before the five o'clock deadline in Denver,
I filed two stories to the metro desk.

My nerves were jangling by the time I shipped the stories
and I had a headache that was almost off the scale. I had been
through a pot and a half of room service coffee and a full pack
of Marlboros – the most I had smoked in one sitting in years.
Pacing the room and waiting for Greg Glenn's callback, I
made a quick call to room service again, explained that I
couldn't leave my room because I was expecting an important
call, and ordered a bottle of aspirin from the hotel's lobby
shop.

After it arrived I downed three tablets with mineral water
from the minibar and almost immediately started feeling
better. Next I called my mother and Riley and alerted them
that my stories would be in the next day's paper. I also told
them there was a chance that reporters from other media
outlets might try to contact them now that the story was out
and to be prepared. Both said they didn't want to talk to any
reporters and I said that was fine, not missing the irony that I
was one myself.

Lastly, I realized I had forgotten to call Rachel to tell her I
was still in town. I called the Phoenix field office of the FBI
but was told by the agent who answered that she was gone.

'What do you mean "gone"? Is she still in Phoenix?'

'I'm not at liberty to say.'

'Can I speak with Agent Backus then?'

'He's gone, too. Who may I ask is calling?'

I hung up and dialed the hotel's front desk and asked for her room. I was told she had checked out. So had Backus. So had Thorson, Carter and Thompson.

'Son of a bitch,' I said after hanging up.

There had been a break. Had to be. For all of them to have checked out, there had to have been a major breakthrough in the investigation. And I realized I had been left behind, that my moment on the inside was surely over now. I got up and paced the room some more, wondering where they would have gone and what could have made them move so quickly. Then I remembered the card Rachel had given me. I dug it out of my pocket and punched the paging number into the phone.

Ten minutes surely seemed enough time to bounce my message off the satellite and then down to her, wherever she was. But ten minutes came and went and the phone didn't ring. Another ten minutes passed and then a half hour. Not even Greg Glenn called. I even picked up the phone to make sure I hadn't broken it.

Restless, but tired of pacing and waiting, I fired up the laptop and logged into the *Rocky* again. I called up my messages but there were none of any importance. I switched to my personal basket, scrolled the files and called up the one labeled HYPSTORIES. The file contained several stories on Horace Gomble, one after the other in chronological order. I began to read from the oldest story forward, my memory of the hypnotist coming back as I went.

It was a colorful history. A physician and researcher for the CIA in the early sixties, Gomble later was a practicing psychiatrist in Beverly Hills who specialized in hypnotherapy. He parlayed his skill and expertise in the hypnotic arts, as he called them, into a nightclub act as Horace the Hypnotist. First it was just appearances on open-mike nights at the clubs in Los Angeles but the act became immensely popular and he started taking it to Las Vegas for weeklong gigs on the strip. Soon Gomble wasn't a practicing shrink anymore. He was a full-time entertainer appearing on the stages of the nicest palaces on the Las Vegas strip. By the mid-seventies his name was on the billing with Sinatra's at Caesar's, albeit in smaller letters. He made four appearances on Carson's show, the last time putting his host in a hypnotic trance and eliciting from him his true thoughts on his other guests that evening. Because of Carson's caustic comments, the studio audience thought it was a gag. But it wasn't. After Carson saw the tape, he canceled the airing of the show and put Horace the Hypnotist on his blacklist. The cancellation made news in the entertainment trade papers and was a knife in the heart of Gomble's career. He never made another network television appearance until his arrest.

His shot at TV gone, Gomble's shtick got old, even in Vegas, and his stages moved further and further away from the strip. Soon he was on the road, working comedy clubs and cabarets, then finally it was the strip club and county fair circuit. His fall from fame was complete. His arrest in Orlando at the Orange County Fair was the exclamation mark at the end of that fall.

According to the trial stories, Gomble was charged with assaulting young girls whom he had chosen as volunteer assistants for matinee performances at the county fair. Prosecutors said he followed a routine of seeking a girl ten to twelve years old from the audience and then taking her backstage to prepare. Once in his private dressing room, he gave the intended victim a Coke laced with codeine and sodium pentothal – a quantity of both was seized during his arrest – and told her he must see if she could be hypnotized before the performance started. With the drugs acting as hypnotic enhancers, the girl was placed in a trance and then assaulted by Gomble. Prosecutors said the molestation primarily involved fellatio and masturbation, actions difficult to prove through physical evidence. Afterward, Gomble repressed memory of the event in the victim's mind with hypnotic suggestion.

It was unknown how many girls were victimized by

Gomble. He was not discovered until a psychologist treating a thirteen-year-old girl with behavioral problems brought out her assault by Gomble during a hypnotherapy session. A police investigation was launched and Gomble was eventually charged with attacks on four girls.

At trial the defense's contention was that the events as described by the victims and police simply did not happen. Gomble presented no fewer than six highly qualified experts in hypnotism who testified that the human mind, while in a hypnotic trance, could not be persuaded or forced under any circumstances to do or even say anything that would endanger the person or be morally repugnant to them. And Gomble's attorney never missed a chance to remind the jury that there was no physical evidence of molestation.

But the prosecution won the case with essentially one witness. He was Gomble's former CIA supervisor, who testified that Gomble's research in the early sixties included experimentation with hypnosis and the use of drug combinations to create a 'hypnotic override' of the brain's moral and safety inhibitions. It was mind control, and the former CIA supervisor said codeine and sodium pentothal were both among the drugs Gomble had used with positive results in his studies.

A jury took two days to convict Gomble of four counts of sexual assault of a child. He was sentenced to eighty-five years in prison to be served at the Union Correctional Institute in Raiford. One of the stories in the file said he had appealed the conviction on the basis of incompetent counsel but his plea was rejected all the way up to the Florida supreme court.

As I reached the bottom of the computer file I noticed the last story was only a few days old. I found this curious because Gomble had been convicted seven years earlier. This story also had come from the *L.A. Times* instead of the *Orlando Sentinel*, which all the previous ones had come from.

Curious, I started reading it and at first believed Laurie Prine had simply made a mistake. It happens often enough. I thought she had shipped me a story unrelated to my request and that somebody else at the *Rocky* had probably asked for.

It was a report on a suspect in the murder of a Hollywood motel maid. I was about to stop reading but then I came across Horace Gomble's name. The story said the suspect in the maid's killing had served time at Raiford with Gomble and even helped him with some undescribed jailhouse legal work. I reread the lines as an idea spun in my mind and then finally couldn't be contained.

Once more I called Rachel's pager after disconnecting the laptop. This time my fingers were shaking as I punched out the number and I could hardly keep still afterward. I paced the room again, staring at the phone. Finally, as if the power of my stare had caused it, the phone rang and I grabbed it up before it had even stopped its first sounding.

'Rachel, I think I've got something.'

'Just hope it isn't syphilis, Jack.'

It was Greg Glenn.

'I thought it was somebody else. Listen, I'm waiting on a call. It's very important and when it comes I should take it.'

'Forget it, Jack. We're pushing the envelope. You ready?'

I looked at my watch. It was ten minutes past the first deadline.

'Okay, I'm ready. The faster the better.'

'Okay, first off, good work, Jack. This ... well, it doesn't make up entirely for not being first, but it's a much better read and much better information.'

'Okay, so what needs to be fixed?' I asked quickly.

I didn't care about his compliment/criticism parlay. I just wanted to be done by the time Rachel answered my page. Because there was only one phone line into the room I couldn't use my laptop to connect with the *Rocky* and view the actual edited version of the story. Instead I called up the original version on the laptop and Glenn read off the changes he had made.

'I want to make the lead a little tighter and stronger, go right out with the fax a little harder. I fiddled around with it and this is what I've got. "A cryptic note from a serial killer who apparently preys on randomly selected children, women and homicide detectives was being analyzed by FBI agents Monday as the latest twist in the investigation of the slayer they have dubbed the Poet." What do you think?'

'Fine.'

He had changed the word 'studied' to 'analyzed.' It wasn't worth protesting. We spent the next ten minutes fine-tuning the main story, going back and forth on nitpicks. He didn't make too many significant changes and with deadline breathing on his neck he didn't have the time to do a lot, anyway. In the end, I thought some of the changes were good and some were made simply for change's sake, a practice all newspaper editors I've worked with seem to share. The second story was a short, first-person account of how my search for understanding of my brother's suicide uncovered the trail of the Poet. It was an understated tooting of the *Rocky*'s horn. Glenn didn't mess with it. When we were done he had me hold on the line while he shipped the stories to the copy desk.

'I think maybe we should keep this line open in case they come up with something on the rim,' Glenn said.

'Who's got it?'

'Brown has the main and Bayer has the side. I'll do the back reading myself.'

I was in good hands. Brown and Bayer were two of the best of the rim rats.

'So, what are you planning for tomorrow?' Glenn asked while we were waiting. 'I know it's early but we also have to talk about the weekend.'

'I haven't thought about that stuff yet.'

'You've got to have a follow, Jack. Something. We don't go out front this big with something and then come back flat-footed the next day. There's gotta be a follow. And for this weekend, I'd like a scene setter. You know, inside the FBI hunt for a serial killer, maybe get into the personalities of the people you've been dealing with. We'll need art, too.'

'I know, I know,' I said. 'I just haven't thought about all of that yet.'

I didn't want to tell him about my latest discovery and the new theory I was brewing. Information like that in an editor's hands was dangerous. The next thing you knew it would be on the daily news budget – practically the same as being written in granite – that I'd have a follow linking the Poet to Horace the Hypnotist. I decided I would wait and talk to Rachel before I told Glenn about that.

'What about the bureau? They going to let you back inside?'

'Good question,' I said. 'I doubt it. I kind of got the sayonara when I left today. In fact, I don't even know where they are. I think they blew town. Something's happening.'

'Shit, Jack. I thought you –'

'Don't worry, Greg, I'll find out where they went. And when I do, I've still got some leverage with them and there are a few things I didn't have room for in the stories today. One way or the other, I'll have something tomorrow. I just don't know what, yet. After that, I'll do the scene setter. But don't count on any art. These people don't like having their pictures taken.'

After a few more minutes Glenn got an all clear from the copy desk and the story was shipped to composing. Glenn said he was going to baby-sit it to production to make sure nothing went wrong. But I was finished for the night. He told me to have a nice dinner on the company expense account and call him in the morning. I told him I would.

As I contemplated whether to page Rachel for a third time, the phone rang.

'Hiya, sport.'

I recognized the sarcasm dripping off the voice.

'Thorson.'

'You got it.'

'What do you want?'

'I'm just letting you know that Agent Walling is tied up and she won't be calling you back any time soon. So do us and yourself a favor and stop calling the pager. It gets annoying.'

'Where is she?'

'That's really none of your business now, is it? You shot your wad, so to speak. You got your story. Now you're on your own.'

'You're in L.A.'

'Message delivered, signing off.'

'Wait! Listen, Thorson, I think I've got something. Let me talk to Backus.'

'No, sir, you aren't talking to anyone on this investigation anymore. You are out, McEvoy. Remember that. All media inquiries on this investigation are now being handled by public affairs at Washington headquarters.'

Anger was balling like a fist inside me. My jaw was clenched tight but I managed to take a shot at him.

'Does that include Michael Warren's inquiries, Thorson? Or does he have a direct line to you?'

'You're wrong about that, fuckhead. I'm no leak. You kind of people make me sick. I've got more respect for some of the scumbags I've put in stir than I have for you.'

'Fuck you, too.'

'See what I mean? You people have no respect whatso –'

'Fuck that, Thorson. Let me talk to Rachel or Backus. I've got a lead they should have.'

'You have something, you give it to me. They're busy.'

It galled me to tell him anything at all but I swallowed back the anger and did what I thought was the right thing.

'I have a name. It could be the guy. William Gladden. He's a pedophile from Florida but he's in L.A. At least he was. He –'

'I know who he is and what he is.'

'You do?'

'Past experience.'

Then I remembered. The prison interviews.

'The rape project? Rachel told me about that. He was one of the subjects?'

'Yes. So forget him, he's not the guy. Thought you were going to be the hero and solve it, didn't you?'

'How do you know he's not the guy? He fits and there's the

possibility he learned hypnotism from Horace Gomble. If you know about Gladden, then you know about Gomble. It all fits. They're looking for Gladden in L.A. He cut up a motel maid. Don't you see? The maid could be the bait murder. The detective – his name is Ed Thomas – could be the intended victim he was talking about in the fax. Let me –'

'You're wrong,' Thorson interrupted loudly. 'We already checked this guy out. You're not the first to come up with him, McEvoy. You're not that special. We checked Gladden out and he's not our guy, okay? We're not stupid. Now drop it and go the fuck back to Denver. When we get the real guy, you'll know.'

'How do you mean you checked Gladden out?'

'I'm not going into it. We're busy and you're no longer inside. You're out and you're staying out. Just don't call the pager anymore. Like I said, it gets annoying.'

He hung up before I could say another word. I slammed the phone into its cradle and it bounced down to the floor. I was tempted to page Rachel again immediately but thought better of it. What could she be doing, I wondered, that would have made her ask Thorson to call me instead of calling me herself? A crushing feeling began to form in my chest and many thoughts went through my mind. Had she merely been baby-sitting me while I was on the case with them? Watching me while I watched them? Had everything just been an act for her?

I broke away from it. There was no way to know the answers until I spoke to her. I had to guard against letting my impressions of Thorson's comments speak for her. Instead, I began to analyze what Thorson had told me. He said Rachel could not call me. She was tied up. What could that mean? Did they have a suspect in custody and she, as lead investigator, was conducting the interrogation? Was the suspect under surveillance? If so, she might be in a car and away from a telephone.

Or by asking Thorson to call me was she sending me a message, communicating something she didn't have the guts to tell me herself?

The nuances of the situation were unreadable to me. I gave up on a deeper meaning and thought about the surface. I thought about Thorson's reaction to my mention of William Gladden. He'd showed no surprise at the name and seemed to easily dismiss it. But in replaying the conversation in my mind, I realized that whether I was right or wrong about Gladden, Thorson would have played it the same way. If I was right, he would have wanted to deflect me. If I was wrong, he would not have missed the opportunity to let me know.

The next thought I focused on was the possibility that I was right about Gladden and that the bureau had somehow made a mistake in dismissing him as a suspect. If this was the case, the detective in Los Angeles could be in danger and not even know it.

It took me two calls to the Los Angeles Police Department to get a number for Detective Thomas at the Hollywood Division. But when I called the number it went unanswered and kicked over to the station's front desk. The officer who answered told me Thomas was unavailable. He would not tell me why or when the detective would be available. I decided not to leave a message.

I paced the room for a few minutes after hanging up and wrestled with thoughts about what to do. I came to the same conclusion from every angle I tried. There was only one way of learning the answers to the questions I had about Gladden and I knew that was to go to Los Angeles. To go to Detective Thomas. I had nothing to lose. My stories were filed and I was off the case. I made some calls and booked the next Southwest flight from Phoenix to Burbank. The airline agent told me Burbank was just as close to Hollywood as L.A. International.

The front-desk clerk was the same man who had checked all of us in on Saturday.

'You're leaving on the fly, too, I see.'

I nodded, realizing he was talking about the FBI agents.

'Yes,' I said. 'They got a head start, though.'

He smiled.

'I saw you on TV the other night.'

At first perplexed, I then realized what he meant. The scene out at the funeral home. Me in the FBI shirt. I knew then that the clerk thought I was an FBI agent. I didn't bother to correct him.

'The boss man wasn't too happy about that,' I said.

'Well, you people must get that a lot when you swoop into town like that. Anyway, I hope you catch him.'

'Yeah, we do, too.'

He went about processing my bill. He asked if I had any room charges and I told him about the room service and the items I had taken from the bar.

'Listen,' I said. 'I guess you also have to charge me for a pillowcase. I had to buy clothes here and didn't have any luggage and . . .'

I held up the pillowcase in which I had packed my few belongings and he chuckled at my predicament. But figuring what to charge me caused confusion and finally he just told me it was on the house.

'I understand you people have to move quickly,' he said. 'The others didn't even have time to check out. Just blew out of town like a Texas tornado, I guess.'

'Well,' I said smiling. 'I hope they at least paid.'

'Oh, yes. Agent Backus called from the airport and said just to keep it on the credit card and send him the receipts. But that's no problem. We aim to please.'

I just looked at him, thinking. Deciding.

'I'm going to be catching up with them tonight,' I finally said. 'You want me to take the receipts?'

He looked up at me from the paperwork in front of him. I could see his hesitation. I held my hand up in a not-to-worry fashion.

'It's all right. It was just a thought. I'll see them tonight and thought it might speed things along. You know, save the postage.'

I didn't know what I was saying but I was already lacking confidence in my decision and wanted to back away.

'Well,' the clerk said, 'I don't really see the harm in it. I've got their paperwork in an envelope ready to go. I guess I can trust you as much as the mailman.'

He smiled and now I smiled back.

'The same guy signs our checks, right?'

'Uncle Sam,' he said brightly. 'Be right back.'

He disappeared into a back office and I looked around the front desk and lobby, halfway expecting Thorson and Backus and Walling to jump out from behind the columns and scream, 'See? We can't trust your kind!'

But nobody jumped out from anywhere and soon the clerk was back with a manila envelope he handed across the counter to me with my own hotel bill.

'Thanks,' I said. 'They'll appreciate it.'

'No problem,' the clerk said. 'Thank you for choosing to stay with us, Agent McEvoy.'

I nodded and shoved the envelope into my computer bag like a thief, then headed to the door.

34
....

The plane was climbing toward thirty thousand feet before I had a chance to open the envelope. There were several pages of bills. One itemized breakdown for each agent's room. This was what I counted on and I immediately was pulled to the bill with Thorson's name on it and began to study the phone charges.

The bill showed no calls to the Maryland area code, 301, where Warren lived. However, there was a call to the 213 area code. Los Angeles. I knew it was not inconceivable that Warren had gone to L.A. to pitch his story to his former editors. He then could have written it from there. The call had been made at 12:41 A.M. Sunday, just an hour or so after Thorson had apparently checked into the hotel in Phoenix.

After using my Visa card to pop the air phone from the seatback in front of me, I slid the credit card through and punched in the number listed on the hotel bill. The call was answered immediately by a woman who said, 'New Otani Hotel, may I help you?'

Momentarily confused, I recovered before she hung up and asked for the room of Michael Warren. I was connected but there was no answer. I realized it was too early for him to be in his room. I depressed the receiver button and called information to get the number of the *Los Angeles Times*. When I called that number I asked for the newsroom and then asked for Warren. I was connected.

'Warren,' I said.

It was a statement, a fact. A verdict. For Thorson as well as Warren.

'Yes, can I help you?'

He didn't know who it was.

'I just wanted to say fuck you, Warren. And to let you know, someday I'm going to write about all this and what you did is going in the book.'

I didn't know exactly what I was saying. I only knew that I felt the need to threaten him and had nothing to do it with. Only words.

'McEvoy? Is this McEvoy?' He paused to inject a sarcastic laugh. 'What book? I've already got my agent on the street with a proposal. What've you got? Huh? What've you got? Hey, Jack, do you even have an agent?'

He waited for an answer and I only had rage. I was silent.

'Yeah, I thought so,' Warren said. 'Look, Jack, you're a nice guy and all, and I'm sorry how this worked out. I really am. But I was in a jam and I just couldn't take that job anymore. This was my ticket out. I took it.'

'You fucking asshole! It was my story.'

I said it too loud. Though I was by myself in a row of three seats, a man across the aisle looked at me angrily. He was seated with an elderly woman who I guessed was his mother and who had never heard such language. I turned away toward the window. There was only blackness out there. I put my hand over my other ear so I could hear Warren's reply above the steady thrum of the plane. His voice was low and steady.

'The story belongs to whoever writes it, Jack. Remember that. Whoever writes it, it's their story. You want to go up against me, that's fine. Then write the fuckin' story instead of calling me up and whining about it. Go ahead, kick my ass. Try it. I'm right here and I'll see you on the front page.'

Everything he had just said was dead right and I knew it the moment he said it. I felt embarrassed that I had even called, and as angry with myself as I was with Warren and Thorson. But I couldn't let it go.

'Well, don't count on getting anything from your source anymore,' I said. 'I'm going to put Thorson in the ground. I got him by the balls. I know he called you late Saturday at the hotel. I got him.'

'I don't know what you're talking about and I don't talk about sources. With anyone.'

'You don't need to. He's mine. Cut and dried. You want to call him after this, you might want to try the bank squad in Salt Lake City. That's where he'll be.'

Using Rachel's reference to a Siberian assignment did not dull the anger much. My jaw was still clenched as I waited for his reply.

'Good night, Jack,' he said finally. 'All I can say is get over it and get a fucking life.'

'Wait a minute, Warren. Answer one question for me.'

There was a pleading whine to my voice that I hated. When he didn't reply I pushed on.

'The page from my notebook that you left in the file room at the foundation, did you leave it on purpose? Was it a setup from the start?'

'That's two questions,' he said and I could hear the smile in his voice. 'I gotta go.'

He hung up.

Ten minutes later, as the plane began to level off, I finally began to smooth out inside, too. Largely with the help of a strong Bloody Mary. The fact that I could now back up my accusation against Thorson with some evidence also served to mollify me. The truth was, I couldn't blame Warren. He had used me, but that's what reporters do. Who knew that better than me?

However, I could blame Thorson and I did. I didn't know how or when I was going to do it but I was going to make sure Thorson's hotel bill and the significance of the phone call came to the attention of Bob Backus. I was going to see Thorson go down.

After I finished the drink, I went back to the bills, which I had stuffed into the seat pocket. With nothing more than idle curiosity at that point, I began with Thorson's and studied the calls he had made before and after the call to Warren.

He had made only three long distance calls during his two-day stay in Phoenix, all of them within a half hour's time. There was the call to Warren at 12:41 A.M., Sunday, a call placed four minutes before to a number with a 703 area code, and a call to a 904 area number at 12:56 A.M. I assumed the 703 number was to the FBI center in Virginia, but because I had nothing else to do, I used the phone again. I keyed in the number and it was answered immediately.

'FBI, Quantico.'

I hung up. I had been right. Next I called the third number, not even knowing where the 904 area code was. After three rings the call was answered with a high-pitched squeal – the language only computers know. I listened until the electronic wail ended. Its mating call unanswered, the computer disconnected me.

Puzzled, I called information for the 904 area and asked the operator what the largest city in the zone was. Jacksonville, I was told. I then asked if the zone included the town of Raiford and was told that it did. I thanked her and hung up.

I knew from the library stories on Horace Gomble that the Union Correctional Institute was located in Raiford. UCI was where Horace Gomble was currently incarcerated and where William Gladden had once been imprisoned. I wondered if Thorson's call to a computer in the 904 area code zone had any connection to the prison or Gladden or Gomble.

One more time I called information for the 904 area. This time I asked for the general number for UCI in Raiford. The exchange prefix I got was 431, the same as the number Thorson had called from his hotel room. I leaned back and brooded about this. Why had he called the prison? Could he have made a direct connection with a prison computer in order to check on Gomble's status there or to look at a file on Gladden? I recalled Backus saying he would have Gomble's status at the prison checked. Possibly, he had given the assignment to Thorson after he picked him up at the airport Saturday night.

I thought of one other possibility for the call. Thorson had told me less than an hour earlier that Gladden had been checked out and dropped as a suspect. Perhaps his call was in some way part of that check. But what part, I couldn't guess. The only thing that seemed clear to me was that I had not been made privy to everything the agents had been doing. I'd been in their midst, but on some things I had simply been kept in the dark.

The other hotel bills provided no surprises. The bills for Carter's and Thompson's rooms were clean. No calls. Backus, according to his bill, had called the same Quantico number at about midnight on both Saturday and Sunday. Curious, I called the number from the plane. It was answered immediately.

'Quantico, Operations Board.'

I hung up without saying anything. I was satisfied that Backus had called Quantico as Thorson had done to return or check messages or take care of other bureau business.

Lastly, I was down to Rachel's bill and an odd feeling of trepidation suddenly came over me. It was a sense I didn't have as I had studied the other bills. This time I felt like a suspicious husband checking on his wife's affairs. There was a voyeuristic thrill to it as well as a sense of guilt.

She'd made four calls from her room. All were to Quantico exchanges and twice she had called the same number as Backus. The Operations Board. I called one of the new numbers she had called and a machine answered the call with her voice.

'This is FBI Special Agent Rachel Walling. I am not available at the moment but if you leave your name and a brief message I will return your call as soon as possible. Thank you.'

She had checked her own office line for messages. I keyed in the last number, which she had called on Sunday evening at 6:10 and a female voice answered.

'Profiling, Doran.'

I disconnected the call without speaking and felt bad about it. I liked Brass, but not enough to possibly tip her off to the fact that I was checking out the calls her fellow agents had made.

Done with the hotel bills, I folded them and put them back in my computer bag, then I snapped the air phone back into its cradle.

35

By the time I pulled up in front of the LAPD's Hollywood Division it was nearly eight-thirty. I didn't know what to expect as I looked at the brick fortress on Wilcox Street. I didn't know whether Thomas would still be there this late, but I hoped that because he was the lead detective working a fresh case – the motel maid killing – that he was still on the clock, preferably behind the bricks working the phones instead of out on the street looking for Gladden.

Inside the front door was a lobby of gray linoleum, two green vinyl couches and the front counter, behind which three uniformed officers sat. There was an entry to a hallway on the left and on the wall above it a sign that said DETEC-TIVE BUREAU above an arrow pointing down the hall. I glanced at the only desk officer not on a phone and nodded as if I was making my nightly visit. I got to about three feet from the hallway when he stopped me.

'Hold on there, partner. Can I help you?'

I turned back to him and pointed up to the sign.

'I need to go to the detective bureau.'

'What for?'

I walked over to the counter so our conversation would not be heard by everyone in the station.

'I want to see Detective Thomas.'

I took out my press identification.

'Denver,' the cop said, in case I had forgotten where I was from. 'Let me see if he's back there. He expecting you?'

'Not that I know of.'

'What's Denver got to do with – yeah, Ed Thomas back there? Got one here from Denver to see him.'

He listened for a few moments, creased his brow at whatever information he was being given and then hung up.

'Okay. Go on down the hall. Second door on the left.'

I thanked him and headed down the hallway. Along both walls were dozens of framed black-and-white publicity shots of entertainers interspersed among photos of police softball teams and officers killed in the line of duty. The door I was told to go to was marked HOMICIDE. I knocked, waited a beat for a reply and then opened the door and stepped in when I didn't get one.

Rachel was sitting behind one of the six desks in the room. The others were empty.

'Hello, Jack.'

I nodded. I wasn't that surprised to see her.

'What are you doing here?'

'That should be obvious, since you've obviously been waiting for me. Where's Thomas?'

'He's safe.'

'Why all the lies?'

'What lies?'

'Thorson said Gladden was not a suspect. He said he was checked out and dropped. That's why I came out. I thought he was either wrong or lying. Why didn't you call me, Rachel? This whole thing –'

'Jack, I was busy with Thomas and I knew if I called anyway, I'd have to lie to you and I didn't want to.'

'So, you just had Thorson do it. Great. Thanks. That makes it better.'

'Stop being a baby. I had more to worry about than your feelings. I'm sorry. Look, I'm here, aren't I? Why do you think that is?'

I hiked my shoulders.

'I knew you'd come no matter what Gordon told you,' she said. 'I know you, Jack. All I had to do was call the airlines. Once I knew your ETA, all I had to do was wait. I only hope that Gladden wasn't out there watching the place. You were on TV with us. That means he probably thinks you are an agent. If he saw you come in here he'll know we're running a setup.'

'But if he was out there and close enough to see me, then you'd have him now, right? Because you've got a twenty-four-hour watch for him on the outside of this place.'

She smiled thinly. I had guessed right.

She picked a two-way radio up off the desk and called her command post. I recognized the voice that came back. It was Backus. She told him she was coming in with a visitor. She then ended the call and stood up.

'Let's go.'

'Where?'

'The command post. Not too far.'

Her voice was curt, clipped. It was cold toward me and I found it hard to believe that I had made love to this woman less than twenty-four hours earlier. It was as if I was a stranger to her now. I kept quiet as we walked through a back hallway of the station and to an employee parking lot in the rear where she had a car waiting.

'I've got a car out front,' I said.

'Well, you'll have to leave it for now. Unless you want to stay on your own and keep doing the cowboy shit.'

'Look, Rachel, if I hadn't been lied to this might not have happened. I might not even have come.'

'Sure.'

She got in and started the car and then unlocked my door. It always annoyed me when people did that to me but I didn't say anything when I got in. She headed out of the lot and up toward Sunset Boulevard with a heavy foot on the gas. She didn't speak until a red light forced her to stop the car.

'How did you know that name, Jack?' she asked.

'What name?' I replied, though I knew.

'Gladden, Jack. William Gladden.'

'I did my homework. How did you people come up with it?'

'I can't tell you.'

'Rachel, . . . Look, this is me, okay? We made, uh . . .' I couldn't say it out loud for fear it would sound like a lie. 'I thought there was something between us, Rachel. Now you're acting like I'm some kind of leper or something. I don't . . .

Look, is it information you want? I'll tell you all I know. I figured it out from the newspapers. Big story on this guy Gladden in the *L.A. Times* on Saturday. Okay? The story said he knew Horace the Hypnotist in Raiford. I just put two and two together. It wasn't hard.'

'Okay, Jack.'

'Now you.'

Silence.

'Rachel?'

'Are we off the record?'

'You know you don't have to ask me that.'

She hesitated a moment and then seemed to relent. She began.

'We arrived at Gladden through two separate leads that just happened to click at the same time. That gives us a high sense of reliability that he's our man. First, the car. Automotive ID traced the stereo serial number to a car which, in turn, was traced to Hertz. You remember this?'

'Yes.'

'Well, Matuzak and Mize went down to the airport and traced the car. Some snowbirds from Chicago had already rerented it. They had to go up to Sedona to get it back. It's been processed. Nothing usable from it. The stereo and window had been replaced. But not by Hertz. Hertz never knew about the break-in. Whoever had the car when the break-in occurred replaced the window and the stereo on their own. Anyway, the rental records put the car in the hands of an N. H. Breedlove for five days this month, including the day Orsulak was killed. This Breedlove turned it in the day after. Matuzak put the name on the computer and got a hit on the ID net. Nathan H. Breedlove was an AKA turned up during the investigation of William Gladden in Florida seven years ago. It was a name used by a man who had placed ads in the papers in Tampa offering his services as a children's photographer. He molested the kids when left alone with them, took dirty pictures. He wore disguises. The Tampa police were looking for this Breedlove at the same time the Gladden case broke. The molestations at the child care center. The investigators always believed Gladden was Breedlove but they never made a case because of the disguises. Besides, they didn't press it because they thought he'd be going away to prison for a long time on the other case.

'Anyway, once we had Gladden's name from the ID net's alias data bank, from there we picked up the wanted that LAPD put out on NCIC last week. And here we are.'

'It seems . . .'

'Too easy? Well, sometimes you make your own luck.'

'You said that before.'

'Because it's true.'

'Why would he use an alias that he must've known was on file somewhere?'

'A lot of these people find comfort in tradition. Plus, he's a cocky son of a bitch. We know that from the fax.'

'But he used a whole new alias when he was arrested by Santa Monica police last week. Why would he –'

'I'm only telling you what we know, Jack. If he's as smart as we think he is, then he probably has several ID packages. They wouldn't be hard to come by. We have the Phoenix field office working on a subpoena for Hertz. We want Breedlove's complete renting history going back three years. He's a Hertz Gold customer no less. Again it shows how smart he is. Most airports, you get off the plane, walk to the Gold lot and your name is on the board. You go to your car and the keys are in it. Most of the time you don't even have to talk to any clerks. You just get in your car, show your license at the gate and you are out of there.'

'Okay, what about the other thing? You said there were two leads to Gladden.'

'The Best Pals. Ted Vincent and Steve Raffa in Florida finally got hold of Beltran's records with the organization this morning. He'd been Best Pal to nine young boys over the years. The second one he sponsored, this is going back something like sixteen years, was Gladden.'

'Jesus.'

'Yeah. It's all starting to fall together.'

I was silent for a few moments as I considered all of the

information she had revealed. The investigation was advancing at exponentially increasing speed. It was seat-belt time.

'How come the field office out here didn't pick up on this guy? He's been in the paper.'

'Good question. Bob's going to have a heart-to-heart with the SAC about that. Gordon's flag landed last night. Somebody should've seen it and put two and two together. But we did it ourselves first.'

A typical bureaucratic snafu. I wondered how much sooner they'd have been on to Gladden if someone in the L.A. office had been a little more alert.

'You know Gladden, don't you?' I said.

'Yes. We had him during the rapist interviews. I told you about that. Seven years ago. He and Gomble, among others at that hellhole in Florida. I think our team – Gordon, Bob, me – spent a week down there, we had so many candidates for interviews.'

I was tempted to bring up Thorson's call to the prison's computer but thought better of it. It was enough just to get her to talk to me again like a human. Telling her I had rifled through the hotel bills was no way to ensure that she would continue. This dilemma also created a problem in regard to nailing Thorson. For the time being I would have to sit on his hotel phone records as well.

'You think there is any connection between Gomble supposedly using hypnotism and what you are seeing on the Poet cases?' I said instead. 'Think maybe Gomble taught him his secret?'

'Possibly.'

She had regressed to the one-word reply.

'Possibly,' I repeated, a thin line of sarcasm in it.

'Eventually, I'll go to Florida to talk to Gomble again. And I'm going to ask him that. Until I get an answer one way or the other, it's possibly. Okay, Jack?'

We pulled into an alley that ran behind a row of old motels and shops. She finally slowed down to the point where I let go of the armrest.

'But you can't go to Florida now, can you?' I asked.

'That's up to Bob. But we're close to Gladden here. For the time being I think Bob wants to put everything we have into L.A. Gladden's here. Or he's close. We can all feel it. We've got to get him. Once we have him, then I'll worry about the other things, the psychological motivation. We'll need to go to Florida then.'

'Why then? To add data to the serial killer studies?'

'No. I mean, yes, there's that, but primarily we'll go for the prosecution. Guy like this, he's got to go the insanity route. It's his only choice. So that means we'll have to build a case on his psychology. One that shows he knew what he was doing and he knew right from wrong. The same old thing.'

Prosecution of the Poet in a courtroom had never entered my mind. I realized that I had assumed that he would not be taken alive. And this assumption, I knew, was based on my own desire that he not be allowed to live after this.

'What's the matter, Jack, you don't want a trial? You want us to kill him where we find him?'

I looked over at her. The lights from a passing window flicked across her face and for a moment I saw her eyes.

'I hadn't thought about it.'

'Sure you have. Would you like to kill him, Jack? If you had a moment with him and there were no consequences, could you do it? Do you think that would make up for things?'

I didn't like discussing this subject with her. I sensed more than just a passing interest from her.

'I don't know,' I finally answered. 'Could you kill him? Have you ever killed anyone, Rachel?'

'Given the chance, I'd kill him in a heartbeat.'

'Why?'

'Because I've known the others. I've looked in their eyes and know what's back there in the darkness. If I could kill them all I think I would.'

I waited for her to continue but she didn't. She pulled the car to a stop next to two other matching Caprices behind one of the old motels.

'You didn't answer the second question.'

'No, I've never killed anyone.'

We went in through a back door into a hallway painted in two tones; dingy lime to about eye level, dingy white the rest of the way up. Rachel went to the first door on the left and knocked and we were let in. It was a motel room, one that would have passed as a kitchenette in the sixties, when it was last refurbished. Backus and Thorson were there waiting, sitting at an old Formica table against the wall. There were two phones on the table that looked as if they had just been added to the room. There was also a three-foot-high aluminum trunk standing on one end with its lid open to reveal a bank of three video monitors. Wires ran out the back of the trunk, along the floor and out the window, which was opened just enough to allow them through.

'Jack, I can't say I'm happy to see you,' Backus said.

But he said it with a wry smile on his face and he stood up and shook my hand.

'Sorry,' I said, not really knowing why. Then, looking at Thorson, I added, 'I didn't mean to blunder into your setup but I was given some bad information.'

The thought of the phone records went through my mind again but I dismissed it. It was not the right time.

'Well,' Backus said, 'I have to admit we were trying a little misdirection there. We just thought it would be best if we could work this out without any distractions.'

'I'll try not to be a distraction.'

'You already are,' Thorson said.

I ignored him and kept my eyes on Backus.

'Have a seat,' he said.

Rachel and I took the two remaining chairs at the table.

'I assume you know what is happening,' Backus said.

'I assume you're watching Thomas.'

I turned so I could see the video monitors and for the first time studied the view each one had. The top monitor showed a hallway not unlike the one outside the room we were in. Several doors going down both sides. All of them closed and with numbers on them. The next tube showed the exterior of a motel front. In the blue-gray haze of the video I could just make out the words on the sign above the door. HOTEL MARK TWAIN. The bottom monitor showed an alley-side view of what I assumed was the same hotel.

'Is this where we are?' I asked, pointing at the display.

'No,' Backus said. 'That is where Detective Thomas is. We're about a block away.'

'Doesn't look very nice. What are they paying these days in this town?'

'It is not his home. But the detectives at Hollywood Station often use the hotel to stash witnesses or sleep over if they're working twenty-hour days on a case. Detective Thomas chose to stay there rather than at home. He has a wife and three children at home.'

'Well, that answers my next question. I'm glad you told him he was being used as bait.'

'You seem measurably more cynical than when we last met this morning, Jack.'

'I guess that's because I am.'

I looked away from him and checked out the video setup again. Backus spoke to my back.

'We have three-point camera surveillance beamed to a mobile dish on our roof here. We also have the field office's critical response unit and LAPD's top surveillance squad watching Thomas around the clock. No one can get near him. Even at the station. He's perfectly safe.'

'Wait until it's over and then tell me that.'

'I will. But in the meantime, you have to step aside, Jack.'

I turned back to him, my best puzzled look on my face.

'You understand what I'm telling you,' Backus said, not buying the face. 'We are at the most critical stage. He is in our sights and, frankly, Jack, you have to get out of the way.'

'I am out of the way and I'll stay out of the way. The same deal, nothing I see goes into the paper until you okay it. But I'm not going back to Denver to wait. I'm too close, too ... This means too much. You've got to let me back inside.'

'This could take weeks. Remember the fax. All it said was that he had his next man in sight. It didn't say when it would happen. There was no time frame. We have no idea when he'll try to hit Thomas.'

I shook my head.

'I don't care. Whatever it takes, I want to be part of the investigation. I've kept up my end of the deal.'

An uneasy silence settled over the room, during which Backus stood up and began pacing on the carpet behind my chair. I looked over at Rachel. She was looking down at the table in a contemplative way. I threw my last chip into the pile.

'I have to write a story tomorrow, Bob. My editor's expecting it. If you don't want it written, bring me in. That's the only way I can convince him to back off. That's the bottom line.'

Thorson made a derisive sound and shook his head.

'This is trouble,' he said. 'Bob, you give in to this guy again and where does it end?'

'The only time there's been trouble,' I said, 'is when I've been lied to or kept out of the investigation, which, by the way, I started.'

Backus looked over at Rachel.

'What do you think?'

'Don't ask her,' Thorson interjected. 'I can tell you right now what she's going to say.'

'If you have something to say about me, say it,' Rachel demanded.

'All right, enough,' Backus said, holding his hands out like a referee. 'You two don't quit, do you? Jack, you're in. For the time being. Same deal as before. That means no story tomorrow. Understood?'

I nodded. I looked over at Thorson, who had already stood up and was heading out the door, defeated.

36

....

The Wilcox Hotel, as I learned it was called, had room for one more – especially when the night clerk learned I was with the government people already staying there and was willing to pay the top price, thirty-five dollars a night. It was the only hotel I'd ever checked into where I felt a nervous sense of foreboding about giving the man behind the front counter my credit card number. This one looked like he was halfway through a bottle on this shift alone. It also appeared as though he had decided on the last four successive mornings that he wasn't quite ready for a shave yet. He never looked at me during the entire check-in process – which took an unusually long five minutes as he hunted for a pen and then accepted a loan of one from me.

'What're you people doin', anyway?' he said as he slid a key with the stamped room number almost worn off it across the equally worn Formica counter.

'They didn't tell you?' I asked, feigning surprise.

'Nope. I'm just checkin' people in is all.'

'It's a credit card fraud investigation. A lot of it going on around here.'

'Oh.'

'By the way, which room is Agent Walling in?'

It took him a half minute to interpret his own records.

'That'd be seventeen.'

My room was small and when I sat on the edge of the bed it sank at least a half foot, the other side rising by an equal amount with the accompanying protest of old springs. It was a ground-floor room with spare but neat furnishings and the stale smell of cigarettes. The yellowed blinds were up and I could see a metal grate over the one window. If there was a fire, I'd be trapped like a lobster in a cage if I didn't get out the door fast enough.

I took the travel-size toothpaste tube and folding toothbrush I had bought out of the pillowcase and went into the bathroom. I could still taste the Bloody Mary from the plane and wanted to get rid of it. I also wanted to be ready for all eventualities with Rachel.

The bathrooms in old hotel rooms are always the most depressing. This one was slightly larger than the phone booths I used to see at every gas station when I was growing up. Sink, toilet and portable shower stall all complete with matching rust stains were set in a crowded configuration. If you were ever sitting on the toilet when somebody came in, you'd lose your kneecaps. When I was finished and had returned to the comparative spaciousness of the room, I looked at the bed and knew I didn't want to sit back down there. I didn't even want to sleep there. I decided to risk leaving the computer and my pillowcase full of clothes and left the room.

My light knock on the door of room seventeen was answered so quickly I thought Rachel had been waiting on the other side. She quickly ushered me in.

'Bob's room is across the hall,' she whispered by way of explanation. 'What is it?'

I didn't answer. We looked at each other for a long moment, each waiting for the other to act. I finally did, stepping close to her and pulling her into a long kiss. She seemed as into it as I was and this quickly calmed many of the worries I had allowed to simmer in my brain. She broke the kiss off and strongly pulled me into an embrace. Over her shoulder I surveyed her room. It was bigger than mine and the furniture was maybe a decade newer but it wasn't any less depressing. Her computer was on the bed and there were some papers spread over the worn yellow spread where a thousand people had lain and fucked and farted and fought.

'Funny,' she whispered, 'I just left you this morning and I found myself already missing you.'

'Same here.'

'Jack, I'm sorry, but I don't want to make love on that bed, in this room or in this hotel.'

'That's okay,' I said nobly, though I regretted the words as I spoke them. 'I understand. Looks like you got a luxury suite compared to mine.'

'We'll have to wait but then we'll make up for it.'

'Yeah. Why are we staying here, anyway?'

'Bob wants to be close. So we can move if they spot him.'

I nodded.

'Well, can we leave for a little while? Want to get a drink? There's got to be someplace around.'

'Probably no better than this. Let's just stay and talk.'

She went to the bed and cleared the papers and the computer, then sat back against the headboard, propped on a pillow. I sat in the room's one chair, its cushion scarred by an ancient knife slash repaired with tape.

'What do you want to talk about, Rachel?'

'I don't know. You're the reporter. I thought you'd ask the questions.'

She smiled.

'About the case?'

'About anything.'

I looked at her for a long moment. I decided to start with something simple and then see how far I could go from there.

'What's this Thomas guy like?'

'He's fine. For a local. Not overly cooperative, but not an asshole.'

'What do you mean not overly cooperative? He's letting you use him as human bait, isn't that enough?'

'I guess. Maybe it's me. I never seem to get along with the locals.'

I moved from the chair onto the bed with her.

'So what? It's not your job to get along with anybody.'

'That's right,' she said, smiling again. 'You know, there's a soda machine in the lobby.'

'You want something?'

'No, but you said something about getting a drink.'

'I was thinking of something stronger. It's all right, though. I'm happy.'

She reached over and did her finger drag through my beard. I caught her hand as she dropped it away and held it for a moment.

'Do you think the intensity of what we're doing and what we're involved with is causing this?' I asked.

'As opposed to what?'

'I don't know. I'm just asking.'

'I know what you're saying,' she said after a long moment. 'I have to admit I've never made love with anybody thirty-six hours after the first time I'd ever seen him in my life.'

She smiled and it sent a beautiful thrill through me.

'Me neither.'

She leaned toward me and we kissed again. I turned and we rolled into a from-here-to-eternity kiss. Only our beach was the old bedspread in a ratty old hotel room three decades past its prime. But all of that didn't matter anymore. Soon I was moving my kisses down her neck and then we made love.

We couldn't both fit in the bathroom or the shower so she went first. As she showered I lay in bed thinking about her and wishing for a smoke.

It was hard to tell because of the sound of the shower but at one point I thought I heard a light knock on the door. Alerted, I sat up on the edge of the bed and started pulling on my pants as I stared at the door. I listened but heard nothing again. Then, I distinctly saw the doorknob move, or thought I did. I got up and moved to the door, pulling up my pants, and tilted my head to the jamb to listen. I heard nothing. There was a peephole but I was reluctant to look through it. The light was on in the room and if I looked through the peephole I would block it, possibly letting whoever was out there know that someone was looking at him.

Rachel cut the shower off at that point. After a few

moments of no noticeable sound from the hallway I moved to the peephole and looked. There was nothing out there.

'What are you doing?'

I turned. Rachel stood by the bed, attempting to show modesty with the tiny towel that came with the room.

'I thought I heard someone knock.'

'Who was it?'

'I don't know. There was no one there when I looked. Maybe it was nothing. All right if I take a shower?'

'Sure.'

I stepped out of my pants and while walking past her stopped. She dropped her towel, exposing her body. She was beautiful to me. I stepped over and we held each other for a long moment.

'Be right back,' I finally said and then headed into the shower.

Rachel was dressed and waiting when I came out. I looked at my watch, which I had left on the bed table, and saw it was eleven. There was a battered old television in the room but I decided not to suggest watching the news. I realized I hadn't eaten dinner but still wasn't hungry.

'I'm not tired,' she said.

'Neither am I.'

'Maybe we could find a place for a drink after all.'

After I dressed, we quietly left the room. She looked out first to make sure Backus or Thorson or anybody else wasn't lurking about. We encountered no one in the hallway or the lobby and outside the street seemed deserted and dark. We walked south to Sunset.

'You got your gun?' I asked, half kidding and half serious.

'Always. Besides, we've got our people around. They probably saw us leave.'

'Really? I thought they were just keeping an eye on Thomas.'

'They are. But they should have a good idea who is on the street at any given time. If they're doing their job.'

I turned and walked backward for a few steps, staring back up the street at the green neon sign for the Mark Twain. I surveyed the street, the cars parked along both sides. Again, I saw no shadows or silhouettes of the watchers.

'How many are out there?'

'Should be five. Two on foot in fixed positions. Two in cars, stationary. One car roving. All the time.'

I turned back around and pulled the collar of my jacket up. It was colder outside than I had expected. Our breath came out in thin clouds, mingled together and then disappeared.

When we got to Sunset I looked both ways and saw a neon sign over an archway a block to the west that said CAT & FIDDLE BAR. I pointed that way and Rachel started walking. We were silent until we got there.

Going through the archway we entered an outdoor garden with several tables below green canvas umbrellas but they were all empty. Past these and through the windows on the other side we could see what looked like a lively and warm bar. We went in, found an empty booth on the opposite side from the dartboards and sat down. It was an English-style pub. When the barmaid came around Rachel told me to go first and I ordered a black and tan. Rachel then did the same.

We looked around the place and small-talked until our drinks arrived. We clinked glasses and drank. I watched her. I didn't think she'd ever had a black and tan before.

'The Harp is heavier. It always stays at the bottom, the Guinness on top.'

She smiled.

'When you said black and tan, I thought that was a brand that you knew. But it's good. I like it but it's strong.'

'One thing the Irish know is how to make a beer. The English have to give them that.'

'Two of these and you'll have to call for backup to get me back.'

'I doubt it.'

We lapsed into a comfortable silence. There was a fireplace in the rear wall and the warmth from its fully engulfed fire extended across the room.

'Is your real name John?'

I nodded.

'I'm not Irish but I always thought Sean was Irish for John.'

'Yes, it's the Gaelic version. Since we were twins my parents decided . . . actually my mother.'

'I think it's nice.'

After a few more drinks from my glass I started asking questions about the case.

'So, tell me about Gladden.'

'There isn't a whole lot to tell yet.'

'Well, you met him. Interviewed him. You must have a feel for him.'

'He wasn't exactly cooperative. His appeal was still pending and he didn't trust us not to use what he said to disrupt that. We all took turns trying to get him to open up. Finally, I think it was Bob's idea, he agreed to talk to us in the third person. As if the perpetrator of the crimes he was convicted of was somebody else.'

'Bundy did that, too, right?'

I remembered that from a book I had read.

'Yes. And others as well. It was just a device to assure them that we were not there to make cases against them. Most of these men have tremendous egos. They wanted to talk to us but they had to be convinced they were safe from legal reprisals. Gladden was like that. Especially since he knew he had a valid appeal still pending.'

'It must be a rare thing that you have a prior relationship, no matter how small, with an active serial killer.'

'Yes. But I have a feeling that if any one of the people we interviewed was set loose like William Gladden, we'd end up hunting for them as well. These people don't get better, Jack, and they don't get rehabbed. They are what they are.'

She said it like a warning, the second such intimation she had made. I thought about it a few moments, wondering if there was more she was trying to tell me. Or, I thought, was she really warning herself?

'So what did he say? Did he tell you about Beltran or Best Pals?'

'Of course not, or I would have remembered when I saw Beltran's name on the victim list. Gladden didn't mention names. But he did give the usual abuse excuse. Said that he was assaulted sexually as a child. Repeatedly. He was at the same age as the children he later victimized in Tampa. You see, that's the cycle. It's a pattern we often see. They become fixated on themselves at the point in their own lives when they were ... ruined.'

I nodded but didn't say anything, hoping she would continue.

'For a three-year period,' she said, 'from ages nine to twelve. The episodes were frequent and included oral and anal penetration. He didn't tell us who the abuser was other than to say it was a nonrelative. According to Gladden, he never told his mother because he feared this man. The man threatened him. He was a figure of some authority in his life. Bob made some follow-up calls about it but never got anywhere with it. Gladden wasn't specific enough for him to track it. Gladden was in his twenties by then and the period of abuse had been years earlier. There would've been statute-of-limitations problems even if we had pursued it. We couldn't even find his mother to ask her about it. She left Tampa after his arrest and all the publicity. We, of course, can now surmise that the abuser was Beltran.'

I nodded. I had finished my beer but Rachel was nursing hers. She didn't like it. I signaled the barmaid and ordered an Amstel Light for her. I said I'd finish her black and tan.

'So how did it end? The abuse, I mean.'

'That's the irony you so often see. It ended when he became too old for Beltran. Beltran rejected him and went on to his next victim. All the boys he sponsored through Best Pals are being located and will be interviewed. I'll bet they all were abused by him. He's the evil seed to all of this, Jack. Make sure you get that across in whatever you write about this. Beltran got what he deserved.'

'You sound like you sympathize with Gladden.'

Wrong thing to say. I saw the anger flare in her eyes.

'You are damn right I sympathize. It doesn't mean I condone a single thing he's done or that I wouldn't drop him with a bullet if I got the chance. But he didn't invent the monster that is inside of him. It was created by someone else.'

'Okay, I wasn't trying to suggest –'

The barmaid came with Rachel's beer and saved me from walking down the wrong path any further. I pulled Rachel's black and tan across the table and took a long drink, hoping we were past my misstep.

'So, aside from what he told you,' I asked, 'what was your take on Gladden? Did he seem to have the smarts that everyone around here is attributing to him?'

She seemed to compose her thoughts before answering.

'William Gladden knew his sexual appetite was legally, socially and culturally unacceptable. He was clearly burdened by this, I think. I believe he was at war within himself, attempting to understand his urges and desires. He wanted to tell us his story, whether it was third person or not, and I think he believed that by telling us about himself he would in some way help himself as well as maybe somebody else down the road. If you look at these dilemmas he had, I think it shows a highly intellectual being. I mean, most of these people I interviewed were like animals. Machines. They did what they did ... almost by instinct or programming, as if they had to. And they did it without much thought. Gladden was different. So, yes, I think he is as smart as we are saying he is, maybe smarter.'

'It's strange what you just said. You know, that he was burdened. Doesn't sound like the guy we're chasing now. The one we're chasing seems to have about as much of a conscience about what he is doing as Hitler had.'

'You're right. But we've seen ample evidence of these types of predators changing, evolving. Without treatment, whether it was drug therapy or not, it is not without precedent that someone with William Gladden's background could evolve into someone like the Poet. Bottom line is, people change.

After the interviews he was in prison another long year before winning his appeal and copping the deal that got him out. Pedophiles are treated the most harshly in prison society. Because of that they tend to band together in knots – just as in free society. That's why you have Gladden being the acquaintance of Gomble as well as other pedophiles in Raiford. I guess what I am saying is that I am not surprised that the man I interviewed so many years ago became the man we call the Poet today. I can see it happening.'

A loud burst of laughter and applause broke out near one of the dartboards and distracted me. It looked like the night's champion had been crowned.

'Enough about Gladden for now,' Rachel said when I looked back at her. 'It's depressing as hell.'

'Okay.'

'What about you?'

'I'm depressed, too.'

'No. I mean, what about *you*. You talk to your editor yet, tell him you're back inside?'

'No, not yet. I'll have to call in the morning and tell him there's no follow coming from me, but that I'm back inside.'

'How will he take that?'

'Not well. He'll want a follow anyway. The story's moving like a locomotive now. The national media's on it and you've got to keep throwing stories into the fire to make the big train move. But what the hell. He's got other reporters. He can put one of them on it and see what they get. Which won't be much. Then Michael Warren will probably crack another exclusive in the *L.A. Times* and I'll really be in the doghouse.'

'You are a cynical man.'

'I'm a realist.'

'Don't worry about Warren. Gor – whoever leaked to him before isn't going to do it again. It would be risking too much with Bob.'

'Freudian slip there, right? Anyway, we'll see.'

'How did you get so cynical, Jack? I thought only those rundown middle-aged cops were like that.'

'I was born with it, I guess.'
'I bet.'

It seemed even colder on the walk back. I wanted to put my arm around her but I knew she wouldn't allow it. There were eyes on the street and I didn't try. As we got close to the hotel I remembered a story and told her.

'You know how when you're in high school and there's always this grapevine that passes information on about who likes whom and who's got a crush on whom? Remember?'

'Yes, I remember.'

'Well, there was this girl and I had a thing, a crush on her. And I was ... I can't remember how but the word went out on the grapevine, you know? And when that happened what you usually did was wait and see how the person responded. It was one of those things where I knew that she knew that I had this desire for her and she knew I knew she knew. Understand?'

'Yes.'

'But the thing was I had no confidence and I was ... I don't know. One day I was in the gym, sitting in the bleachers. I think I was in there early for a basketball game or something and it was filling up with people. Then she comes in, she's with a friend, and they're walking along the bleachers looking for a place to sit. It was one of those do-or-die moments and she looks right at me and waves ... And I froze. And ... then ... I turned and looked behind me to see if she was waving to somebody else.'

'Jack, you fool!' Rachel said, smiling and not taking the story to heart as I had done for so long. 'What did she do?'

'When I turned back around she had looked away, embarrassed. See, I had embarrassed her by setting the whole thing into motion and then turning away ... snubbing her ... She started going out with somebody else after that. Ended up marrying him. It took me a long time to get over her.'

We took the last steps to the hotel door silently. I opened the door for Rachel and looked at her with a pained, embarrassed smile. The story could still do that to me all these years later.

'So that's the story,' I said. 'It proves I've been a cynical fool all along.'

'Everybody has stories from growing up like that,' she said in a voice that seemed to dismiss the whole thing.

We crossed the lobby and the night man looked up and nodded. It seemed as if his whiskers had grown even longer in the few hours since I had first seen him. At the stairs Rachel stopped and in a whispered voice designed to leave the night man out of earshot told me not to come up.

'I think we should go to our own rooms.'

'I can still walk you up.'

'No, that's okay.'

She looked back at the front desk. The night man had his head down and was reading a gossip tabloid. Rachel turned back to me, gave me a silent kiss on the cheek and whispered good night. I watched her go up the stairs.

I knew I wouldn't be able to sleep. Too many thoughts. I had made love to a beautiful woman and spent the evening falling in love with her. I wasn't sure what love was but I knew acceptance was part of it. That's what I sensed from Rachel. It was a quality that had been a rarity in my life and I found its nearness thrilling and disquieting in the same instant.

As I stepped out to the front of the hotel to smoke a cigarette the feeling of disquiet grew and then infected my mind with other thoughts. The ghost story intruded and my embarrassment and thoughts of what might have been still grabbed me so many years after that day on the bleachers. I marveled at the hold of some memories and at how well and precisely they can be relived. I hadn't told Rachel everything about the high school girl. I hadn't told her the ending, that the girl was Riley and that the boy she went out with and then married was my brother. I didn't know why I had left that part out.

I was out of cigarettes. I stepped back into the lobby to ask the night man where I could get a pack. He told me to go back to the Cat & Fiddle. I saw he had an open pack of Camels on the counter next to his stack of tabloids but he didn't offer me any and I didn't ask for one.

As I walked Sunset alone I thought about Rachel again and became preoccupied with something I had noticed during our lovemaking. Each of the three times we had been together in bed she had been fully giving of herself, yet I would say she was decidedly passive. She deferred control to me. I waited for the small nuances of change on the second and third times we made love, even hesitating in my own movements and choices in order to allow her to take the lead, but she never did. Even at the sacred moment when I entered her, it was my hand fumbling at the door. Three times. No woman that I had been with before on that number of occasions had done the same.

There was nothing wrong with this and it did not bother me in the least, but still I found it to be a curiosity. For her passivity in these horizontal moments was diametrically opposed to her demeanor in our vertical moments. When we were away from the bed she certainly exercised or sought to exercise her control. It was the sort of subtle contradiction that I believed made her so enthralling to me.

As I stopped to cross Sunset to the bar, my peripheral vision picked up movement to the far left as I glanced back to check traffic. My eyes followed the movement and I saw the form of a person ducking back into the shadowed doorway of a closed shop. A chill raced through me but I didn't move. I watched the spot where I had seen the movement for several seconds. The doorway was maybe twenty yards from me. I felt sure it had been a man and he was probably still there, possibly watching me from the darkness while I watched for him.

I took four quick, determined steps toward the doorway but then stopped dead. It had been a bluff but when no one ran from the doorway, I had only bluffed myself. I felt my heartbeat rising. I knew it might only be a homeless man looking for a spot to sleep. I knew there might be a hundred explanations. But just the same I was scared. Maybe it was a transient. Maybe it was the Poet. In a split second a myriad of possibilities took over my mind. I was on TV. The Poet saw TV. The Poet had made his choice. The dark doorway was on the path between me and the Wilcox Hotel. I could not go back. I quickly turned and stepped into the street to cross to the bar.

The blast of a car horn greeted me and I jumped back. I had not been in any danger. The car that sped past trailing the laughter of teenagers was two lanes away but maybe they had seen my face, seen the look, and known I was easy prey for a scare.

I ordered another black and tan at the bar along with a basket of chicken wings, and got directions to the cigarette machine. I noticed the unsteadiness of my hands as I lit the match after finally getting a cigarette into my mouth. Now what, I thought as I exhaled the stream of blue smoke toward my reflection in the mirror behind the bar.

I stayed until last call at two and then left the Cat & Fiddle with the exodus of die-hards. There was safety in numbers, I had decided. By loitering behind the crowd, I was able to identify a group of three drunks walking east toward Wilcox and fell in a few yards behind them. We passed the doorway in question from the other side of Sunset and as I looked across the four lanes I could not tell if the darkened alcove was empty. But I didn't linger. At Wilcox I broke away from my escort and trotted across Sunset and up to the hotel. I didn't breathe normally until I entered the lobby and saw the familiar, safe face of the night man.

Despite the lateness of the hour and the heavy beer I had filled myself with, the scare I had submitted myself to robbed me of any fatigue. I could not sleep. In my room I undressed, got into bed and turned off the light but I knew as I was doing it that it was fruitless. After ten minutes I faced the facts of my situation and turned on the light.

I needed a distraction. A trick that would allow my mind to rest easily and for me to sleep. I did what I had done on countless prior occasions of similar necessity. I pulled my computer up onto the bed. I booted it, plugged the room's phone line into the modem outlet and dialed long distance into the *Rocky*'s net. I had no messages and wasn't really expecting any but the motions of doing it began to calm me. I scrolled the wires a little bit and came across my own story, in abbreviated form, on the AP national wire. It would hit the ground tomorrow and burst like a shell. Editors from New York to here in L.A. would know my byline. I hoped.

After signing off and shutting down the connection, I played a few hands of computer solitaire but became bored with losing. Looking for something else to distract me, I reached into the computer bag for the hotel receipts from Phoenix but couldn't find them. I checked every pocket of the bag but the folded sheaf of papers wasn't there. I quickly grabbed the pillowcase and frisked it like a suspect but there were only clothes.

'Shit,' I said out loud.

I closed my eyes and tried to envision what I had done with the pages on the plane. A sense of dread came over me as I remembered at one point stuffing them into the seat pocket. But then I recalled that, after talking to Warren, I had retrieved them to make the other calls. I conjured a vision of putting the pages back into the computer bag as the plane was on final approach. I was sure I had not left them on the plane.

The alternative to this, I knew, was that someone had been in my room and taken them. I paced around a little bit, not sure what I could do. I had had what could be construed as stolen property stolen from me. Who could I complain to?

Angrily, I opened the door and walked down the hallway to the front desk. The night man was looking at a magazine called *High Society* which had a cover photo of a nude woman skillfully using her arms and hands to strategically cover enough of her body to allow the magazine to be sold on the newsstand.

'Hey, did you see anybody go down to my room?'

He hiked his shoulders and shook his head.

'Nobody?'

'On'y ones I seen around was that lady that was with you, and you. Tha's it.'

I looked at him for a moment, waiting for more, but he had said his piece.

'Okay.'

I went back to my room, studying the keyhole for signs of a pick before going inside. I couldn't tell. The keyhole was worn and scratched but it could have been that way for years. I wouldn't know how to identify a picked lock if my life depended on it but I looked anyway. I was mad.

I was tempted to call Rachel and tell her about the burglary of my room but my dilemma was that I couldn't tell her about what had been taken in the burglary. I didn't want her to know what I had done. The memory of that day on the bleachers and other lessons learned since went through my mind. I got undressed and got back into bed.

Sleep eventually came but not before I had visions of Thorson in my room going through my things. When it finally came, the anger had not left me.

37

········

I was awakened by a sharp banging on my door. I opened my eyes and saw light bleeding brightly around the curtains. The sun was already well up and I realized I should have been also. I pulled on my pants and was still buttoning a shirt as I opened the door without looking through the peephole. It wasn't Rachel.

''Morning, sport. Rise and shine. You're with me today and we've got to get going.'

I stared blankly at him. Thorson reached over and knocked on the open door.

'Hello? Anyone home?'

'What do you mean I'm with you?'

'Just like it sounds. Your girlfriend has some things she has to do alone. Agent Backus has assigned you to be with me today.'

My face must have shown my thoughts on the prospect of spending the day with Thorson.

'I'm not exactly thrilled to pieces myself,' he said to me. 'But I do what I'm told. Now, if you just want to stay in bed all day, that'd be no skin off my back. I'd just tell –'

'I'm getting dressed. Give me a few minutes.'

'You've got five minutes. I'll meet you in the alley at the car. If you're not there you're on your own.'

After he was gone I looked at my watch on the bed table. It was eight-thirty, not as late as I had thought. I took ten minutes instead of five. I held my head under the shower and thought about being with Thorson for the day, dreading every moment of it. But most of all I thought about Rachel and wondered what assignment Backus had given her and why it didn't include me.

After leaving my room I went up to her door and knocked but got no answer. I listened at the door for a few moments and heard nothing. She was gone.

Thorson was leaning on the trunk of one of the cars when I got out to the alley.

'You're late.'

'Yeah. Sorry. Where's Rachel?'

'Sorry, sport, talk to Backus. He seems to be your bureau rabbi.'

'Look, Thorson, my name isn't sport, okay? If you don't want to call me by my name, just don't call me anything. I'm late because I had to call my editor and tell him there was no story coming. He wasn't happy.'

I went to the passenger door and he went around to the driver's side. I had to wait for him to unlock it and it seemed like he took forever to notice I was waiting.

'I don't really give a shit how your editor was this morning,' he said over the car before sliding in.

Inside the car, I saw two containers of coffee sitting on the dashboard, steam from them fogging the windshield. I looked at them the way a junkie looks at the spoon held to the candle but didn't say anything. I assumed they were part of some game Thorson was going to try to play.

'One of those is yours, sp – uh, Jack. You want cream or sugar, check the glove box.'

He started the car. I looked at him and then back at the coffee. Thorson reached over and took one of the containers and opened it. He took a small sip, like a swimmer dipping a toe into the water to test the temperature.

'Ahh,' he said. 'I take mine hot and black. Just like my women.'

He looked over and winked in a man-to-man gesture.

'Go ahead, Jack, take the coffee. I don't want it to spill when I move the car.'

I took the container and opened it. Thorson started driving. I took a small sip, but I did it more like the Czar's official food taster. It was good and the caffeine hit came quickly.

'Thanks,' I said.

'No problem. Can't get started without the stuff myself. So what happened, bad night?'

'You could say that.'

'Not me. I can sleep anywhere, even a dump like that. I slept fine.'

'Didn't do any sleepwalking, did you?'

'Sleepwalking? What do you mean?'

'Look, Thorson, thanks for the coffee and all but I know it was you who called Warren and I know it was you who was in my room last night.'

Thorson pulled to a stop at a curb marked for deliveries only. He threw the car into park and looked at me.

'What did you say? What're you saying?'

'You heard what I said. You were in there. I might not have the proof now but if Warren comes up with anything ahead of me, I'll go to Backus anyway and tell him what I saw.'

'Listen, sport, see that coffee? That was my peace offering. If you want to throw it in my face, fine. But I don't know what the fuck you are talking about and for the last time, I don't talk to reporters. Period. I'm only talking to you now because you have special dispensation. That's it.'

He jammed the car into drive and lurched out into traffic, prompting an angry rebuke from the horn of another driver. Hot coffee slopped onto my hand but I kept silent about it. We drove in silence for several minutes, entering a canyon of concrete and glass and steel. Wilshire Boulevard. We were heading toward the towers of downtown. The coffee no longer tasted good to me and I put the cap back on it.

'Where are we going?' I finally asked.

'To see Gladden's lawyer. After that we're going out to Santa Monica, talk to the dynamic duo that had this dirtbag in their hands and let him go.'

'I read the *Times* story. They didn't know who they had. You can't really blame them.'

'Yeah, that's right, nobody's ever to blame.'

I had completely succeeded in taking Thorson's offering of goodwill and flushing it down the toilet. He had turned sullen and bitter. His usual self as far as I could tell, yet it was still my fault.

'Look,' I said, putting my coffee on the floor and holding my hands in an I-give-up gesture, 'I'm sorry, okay? If I'm wrong about you and Warren and everything else, I'm sorry. I was just looking at things the way they seem to me. If I'm wrong, I'm wrong.'

He said nothing and the silence became oppressive. I felt like the ball was still in my court, that there was more I needed to say.

'I'll drop it, okay?' I lied. 'And I'm sorry about . . . if you're upset about me and Rachel. Things just happened.'

'Tell you what, Jack, you can keep your apology. I don't care about you and I don't care about Rachel. She thinks I do and I'm sure she's told you that. But she's wrong. And if I were you, I'd watch my ass with her. There's always something else going on with her. Remember I told you that.'

'Sure.'

But I drop-kicked that stuff as soon as he said it. I wasn't going to let his bitterness infect my thoughts about Rachel.

'You ever heard of the Painted Desert, Jack?'

I looked at him, my eyes squinted in confusion.

'Yeah, I've heard of it.'

'Been there?'

'No.'

'Well, if you're with Rachel, then you're there now. She's the Painted Desert. Beautiful to look at, yeah. But, man, once you're there, she's desolate. There's nothing there past the beauty, Jack, and it gets cold at night in the desert.'

I wanted to hit him with some kind of comeback that would be the verbal equivalent of a roundhouse punch. But the depth of his acid and anger stunned me into silence.

'She can play you,' he continued. 'Or play *with* you. Like a toy. One minute she wants to share it, the next she doesn't. She disappears on you.'

I still said nothing. I turned and looked out the window so I wouldn't even have him in my peripheral vision. In a couple of minutes he said we were there and he pulled into the parking garage of one of the downtown office buildings.

After consulting a directory in the lobby of the Fuentes Law Center, we silently rode the elevator up to the seventh floor. To the right we found a door with a mahogany plaque set to the side of it that announced the law offices of Krasner & Peacock. Inside, Thorson placed his opened badge and ID wallet on the counter in front of the receptionist and asked to see Krasner.

'I'm sorry,' she said, 'Mr Krasner is in court this morning.'

'Are you sure?'

'Of course I'm sure. He's in arraignments. He won't be back until after lunch.'

'Down here? Which courthouse?'

'Down here. The CCB.'

We left the car where it was and walked to the Criminal Courts Building. Arraignments were held on the fifth floor in a huge, marble-walled courtroom heavily crowded with lawyers, the accused and the families of the accused. Thorson approached a deputy marshal sitting behind a desk at the first row of the gallery and asked her which of the lawyers milling about was Arthur Krasner. She pointed to a short man with thinning red hair and a red face who was standing near the court railing talking with another man in a suit, undoubtedly another lawyer. Thorson headed toward him, mumbling something about his looking like a Jewish leprechaun.

'Mr Krasner?' Thorson said, not waiting for a lull in the conversation the two men were having.

'Yes?'

'Can I have a word with you out in the hallway?'

'Who are you?'

'I can explain in the hallway.'

'You can explain now or you can go out to the hallway by yourself.'

Thorson opened his wallet, Krasner looked at the badge and read the ID, and I watched his small porcine eyes move back and forth as he thought.

'That's right, I think you know what it's about,' Thorson said. Looking at the other lawyer, he said, 'Will you excuse us now?'

In the hallway Krasner had regained some of his lawyerly bluff.

'All right, I have an arraignment in there in five minutes. What's this about?'

'I thought we were past that,' Thorson said. 'It's about one of your clients, William Gladden.'

'Never heard of him.'

He made a move to go past Thorson to the courtroom door. Thorson nonchalantly reached out and put a hand on the other man's chest, stopping him dead.

'Please,' Krasner said. 'You have no right to touch me. Don't touch me.'

'You know who we're talking about, Mr Krasner. You are in serious trouble for hiding this man's true identity from the court and the police.'

'No, you are wrong. I had no idea who he was. I took the case at face value. Who he turned out to be was not my concern. And there is not one scintilla of evidence or even a suggestion that I knew otherwise.'

'Never mind the bullshit, Counselor. You can save it for the judge in there. Where is Gladden?'

'I have no idea and even if I did I –'

'You wouldn't say? That's the wrong attitude, Mr Krasner. Let me tell you something, I've gone over the record of your representation of Mr Gladden and things don't look good, if you know what I mean. Not kosher is what I am saying. This could be a problem for you.'

'I don't know what you're talking about.'

'How did he come to call you after his arrest?'

'I don't know. I didn't ask.'

'Was it a referral?'

'Yes, I think so.'

'From who?'

'I don't know. I said I didn't ask.'

'Are you a pedophile, Mr Krasner? Is it little girls or little boys that turn you on? Or maybe both?'

'What?'

Little by little Thorson had backed him up against the marble wall of the hallway with his verbal assault. Krasner was beginning to look spent. He was holding his briefcase in front of his body now, almost as a shield. But it wasn't thick enough.

'You know what I'm talking about,' Thorson said, bearing down on him. 'Of all the lawyers in this town, why'd Gladden call you?'

'I told you,' Krasner yelled, drawing looks from everyone passing in the hall. He continued in a whisper. 'I don't know why he chose me. He just did. I'm in the book. It's a free country.'

Thorson hesitated, allowing Krasner to say more but the lawyer didn't take the bait.

'I looked at the records yesterday,' Thorson said. 'You had him out two hours and fifteen minutes after bail was set. How did you make the bond? The answer is you already had the money from him, didn't you? So the real question is, how'd you get the money from him if he spent the night in jail?'

'Wire transfer. Nothing illegal. We talked the night before about my fee and what the bond might be and he had it wired the following morning. I had nothing to do with it. I . . . You can't stand here and slander me in this way.'

'I can do whatever I want to do. You fucking disgust me. I checked you out with the locals, Krasner. I know about you.'

'What are you talking about?'

'If you don't know now, you're going to know soon enough. They're coming for you, little man. You put this guy back on the street and look what he did. Look what he fucking did.'

'I didn't know!' Krasner said in a whine that pleaded for forgiveness.

'Sure, nobody ever knows. You have a phone?'

'What?'

'A phone. A telephone.'

Thorson slapped an open hand against Krasner's briefcase, a move that made the little man jump as if shocked with a cattle prod.

'Yes, yes, I have a phone. You don't have to –'

'Good. Get it out, call your receptionist and tell her to pull the wire transfer records from your file. Tell her I'll be there in fifteen minutes for a copy of it.'

'You can't take – I have an attorney/client relationship with this individual that I must protect no matter what he's done. I –'

Thorson slapped a backhand off the briefcase again, which shut Krasner up in mid-sentence. I could see Thorson received a genuine sense of accomplishment from pushing the little lawyer around.

'Make the call, Krasner, and I'll tell the locals you helped out. Make the call or the next person to die is on you. Because now you do know who and what we're talking about here.'

Krasner slowly nodded and began opening his briefcase.

'That's it, Counselor,' Thorson said. 'Now you see the light.'

As Krasner called his receptionist and issued the order in a shaky voice, Thorson stood silently watching. I had never seen or heard of anyone using the bad cop routine without the good cop counterpart and still so expertly finesse the information needed from a source. I wasn't sure if I admired Thorson's skill or was appalled by it. But he had turned the posturing bluff artist into a shaking mess. As Krasner was folding the phone closed, Thorson asked what the amount of the wire transfer had been.

'Six thousand dollars even.'

'Five for bail and one for you. How come you didn't squeeze him?'

'He said it was all he could afford. I believed him. May I go now?'

There was a resigned and defeated look on Krasner's face.

Before Thorson answered his question the door to the courtroom opened and a bailiff leaned out.

'Artie, you're up.'

'Okay, Jerry.'

Without waiting for further comment from Thorson, Krasner began moving toward the door again. And once again Thorson stopped him with a hand on the chest. This time Krasner made no protest about being touched. He simply stopped, leaving his eyes staring dead ahead.

'Artie – can I call you Artie? – you better do some soul-searching. That is if you have one. You know more than you've said here. A lot more. And the more time you waste, the more there's a chance that a life will be wasted. Think about that and give me a call.'

He reached over and slid a business card into the handkerchief pocket of Krasner's suit coat, then patted it gently.

'My local number is written on the back. Call me. If I get what I need from somewhere else and find out you had the same information, I will be merciless, Counselor. Fucking merciless.'

Thorson then stepped back so the lawyer could slowly make his way back into the courtroom.

We were back out on the sidewalk before Thorson spoke to me.

'Think he got the message?'

'Yeah, he got it. I'd stay by the phone. He's gonna call.'

'We'll see.'

'Can I ask you something?'

'What?'

'Did you really check him out with the locals?'

Thorson smiled by way of an answer.

'The part about him being a pedophile. How do you know that?'

'Just takin' a shot. Pedophiles are networkers. They like to surround themselves with their own kind. They have phone nets, computer nets, a whole support system. They view it as them against society. The misunderstood minority, that kind of bullshit. So I figured maybe he got Krasner's name on a referral list somewhere. It was worth the shot. The way I read Krasner, I think it hit him. He wouldn't have given up the wire records if it didn't.'

'Maybe. Maybe he was telling the truth about not knowing who Gladden was. Maybe he just has a conscience and doesn't want to see anybody else hurt.'

'I take it you don't know that many lawyers.'

Ten minutes later we were waiting for the elevator outside the Krasner & Peacock law offices, Thorson looking at the wire transfer receipt for the sum of $6,000.

'It's a bank out of Jacksonville,' he said without looking up. 'We'll have to get Rach on it.'

I noticed his use of the diminutive of her name. There was something intimate about it.

'Why her?' I asked.

''Cause she's in Florida.'

He looked up from the receipt at me. He was smiling.

'Didn't I tell you?'

'No, you didn't tell me.'

'Yeah, Backus sent her out this morning. She went to see Horace the Hypnotist and work with the Florida team. Tell you what, let's stop in the lobby and use the phone, see if I can get somebody to get this account number to her.'

38

· · · · · · · ·

Very little was said between us on the way out from downtown to Santa Monica. I was thinking about Rachel in Florida. I couldn't understand why Backus would send her when the front line seemed to be out here. There were two possibilities, I decided. One was that Rachel was being disciplined for some reason, possibly me, and taken off the front line. The other was that there was some new break to the case I didn't know about and was purposely not being told. Either choice was a bad one, but I found myself secretly choosing the first.

Thorson seemed lost in thought during most of the drive, or perhaps just tired of being around me. But when we parked out front of the Santa Monica Police Department, he answered the question I had before I even asked it.

'We just need to pick up the property they took from Gladden when he was arrested. We want to consolidate it all.'

'And they're going to let you do that?'

I knew how small departments, in fact, all departments, tended to react to being bigfooted by the Big G.

'We'll see.'

At the front counter of the detective bureau, we were told that Constance Delpy was in court but her partner, Ron Sweetzer, would be with us shortly. Shortly to Sweetzer turned out to be ten minutes. A period of time that didn't sit well with Thorson. I got the idea that the FBI, in the embodiment of Gordon Thorson at least, didn't appreciate having to wait for anybody, especially a small-town gold badge.

When Sweetzer finally appeared, he stood behind the counter and asked how he could help us. He gave me a second glance, probably computing how my beard and clothes did not jibe with his image of the FBI. He said nothing and made no movement that could have been translated as an invitation back to his office. Thorson responded in kind with short sentences and his own brand of rudeness. He took a folded white page from his inside pocket and spread it on the counter.

'That's the property inventory from the arrest of William Gladden, AKA Harold Brisbane. I'm here to accept custody of the property.'

'What are you talking about?' Sweetzer said.

'I'm talking about what I just said. The FBI has entered the case and is heading the nationwide investigation of William Gladden. We need to have some experts look over what you've got here.'

'Wait a minute, Mr Agent. We've got our own experts and we've got a case against this guy. We're not turning over the evidence to anybody. Not without a court order or the DA's approval.'

Thorson took a deep breath but he seemed to me to be going through an act he had performed countless times before. The bully who comes into town and picks on the little guy.

'First of all,' he said, 'you know and I know your case is for shit. And secondly, we're not talking about evidence, anyway. You've got a camera, a bag of candy. That's not evidence of anything. He's charged with fleeing an officer, vandalism and polluting a waterway. Where's the camera come into it?'

Sweetzer started to say something, then stopped, apparently stymied for a reply.

'Just wait here, please?'

Sweetzer started away from the counter.

'I don't have all day, Detective,' Thorson said after him. 'I'm trying to catch this guy. Too bad he's still on the loose.'

Sweetzer angrily swung around.

'What's that supposed to mean? What the *fuck* does that mean?'

Thorson held his hands up in a no-harm gesture.

'Means exactly what you think it means. Now go ahead, get your CO. I'll talk to him now.'

Sweetzer left and in two minutes returned with a man ten years older, thirty pounds heavier and twice as angry.

'What's the problem here?' he said in a short, clipped voice.

'There's no problem, Captain.'

'It's Lieutenant.'

'Oh, well, Lieutenant, your man here seems confused. I've explained that the FBI has stepped into the investigation of William Gladden and is working hand in hand with the Los Angeles police and other departments across the country. The bureau also extends that hand to Santa Monica. But Detective Sweetzer seems to think that by holding on to the property seized from Mr Gladden, he is helping the investigation and eventual capture of Mr Gladden. In reality, he is impeding our efforts. I'm surprised, frankly, to be treated this way. I've got a member of the national media with me and I didn't expect that he'd see something like this.'

Thorson gestured toward me and Sweetzer and his lieutenant studied me. I felt myself getting angry at being used. The lieutenant looked from me back to Thorson.

'What we don't understand is why you need to take this property. I've looked at the inventory. It's a camera, a pair of sunglasses, a duffel bag and a bag of candy, that's it. No film, no pictures. Why does the FBI have to take this from us?'

'Have you submitted candy samples to a chemical analysis lab?'

The lieutenant looked at Sweetzer, who shook his head slightly as if it were some kind of a secret signal.

'We will do that, Lieutenant,' Thorson said. 'To determine if the candy was in any way doctored. And the camera. You are not aware of this but there have been some photos recovered in our investigation. I cannot go into the content of these photos but suffice it to say they are of a highly illegal nature. But the point is, analysis of these photos shows an imperfection in the lens of the camera with which these photos were taken. It's like a fingerprint on every photo. We can match those photos to a camera. But we need the camera to do it. If you allow us to take it and we make a match, we will be able to prove this man took the photos. There will then be additional charges when we catch him. It will also help us determine exactly what this man has been up to. This is why we request that you turn this property over. Really, gentlemen, we want the same thing.'

The lieutenant didn't say anything for a long moment. Then he turned and started away from the counter. To Sweetzer, he said, 'Make sure you get a chain-of-evidence receipt.'

Sweetzer's face fell and he followed the lieutenant away from the counter, not protesting but whispering something about not getting the explanation Thorson had just made before dragging the lieutenant into it. After both of them had turned a corner back into the bureau, I moved up next to Thorson at the counter so I could whisper.

'Next time you're going to use me like that, give me some warning,' I said. 'I don't appreciate it at all.'

Thorson smirked.

'The good investigator uses any and all tools available to him. You were available.'

'Is that true about photos being recovered and camera analysis?'

'Sounded good, didn't it?'

The only way Sweetzer could salvage any kind of pride from the transaction was to leave us waiting at the counter for another ten minutes. Finally, he came out with a cardboard box and slid it across the counter. He then told Thorson to sign a property receipt. Thorson started to open the box first. Sweetzer put his hand on the lid to stop him.

'It's all there,' Sweetzer said. 'Just sign the receipt so I can get back to work. I'm busy.'

Thorson, having won the war, gave him the last battle and signed the receipt.

'I trust you. It's all in here.'

'You know, I used to want to be an FBI agent.'

'Well, don't feel bad about it. Lot of people fail the test.'

Sweetzer's face flushed pink.

'It wasn't that,' he said. 'I just decided that I liked being a human too much.'

Thorson raised his hand and pointed a finger like a gun.

'Good one,' he said. 'Have a nice day, Detective Sweetzer.'

'Hey,' Sweetzer said, 'if you fellows over there at the bureau need anything else, and I mean anything at all, be sure to hesitate to call.'

On the way back to the car I couldn't resist.

'I guess you never heard that you supposedly can catch more flies with sugar than with lemon.'

'Why waste the sugar on flies?' he replied.

He didn't open the property box until we were in the car. After he removed the lid I saw there were the items already discussed wrapped in plastic bags and a sealed envelope marked CONFIDENTIAL: FBI EYES ONLY. Thorson ripped open the envelope and from it took out a photograph. It was a Polaroid, probably taken with a jail booking camera. It was a close-up shot of a man's buttocks, hands grasping and spreading them to afford a clear, deep view of the anus. Thorson studied it a moment and then tossed it over the seat into the back.

'That's strange,' he said. 'I wonder why Sweetzer included a picture of his mother?'

I gave a short laugh and said, 'There's the most telling example of interagency cooperation I've ever seen.'

But Thorson ignored the comment or didn't hear it. His face turned somber and from the box he pulled a plastic bag containing the camera. I watched him stare at it intently. He turned it in his hands, studying it. I saw his face grow dark.

'Those fucking assholes,' he said slowly. 'They've been sitting on this all this time.'

I looked at the camera. There was something odd about its bulky shape. It looked like a Polaroid but had a standard-looking 35mm lens on it.

'What is it? What's wrong?'

'Know what this is?'

'No, what?'

Thorson didn't answer. He pressed a button to turn the camera on. Then he studied the computerized display on the back.

'No pictures,' he said.

'What is it?'

He didn't answer. He put the camera back in the box, closed it and started the car.

Thorson drove the car down the street from the police station like a fire engine heading to a four-alarm. He pulled into a gas station on Pico Boulevard and jumped out while the car was still jerking in response to his skidding stop. He ran to the phone and punched in a long distance number without putting in any coins. While he waited for a response he took out a pen and a small notebook. I saw him write something down after saying a few words into the phone. When he keyed in another long distance number without putting in coins, I guessed he had gotten directory assistance for a toll-free 800 number.

I was tempted to get out of the car and go up to him so that I could hear his conversation but decided to wait. In a minute or so I saw him writing information into his notebook. While he did that I looked at the evidence box Sweetzer had given him. I wanted to open it and look at the camera again but thought this might anger Thorson.

'You mind telling me what's going on?' I asked as soon as he was behind the wheel again.

'Sure I mind, but you're going to find out anyway.' He opened the box and lifted out the camera again. 'Know what this is?'

'You asked that. A camera.'

'Right, but what kind of camera is what's important.'

As he turned it in his hands I saw the manufacturer's symbol imprinted on the front. A large lowercase *d* in pale blue. I knew it was the symbol of the computer manufacturer called digiTime. Printed beneath the corporate symbol was *Digishot 200*.

'This is a digital camera, Jack. That hillbilly Sweetzer didn't know what the fuck he had. We just have to hope we're not too late.'

'You're losing me. I guess I'm just a hillbilly, too, but can you –'

'You know what a digital camera is?'

'Yeah, it doesn't use film. They've been experimenting with them at the paper.'

'Right, no film. The image the camera shoots is captured on a microchip instead. The image can then be put into a computer, edited, blown up, whatever, then printed. Depending on your equipment – and this is top-of-the-line equipment, comes with a Nikon lens – you can come up with high-resolution photographs. As good as the real thing.'

I had seen prints taken on digital at the *Rocky*. Thorson was correct in his assessment.

'So what's it mean?'

'Two things. Remember what I told you about pedophiles? The networking they do?'

'Right.'

'Okay, we pretty much know Gladden has a computer because of the fax, right?'

'Right.'

'And now we know he had a digital camera. With the digital camera, his computer and the same modem he used to send the fax, he could send a photo anywhere he wanted to in the world, to anybody who had a phone and a computer and the software to receive it.'

It hit me then in a split second.

'He's sending people pictures of kids?'

'No, he's *selling* them pictures of kids. That's my guess. The questions we had about how he lives and gets money? About this account in Jacksonville he wired money from? This is the answer. The Poet makes his money selling pictures of kids, maybe even the kids he killed. Who knows, maybe even the cops he killed.'

'There are people who would . . .'

I didn't finish. I knew the question was stupid.

'If there is one thing I know from this job it's that there is an appetite and therefore a market for anything and everything,' Thorson said. 'Your darkest thought is not unique. The worst thing you can possibly imagine, whatever it is, no matter how bad, there is a market for it . . . I gotta make another call, get this list of dealers split up.'

'What was the second thing?'

'What?'

'You said there were two things significant about —'

'It's a break. It's a big fucking break. That is, if we're not too late because Santa Monica's been sitting on the goddamn camera. If Gladden's income, his traveling money, comes from selling photos to other pedophiles, shipping them through the Internet or some private bulletin board, then he lost his main tool last week when the cops took this away.'

He tapped the top of the cardboard box on the seat between us.

'He's got to replace it,' I said.

'You got it.'

'You're going to go to the digiTime dealers.'

'You're a smart guy, sport. How come you became a reporter?'

This time I didn't protest the use of his name for me. There wasn't the same malice as when he had called me by it before.

'I called the digiTime 800 number and got eight dealers who sell the digiShot 200 in L.A. I figure he's got to go for the same model. He'd already have all the other equipment. I've got to make that call to split these up. You got a quarter, Jack? I'm out.'

I gave him the quarter and he jumped out of the car and went back to the phone. I imagined he was calling Backus, gleefully telling him about the break and splitting up the list. I sat there thinking that Rachel should have been the one standing there on the phone. In a few minutes, Thorson was back.

'We're checking out three of them. All over here on the west side. Bob's giving the other five to Carter and some guys from the FO.'

'Do you have to order these cameras or do they keep them in stock?'

Thorson pulled back into the traffic and headed east on Pico. He referred to one of the addresses he had written down in his notebook as he talked and drove.

'Some places keep them in stock,' he said. 'If they don't they can get 'em pretty quick. That's what the digiTime operator said.'

'Then what are we doing? It's been a week. He would've got one by now.'

'Maybe, maybe not. We're playing a hunch. This is not a cheap piece of equipment. You buy it in a kit with the downloading and editing software and the serial cable to connect it to your computer, the leather case and flash and all the extras, you're getting up well over a grand. Probably fifteen hundred. But ...'

He raised his finger to make the point.

'What if you already have all the extras and all you want is the camera? No cable. No software. None of that stuff. What if you just shelled out six grand for bail and a lawyer and you're hurting for cash and not only don't need all those extras but can't afford them?'

'You special-order just a camera and save a lot of money.'

'That's right. That's my hunch. I think that if making bail came close to busting our friend Gladden just like that shyster lawyer said it did, then he'd be looking to save a dollar here and there. If he replaced the camera, I'm betting he made the special order.'

He was juiced and it was contagious. I had caught his excitement and was beginning to look at Thorson in perhaps a truer light. I knew these were the moments he lived for. Moments of understanding and clarity. Of knowing he was close.

'McEvoy, we are on a roll,' he suddenly said. 'I think you might be good luck after all. Just make it good enough that we're not too late.'

I nodded my agreement.

We drove for a few minutes in silence before I questioned him again.

'How do you know so much about digital cameras?'

'It's come up before and it's becoming more prevalent. At Quantico we have a unit now that does nothing but computer crime. Internet crime. A lot of what they do bleeds over into pornography, child crimes. They put out bureau-wide briefings to keep people current. I try to keep current.'

I nodded.

'There was this old lady – a schoolteacher, no less – up near Cornell in New York checks the download file in her home computer one day and sees a new entry she doesn't recognize. She prints it out and what she gets is a murky black-and-white but clearly identifiable picture of a boy of about ten copping some old guy's joint. She calls the locals and they figure out it got to her computer by mistake. Her Internet address is just a number and they figure the sender transposed a couple digits or something. Anyway, the routing history of the file is right there and they trace it back to some gimp, a pedophile with a nice long record. Out here in fact, he was from L.A. Anyway, they do the search-and-bust and take him down pretty neat. The first digital bust. The guy had something like five hundred different photos in his computer. Christ, he needed a double hard drive. I'm talking about kids of every age, persuasion, doing things normal grownups don't even do . . . Anyway, good case. He got life, no parole. He had a digiShot, though that might've been a 100 model. They put the story out last year in the FBI *Bulletin*.'

'How come the picture the teacher got was so murky?'

'She didn't have the printer for it. You know, you need a nice colorgraphics printer and high-gloss paper. She had neither.'

*

The first two stops were dead ends. One store hadn't sold a digiShot in two weeks and the other had sold two in the last week. However, those two cameras had gone to a well-known Los Angeles artist whose collage portraits made of Polaroid photos were celebrated and displayed in museums around the world. He now wanted to dabble in a newer photographic medium and was going digital. Thorson didn't even bother writing down notes for further follow-up.

The last stop on our list was a street-front shop called Data Imaging Answers on Pico, two blocks from the Westwood Pavilion shopping center. After pulling to the curb in a no-parking zone out front, Thorson smiled and said, 'This is it. This is the one.'

'How do you know?' I asked.

'Walk-in store on a busy street. The other two were more like mail-order offices, not storefronts. Gladden would have wanted the storefront. More visual stimulation. People passing outside, people coming in and out, more distractions. It would be better for him. He doesn't want to be remembered.'

It was a small store with two desks in the showroom and several unopened boxes stacked about. There were two circular counters with computer terminals and video equipment on display along with stacks of computer equipment catalogs. A balding man wearing thick glasses with black frames was sitting at one of the desks and looked up as we entered. There was no one at the other desk and it looked unused.

'Are you the manager?' Thorson inquired.

'Not only that, I'm the owner.' The man stood up with proprietary pride and smiled as we approached his desk. 'Not only that, I am the number one employee.'

When we didn't join in his guffaw he asked what he could do for us.

Thorson showed him the inside of his badge wallet.

'FBI?'

It seemed incomprehensible to him.

'Yes. You sell the digiShot 200, correct?'

'Yes, we do. Top-of-the-line digital camera. But I'm out of stock at the moment. Sold my last one last week.'

I felt my guts seize. We were too late.

'I can have one in three or four days. In fact, seein' that it's the FBI I might get them to ship two-day. No charge extra, of course.'

He smiled and nodded but his eyes had a quizzical look behind the thick glasses. He was nervous dealing with the FBI, especially not knowing what it was all about.

'And your name is?'

'Olin Coombs. I'm the owner.'

'Yes, you said that. Okay, Mr Coombs, I'm not interested in buying anything. Do you have the name of the person who bought your last digiShot?'

'Uh...' He creased his brow, probably wondering if he should ask if it was legal for the FBI to ask for such information. 'Of course I keep records. I can get that for you.'

Coombs sat down and opened a drawer in his desk. He looked through a hanging file until he found what he was looking for, pulled out a sheet of paper and laid it flat on the desk. He then turned it around so Thorson didn't have to read it upside down. Thorson leaned over, studied the document and I saw his head make a slight turn to the right and then back. Looking at the receipt, it looked to me as if numerous pieces of equipment had been purchased along with the digiShot camera.

'This isn't what I'm looking for,' Thorson said. 'I'm looking for a man that we believe wanted to purchase a digiShot camera only. This is the only one you've sold in the last week?'

'Yes – uh, no. It's the only one with delivery. We've sold two others but they had to be ordered.'

'And they haven't been delivered yet?'

'No. Tomorrow. I'm expecting a truck in the morning.'

'Either of those two just order the camera?'

'The camera?'

'You know, none of the other stuff. The software, the cable, the whole kit.'

'Oh, yes. Uh, as a matter of fact, there is ...'

His words trailed off as he opened the drawer again and pulled out a clipboard with several pink forms on it. He started peeling them back and reading.

'I have a Mr Childs. Just wanted the camera, nothing else. Paid cash in advance. Nine ninety-five plus California sales tax. Came to –'

'Did he leave a number or address?'

I stopped breathing. We had him. This had to be Gladden. The irony of the name he had given was not lost on me. I felt a chill roll across my back.

'No, no number or address,' Coombs said. 'I wrote a note to myself. It says Mr Wilton Childs will call to check on the equipment's arrival. I told him to call tomorrow.'

'Then he'll come pick it up?'

'Yes, if it's here by then he'll come pick it up. Like I said, we don't have an address so we can't deliver it.'

'Do you remember what he looked like, Mr Coombs?'

'Looked like? Uh, well, yes I suppose so.'

'Can you describe him?'

'He was a white fellow, I remember that. He . . .'

'Blond hair?'

'Uh, no. It was dark. And he was growing a beard, I remember that.'

'How old?'

'About twenty-five or perhaps thirty.'

That was good enough for Thorson. It was in the ballpark and the rest of the information fit. He pointed at the empty desk.

'Anybody using that desk?'

'Not at the moment. Business is not so good.'

'Then is it all right if we do?'

39

• • • • • • • •

There was a discernible electric buzz in the air as everyone gathered around a table in the conference room with the million-dollar view. After being brought up to speed by a phone call from Thorson, Backus had decided to move his operation command post from the Wilcox Hotel to the FBI offices in Westwood. We gathered on the seventeenth floor of the federal building in a conference room with a panoramic view of the city. I could see Catalina Island floating out in a golden ocean reflecting the spectacular burnt-orange-and-red start of another sunset.

It was four-thirty Pacific time and the meeting had been scheduled late to give Rachel as much time as possible to obtain and execute a search warrant for records of Gladden's bank account in Jacksonville.

In the conference room, Backus was joined by Thorson, Carter, Thompson, six agents I hadn't been introduced to but who I assumed were locals, and me. Quantico and all the field offices involved in the investigation were also on the conference line. And even these unseen people seemed excited. Brass Doran kept saying over the speaker, 'Are we ready to start yet?'

Finally, Backus, sitting at the center of the table, closest to the speakerphone, called everyone to order. Behind him, on an easel, was a crude top-view diagram of the Data Imaging Answers store and the block of Pico Boulevard where it was located.

'Okay, people, things are happening,' he said. 'This is what we worked for. So let's talk about it and then let's do it and let's do it right.'

He stood up. Maybe the moment was getting to him as well.

'We have a priority one lead we're working and we want to hear from Rachel and Brass. First, though, I'm going to have Gordon give the rundown on what we've got set up for tomorrow.'

As Thorson told the captive audience about our day's work and discoveries, my mind wandered. I thought of Rachel somewhere in Jacksonville, twenty-five hundred miles from her investigation and listening to a man she didn't like and probably even despised talk about the major break he had made. I wanted to talk to her and try in some way to console her, but not with twenty-five people listening. I wanted to ask Backus where she was so I could call afterward but knew I couldn't do that, either. Then I remembered the pager. I would do that later.

'We are shifting our critical incident team off Thomas,' Thorson said. 'The LAPD surveillance team is doubling up and will stay with Thomas. We are redirecting our people to be used in a twofold plan to facilitate the arrest of this offender. First off, we now have caller ID on the phones at Data Imaging. We will have a mobile receiver and LED readout to monitor incoming calls on both lines and the field office is providing all available hands for response teams. We're going to trace this subject's call when he checks in to see if his product is in and try to hold him at the phone until our people can get there. If they do, standard felony arrest procedures will follow. Any questions so far?'

'Air support?' an agent asked.

'We're working on it. I'm told we can count on one bird but we are going for two. All right then, step two is if we are unable to effect capture of the subject through caller ID. At Digital Imaging Answers – let's call it DIA for short – I'll be inside with Coombs, the owner. If we get the call from this guy, he will be told that the camera he ordered is ready for pickup. We'll try to press for a pickup time but not too hard, just keeping it natural.

'If the subject slips through the first net, the plan is to set up on him once he comes to the store. The store's been wired – sound and video. If he comes in, I'll just give him his camera and send him on his way, another satisfied customer. The felony arrest will take place at the time Don Sample, he's our critical team leader, thinks is appropriate and gives the word. Obviously, that will be the first controlled setting our man takes us to. We hope that will be his car. But you all know the procedures for other contingencies. Questions?'

'Why not prone his ass right there in the store?'

'We feel we need Coombs to be there so as not to spook the subject. He bought the camera from Coombs, Coombs should be there. I don't want to try to take this guy down that close to a civilian. Also, it's a small store and we may be pressing it having even one agent in there. You put more in and it's going to look suspicious to this guy. So why don't we just give him the camera and take him down out there on the street, where we can control things a little better?'

With Thorson, Backus and Sample handing off to each other, they outlined the plan in more detail. Coombs would be in the store with Thorson to handle the daily business and real customers throughout the day. But when the outside surveillance teams reported the approach of any customer even remotely matching Gladden's description, Thorson would remain up front to handle the transaction while Coombs excused himself, retreated to a small rear storage room and locked himself in. Another agent, posing as a customer, would enter through the front door as backup after Gladden entered. The interior of the store would be monitored by a video setup. The exterior would be monitored by roving and stationary agents ready to deal with all contingencies once Gladden was identified. Additionally, a female agent in a Los Angeles parking enforcement uniform and car would continuously patrol the block where DIA was located.

'I don't think I need to remind everybody just how dangerous this individual is,' Backus said when the briefing was done. 'Everybody pack some extra common sense tomorrow. Watch out for yourself and your partner. Questions?'

I waited a beat to see if there were any questions from agents. When there weren't, I spoke up.

'What if the digiShot doesn't come in tomorrow like Mr Coombs said it was supposed to?'

'Oh, yes, good point,' Backus said. 'We're not taking any chances. The Internet group at Quantico has one of these cameras and it's coming out tonight on a plane. We'll use that whether the one he really ordered comes in or not. Ours will be wired with a homer just in case, God forbid, he gets by us. We'll be able to track him. Anything else?'

'Has any thought been given to not taking him down?'

It was Rachel's voice on the speakerphone.

'How do you mean?'

'Just playing devil's advocate, it looks like we've got this pretty well buttoned down. This could be a rare opportunity for us to watch a serial killer and observe his hunting and victim acquisition patterns. It could be invaluable to our studies.'

Her question set off a debate among the agents over the plan.

'And risk the chance that we lose him and he kills some kid or another cop?' Thorson responded. 'No thanks – especially with the Fourth Estate here watching.'

Almost everybody came down on Thorson's side of it, the feeling being that a monster like Gladden, though a worthy research subject, should be studied only in the closed setting of a prison cell. The risks of his potential escape far outweighed the riches that might be gained by watching him at work in an open environment.

'Look, people, the plan has been set,' Backus finally said, closing the subject. 'We've considered the alternatives that have been suggested and I feel that going at him in the way we have outlined is the best and safest plan. So let's move on. Rachel, what have you got for us?'

I watched the body language of the agents in the room change as their attention went from Backus and Thorson to the white phone positioned at the center of the table. People seemed to lean toward it. Backus, still standing, leaned down with his palms on the tabletop.

'Let me start with the bank,' Rachel said. 'I just got these records about ninety minutes ago, so there hasn't been a lot of time. But, preliminarily, it looks like we have withdrawals wired to three of our cities, Chicago, Denver and L.A. The dates look good. He got money in those cities within days, just before or after, the bait murders in each. There are two wires to L.A. One coincides with the bail last week, and then on Saturday there was another transfer of twelve hundred. He picked the money up at the same bank. A Wells Fargo on Ventura Boulevard in Sherman Oaks. I was thinking this might be another way of taking him if he doesn't show up tomorrow for his camera. We could watch the account and intercept him next time he gets money. Only problem with that is that he's running low on funds. After pulling out that twelve hundred, he's down to about two hundred in the account.'

'But he's going to try to make some more with the new camera,' Thorson said.

'Going on to the deposits,' Rachel continued. 'These are very interesting but I just haven't had the time to really . . . uh, in the last two years there has been about forty-five thousand dollars wired to the account. Deposits coming from all over the place. Maine, Texas, California – several from California, New York. There doesn't seem to be a correlating pattern to our killings. Also, I found one overlap. Last November one there were wire deposits made from New York and Texas on the same day.'

'He's obviously not making the deposits,' Backus said. 'Or at least not all of them.'

'Those are payments,' Brass said over the conference line. 'From selling the photos. Payments wired in directly by the buyers.'

'Exactly,' Rachel said.

'Will we . . . can we trace back these wires and get to these purchasers?' Thompson asked.

'Uh,' Rachel replied when no one else did. 'We can try. I mean, we can trace them back but I wouldn't count on much. If you have cash, you can walk into almost any bank in the country and make a wire transfer as long as you have the destination account number and you pay the service charge. You have to give bare-bones sender's information but you don't have to show ID. People buying child pornography and possibly – probably – much worse are likely to use false names.'

'True.'

'What else, Rachel?' Backus asked. 'Anything else from the subpoena?'

'There is a P.O. box for the account mail. It's local and it's probably a mail drop. I'll be checking it out in the morning.'

'Okay. Do you want to report on Horace Gomble or save that until you've put your thoughts together?'

'No, I'll tell you the high points, which weren't many. My old pal Horace was not too happy to see me again. We sparred for a while and then his ego got the better of him. He acknowledged that he and Gladden had discussed the practice of hypnosis when they were cellmates. He admitted finally that he traded lessons for Gladden's legal work on his appeal. But he would go no further than that. I sensed . . . I don't know.'

'What, Rachel?'

'I don't know, some kind of appreciation for what Gladden was doing.'

'You told him?'

'No, I didn't tell him, but it was obvious to him that I was there for a reason. Still, it seemed like he knew something more. Maybe Gladden told him before he left Raiford what he planned to do. Told him about Beltran. I don't know. He also might've seen CNN today – if they have cable in the dorm. They picked up Jack McEvoy's story big time. I saw it at the airport. Of course, nothing in it links the Poet to Gladden, but Gomble could have figured it out. CNN used the tape from Phoenix again. If he saw that and then I showed up, he'd know what it was about without me saying a word.'

It had been the first I'd heard about any response to my story. In fact, I had totally forgotten about it because of the events of the day.

'Any chance Gladden and Gomble have been communicating?' Backus asked.

'I don't think so,' Rachel said. 'I checked with the hacks. Gomble's mail is still filtered. Coming in and out. He's managed to work his way up to trustee status, works in the prison's receiving shop. I guess there is always the possibility that incoming shipments might contain some kind of message but it seems doubtful. I also doubt Gomble would want to risk his position. He's got it pretty nice after seven years in. Nice job with a little office. He's supposedly in charge of supplying the prison canteen. In that society, that would make him a power. He's got a single cell now and his own TV. I don't see the reason to communicate with a wanted man like Gladden and risk all of that.'

'Okay, Rachel,' Backus said. 'Anything else?'

'That's it, Bob.'

Everyone was silent for a few moments, digesting what had been said so far.

'That brings us finally to the model,' Backus said. 'Brass?'

Again all eyes went to the phone on the table.

'Yes, Bob. The profile is coming together and Brad is adding some of the new details even as we speak. This is what we think we have. We might have a – this could be a situation where the offender went back to the man who set him on the path, who abused him and thereby nurtured the aberrant fantasies he later felt compelled to act upon as an adult.

'It's a play on the patricide model we have all seen before. We are almost solely focusing on the Florida cases. What we see here is the offender, in effect, seeking out his replacement. That is, the boy, Gabriel Ortiz, who currently held the attentions of Clifford Beltran, the father figure who abused him and then discarded him. It is the feeling of rejection the offender encountered that may motivate everything.

'Gladden killed the object of his abuser's current affection and then came back around and killed the abuser himself. It looks to me like an exorcism, if you will, the cathartic rush of eliminating the cause of all that was wrong in his life.'

There was a long period of quiet while I thought Backus

and the others waited to see if Brass would continue. Backus finally spoke up.

'And then, what you're saying is, he repeats the crime over and over.'

'Correct,' Brass said. 'He is killing Beltran, his abuser, over and over. It is how he gains his peace. But, of course, the peace doesn't last long. He has to go back out and kill again. These other victims – the detectives – are innocents. They did nothing other than their jobs to be chosen by him.'

'What about the bait cases in the other cities?' Thorson asked. 'They don't all fit the archetype of the first boy.'

'I don't think the bait cases would be as important anymore,' Brass said. 'What is important is that he draws out a detective, a good detective, a formidable foe. This way the stakes are high and the purging he needs is there. As far as the bait cases go, they may have simply evolved into a means to the end. He uses the children to make money. The photos.'

As high as the group had been with the prospect of a major break or even conclusion to the investigation coming the following day, a gloom now descended over everyone. It was the gloom of knowing what horrors there were out there in the world. This was just one case. There would always be others. Always.

'Keep working it, Brass,' Backus finally said. 'I'd like you to send a psychopathologic report as soon as possible.'

'Will do. Oh, and one other thing. This is good.'

'Then go ahead.'

'I just pulled the hard file on Gladden that was put together after some of you visited him six years ago for the rapist profile data project. There's really nothing here that wasn't on the computer already. But there is a photograph.'

'Right,' Rachel said. 'I remember. The hacks let us go into the block after lockdown to take a picture of them, Gladden and Gomble, in their cell together.'

'Yes, that's what this is. And in the photograph there are three bookshelves situated over the toilet. I would assume these were shared shelves, both men's books. But anyway, the spines of these books are clearly visible. Most are law books that I am assuming Gladden must have used while working on his own appeal and for other inmates. Also, there is *Forensic Pathology* by DiMaio and DiMaio, *Techniques of Crime Scene Investigation* by Fisher, and *Psycho-Pathologic Profiling* by Robert Backus Sr. I'm familiar with these books and I think Gladden could have learned enough from these, particularly the book by Bob's father, to possibly know how to make each of the bait killings and crime scenes different enough from each other so that a VICAP hit could be avoided.'

'Shit,' Thorson said. 'What the fu – what was he doing with those books?'

'I assume by law the prison had to allow him access to them so that he could properly prepare his appeal,' Doran replied. 'Remember, he was pro se. He was certified in court as his own attorney.'

'Okay, good work, Brass,' Backus said. 'That's a help.'

'It's not all, either. There were two other books of note on the shelf. *Edgar Allan Poe, the Poems* and *The Complete Works of Edgar Allan Poe.*'

Backus whistled his delight.

'Now, that's really starting to tie things up,' he said. 'I assume we can find all the quotes in these books?'

'Yes. One of these is the book Jack McEvoy used already to verify the quotes.'

'Right. Okay, can you shoot us out a copy of that photo?'

'Will do, boss.'

The excitement in the room and coming over the phone lines seemed almost palpable. It was all coming together, all the pieces. And tomorrow the agents were going to go out and get this son of a bitch.

'I love the smell of napalm in the morning,' Thorson said. 'Smells like . . .'

'Victory!' shouted those in the room and on every phone.

'Okay, folks,' Backus said, clapping his hands twice. 'I think we've covered enough for now. Let's keep sharp. Let's keep this spirit. Tomorrow could be the day. Let's say it *is* the day. And you people listening in the cities, don't stop for one minute. Keep working your end. If we get this guy, we'll still need physical evidence connecting him to the other crimes. We need to place him in every city for trial.'

'If there is a trial,' Thorson said.

I looked at him. The humor he had shown a moment before had now evaporated. His jaw was set. He got up and headed out of the conference room.

I spent the evening alone in my room, filling my computer with notes from the conference meeting and waiting for Rachel to call. I had paged her twice.

Finally, at nine – midnight in Florida – she called.

'I can't sleep and I just wanted to make sure you didn't have another woman with you in there.'

I smiled.

'Not very likely. I've been waiting for you to call. Didn't you get my pages or are you just busy with another man?'

'No, let me check.'

She put the phone down for a few moments.

'Darn, the battery's down. I've got to get another. Sorry.'

'You talking about the pager or the other man?'

'Funny guy.'

'So why can't you sleep?'

'I keep thinking about Thorson in that store tomorrow.'

'And?'

'And I have to admit I'm fucking jealous. If he gets the arrest on this ... I mean, it's my case and I'm two thousand fucking miles away from it.'

'Maybe it won't happen tomorrow. Maybe you'll be back in time. Even if you're not, it's not going to be him. It's going to be the critical team.'

'I don't know. Gordon's got a way of getting in there. And I have a bad feeling. It's tomorrow.'

'Some people might call that a good feeling, knowing that this guy's going to be taken off the street.'

'I know, I know. Still, why him? I think he and Bob ... I didn't really get it clear from Bob why he sent me to Florida instead of someone else, instead of Gordon. He took the case away from me and I just let him.'

'Maybe Thorson told him about you and me.'

'I was thinking that. He would, too. But I don't see Bob doing what he did and not talking to me about it, not telling me why first. He's not that way. He doesn't take a side until he hears both sides.'

'I'm sorry, Rachel. But look, everybody knows it's your case. And it was your break with that Hertz car that brought everybody to L.A.'

'Thanks, Jack. But it was just one of the breaks. And it doesn't matter. Making the arrest is like what you said about getting the story first. Doesn't really matter what's happened before.'

I knew I wasn't going to be able to make her feel better about the situation. She had brooded over it all night and there weren't enough words for me to change her mind. I decided to change the subject.

'Anyway, that was good stuff you got today. It seems like everything is coming together. We haven't even caught the guy and so much is known about him.'

'I guess. After hearing everything Brass said, do you have sympathy for him, Jack? For Gladden?'

'The man who killed my brother? Nope. No sympathy at all.'

'I didn't think so.'

'But you still do.'

She took a long time answering.

'I think of a little child that could have been a lot of different things until that man did what he did. Beltran set the child on the path. He's the real monster in all of this. Like I said before, if anybody got what he deserved, it was him.'

'Okay, Rachel.'

She started laughing.

'Sorry, I guess I'm finally getting tired. I didn't mean to be so intense all of a sudden.'

'It's okay. I know what you meant. There is a means to

every end. A root to any cause. Sometimes the root is more evil than the cause, though it's the cause that is usually the most vilified.'

'You have a way with words, Jack.'

'I'd rather have my way with you.'

'You have that, too.'

I laughed and thanked her. Then we were silent for a few moments, the line open between us, stretching two thousand miles. I felt comfortable. No need to talk.

'I don't know how close they'll let you get tomorrow,' she said. 'But be careful.'

'I will. You too. When will you be back?'

'I hope by tomorrow afternoon. I told them to have the jet ready by twelve. I'm going to check out Gladden's mail drop and then get on the plane.'

'Okay. Why don't you try to go to sleep now?'

'Okay. I wish I was with you.'

'Me, too.'

I thought she was about to hang up but she didn't.

'Did you talk about me with Gordon today?'

I thought about his comment, calling her the Painted Desert.

'No. We had a pretty busy day.'

I don't think she believed me and I felt bad about lying.

'I'll see you, Jack.'

'Okay, Rachel.'

I thought about the phone conversation for a while after hanging up. Our conversation made me feel kind of sad and I couldn't pinpoint the true reason. After a while, I got up and left the room. It was raining. From the doorway of the hotel I checked the street and saw no one hiding, no one waiting for me. I shrugged off the fears of the night before and stepped out.

Walking close to the buildings to avoid as much of the rain as I could, I went to the Cat & Fiddle and ordered a beer at the bar. The place was crowded despite the rain. My hair was wet and in the mirror behind the bar I saw dark circles cut under my eyes. I touched my beard the way Rachel had caressed it. When I was done with the black and tan I ordered another.

40
·········

The incense had long burned away by Wednesday morning. Gladden moved about the apartment with a T-shirt tied around his head, covering his mouth and nose, making him look like a bank robber from the Old West. He had sprinkled perfume he had found in the bathroom on the shirt and around the apartment, like a priest with holy water, but just like holy water, it didn't help him much. The smell was still everywhere, haunting him. But he didn't care anymore. He had made it through. It was time to leave. Time to change.

In the bathroom, he once again used a pink plastic razor he had found on the bathtub ledge to shave. He then took a long, hot and then cold, shower and afterward moved about the apartment naked, letting the air dry his body. He had taken a mirror off the wall of the bedroom earlier and propped it up against the living room wall. He now practiced walking in front of it again, back and forth, back and forth, watching his hips.

When he was satisfied he had it down, he went into the bedroom. The processed air chilled his naked body and the smell nearly made him convulse. But he stood his ground and looked down at her. She was gone now. The body on the bed was bloated and had lost all recognizable values. The eyes were coated in a milky caul. Bloody decomposition fluids had purged from everywhere, even the scalp. And the bugs had her now. He couldn't see them but he could hear them. They were there. He knew. It was in the books.

As he closed the door he thought he heard a whisper and he looked back in. It was nothing. Just the bugs. He closed the door and put the towel back in place.

41

....

The man we believed to be William Gladden called Data Imaging Answers at 11:05 on Wednesday morning, identifying himself as Wilton Childs and inquiring about the digiShot camera he had ordered. Thorson took the call and, according to plan, asked if Childs could call back in five or ten minutes. Thorson explained that a shipment of merchandise had just been delivered and he hadn't had a chance to look through it all. Childs said he would call back.

Meantime, Backus monitored the caller ID display and quickly gave the number Childs/Gladden had called from to an AT&T operator standing by on the law enforcement request desk. The operator punched the number into her computer and reported that it belonged to a pay phone on Ventura Boulevard in Studio City before Thorson had even hung up.

One of the roving two-car teams of FBI agents was on the 101 freeway in Sherman Oaks, about five minutes away from the pay phone with good traffic. They gassed it down to the Vineland Boulevard exit without use of sirens, exited to Ventura Boulevard and took positions within sight of the pay phone, which was on a wall outside the office of a $40-a-night motel, porno movies included. No one was at the phone by the time they got there but they waited. Meantime, another roving team was en route from Hollywood as backup and a helicopter was circling on standby over Van Nuys, ready to move over the scene when the ground agents moved in.

The agents in place waited. And so did I, in a car with Backus and Carter a block from Data Imaging. Carter turned the car on, ready to roll if the word came over the radio that the others had Gladden in sight.

Five minutes passed and then ten. It was all·very intense, even sitting blind with Backus and Carter. The backup cars had enough time to take positions a few blocks behind the first team's cars on Ventura. There were now eight agents within a block of the pay phone.

But at 11:33, when the phone on Thorson's desk at Data Imaging rang, the agents in place were still watching an unused pay phone. Backus picked up the two-way.

'We've got a ring here. Anything?'

'Nada. No one's using this phone.'

'Be ready to move.'

Backus put the two-way down and picked up the mobile phone, hitting the preset key for calling the AT&T law enforcement desk. I was leaning over from the backseat, watching him and the video monitor on the transmission hump beneath the dashboard. It was a black-and-white fish-eye view of the whole Digital Imaging showroom. I saw Thorson pick the phone up on the seventh ring. Though both phone lines into the store were tapped, we could only hear Thorson's side of the conversation in the car. Thorson gave the high sign on the video, raising his hand over his head and making a circling motion with his finger. It was the sign that Childs/Gladden was calling again. Backus began the same rundown with caller ID that he had done before.

Not wanting to possibly spook Childs/Gladden, Thorson engaged no delay tactics on the second call. He also had no way of knowing that the call was coming from a different phone this time. For all he knew, agents were moving in on Gladden as he spoke to him.

But they weren't. As Thorson was telling the caller that his digiShot 200 had arrived and was ready for pickup, Backus was learning from the AT&T operator that the new call was being placed from another pay phone at Hollywood Boulevard and Las Palmas Street.

'Shit,' Backus said after hanging up. 'He's in Hollywood. I just pulled everyone out of there.'

Was it by design or luck that Gladden had escaped? No

one knew, of course, but it was eerie, sitting there in the car with Backus and Carter. The Poet had kept moving and so far had avoided the net. Backus went through the motions of sending the roving teams to the intersection in Hollywood but I could tell by his voice he knew there wasn't much of a percentage in it. The caller would be gone. The only chance now would be to take him after he came for the camera. If he came.

On the phone in the store, Thorson was delicately attempting to pin the caller down on what time he would be by to pick up his camera but trying to act uninterested about it. Thorson was a good actor, it seemed to me. After a few moments he hung up.

He immediately looked toward the fish-eye lens of the camera and calmly said, 'Talk to me people. What's going on?'

Backus used the mobile phone to call the store and fill Thorson in on the near miss. I watched on the video as Thorson balled his hand into a fist and lightly bounced it once on the desk. I couldn't tell if it was a sign of disappointment that the arrest had not gone down or maybe a sign of thanks that he would now get the chance to come face to face with the Poet.

Most of the next four hours was spent in the car with Backus and Carter. At least I had the backseat so I could stretch. The only break came when they sent me around the corner to a deli on Pico to pick up sandwiches and coffee. I went quickly and missed nothing.

It was a long day, even with the hourly drive-bys Carter made of the store and the arrival of several customers at different times, which always proved to be tense moments until they were identified as real customers, not Gladden.

By four, Backus was already talking over plans for the next day with Carter, not giving in to the thought that maybe Gladden wasn't coming, that maybe he knew something was amiss and had outsmarted the bureau. He told Carter that he had decided he wanted to open a two-way mike so that he didn't have to use one of the phone lines to communicate with Thorson in the store.

'I want that fixed by tomorrow,' he said.

'You got it,' Carter answered. 'After we close this down, I'll go in with technical and get it all fixed up.'

The car dropped into silence again. I could tell Backus and Carter, the veterans of too many stakeouts to recall, were used to long stretches of silent company. To me, though, it made the time pass all the more slowly. Occasionally I attempted conversation but they never carried it further than a few words.

Shortly after four a car pulled to the curb behind us. I turned around to look and saw it was Rachel. She got out and got into our car next to me.

'Well, well,' Backus said. 'I had a feeling you wouldn't stay away for long, Rachel. Are you sure you covered everything you needed to cover in Florida?'

He was being even but I sensed that he was annoyed that she had rushed back. I think he wanted her in Florida.

'Everything's fine, Bob. Anything happening here?'

'Nope, it's been slow.'

When Backus turned back around, she reached over and squeezed my hand on the seat and made a curious face at me. It took me a few moments to realize why.

'Did you check the mail drop, Rachel?'

She broke her look away from me and looked at the back of Backus's head. He had not turned around and she was sitting directly behind him.

'Yes, Bob, I did,' she said in a voice slightly tinged with exasperation. 'It was a dead end. There was nothing in the box. The owner said that he believed a woman, an older woman, came in every month or so and cleaned it out. He said the only mail that ever came looked like bank statements. I think it was Gladden's mother. She's probably living somewhere around there but I couldn't find a listing and there was nothing from Florida DMV.'

'Maybe you should've stayed a little longer and looked a little harder.'

She was silent a moment. I knew she was still confused by the way Backus was now treating her.

'Maybe,' she said. 'But I think that's something the agents in Florida can handle. I'm the lead agent on this case. Remember, Bob?'

'Yes, I remember.'

The car was silent for a few minutes after that. I spent most of that time staring out my window. When I sensed the tension had dissipated a bit I looked over at Rachel and raised my eyebrows. She raised her hand to reach to my face but then thought better of it and put it down.

'You shaved.'

'Yeah.'

Backus turned around and looked at me, then returned to his normal position.

'I thought something was different,' he said.

'How come?' Rachel asked.

I hiked my shoulders.

'I don't know.'

A voice crackled over the radio.

'Customer.'

Carter picked up the mike and said, 'What've we got?'

'White male, twenties, blond hair, carrying a box. No vehicle observed. He's either going in Data or next door for a haircut. He could use one.'

There was a hair salon directly west of Data Imaging Answers. On the east side was an out-of-business hardware store. The observation agents had been calling out the potential customers all day; most of them ended up going into the salon rather than DIA.

'He's going in.'

I leaned over the seat to look at the monitor and saw the man enter the store with the box. The video frame was a black-and-white image that encompassed the whole showroom. The figure was too grainy and small to be identified as Gladden or not. I held my breath as I had each time a customer had entered. The man walked directly to the desk where Thorson sat. I saw Thorson move his right hand to his midsection, ready to go inside his coat for his weapon if needed.

'Can I help you?' he asked.

'Yes, I have these great monthly planners here.' He started reaching into the box. Thorson started standing. 'I'm selling them to a lot of your neighbors here.'

Thorson grabbed the man's arm to stop him from reaching, then tilted the box down so he could see inside it.

'I'm not interested,' he said after inspecting the contents.

The salesman, slightly taken aback by Thorson grabbing him, recovered and completed the sales pitch.

'Are you sure? Just ten bucks. Something like this'll run you thirty, thirty-five dollars in the office supply store. It's genuine Naugahyde and it's –'

'Not interested. Thank you.'

The salesman turned to Coombs sitting behind the other desk.

'How 'bout you, sir? Let me show you the deluxe mo –'

'We're not interested,' Thorson barked. 'Now if you would please leave the store, we're busy here. There's no soliciting here.'

'Yeah, I can see. Well, have a nice day to you, too.'

The man left the store.

'People,' Thorson said.

He shook his head as he sat down and didn't say anything more. Then he yawned. Watching it made me yawn, then Rachel caught it from me.

'The excitement is getting to Gordo,' Backus commented.

Me, too. I needed a caffeine fix. If I had been in the newsroom, I would have had at least six cups by this time of day. But because of the stakeout, there had been only one run for food and coffee and that had been three hours earlier.

I opened the door.

'I'm going for coffee. You guys want any?'

'You're gonna miss it, Jack,' Backus kidded.

'Yeah, right. Now I know why so many cops get hemorrhoids. Sitting and waiting for nothing.'

I got out, my knees cracking as I straightened my body. Carter and Backus said they'd pass on the coffee. Rachel said she would love some. I was hoping she wouldn't say she'd go with me and she didn't.

'How do you like it?' I asked, though I knew the answer.

'Black,' she said, smiling at my act.

'Okay. Be right back.'

42

....

Carrying four containers of black coffee in a small card-board box, I stepped through the door of the Data Imaging Answers store to see Thorson's shocked face. Before he could say anything the phone on his desk started ringing. He picked it up and said, 'I know.'

He held the phone out for me.

'For you, sport.'

It was Backus.

'Jack, get the hell out of there right now!'

'I will. I just wanted to drop off some coffee to these guys. You saw Gordo, he's falling asleep, it's so boring in here.'

'Very funny, Jack, but get out. Our agreement was that you would do things my way and I would protect the story. Now, please, do as – you've got a customer. Tell Thorson. It's a woman.'

I held the phone against my chest and looked at Thorson.

'Customer on the way. But it's a woman.'

I held the receiver back up.

'Okay, I'm out of here,' I said to Backus.

I hung the phone up and took one of the coffee containers out of the box and put it on Thorson's desk. I heard the door open behind me, the sound of traffic going by on Pico getting momentarily louder and then buffered again by the closed glass. Without turning around to look at the customer I went over to the desk where Coombs was sitting.

'Coffee?'

'Thank you very much.'

I put another cup down and reached into the box for packets of sugar and powdered cream and a stirring straw.

When I turned around I saw the woman standing in front of Thorson's desk, digging through a big black purse. She had fluffy blond hair in a Dolly Parton cascade. An obvious wig. She wore a white blouse over a short skirt and black stockings. She was tall, even with the high heels. I noticed that when she had opened the door to the shop a strong odor of perfume entered with her.

'Ah,' she said, finding what she was looking for. 'I'm here to pick this up for my boss.'

She placed a folded yellow sheet on the desk in front of Thorson. He looked over at Coombs, an attempt to signal that Coombs should take over this transaction.

'Take it easy, Gordo,' I said.

As I started for the door I looked over at Thorson, expecting him to reply to my repeated use of the nickname Backus had used for him. I saw Thorson looking at the now unfolded sheet she had given him and his eyes fixed on something. I saw his eyes glance at the west wall of the store. I knew he was looking at the camera. At Backus. He then looked up at the woman. I was behind her at this point and could only see Thorson's eyes just over her shoulder. He was rising and I saw his mouth coming open in a silent O. His right arm was coming up and he was reaching inside his jacket. Then I saw her right arm coming up from the bag. When it cleared her torso I saw the knife grasped in her hand.

She brought the knife down well before Thorson had his arm out of his jacket. I heard his strangled cry as the knife plunged into his throat. He started falling back, a spray of arterial blood going up, hitting her in the shoulder as she leaned all the way over the desk reaching for something.

She straightened up and spun around, Thorson's gun in hand.

'Nobody fuckin' move!'

The woman's voice was gone, replaced by the near hysterical and taut voice of the cornered male animal. He aimed the gun at Coombs and then swung it around at me.

'Get away from that door. Get in here!'

I dropped the box with the two coffee containers, raised my

hands and moved away from the door, further into the show-room. The man in the dress then wheeled again on Coombs, who shrieked.

'No! Please, they're watching, no!'

'Who's watching? Who?'

'They're watching on the camera!'

'Who?'

'The FBI, Gladden,' I said in as calm a tone as I could muster, which probably wasn't too far removed from the same shriek that Coombs had emitted.

'Can they hear?'

'Yes, they can hear.'

'FBI!' Gladden yelled. 'FBI, you got one dead already. You come in here and you'll get two more.'

He then turned to the display table and aimed Thorson's gun at the video camera with the red light on. He fired three times until he hit it and it flew backward off the table, breaking apart.

'Get over here,' he yelled at me. 'Where are the keys?'

'Keys to what?'

'The goddamn store.'

'Take it easy. I don't work here.'

'Then who does?'

He turned the gun on Coombs.

'In my pocket. The keys are in my pocket.'

'Go lock that front door. You try to run through and I'll shoot you down like the camera.'

'Yes, sir.'

Coombs did as he was told and then Gladden ordered both of us to the back of the showroom and told us to sit on the floor against the door to the rear storage room, blocking any-body from charging through. He then turned over both desks so they would act as blinds and maybe even barriers against bullets from outside the front windows. He crouched down behind the desk where Thorson had been.

I could see Thorson's body from my position. Most of his previously white shirt was soaked in blood. There was no movement and his eyes were half closed and fixed. The handle of a knife still protruded from his throat. I shuddered at the sight, realizing that a moment ago the man was alive and that whether I liked him or not, I knew him. Now he was dead.

The thought occurred to me then that Backus must be panicked. With the video out, he might not know Thorson's status. If he believed Thorson was alive and there was a chance he could be saved, I could expect the critical response team to start coming through with stun grenades and everything else at any moment. If they believed Thorson to be dead, I might as well settle in for what could be a long night.

'You don't work here,' Gladden said to me. 'Who are you? Do I know you?'

I hesitated. Who was I? Did I tell this man the truth?

'You're FBI.'

'No. I'm not FBI. I'm a reporter.'

'A reporter? You came for my story, is that it?'

'If you want to give it. If you want to talk to the FBI, put that phone over there on the floor back on its hook. They'll call on that line.'

He looked over at the phone that had come apart on the floor when he had overturned the desk. Just then it began emitting the sharp tone signaling it was off the hook. He could reach the line without moving out of cover. He dragged the phone over and hung it up. He looked at me.

'I recognize you,' he said. 'You –'

The phone rang and he picked it up.

'Talk,' he commanded.

There was a long silence until he finally responded to whatever had been said.

'Well, well, Agent Backus, good to make your acquaintance again. I have learned a lot about you since we last met in Florida. And Dad, of course. Read his book. I always hoped we would talk again ... You and I. ... No, you see, that would be impossible because I have these two hostages here. You fuck with me, Bob, and I fuck with them in ways you won't believe when you come in here. You remember Attica? Think

391

about that, Agent Backus. Think about how Dad would handle this. I gotta go.'

He hung up and looked at me. He pulled the wig off and threw it angrily across the showroom.

'How the hell did you get in here, reporter? The FBI doesn't let –'

'You killed my brother. That's what got me in.'

Gladden looked at me a long moment.

'I didn't kill anyone.'

'They've got you cold. No matter what you do to us, they've got you, Gladden. And they're not going to let you out of here. They –'

'All right, shut the fuck up! I don't have to listen to that.'

Gladden picked up the phone and dialed a number.

'Let me talk to Krasner, it's an emergency ... William Gladden ... Yeah, that one.'

We looked at each other while he waited for the lawyer to pick up. I tried to show a calm exterior but inside my brain was racing. I didn't see any way out of this without somebody else dying. Gladden didn't seem like the type who could be talked into raising his hands and giving up so he could be strapped into the electric chair or the gas chamber in a few years, depending on which state got the first shot at him.

Krasner apparently came on the line and for the next ten minutes Gladden heatedly reviewed the situation for him, getting angry at whatever course of action Krasner suggested he take. Finally, he slammed the phone down.

'Fuck that.'

I kept quiet. I figured that every minute that went by was in my favor. The FBI had to be formulating something out there. The sharpshooters, the surgical entry team.

The light was dimming outside. I looked through the front plate-glass window and to the plaza shopping center across the street. My eyes followed the roofline but I saw no figures, not even the telltale barrel of a sniper's rifle. Not yet.

I looked away and then quickly back. I realized there was no traffic going by on Pico. They had closed the road. Whatever was going to happen was going to happen soon. I looked over at Coombs, wondering if there was some way of letting him know to brace himself.

Coombs had sweated through his shirt. The knot of his tie, the recipient of all the sweat sliding down his cheeks and neck, was soaked. He looked like someone who had just spent the better part of an hour throwing up. He was sick.

'Gladden, show 'em something. Let Mr Coombs go. He doesn't have anything to do with this.'

'No, I don't think so.'

The phone rang and he picked it up and listened without saying anything. Then he softly placed the receiver down on the hook. The phone rang again in a few moments and he answered and quickly pushed the hold button. He punched the key for picking up the other line and put that on hold as well. Now no one could call in.

'You're fucking up,' I said. 'Let them talk to you, they'll figure something out.'

'Listen, when I want your advice I'll beat it out of you. Now, shut the fuck up!'

'Okay.'

'I said shut up!'

I raised my hands in an I-give-up gesture.

'You fucking media assholes never know what you're talking about anyway. You – what's your name, anyway?'

'Jack McEvoy.'

'You got ID?'

'In my pocket.'

'Throw it over here.'

I slowly pulled my wallet out and slid it across the rug to him. He opened it and looked through the press passes.

'I thought you – Denver? What the fuck you doing in L.A.?'

'I told you. My brother.'

'Yeah, and I told you. I didn't kill anybody.'

'What about him?'

I nodded toward Thorson's still inert body. Gladden looked at the body and then back at me.

'He made the play. I finished it. Rules of the game.'

'The guy's dead. It's no fucking game.'

Gladden raised the gun and pointed it at my face.

'If I say it's a game, then it's a game.'

I said nothing in response.

'Please,' Coombs said. 'Please . . .'

'Please what? Just shut the fuck up. You . . . uh, paperboy, what are you going to write when this is over? Assuming you can still write.'

I thought for at least a minute and he let me.

'I'll tell why if you want me to,' I said finally. 'It's always the most interesting question. Why did you do it? I'd tell that. Is it because of that guy in Florida? Beltran?'

He snorted in derision, more in displeasure that I had mentioned the name, not that I knew it.

'This isn't an interview. And if it is, no fucking comment.'

Gladden looked down at the gun in his hands for what seemed like a long time. I think at that point he felt the futility of the situation pressing down on him. He knew he wasn't going anywhere and I got the sense that he'd known his trail would eventually end in a scene like this. It seemed he was at a weak point and I tried again.

'You should pick up that phone and tell them you want to speak to Rachel Walling,' I said. 'Tell 'em you'll talk to her. She's an agent. You remember her? She came to you at Raiford. She knows all about you, Gladden, and she'd help.'

He shook his head no.

'I had to kill your brother,' he said softly, without looking at me. 'I had to do it.'

I waited and that was all he said.

'Why?'

'The only way to save him.'

'Save him from what?'

'Don't you see?' He looked up at me now, deep pain and anger in his eyes. 'From becoming like me. Look at me! From becoming like me!'

I was about to ask another question when there was the sudden sound of shattering glass. I looked toward the front and saw a dark object about the size of a baseball bounce across the room toward the overturned desk near Gladden. I registered what it was and began to roll and bring my arms up to cradle my head and shield my eyes just as there was a tremendous detonation in the showroom, a blast of light that burned through my closed eyes and a following concussion so strong it sent a pounding energy wave through me like a punch to my whole body.

The rest of the windows shattered and as I completed my roll I opened my eyes enough to get a bead on Gladden. He was squirming on the floor, his eyes wide but not focused and his hands held to his ears. But I could tell he had been too late in recognizing what was happening. I had been able to block at least some of the impact of the concussion grenade. He looked as if he had taken the full brunt of it. I saw the gun lying loose on the floor next to his legs. Without pausing to consider my chances, I quickly crawled toward it.

Gladden sat up as I got to him and we both lunged for the gun, our hands reaching it at the same time. We fought for control and rolled over each other. My thought was to get to the trigger and just start firing. It didn't matter if I hit him, as long as I didn't hit myself. I knew the concussion grenade would be followed by the charge of the agents. If I could empty the gun, it wouldn't matter who had it. It would be over.

I managed to squeeze my left thumb in behind the trigger guard but the only place my right hand could grasp was the end of the barrel. The gun was between our chests, pointing toward our chins. At the moment I judged – hoped – I was out of the line of fire, I squeezed with my left hand while opening my right hand. The gun discharged and I felt a sharp pain as the bullet clipped the webbing between my thumb and palm and the escaping gases scorched my hand. At the same moment I heard Gladden howl. I looked up to his face and saw blood spreading from his nose. What was left of it. The bullet had ripped off the rim of his left nostril and cut a slashing crease up his forehead.

I felt his grip momentarily weaken and in one burst of strength – possibly my last – I wrenched away control of the gun. I was pulling myself away from him, registering the sound of footsteps in glass and unintelligible yells when Gladden made another lunge for the gun in my hands. My thumb was still caught in the trigger guard, all the way past the joint. It was pressed against the trigger and there was no room left for movement. Gladden tried to wrench the gun back and in doing so it discharged once again. Our eyes met at that moment and there was something telling in his. They told me that he had wanted the bullet.

Immediately his grip on the gun relaxed and he fell back away from me. I saw the gaping wound in his chest. His eyes stared at me with the same look of resolve I had seen moments before. Like he knew what was going to happen. He reached to his chest and looked down at the blood pumping into his hand.

Suddenly I was grabbed from behind and pulled away from him. A hand firmly gripped my arm and another carefully removed the gun from my hand. I looked up and saw a man wearing a black helmet and matching black jumpsuit with a large armored vest on the outside. He held some kind of assault weapon and wore a radio headset, a thin black bar curving in front of his mouth. He looked down at me and touched the transmit button at his ear.

'We're all secure here,' he said. 'We've got two down and two walking. Come on in.'

43
········

There was no pain and that surprised him. The blood, gushing through his fingers and over his hands, was warm and comforting. He had a giddy feeling of having just passed some test. He had made it. Whatever that was. The sound and movement around him were all dulled and in slow motion. He looked about and saw the one who had shot him. Denver. For a moment their eyes locked but then someone got in the way. The man in black bent down over him and did something. Gladden looked down and saw the handcuffs on his wrists. He smiled at the stupidity of it. No handcuffs could hold him where he was going now.

Then he saw her. A woman crouching over the one from Denver. She squeezed his hand. Gladden recognized her. She was one of those who had come to him so many years before in prison. He remembered now.

He was getting cold. His shoulders and neck. His legs, they were numb. He wanted a blanket but no one was looking at him. No one cared. The room was getting brighter, like TV cameras. He was slipping away and knew it.

'This is what it is like,' he whispered but no one seemed to hear.

Except the woman. She turned at the sound of his soft words. Their eyes connected and after a moment Gladden thought he saw the slight nod, the knowledge of recognition.

Recognition of what, he wondered. That I'm dying? That there was purpose to my being here? He turned his head toward her and waited for the life to finish flowing from him. He could rest now. Finally.

He looked at her once more but she was looking down at

the man again. Gladden studied him, the man who had killed him, and an odd thought pushed its way through the blood. He seemed too old to have had a brother that young. There must be a mistake somewhere.

Gladden died with his eyes open, staring at the man who had killed him.

44
········

It was a surrealistic scene. People running around the showroom, yelling, huddled over the dead and the dying. My ears ringing, my hand throbbing. It seemed almost to be in slow motion. At least that is the way it is in my memory. And out of all of this Rachel appeared, stepping through the glass like a guardian angel sent to shepherd me away. She reached down and grabbed my uninjured hand and squeezed it. Her touch was like a code-blue paddle shocking me back from a flat line. I suddenly realized what had happened and what I had done, and I was overcome with the joy of simply surviving. Thoughts of justice and vengeance were far away.

I looked over at Thorson. The paramedics were working on him, one of them sitting astride him, putting all her weight behind the heart massage, the other holding the oxygen mask in place. Still another zipping his prone body into a pressure suit. Backus knelt next to his fallen agent, holding his hand and rubbing his wrist, yelling, 'Breathe, damnit, breathe! Come on, Gordo, breathe!'

But it was not to be. They couldn't bring poor Thorson back from the dead. They all knew it but no one stopped. They kept working on him and when the stretcher and gurney were brought in through the blasted-out front window and he was loaded aboard, the paramedic took her spot straddled on top of him again. Her elbows locked, her hands locked together and pushing up and down, up and down, on his chest. They were wheeled out like that.

I watched Rachel watch the procession with not sad but distant eyes, then her stare fell from her former husband's exit to his killer on the floor next to me.

I looked over at Gladden. He had been cuffed and no one was working on him yet. They were going to let him die. Any thoughts of what they might be able to learn from him went out the window when he drove that knife into Thorson's throat.

I looked at him and thought, in fact, that he already was dead, his eyes staring blankly at the ceiling. But then his mouth moved and he said something I couldn't hear. Then his head slowly turned toward me. At first, his eyes held on Rachel. It lasted only a moment but I saw their eyes lock and some kind of communication pass between them. Recognition maybe. Perhaps he remembered her. Then he slowly turned his eyes until he stared directly at me again. I was looking at his eyes when the life ran out of them.

After Rachel walked me out of Data Imaging, I was taken in an ambulance to a hospital called Cedars-Sinai. By the time I arrived, Thorson and Gladden had already been there and had been pronounced dead. In an emergency room suite a doctor looked my hand over, irrigated the wound with something that looked like a piece of a black soda straw and then sewed it shut. He put some kind of balm on the burns and then wrapped bandages around the whole thing.

'The burns are nothing,' he said as he wrapped. 'Don't worry about them. But the wound's going to be tough. On the positive, it's through and through, no bones involved. But on the negative, the bullet chopped through that tendon there and you're going to have restricted thumb movement if you leave it the way it is. I can put you in touch with a specialist who can probably reattach the tendon or make a new one for you. With the surgery and some exercise it should be okay.'

'What about typing?'

'Not for a while.'

'No, I mean as exercise.'

'Yeah, maybe. You'll have to ask your doctor.'

He patted my shoulder and left the room. I was alone for ten minutes, sitting on the examination table, before Backus and Rachel came in. Backus had the washed-out look of a man who has seen all his plans turn to shit.

'How're you doing, Jack?' he asked.

'I'm okay. I'm sorry about Agent Thorson. It was ...'

'I know. These things ...'

Nobody spoke for a few moments. I looked at Rachel and our eyes held each other's.

'Are you sure you're all right?'

'Yeah, fine. I won't be typing for a while but ... I guess I'm the lucky one. What happened to Coombs?'

'He's still in shock at what happened but he's all right.'

I looked at Backus.

'Bob, there was nothing I could do. Something happened. It looked like they suddenly knew who each other was. I don't know. Why didn't Thorson go ahead with the plan? Why didn't he just give him the camera instead of going for his gun?'

'Because he wanted to be the hero,' Rachel said. 'He wanted the arrest. Or the kill.'

'Rachel, we don't know that,' Backus said. 'We never will. The one question that can be answered, though, is why did you go in there in the first place, Jack? Why?'

I looked down at my bandaged hand. With my good hand I touched my cheek.

'I don't know,' I answered. 'I saw Thorson yawn on the monitor and thought ... I don't know why I did it. He brought me coffee once ... I was returning the favor. I didn't think Gladden was going to show.'

I lied. But I could not articulate my true motives or emotions. All I knew was that I had a sense that if I went into that store Gladden might come. And I wanted him to see me. Without disguise. I wanted him to see my brother.

'Well,' Backus said after a spell of silence. 'Think you'll be up for spending some time with a stenographer tomorrow? I realize you are hurt but we'd like to get your statement so we can get this all squared away. We'll have to submit something to the local district attorney.'

I nodded.

'Yeah, I'll be there.'

'You know, Jack, when Gladden took out the camera, he took down the sound as well. We don't know what was said in there. So tell me, did Gladden say anything?'

I thought a moment. The memory was still coming back to me.

'First he said he didn't kill anybody. Then he admitted killing Sean. He said he killed my brother.'

Backus arched his eyebrows as if surprised and then nodded.

'Okay, Jack, we'll see you then.' He turned to Rachel. 'You said you'll get him back to the room?'

'Yes, Bob.'

'Okay.'

Backus left the room with his head down and I felt bad. I didn't think he had accepted my explanation and I wondered if he would always blame me for how horribly wrong things had gone.

'What will happen to him?' I asked.

'Well, the first thing is there's a lobby full of media out there and he's got to tell them how this got all fucked up. After that I'm sure the director will want Professional Standards to come out to investigate the planning of this. It's not going to get any better for him.'

'It was Thorson's plan. Can't they just –'

'Bob approved it. If somebody has to take a fall, Gordon isn't around anymore.'

Looking through the open door where Backus had just walked I saw a doctor stop and look in. He carried a stethoscope in his hand and several pens in the pocket of his white jacket.

'Everything okay in here?' he inquired.

'Fine.'

'We're fine,' Rachel added.

She turned away from the door and looked at me.

'You sure?'

I nodded.

'I'm so glad you are okay. That was a foolish thing you did.'

'I just thought he could use the coffee. I didn't ex –'

'I mean going for the gun. Getting it from Gladden.'

I shook my shoulders. Maybe it was foolish, I thought, but maybe it saved my life.

'How did you know, Rachel?'

'Know what?'

'You asked me what would happen if I ever faced him. It was like you knew.'

'I didn't know, Jack. It was just a question.'

She reached up and traced my jawline like she did when I'd had the beard. Then with her finger she tilted my chin up until I was looking at her. She moved in between my legs and pulled me into a deep kiss. It was healing and sensual at the same time. I closed my eyes. My good hand went up under her jacket and I rested it lightly on her breast.

When she pulled away I opened my eyes and over her shoulder I saw the doctor who had poked his head in earlier turning away.

'Peeping Tom,' I said.

'What?'

'That doctor. I think he was watching us.'

'Never mind him. Are you ready to go?'

'Yeah, I'm ready.'

'Did you get a prescription for pain?'

'I'm supposed to get some pills before I sign out.'

'You can't sign out. The media's up there and they'll be all over you.'

'Damn, I forgot. I've got to call in.'

I looked at my watch. It was almost eight in Denver. Greg Glenn was probably there, waiting to hear from me, refusing to release the front page to the printers until he'd heard from me. I figured the latest he could go would be nine. I looked around. There was a phone on the wall above a supplies and equipment counter at the back of the room.

'Could you go tell them I can't sign out up there?' I asked. 'In the meantime I'll just call in at the *Rocky* and tell them I'm still alive.'

*

Glenn was almost delirious when I got through to him.

'Jack, where the hell you been?'

'I've sort of been tied up. I –'

'Are you okay? The wires say you were shot.'

'I'm okay. I'll be typing one-handed for a while.'

'The wires say the Poet's dead. AP quotes one source who says you . . . uh, killed him.'

'AP's got a good source.'

'Jesus, Jack.'

I didn't reply.

'CNN's been going live from the scene every ten minutes but they don't have shit. There's supposed to be a press conference at the hospital.'

'Right. And if you can get me hooked up with somebody to take some rewrite, I can give you enough of the story for the front page. It will be better than anyone else gets tonight.'

He said nothing in response.

'Greg?'

'Wait a minute, Jack. I have to think. You . . .'

He didn't finish but I waited him out.

'Jack, I'm going to put you on the line with Jackson. Tell what you can to him. He'll also take notes off the press conference if CNN carries it.'

'Wait a minute. I don't want to give anything to Jackson. Just give me a copy messenger or a clerk and I'll dictate the story. It's going to be better than what they put out at the press conference.'

'No, Jack, you can't. It's different now.'

'What are you talking about?'

'You're not covering the story anymore. You are part of it. You killed the guy who killed your brother. You killed the Poet. The story's about you now. You can't write it. I'm putting you on with Jackson. But do me a favor. Stay away from the other reporters out there. Give us a one-day exclusive on our own guy, at least.'

'Look, I've always been part of this story.'

'Yeah, but you didn't shoot anybody. Jack, that's not what

reporters do. That's what cops do and you crossed that line. You're off the story. I'm sorry.'

'It was him or me, Greg.'

'I'm sure it was and thank God it was him. But that doesn't change things, Jack.'

I said nothing. In my mind I knew he was right about me not writing it. I just couldn't believe it. It was my story and now it was gone. I was inside still but I was out.

Just as Rachel came back in the room with a clipboard and several forms for me to sign, Jackson came on the line. He told me what a great story it was going to be and started asking questions. I answered them all and told him some things unasked. I signed the forms where Rachel pointed as I talked.

The interview was quick. Jackson said he wanted to watch the press conference on CNN so he would have official comment and confirmation to go with my version of events. He asked if I would call back in an hour in case of follow-up questions and I agreed. We then hung up and I was thankful to get off the line.

'Well, now that you just signed away your life and your firstborn son, you're free to go,' Rachel said. 'You sure you don't want to read any of this stuff?'

'Nah, let's go. You get the painkillers? My hand's beginning to hurt again.'

'Yes, right here.'

She pulled a vial out of her coat pocket and handed it to me along with a stack of pink phone message slips, apparently taken at the hospital's front desk.

'What are . . .'

There were calls from news producers at the three networks, 'Nightline' with Ted Koppel, and two of the morning shows, and from reporters at the *New York Times* and the *Washington Post*.

'You're a celebrity, Jack,' Rachel said. 'You went face to face with the devil and survived. People want to ask you how that felt. People always want to know about the devil.'

I shoved the messages into my back pocket.

'You going to call them?'
'Nope. Let's go.'

On the way back to Hollywood I told Rachel I didn't want to spend the night in the Wilcox Hotel. I said I wanted to order room service and then lie in a comfortable bed and watch TV with a remote in my hand, amenities that the Wilcox obviously didn't offer. She saw my point.

After we stopped at the Wilcox so I could get my things and check out, Rachel drove down Sunset Boulevard toward the strip. At the Chateau Marmont she stayed in the car while I went to the desk. I said I wanted a room with a view and didn't care what it cost. They gave me a room with a balcony that cost more than I'd ever spent for a hotel in my life. The balcony was overlooking the Marlboro Man and the rest of the billboards on the strip. I liked looking at the Marlboro Man. Rachel didn't bother getting her own room.

We didn't talk much while we ate our room service dinner. Instead, we maintained the kind of comfortable silence that couples of many years achieve. Afterward, I took a long bath and listened over the bathroom speaker to the CNN report on the shootout at Digital Imaging. There was nothing new. More questions than answers. A good portion of the news conference was focused on Thorson and the ultimate sacrifice he had made. For the first time I thought about Rachel and how she was dealing with this. She had lost her ex-husband. A man she had grown to despise but someone she had shared an intimate relationship with just the same.

When I came out of the bathroom I wore the terry-cloth bathrobe the hotel provided. She was lying on the bed, propped against the pillows, and still watching the television.

'The local news is about to start,' she said.

I crawled across the bed and kissed her.

'You okay?'

'Yeah, why?'

'I don't know. Uh, whatever the relationship was that you had with Thorson, I'm sorry. Okay?'

'So am I.'

'I was thinking . . . you want to make love?'

'Yes.'

I turned off the television and the lights. At one point in the dark I tasted tears on her cheeks and she held me tighter than she had ever done before. There was a bittersweet feel to our lovemaking. It was as if two sad and lonely people had crossed paths and had agreed to help heal each other. Afterward, she huddled against my back and I tried to sleep but I couldn't. The demons of the day were still wide awake inside.

'Jack?' she whispered. 'Why did you cry?'

I was silent for a few moments, trying to find the words that would explain an answer.

'I don't know,' I finally said. 'It's hard. All along, I think, I was hoping in a daydreaming sort of way that I would get the chance to . . . Just be glad you've never done what I did today. Just be glad.'

Still later sleep would not come, even after I had taken one of the pills from the hospital. She asked me what my thoughts were.

'I'm thinking about what he said to me at the end. I don't understand what he meant.'

'What did he tell you?'

'He said he killed Sean to save him.'

'From what?'

'From becoming like him. That's what I don't understand.'

'We probably never will. You should just let it go now. It's over.'

'He said something else. At the end. When everyone was there. Did you hear it?'

'I think so.'

'What was it?'

'He said something like, "This is what it's like." That's all.'

'What does it mean?'

'I think he was solving the mystery.'

'Death.'

'He saw it coming. He saw the answers. He said, "This is what it's like." Then he died.'

45
....

In the morning we found Backus already waiting in the conference room on the seventeenth floor of the federal building. It was another clear day and I could see the top of Catalina rising behind the marine layer of morning fog out on the Santa Monica Bay. It was eight-thirty but Backus had his jacket off and looked as though he had already been at it for several hours. His spot at the meeting table was cluttered with a spread of paperwork, two open laptops and a stack of pink phone message slips. His face was drawn and sad. It looked as though the loss of Thorson would leave a permanent mark on him.

'Rachel, Jack,' he said by means of salutation. It wasn't a good morning and he didn't say that. 'How's the hand?'

'It's okay.'

We had brought containers of coffee with us but I saw he had none. I offered him mine but he said he'd already had too much.

'What have we got?' Rachel asked.

'Did you two check out? I tried to call you this morning, Rachel.'

'Yes,' she said. 'Jack wanted something a little more comfortable. We moved over to the Chateau Marmont.'

'Pretty comfortable.'

'Don't worry. I won't submit it for reimbursement.'

He nodded and I got the idea from the way he looked at her that he knew she hadn't gotten her own room and had nothing to submit anyway. It was the least of his worries, though.

'It's coming together,' he said. 'Another one for the studies,

I suppose. These people – if you can call them that – never cease to amaze me. Every one of them, their stories … each one of them's a black hole. And there's never enough blood to fill it.'

Rachel pulled out a chair and sat across from him. I sat next to her. We didn't say anything. We knew he wanted to go on. He reached over with a pen and tapped the side of one of the laptops.

'This was his,' he said. 'It was recovered from the trunk of his car last night.'

'A Hertz car?' I asked.

'No. He arrived at Data Imaging in an eighty-four Plymouth registered to a Darlene Kugel, thirty-six, of North Hollywood. We went to her apartment last night, got no response and went in. She was in the bed. Her throat was cut, probably with the same knife he used on Gordon. She'd been dead for days. It looked like he'd burned incense, slopped perfume around to hide the smell.'

'He stayed in there with her body?' Rachel asked.

'Looks like it.'

'Were those her clothes he was wearing?' I asked.

'And the wig.'

'What was he doing dressed like her, anyway?' Rachel asked.

'Don't know and never will now. My guess is he knew everybody was looking for him. Police, the bureau. He thought it was a way to leave her place, get the camera and then maybe get out of town.'

'Probably. What did you get from her place?'

'There was nothing that was of much use inside, but her unit had two parking spaces assigned to it in the garage and we found an eighty-six Pontiac Firebird in one of them. Florida plate, it came back to Gladys Oliveros of Gainesville.'

'His mother?' I asked.

'Yes. Moved there when he went to prison so she'd be close for visits, I guess. Remarried and changed her name. Anyway, we opened the trunk of the Pontiac and found the computer, some other things, including the books Brass found in the picture from the cell. There was an old sleeping bag. There's blood on it and the lab has it. The initial report is that there is kapok in the insulation.'

'It means he put some of his victims in the trunk,' I said.

'Which accounts for the hours they were missing,' Rachel added.

'Wait a minute,' I said. 'If he had his mother's car, what about the car from Hertz in Phoenix? Why would he rent a car if he already had one?'

'Just another way of confusing the trail, Jack. Use mother's to move from city to city, but then he rents one when he moves in for the kill on the cop.'

My confusion over the logic of that theory showed on my face. But Backus dismissed it.

'Anyway, we haven't gotten the Hertz records yet, so let's not get sidetracked. For the moment, the computer is what's important.'

'What's in it?' Rachel asked.

'The office here has a computer unit, works with the group in Quantico. One of the agents, Don Clearmountain, took this last night and broke down the coding by about three this morning. He copied the hard disk to the mainframe here. Anyway, it's full of photographs. Fifty-seven of them.'

Backus used his thumb and forefinger to pinch the bridge of his nose. He had aged since I'd last seen him at the hospital. Aged badly.

'Children?' Rachel asked.

Backus nodded.

'Jesus. The victims?'

'Yes ... before and after. It's horrible stuff. Truly horrible.'

'And he was transmitting these somewhere? Like we thought?'

'Yes, the computer has a cellular modem as Gordon ... as he guessed. It, too, is registered out of Gainesville to Oliveros. We just got the records a little while ago.'

He indicated some of the paperwork in front of him.

'There are a lot of calls,' he said. 'All over the place. He was into some kind of net. A network where the users were interested in these kinds of photographs.'

He looked up from the papers at us, his eyes sick but defiant.

'We are tracing them all now. We're going to make a lot of arrests. A lot of people will pay for this. What happened to Gordon will not be for nothing.'

He nodded more to himself than us.

'We can compare the transmissions and the users to the bank deposits I found in Jacksonville,' Rachel said. 'I bet we'll be able to know just how much they paid for the photos and when.'

'Clearmountain and his people are already working on it. They're down the hall in the Group Three offices if you want to stop in.'

'Bob?' I said. 'Did they look at all fifty-seven photos?'

He looked at me a moment before answering.

'I did, Jack. I did.'

'They were only the kids?'

I felt my chest tightening. Whatever I had told myself about being emotionally deadened to my brother and what had happened was a lie.

'No, Jack,' Backus said. 'There are no pictures of those victims. None of the police officers, none of the other adult victims. I guess . . .'

He didn't finish.

'What?' I asked.

'I guess those kinds of photos would not have been profitable to him.'

I looked down at my hands on the table. My right hand was beginning to ache and felt clammy under the white bandages. I felt relief go through me. I think it was relief. What else is it that you feel when you learn that there are no photographs of your murdered brother's body out there all over the country, floating out there on the Internet and ready to be downloaded by any sick individual with a taste for it.

'I think when this gets out about this guy, there'll be a lot of people who'll want to throw a parade for you, Jack,' Backus said. 'Put you in a convertible and drive you down Madison Avenue.'

I looked at him. I didn't know if it was an attempt at humor but I didn't smile.

'Maybe sometimes vengeance is just as good as justice,' he said.

'They're pretty much the same if you ask me.'

After a few moments of silence, Backus changed the subject.

'Jack, we have to get your formal statement. I've got one of the office's stenographers set up for nine-thirty. Are you ready?'

'Ready as I'll ever be.'

'We just want the linear story. From A to B, don't leave any detail out. I thought, Rachel, you'd handle that, ask the questions.'

'Sure, Bob.'

'I'd like to get this wrapped up today and submitted to the DA tomorrow. Maybe we can all go home then.'

'Who's doing the package for the DA?' Rachel asked.

'Carter.'

He looked at his watch.

'Uh, you have a few minutes but why don't you go down the hall and ask for Sally Kimball. She might be ready to go now.'

Dismissed, we stood and headed for the door. I watched Rachel, trying to judge whether she was annoyed at being assigned to taking my statement while the local agents were tracing Gladden's computer records, which seemed at the moment to be the more exciting branch of the investigation. She showed nothing and at the door of the conference room she turned and told Backus she'd be around if he needed anything else.

'Thanks, Rachel,' he said. 'Oh, and Jack, these are for you.'

He held up the stack of pink message slips. I went back to the table and took them.

'And this.'

He raised my computer satchel from the floor next to his seat and handed it across the table to me.

'You left that in the car yesterday.'

'Thanks.'

I studied the stack of pink slips. There must have been a dozen of them.

'You're a popular man,' Backus said. 'Don't let it go to your head.'

'Only if they give me that parade.'

He didn't smile.

While Rachel went to look for the stenographer I stood in the hallway and looked through the messages. They were mostly repeats from the networks but a few print reporters had called, even one from my hometown competition, the *Denver Post*. The tabloids, of both the print and television variety, had left messages. There was also a call from Michael Warren. I noted from the 213 callback number that he was still in town.

The three messages that intrigued me the most weren't from the news media. Dan Bledsoe had called just an hour earlier from Baltimore. And there were two messages from book publishers, one from a senior editor at a New York-based house and one from an assistant to the publisher at another house. I recognized both imprints and felt a mixture of trepidation and thrill course through my chest.

Rachel came up to me then.

'She's going to be a couple minutes. There's an office down here we're going to use. Let's wait there.'

I followed her.

The room was a smaller version of the one we had met Backus in, with a round table and four chairs, a side counter with a phone, and a picture window with a view east toward downtown. I asked Rachel if it would be all right if I used the phone while we waited and she said go ahead. I keyed in the number Bledsoe had left and he picked up after one ring.

'Bledsoe Investigations.'

'It's Jack McEvoy.'

'Jack Mac, how you doing?'

'I'm fine. How are you?'

'A lot better since I heard the news this morning.'

'Well, I'm glad, then.'

'You did good, Jack, putting that guy in the hole. You did real good.'

Then how come I don't feel so good, I thought but didn't say.

'Jack?'

'What?'

'I owe you one, buddy. And Johnny Mac owes you one.'

'No you don't. We're even, Dan. You helped me.'

'Well, just the same, you get back out here one day and we're going to go for crabs at the tavern. It'll go on my tab.'

'Thanks, Dan. I'll be out.'

'Hey, what about this G-girl who's been in the papers and TV? Agent Walling. She's a looker.'

I looked over at Rachel.

'Yeah, she is.'

'I seen the clip on CNN of her walking you out of that store last night. You be careful, young man.'

He managed to get a smile out of me. I hung up and looked at the two messages from the publishers. I was tempted to return the calls but thought better of it. I didn't know much about the publishing industry, but back when I was writing my first novel – the one later left unfinished and hidden in a drawer – I'd done a little research and decided that if I ever finished the book I'd get an agent before I went to the publishers. I had even picked the agent I would seek to represent me. Only I had never finished a book to send to him. I decided I would look up his name and number again and call him later.

Next to consider was the call from Warren. The stenographer still had not arrived in the office so I hit the buttons for the number he had left. An operator answered and when I asked for Warren I saw Rachel immediately look up at me with quizzical eyes. I winked at her as the voice on the line told me Warren was out of the office. I told her my name but left no message or callback number. Warren would have to think about missing the call when he got that.

'Why were you calling him?' Rachel asked after I hung up. 'I thought you two were enemies.'

'I guess we are. I was probably going to tell him to go fuck himself.'

It took me an hour and fifteen minutes to tell my story in full detail to Rachel with the stenographer taking it down. Rachel primarily asked leading questions, designed to move me along through the story in chronological order. When I got to the shooting, her questions were more specific and for the first time she asked what my thoughts were at the time of specific actions.

I told her I went for the gun to simply get it away from Gladden, nothing more. I told her of my idea to empty the weapon once the struggle ensued and how the second shot was not deliberate.

'It was more him pulling the gun than me pulling the trigger, you know? He just tried for it one more time and my thumb was still in the guard. When he pulled, it went off. He kind of killed himself. It was like he knew what was going to happen.'

We went a few more minutes after that, with Rachel asking some follow-up questions. She then told the stenographer she would need the transcript the next morning for inclusion in the charging package that would be submitted to the district attorney.

'What do you mean, "charging package"?' I asked after the stenographer had left the room.

'It's just a term. We call it that whether we are seeking a charge or an indictment or not. Relax. We obviously aren't seeking anything here but a finding of self-defense, justifiable homicide. Don't worry, Jack.'

It was early but we decided to get lunch. Rachel said she'd drop me by the hotel afterward. She had work to do back at the field office but I'd be done for the day. We were walking down the hallway when she noticed the door marked Group Three was open and she looked in. There were two men in the room, both sitting at computers, paperwork on the keyboards and on top of the terminals. I noticed a copy of the same book I had on Edgar Allan Poe on top of one of the agent's monitors. He was the first to notice us.

'Hi, I'm Rachel Walling, how is it going?'

The other looked up then and they said their hellos along with their names. Rachel then introduced me. The agent who had first looked up and had identified himself as Don Clearmountain spoke.

'We're doing good. End of the day we'll have a list of names and addresses. We'll ship them to the nearest FOs and they should have enough for search warrants.'

I visualized teams of agents hitting doors and pulling the pedophiles who had bought digital photos of murdered children out of their beds. It would be a nationwide reckoning. I began to visualize the headlines. The Dead Poet's Society. That's what they'd call these men.

'But I've got something else working here that is really pretty special,' Clearmountain said.

The computer agent had a hacker's smile on his face as he looked at us. It was an invitation and Rachel moved into the room, me right behind her.

'What is it?' she said.

'Well, what we have here are a bunch of numbers that Gladden shipped digital photos to. Then we also have the wire deposit records of the bank in Jacksonville. We collated it and it all fits together pretty well.'

He took a stack of pages off the keyboard of the other agent, looked through it and selected a sheet.

'For example, on December fifth of last year there was a deposit of five hundred dollars made to the account. It was wired from the Minnesota National Bank in St. Paul. The sender was listed as Davis Smith. Probably a false name. The next day, Gladden's cellular modem placed a call to a number we've traced to a fellow named Dante Sherwood in St. Paul. The connection lasted four minutes, about what it takes to transmit and download a photograph. We've got literally dozens of transactions like this. One-day correlations between deposits and transmissions.'

'Great.'

'Now, the question all of this raises is, how did all these buyers know about Gladden and what he had to sell? In other words, where was the marketplace for these photos?'

'And you found it.'

'Yes, we did. The number called most often on the cellular modem. It's a computer bulletin board. It's called the PTL Network.'

Rachel's face showed her surprise.

'Praise The Lord?'

'You wish. Actually, we think it means Pre-Teen Love.'

'Gross.'

'Yeah. It was actually kind of easy to figure out. Not that original and most of these boards use these kinds of euphemisms. It was getting into the network that took us all morning.'

'How'd you do it?'

'We came up with Gladden's passwords.'

'Wait a minute,' Rachel said. 'What happened last night has been all over the news across the whole country. Wouldn't whoever was operating this bulletin board have wiped him out? You know, killed his access and his password before we got in?'

'He should've but he didn't.' Then Clearmountain looked at the other agent and they shared conspiratorial smiles. There was something still not said. 'Maybe the systems operator was sort of tied up and couldn't get to it in time.'

'Okay, tell me the rest,' Rachel said impatiently.

'Well, we tried everything to get in, variations on Gladden's name, DOB, social security, all the usual tricks. Nothing. We were thinking the same thing you were, that he was deleted from the system.'

'But?'

'But then we went to Poe.'

Clearmountain took the heavy book off his monitor and held it up.

'It's a two-password entry system. We got the first one easy. It was Edgar. But then the second, that's where we had trouble. We tried Raven, Eidolon, Usher, everything we could pull out of this book. Then we doubled back and went through Gladden's names and numbers again. Still nothing. Then – bingo! – we nailed it. Joe did while he was having coffee cake.'

Clearmountain pointed to the other agent, Joe Perez, who smiled and took a bow in his seat. For computer cops, I guessed that what he had done was like making a felony arrest for a street cop. He looked as proud as a boy who scores in a hotel room on prom night.

'I was just reading about Poe while taking a break,' Perez explained. 'My eyes get tired looking at a monitor too long.'

'Lucky for us he decided to rest them looking at a book,' Clearmountain said, regaining the narrative. 'Joe, in the biographical section, comes across a reference to Poe having once used an alias to enlist in the army or something. Edgar Perry. We stuck it in and like I said, bingo! We were in.'

Clearmountain turned and exchanged a high five with Perez. They looked like a couple of nerds in heat. Today's FBI, I thought.

'What did you find?'

'There are twelve message boards. Most are for discussion about specific tastes. In other words, girls under twelve, boys under ten, that sort of thing. There is a lawyer referral board. We found Gladden's lawyer, Krasner, listed on it. Then there's also a kind of bio board with a lot of strange shit on it, essays and such. There's a few that have to be by our man. Look at this.'

He looked through the stack of papers again and pulled out a printout. He started reading from it.

'This is from one of them. "I think they know about me. My time in the light of public fascination and fear is near. I am ready." Then further down he goes, "My suffering is my passion, my religion. It never leaves me. It guides me. It is me." It's full of that kind of stuff and the author at one point calls himself Eidolon. So we think it's gotta be him. You BSS people are going to get a lot of stuff for the research banks out of this.'

'Good,' Rachel said. 'What else?'

'Well, one of the boards is a barter board. You know, where people post things to sell or buy.'

'Like photos and IDs?'

'Yup. There's somebody on there selling Alabama DLs. I assume we're going to have to shut that sucker down in a hurry. And there was a file for selling what Gladden had in his computer. Minimum price was five hundred dollars per picture. Three for a grand. You wanted something, you left a message with a computer number. You wired the money to a bank account and your pictures showed up in your computer. On the barter board, this advertiser said he could provide photos to meet specific tastes and desires.'

'Like he was taking orders and then he'd go out and . . .'

'Right.'

'You tell Bob Backus about this yet?'

'Yeah, he was just in here.'

Rachel looked at me.

'That parade is sounding better and better all the time.'

'You're forgetting the neatest part,' Clearmountain said.

'And what parade?'

'It's nothing. What's the neatest part?'

'The bulletin board. We traced the number to a location.'

'And?'

'Union Correctional Institution, Raiford, Florida.'

'Oh, my God! Gomble?'

Clearmountain smiled and nodded.

'That's what Bob Backus thinks. He's going to have somebody check it out. I already called the prison and asked the captain of the day where that line went to. He said it was to the supplies office. And, see, I had noticed that all of Gladden's calls to that number were placed after five P.M.

eastern time. The captain told me that the supply office was closed and locked up every day at five. Opens up at eight every morning. I also asked him if there was a computer in that office for keeping track of orders and supplies and such and he said there sure was. I said what about a phone and he said there was one but it wasn't connected to the computer. But believe me, this is not a guy who knows a modem from a hole in the ground. This is a guy who volunteers to go to prison every day. Think about that. I told him to check again on the phone line, like some night after that office is closed up and –'

'Wait a minute. He isn't –'

'Don't worry, he's not going to do anything. I told him not to mess with things until he hears from us. For now, the network should remain on line, after five in the East, that is. I asked him who works in there and he told me Horace Gomble. He's a trustee. I see you are already familiar with him. I guess each night he sticks the phone line into the computer before he locks up and goes back to his cell.'

Rachel canceled lunch with me because of the new developments. She said I'd have to grab a cab back to the hotel and that she'd call me when she could. She said she might be going back to Florida but would let me know. I wanted to stay, too, but fatigue was finally setting in from my sleepless night.

I took the elevator down and was walking through the lobby of the federal building, thinking about calling Greg Glenn and checking my messages, when I heard a familiar voice behind me.

'Hey, hot shot, howzit hanging?'

I turned around and Michael Warren walked up to me.

'Warren. I just tried to call you at the *Times*. They said you were out.'

'I was here. Supposed to be another press conference at two. Thought I'd come early and see what I could dig up.'

'Like another source maybe?'

'I told you, Jack, I'm not talking to you about that.'

'Yeah, well, I'm not talking to you either.'

I turned and started away. He called after me.

'Then why'd you call me? To gloat?'

I looked back at him.

'Something like that. I guess. But you know, Warren, I'm not really mad at you. You went after a story that was given to you and that's cool. I can't blame you. Thorson had his own agenda and you didn't know about that. He used you but we all get used. I'll see you.'

'Wait a minute, Jack. If you're not pissed off, why don't you talk to me?'

'Because we're still competitors.'

'No we're not, man. You're not even on the story anymore. I had the front page of the *Rocky* faxed to me this morning. They gave it to somebody else. Only place your name appears is in the story. No bylines, Jack. You're not on the story. You *are* the story. So why don't we go on the record here and let me ask you a few questions?'

'Like "How do you feel?" Is that what you want to ask?'

'That's one of them, yeah.'

I looked at him a good long moment. No matter how much I didn't like him or what he had done, I couldn't deny the empathy I had for his position. He was doing what I had done so many times before. I looked at my watch and out at the parking circle beyond the lobby. There were none of the waiting cabs I had seen the day before.

'You got a car?'

'Yeah, company car.'

'Give me a ride to the Chateau Marmont. We'll talk on the way.'

'On the record?'

'On the record.'

He turned on a tape recorder and put it on the dashboard. He just wanted the basics from me. He wanted to quote me about what I had done the night before rather than rely on a secondhand source like an FBI spokesman. That was too easy and he was too good a reporter to settle for a spokesman.

Whenever possible he went straight to the source. I understood this. I was the same way.

Telling him the story somehow made me feel good. I enjoyed it. It wasn't anything I hadn't already given Jackson at my own paper, so it wasn't like I was revealing company secrets. But Warren had been around at almost the start of the trail and I liked being the one who told him where it had led and how it had ended.

I didn't tell him about the latest developments, about the PTL network and Gomble running it from a prison. That was too good to give away. I planned on writing that one myself, whether it was for the *Rocky* or one of those publishers in New York.

Finally, Warren drove up the short hill to the entrance of the Chateau Marmont. A doorman opened the door but I didn't get out. I looked at Warren.

'Anything else?'

'No, I think I got it. I have to get back to the federal building for the press conference anyway. But this is going to be great.'

'Well, you and the *Rocky* are the only ones that got it. I'm not planning to go to "Hard Copy" unless it's six figures.'

He looked at me, surprised.

'Just kidding, Warren. I'd break into the records room with you at the foundation but, hey, I draw the line at selling my story to the tabs.'

'What about the publishers?'

'I'm working on it. You?'

'I gave up once your first story came out. My agent said the editors he talked to were more interested in you than me. You had the brother, you know? You were obviously on the inside. Only thing I'd be able to sell was one of those quick-and-dirty jobs. I'm not interested. I've got a reputation.'

I nodded and turned to get out of the car.

'Thanks for the ride.'

'Thanks for the story.'

I was out and about to close the door when Warren started to say something but then stopped.

'What is it?'

'I was going ... ah, hell, look, Jack, about the source on that story. If —'

'Forget it, man, it doesn't matter anymore. Like I said, the guy's dead and you did what any reporter would do.'

'No, wait. That's not what I'm saying ... I don't give up sources, Jack, but I can tell you who isn't a source. And Thorson wasn't my source, okay? I didn't even know the guy.'

I just nodded, saying nothing. He didn't know that I had seen the hotel phone records and that I knew he was lying. A new Jaguar pulled under the parking overhang and a couple dressed head to toe in black started getting out. I looked back at Warren, wondering what he was trying to do. What scam could he be pulling by lying now?

'That it?'

Warren turned a hand upside down and nodded.

'Yeah, that's it. Being that he's dead and you were there, I thought you might want to know.'

I looked at him for another moment.

'Okay, man,' I said. 'Thanks. I'll see you around.'

I straightened up and closed the door, then bent down to look at Warren through the window and gave a wave. He snapped off a military-style salute and drove away.

46
. . . .

In my room I connected my computer to the phone line and dialed into the *Rocky*'s computer. I had thirty-six E-mail messages waiting for me. I hadn't checked in two days. Most of the in-house messages were congratulatory, although they weren't explicitly worded as such because the senders probably hesitated to do so, wondering if it was proper to congratulate me for killing the Poet. There were two from Van Jackson asking me where I was and to call and three from Greg Glenn asking the same. The *Rocky* operator had also dumped my phone messages into my E-mail basket and there were several from reporters across the country and from Hollywood production companies. My mother and Riley had also called. There was no doubt I was in demand. I saved all the messages in case I wanted to call back and signed off.

Greg Glenn's direct line rang through to the operator. She said Glenn was in a story meeting and she had standing orders not to ring into the conference room. I left my name and number and hung up.

After waiting fifteen minutes for Glenn to return my call and trying not to think about what Warren had told me at the end of our ride, I got impatient and left the room. I started walking down the strip and eventually stopped at Book Soup, a bookstore I had noticed earlier during the ride with Warren. I went to the mystery section and found a book I had once read which I knew was dedicated to the author's agent. My theory was that this was at least the sign of a good agent. With the name in hand, I next went to the research section and looked up the agent in a book listing literary agencies, their addresses and phone numbers. I committed the phone number to memory, left the store and walked back to the hotel.

The red light on the phone was flashing when I got back to my room and I knew it was probably Glenn, but I decided to call the agent first. It was five o'clock in New York and I didn't know what hours he kept. He answered after two rings. I introduced myself and quickly went into my pitch.

'I wanted to see if I could talk to you about representing me in regard to a, uh, I guess it would be called a true crime book. Do you do true crime?'

'Yes,' he said. 'But rather than discuss this on the phone I would really prefer that you send me a query letter telling me about yourself and the project. Then I can respond.'

'I would but I don't think there is time. I've got publishers and movie people calling me and I have to make some decisions quickly.'

That set the hook. I knew it would.

'Why are they calling you? What's it about?'

'Have you read or seen anything on TV about this killer out in L.A., the Poet?'

'Yes, of course.'

'I'm the one who, uh, shot him. I'm a writer – a reporter. My brother –'

'You're the one?'

'I'm the one.'

Though he was interrupted often by other calls, we talked for twenty minutes about the possible book project and the interest I'd already gotten from the movie production people. He said he worked with an agent in Los Angeles who could handle the interest from that industry. In the meantime, he wanted to know how quickly I could send him a two-page proposal. I told him I'd get it to him within the hour and he gave me the number of his computer's fax modem. He said that if the story was as good as he had seen on TV, he thought that he could have the book sold by the end of the week. I told him the story was better.

'One last thing,' he said. 'How did you get my name?'

'It was in *A Morning for Flamingos*.'

The red light on the phone continued to wink at me but I ignored it after hanging up and went to work on my laptop writing the proposal, trying to consolidate the last two weeks into two pages. It was a difficult process, not helped by having only one usable hand, and I went long, finishing with four pages.

By the time I was done, my hand was beginning to throb even though I had tried not to use it. I took another one of the pills the hospital had given me and had gone back to the computer, proofreading my proposal, when the phone rang.

It was Glenn and he was livid.

'Jack!' he cried out. 'I've been waiting on your call! What the fuck are you doing?'

'I did call! I left a message. I've been sitting here an hour waiting for you to call back.'

'I did, goddamnit! You didn't get *my* message?'

'No. You must've called when I went down the hall for a Coke. But I didn't get any –'

'Never mind, never mind. Look, what do we have for tomorrow? I've got Jackson on it here and Sheedy took a plane out this morning. She's going to a press conference at the bureau. But what can you give us that's new? Every paper in the country is following our ass and we need to stay in front of them. What's new? What do you have that they don't have?'

'I don't know,' I lied. 'Not a lot's going on. The bureau people are still tying up the details, I guess . . . I'm still off the story?'

'Look, Jack, I don't see how you can write this. We went over this yesterday. You're too involved. You can't expect me to let –'

'Okay, okay, I was just asking. Um . . . uh, there's a couple things. First, they traced this guy Gladden back to an apartment last night and they found a body there. Another victim. You can start with that. But that might be what the press conference is about. Then, also, tell Jackson to call the field office out here and ask about the computer they found.'

'The computer?'

'Yeah, Gladden had a laptop in his car. They had their computer geeks going over it all night and this morning. I don't know, it might be worth a call. I don't know what they found.'

'Well, what have you been doing?'

'I had to go down there and give a statement. Took all morning. They have to go to the district attorney and ask for a justifiable homicide ruling or something. I came back here when I was done.'

'They're not telling you what's going on?'

'No, I only overheard a couple of agents talking about the body and the thing about the computer, that's all.'

'Okay, well that's a start.'

I was smiling and trying to keep it out of my voice. I didn't care about revealing the discovery of the Poet's last victim. That was probably going to come out anyway. But someone like Jackson calling cold wouldn't be able to even get confirmation that there was a computer, let alone what was in it. The bureau wouldn't put that out until it was good and ready to.

'Sorry that's all I've got, Greg,' I said. 'Tell Jackson I'm sorry. So what's Sheedy going to do besides the press conference?'

Sheedy was an up-and-comer. She had recently been appointed to the go team – reporters who have packed suitcases in their car trunks and are ready to hit the road within minutes of any calamity, disaster or other breaking news story outside of Denver. I had been a go team reporter once. But after covering my third airliner crash and talking to people whose loved ones had been reduced to crispy critters or found in small parts, the job got old and I went back to the cop beat.

'I don't know,' Glenn said. 'She'll hunt around. When are you coming back?'

'They want me to stay around in case the district attorney's office wants to interview me. I think by tomorrow I'll be done.'

'Okay, well, if you hear anything let me know right away. And give them shit down at the front desk for not giving you my message. I'll pass this computer thing on to Jackson. I'll seeya, Jack.'

'Okay. Oh, and Greg? My hand's okay.'

'What?'

'I knew you were concerned. But it's feeling a lot better. It will probably be fine.'

'Jack, I'm sorry. It's been one of those days.'

'Yeah. I know. I'll see you.'

47

The pain pill I had taken was beginning to kick in. The discomfort in my hand was subsiding and a calm current of relaxation was overtaking me. After I hung up with Glenn I connected the phone line back into my computer, engaged the fax program and transmitted the book proposal to the number the literary agent had given me. As I listened to the braying sound of the computers coupling, a thought hit me like a bolt. The calls I had made on the flight out to L.A.

I had been so concerned about proving and exposing Thorson as the leak to Warren, I had paid only passing attention to the other calls on his hotel bill, the calls I had repeated myself on the plane to L.A. One of them had been answered by the high-pitched tone of a computer in Florida, possibly at UCI in Raiford.

I grabbed my computer satchel off the bed, pulled out my notebooks and flipped through both of them but found no notes on the calls I had made on the plane. I remembered then that I had not written notes or the phone numbers down because I had not expected someone to steal the hotel bills from my room.

Clearing my mind of everything else, I tried to review the exact course of events on the plane. The main concern I'd had at the time was the record of the call to Warren that was on Thorson's bill. That had confirmed for me that Thorson was Warren's source. The other calls made from his room – though made within minutes of each other – had held little interest to me at the time.

I had not seen the number that Clearmountain had said was called the most often from Gladden's computer. I thought about calling him and asking for the number but I doubted that he would hand it over to a reporter without seeking approval from Rachel or Backus. And that would tip my hand, something that an instinct told me not to do yet.

I slid my Visa card out of my wallet and turned it over. After reconnecting the phone I dialed the 800 number on the credit card and told the operator I had a billing inquiry. After three minutes of Muzak, another operator came on the line and I asked if it was possible to check on charges added to my credit account as recently as three days earlier. After verifying my identity through my social security number and other details, she said she could check my records on the computer to see if the charges had been posted and I told her what I was looking for.

The calls had just been posted on the Visa billing computer. And the phone numbers I had called were also part of the billing record. In five minutes I had copied all the numbers I had called on the plane into my notebook, thanked the operator and hung up.

Once again I plugged the phone line into my computer. I opened the terminal window, typed in the phone number that had been called from Thorson's room and ran the program. I looked at the bedside clock. It was three here, six in Florida. There was one ring and then a connection. I heard the familiar squeal of computers meeting and then mating. My screen went blank and then a template printed across it.

WELCOME TO THE PTL CLUB

I exhaled, leaned back and felt a surge of electricity go through me. After a few seconds the screen moved up and there was a coded prompt for a user's password. I typed in EDGAR, noticing that my good hand was shaking as I did this. Edgar was approved and followed by a prompt for a second password. I typed in PERRY. In a moment this, too, was approved and followed by a warning template.

PRAISE THE LORD!

RULES OF THE ROAD

1. NEVER EVER USE A REAL NAME
2. NEVER PROVIDE SYSTEMS NUMBERS TO ACQUAINTANCES
3. NEVER AGREE TO MEET ANOTHER USER
4. BE AWARE THAT OTHER USERS MAY BE FOREIGN BODIES
5. SYSOP RESERVES THE RIGHT TO DELETE ANY USER
6. MESSAGE BOARDS MAY NOT BE USED FOR DISCUSSION OF ANY ILLEGAL ACTIVITIES — THIS IS FORBIDDEN!
7. PTL NETWORK IS NOT RESPONSIBLE FOR CONTENT
8. PRESS ANY KEY TO CONTINUE

I hit RETURN and got a table of contents for the various message boards available to users. These were, as Clearmountain had said, a cornucopia of subjects catering to the modern pedophile. I hit the escape key and the computer asked if I wanted to exit PTL. I hit the yes prompt and disconnected. I wasn't interested in exploring the PTL Network at the moment. I was more interested in the fact that Thorson, or whoever had made that call early Sunday morning, knew about the PTL Network and even had access to it at least four days ago.

The call to the PTL board had been placed from Thorson's room so it seemed obvious that he had made the call. But I carefully considered other factors. The call to the PTL board had been made, as I recalled, within minutes of the call from the same room to Warren in Los Angeles. Thorson had vehemently denied being Warren's source on at least three occasions. Warren twice denied it as well, including after Thorson was dead and it didn't matter anymore if he had been the source. The seed planted by Warren during that second denial just a few hours before weighed on me now. It was blossoming in my mind into a flower of doubt I could not put aside.

If Warren and Thorson were to be believed, who had made the calls from Thorson's room? As the possibilities played through my mind they invariably came back with a dull thud in my chest to one person. Rachel.

It was the fermentation of various and unrelated facts that led me down this path.

First, Rachel had a laptop computer. This, of course, was the weakest piece. Thorson, Backus, everyone possessed or had access to a computer that would have allowed them to make the linkage to the PTL board. But second, Rachel was not in her room late Saturday night when I called and then even knocked. So where was she? Could she have gone to Thorson's room?

I considered the things Thorson had said to me about Rachel. He had called her the Painted Desert. But he had said something else. *She can play with you ... like a toy. One minute she wants to share it, the next she doesn't. She disappears on you.*

And last, I thought of seeing Thorson in the hallway that night. I knew it had been after midnight by then and roughly near the times of the long distance calls placed from his room. As he had passed me in the hall I noticed he carried something. A small bag or a box. I now remembered the sound of the little zippered pocket opening in Rachel's purse and the condom – the one she carried for emergencies – being placed in my palm. And I thought of a way Rachel could have gotten Thorson out of his own room so that she could use the phone.

A feeling of pure dread began to descend on me now. Warren's flower was in full bloom and was choking me. I stood up to pace a little but felt light-headed. I blamed it on the painkiller and sat back down on the bed. After a few moments' rest, I reconnected the phone and called the hotel in Phoenix, asking for the billing office. A young woman took the call.

'Yes, hello, I stayed at your hotel over the weekend and

didn't really look at my bill until I got back. I had a question about a few phone calls I was billed for. I've been meaning to call but keep forgetting. Is there someone I could talk to about that?'

'Yes, sir, I would be glad to help. If you give me your name I can call up your statement.'

'Thanks. It's Gordon Thorson.'

She didn't reply and I froze, thinking maybe she recognized the name from the TV or a newspaper as the agent slain in L.A., but then I heard her begin tapping on a keyboard.

'Yes, Mr Thorson. That was room three twenty-five for two nights. What seems to be the problem?'

I wrote the room number down in my notebook, just to be doing something. Following the journalist's routine of making a record of facts helped calm me.

'You know what? I can't – I'm looking around my desk here for my copy and I seem to have misplaced . . . Darn it! I can't find it now. Uh, I'll have to call you back. But in the meantime maybe you can look it up and have it ready. What I was concerned about was that there were three calls made after midnight on Saturday that I just don't remember making. I have the numbers written down here some – here they are.'

I quickly gave her the three numbers I had gotten from the Visa operator, hoping I'd be able to finesse my way through this.

'Yes, they are on your billing. Are you sure you –'

'What time were they made? See, that's the problem. I don't conduct business in the middle of the night.'

She gave me the times. The call to Quantico was logged at 12:37 A.M., followed by the call to Warren at 12:41 A.M. and then the call to the PTL Network line at 12:56 A.M. I stared at the numbers after writing them down.

'You don't believe you made these?'

'What?'

'I said you don't believe you made these?'

'That's right.'

434

'Was there anyone else in the room with you?'

That was the point, wasn't it, I thought but didn't say.

'Uh, no,' I said, and then quickly added, 'Can you just double-check those for me and if there is nothing wrong with your machines, I'll be glad to pay. Thank you.'

I hung up and looked at the times I had written in my notebook. They fit. Rachel had stayed in my room until almost midnight. The next morning she told me she had bumped into Thorson while in the hall after leaving. Maybe she had lied to me. Maybe she had done more than bump into him. Maybe she had gone to his room.

With Thorson dead, there was only one way of pursuing this theory outside of going to Rachel, which I couldn't do yet. I picked the phone up once again and called the FBI office in the federal building. The operator, under strict orders to screen calls to Backus, especially from the media, was not going to put me through until I told her I was the one who had killed the Poet and that I had an urgent need to speak to the special agent. Finally, I was put through and Backus picked up.

'Jack, what's the problem?'

'Bob, listen to me, I'm very serious. Are you alone?'

'Jack, what –'

'Just answer the question! Look, I'm sorry, I didn't mean to yell. I've just got – Look, just tell me, are you alone?'

There was a hesitation and his voice was skeptical when it returned.

'Yes. Now what's this about?'

'We've talked about the trust in our relationship. I've trusted you and you've trusted me. I want you to trust me again, Bob, for the next few minutes and just answer my questions without asking me any questions. I will explain it all after. Okay?'

'Jack, I'm very busy here. I don't under –'

'Five minutes, Bob. That's all. It's important.'

'What's your question?'

'What happened to Thorson's things? His clothes and things from his hotel. Who got it after he . . . died?'

'I gathered it all together last night. I don't see what this has to do with anything. His property is nobody's business.'

'Indulge me, Bob. This isn't for a story. It's for me. And for you. I have two questions. First, did you find the hotel receipts, the bills, from Phoenix with his stuff?'

'From Phoenix? No, they weren't there and they weren't supposed to be. We checked out on the fly, never went back. I'm sure the bill is being sent to my office in Quantico. What is on your mind, Jack?'

The first piece clicked into place. If Thorson didn't have the bills, he likely wasn't the one who had taken them from my room. I thought about Rachel again. I couldn't help it. The first night in Hollywood, after we had made love, she got up and took the first shower. Then it was my turn. I envisioned her taking the room key from the pocket of my pants, going downstairs and slipping into my room to conduct a quick search of my things. Maybe she was just looking around. Maybe she knew somehow that I had the hotel bills. Maybe she had called the hotel in Phoenix and had been told.

'Next question,' I said to Backus, ignoring his own question. 'Did you find any condoms with Thorson's things?'

'Look, I don't know what kind of morbid fascination you have with this but I'm not going to go on with it. I'm hanging up now, Jack, and I don't want you –'

'Wait a minute! What morbid fascination? I'm trying to figure out something you people have missed! Did you talk to Clearmountain today about the computer? About the PTL Network?'

'Yes, I've been fully briefed. What's it got to do with a box of condoms?'

I noticed he had inadvertently answered my question about condoms. I had not said anything about a box.

'Did you know that a call was placed to the PTL Network from Thorson's room in Phoenix on Sunday morning?'

'That's preposterous. And how the hell would you know something like that?'

'Because when I checked out of that hotel, the clerk thought I was an FBI agent. Remember? Just like that reporter at the funeral home. He gave me the hotel bills to take to you people out here. He thought it would save the time of mailing them.'

There was a long silence after this confession.

'Are you saying you stole the hotel bills?'

'I'm saying what I just said. They were given to me. And on Thorson's bill there were calls to both Michael Warren and the PTL. And that's funny, since you people supposedly didn't know about the PTL until today.'

'I'm sending someone over to pick up those bills.'

'Don't bother. I don't have them. They were stolen from my room in Hollywood. You've got a fox in the henhouse, Bob.'

'What are you talking about?'

'Tell me about the box of condoms you found in Thorson's things and I'll tell you what I'm talking about.'

I heard him exhale in a tired, I-give-up fashion.

'There was a box of condoms, okay? It wasn't even opened. Now, what's it mean?'

'Where is it now?'

'It's in a sealed cardboard box with the rest of his things. It goes back to Virginia with his body tomorrow morning.'

'Where's this sealed box?'

'Right here with me.'

'I need you to open it, Bob. Look at the condoms, see if there is a price tag or anything that shows where he got them.'

As I listened to the sounds of him tearing cardboard and tape my mind served up my memory of the sight of Thorson coming down the hall with something in his hand.

'I can tell you right now,' Backus said as he was opening the property box, 'they were in a bag from a drugstore.'

I felt my heart leap and next I heard the crinkling sound of a bag opening.

'Okay, I've got it,' Backus said in a voice showing his strained patience. 'Scottsdale Drugs. Open twenty-four hours. Box of twelve condoms, nine ninety-five. You want to know the brand, too, Jack?'

I ignored his sarcasm but his question gave me an idea for later.

'There's a receipt?'

'I just read it to you.'

'What about the date and time of purchase, that on there? Most of these computer registers put it on there.'

Silence. So long I wanted to scream.

'Sunday morning, twelve fifty-four.'

I closed my eyes. While Thorson was buying a box of condoms, of which he wouldn't even use one, someone was in his room making phone calls.

'Okay, Jack, what's it mean?' Backus asked.

'It means everything is a lie.'

I opened my eyes and pulled the phone from my ear. I looked at it like it was some alien thing attached to my hand and slowly dropped it back into its cradle.

Bledsoe was still in his office and answered on the first ring.

'Dan, it's Jack again.'

'Jack Mac, what's up?'

'You know that beer you said you owed me? I thought of something else you can do for me instead.'

'You got it.'

I told him what I needed him to do and he didn't hesitate, even when I told him I needed it done now. He said he couldn't promise results but that he'd get back to me one way or the other as soon as possible.

I thought about the first call made while Thorson was out of his room. It had been to the general public line at the Quantico center. It hadn't struck me as odd when I called the number on the plane. But now it did. Why would someone call the general number in the middle of the night? I knew now that the answer could only be that the caller did not want to call a direct number at the center, thereby revealing knowledge of that number. Instead, through her computer, she

438

called the general number and when the operator recognized the fax mating beep, the call was transferred to one of the general fax lines.

I recalled that during the Sunday morning meeting on the fax from the Poet, Thorson had recited the details after getting the rundown from Quantico. The fax had come through on the general number and had been transferred to a fax machine.

Without a word an operator at Quantico switched me to the BSS offices when I called and asked for Agent Brad Hazelton. The phone rang three times and I thought I was too late, that he had gone home for the day, when he finally picked up.

'Brad, it's Jack McEvoy. In Los Angeles.'

'Hey, Jack, how're you doing? Pretty close call for you yesterday.'

'I'm doing okay. I'm sorry about Agent Thorson. I know everybody works very closely together there ...'

'Well, he was pretty much an asshole but nobody deserves what happened to him. It's pretty awful. Not a lot of smiling faces around here today.'

'I can imagine.'

'So what's going on?'

'Well, it's just a couple of minor points. I'm putting to-gether a chronology of events so that I have this story down straight. You know, if I ever get to write the whole thing.'

I hated lying to this man who had only been friendly to me, but I couldn't afford to tell him the truth because then he certainly wouldn't help me.

'And, anyway, I seem to have misplaced my notes on the fax. You know, the fax the Poet sent to Quantico on Sunday. I remember Gordon said he got the details from either you or Brass. What I wanted to know is the exact time it came in. If you have it.'

'Uh, hold on, Jack.'

He was gone before I could say I would hold. I closed my eyes and spent the next few minutes wondering whether he was actually looking up the information or first checking to see if he could give it to me.

Finally, he came back on the line.

'Sorry, Jack, I had to look through all the papers here. The fax came to machine number two in the academy offices wire room at three thirty-eight Sunday morning.'

I looked at my notes. Subtracting the three-hour time difference, the fax came in at Quantico one minute after the call to the general number had been placed from Thorson's room.

'Okay, Jack?'

'Oh, yeah, thanks. Uh, I had one other question.'

'Shoot – oh, shit, sorry.'

'That's okay. Uh, the question I have is, um ... Agent Thompson sent back an oral swab from the victim in Phoenix. Orsulak.'

'Yes, Orsulak.'

'Uh, he wanted to identify the substance. He believed it was the lubricant from a condom. The question I had was whether it was identified as coming from a specific brand of condom. Can that be done? Was it done?'

Hazelton didn't answer at first and I almost jumped into the silence. But then he spoke.

'That's a strange question, Jack.'

'Yeah, I know but, uh, the details of the case, and how you people do things, really fascinates me. It's important to have them right – it makes a better story.'

'Hold on another second.'

Again he was gone before I could agree to hold. This time he came back very quickly.

'Yes, I have that information. Do you want to tell me why you really want it?'

Now it was my turn to be silent.

'No,' I finally said, trying the honesty route. 'I'm just trying to work something out, Brad. If it goes the way I think it's going, the FBI's going to be the first to know about it. Believe me.'

Hazelton paused for a moment.

'Okay, Jack, I'll trust you. Besides, Gladden's dead. It's not like I'm giving away trial evidence and there's not much you can prove with this anyway. The substance was narrowed down to being similar to two different brands. Ramses Lubricated and Trojan Golds. Problem is they are two of the most popular brands in the country. It is not what we'd call unequivocal evidence of anything.'

Maybe it wasn't evidence you could take into a courtroom, but Ramses Lubricated was the brand that Rachel had handed me from her purse on Saturday night in my hotel room. I thanked Hazelton without further discussion and hung up.

It was all there and it all seemed to fit. No matter how many ways over the next hour that I tried to destroy my own theory, I couldn't. It was a theory built on a foundation of suspicion and speculation but it worked like a machine, all the parts meshing together. And I had nothing to throw into its gears that could bring it to a grinding halt.

The last part I needed was Bledsoe. I paced the room waiting for his call, the feeling of anxiety churning in my stomach like something that was alive. I went out on the balcony for fresh air but that didn't help. Staring at me was the Marlboro Man, his thirty-foot-high face holding dominion over the Sunset Strip. I went back inside.

Instead of the cigarette I wanted, I decided on a Coke. I left the room, turning the night lock so the door wouldn't close all the way and trotted down the hallway to the vending machines. In spite of the painkiller, my nerves were jangling. But I knew that this intensity would translate to fatigue in a little while if I didn't ante up with a shot of sugar and caffeine. Halfway back to my room, I heard the phone ringing and I ran. I went for the phone before even closing the door, grabbing it on what I thought might be the ninth ring.

'Dan?'

Silence.

'It's Rachel. Who is Dan?'

'Oh.' I could barely catch my breath. 'He's, uh – He's just a friend at the paper. He was supposed to call.'

'What's the matter with you, Jack?'

'I'm out of breath. I was down the hall getting a Coke and I heard the phone.'

'Jesus, it must've been the hundred-yard dash.'

'Something like that. Hold on.'

I went back to the door and closed it, then put my actor's face on as I went back to the phone.

'Rachel?'

'Listen, I just wanted you to know I'm leaving. Bob wants me to go back to Florida and handle this PTL thing.'

'Oh.'

'It will probably be a few days.'

The message light on my phone came on. Bledsoe, I thought, and silently cursed the timing of his call.

'Okay, Rachel.'

'We'll have to get together somewhere afterward. I was thinking of taking a vacation.'

'I thought you just did.'

I remembered the notation on the calendar I had seen on her desk in Quantico. It struck me for the first time that that was when she must have gone to Phoenix to stalk and kill Orsulak.

'I haven't had a real vacation in a long time. I was thinking about Italy maybe. Venice.'

I didn't challenge her on the lie. I remained silent and she lost her patience. My acting wasn't working.

'Jack, what's the matter?'

'Nothing.'

'I don't believe you.'

I hesitated and then said, 'There is one thing that's been kind of bothering me, Rachel.'

'Tell it to me.'

'The other night, our first night together, I called your room after you left. I just wanted to say good night, you know, and tell you how much I enjoyed what we did. And there was no answer. I even went to your door and knocked. No answer. Then the next morning you said you had seen Thorson in the hall. And I don't know, I guess I've been thinking about that.'

'Thinking what, Jack?'

'I don't know, just thinking. I was wondering where you were when I called and when I knocked.'

She was silent for a moment and when she finally spoke her anger crackled through the phone like a fire.

'Jack, you know what you sound like? A jealous high school boy. Like the boy on the bleachers you told me about. Yes, I saw Thorson in the hall and, yes, I'll even admit that he thought I was looking for him, that I wanted him. But that's as far as it went. I can't explain why I didn't get your call, okay? Maybe you called the wrong room and maybe it was when I was taking a shower and thinking about how nice the night had been, too. And maybe I shouldn't have to defend myself or explain myself to you. If you can't deal with your petty jealousies then find a different woman and get a different life.'

'Rachel, look I'm sorry, okay? You asked me what was wrong and I told you.'

'You must have taken too many of those pills the doctor gave you. My advice is that you sleep it off, Jack. I have a plane to catch.'

She hung up.

'Goodbye,' I said into the silence.

48

....

The sun was going down and the sky was the color of ripe pumpkin with slashes of phosphorescent pink. It was beautiful and even the clutter of billboards up and down the strip looked beautiful to me. I was back out on the balcony, trying to think, trying to figure things out, waiting for Bledsoe to call back. He was the one who had left the message while I talked to Rachel. His message said he was out of the office but would call back.

I looked at the Marlboro Man, his crinkled eyes and stoic chin unchanged by time. He'd always been one of my heroes, an icon, no matter that he was always as shallow as a magazine page or a billboard sign. I remembered being at the dinner table, my position every night always to my father's right. Him always smoking and the ashtray always to the right of his plate. Me learning to smoke by virtue of that. He looked like the Marlboro Man to me, my father. Back then, at least.

Back in the room, I called home and my mother answered. She went into histrionics asking whether I was all right and gently scolded me for not calling sooner. Finally, after I had calmed her and assured her that I was okay, I asked her to put my father on the line. We had not spoken since the funeral – if we had even spoken then.

'Dad?'

'Son. You sure you're okay?'

'I'm fine. You okay?'

'Oh, sure. We were just worried about you, that's all.'

'Well, don't. Everything's fine.'

'It's a crazy thing, isn't it?'

'You mean about Gladden? Yeah.'

'Riley's here with us. She's going to spend a few days.'

'That's good, Dad.'

'Do you want to talk to her?'

'No, I wanted to talk to you.'

That silenced him, maybe made him nervous.

'You in Los Angeles?'

He said it with a hard G.

'Yeah, at least a day or two more. I just ... I called because I wanted – I've been thinking about things and I wanted to say I'm sorry.'

'Sorry for what, Son?'

'Anything, everything. Sarah, Sean, you name it.' I laughed the way you laugh when something isn't funny, when it's uncomfortable. 'I'm sorry for everything.'

'Jack, you sure you're okay?'

'I'm fine.'

'Well, you don't have to say you're sorry for anything.'

'Yes, I do. I do.'

'Well ... we're sorry, too, then. I'm sorry.'

I let a little bit of silence underline that.

'Thanks, Dad. I'm gonna go. Tell Mom I said good-bye and tell Riley I said hello.'

'I will. Why don't you come down here when you get back? Spend a couple days, too.'

'I will.'

I hung up. Marlboro Man, I thought. I looked out the open balcony door and saw his eyes peeking over the railing, watching me. My hand was hurting again. So was my head. I knew too much and didn't want to. I took another pill.

At five-thirty Bledsoe finally called. The news he had was not good. It was the final piece, the final tearing of the veil of hope I'd held on to. As I listened to him it felt like the blood was draining from my heart. I was alone again. And what was worse was that the one I had desired had not simply rejected me. She had used and betrayed me in a way I would've thought no woman could do.

'This is what I got, buddy,' Bledsoe said. 'Hang on to your hat, is all I can say.'

'Give it to me.'

'Rachel Walling. Her father was Harvey Walling. I didn't know him. When he was in dicks, I was still in patrol. I talked to one of the old guys from dicks and he said your guy was called Harvey Wallbanger. You know, after the drink. He was sort of an odd duck, loner type.'

'What about his death?'

'I'm getting to that. I had a buddy pull the old file out of archives. Happened nineteen years ago. Funny I don't remember it. I guess I was working with my head down. Anyway, I met my pal over at the Fells Point Tavern. He brought the file. And, first off, this was definitely her old man. Her name's in there. She was the one who found him. He'd shot himself. Temple shot. It went suicide but there were some problems.'

'What?'

'Well, no note for one thing. And for another, he'd worn gloves. It was in the winter, yes, but he did it inside. First thing in the morning. The investigator wrote down in the reports that he didn't like that part of it.'

'Was there gunshot residue on one of the gloves?'

'Yeah, it was there.'

'Was she – was Rachel home when it happened?'

'She said she was upstairs in her bedroom sleeping when she heard the shot. In her king-size bed. She got scared, said she didn't come down for an hour after the shot. Then she found him. This is according to the reports.'

'What about the mother?'

'There was no mother. She'd taken off years before. Rachel was left alone with the father then.'

I thought about that for a few moments. His mention of the size of her bed and something about the way he'd said the last line bothered me.

'What else, Dan? You're not telling me everything.'

'Jack, let me ask you something. Are you involved with this woman? Like I told you, I saw on the CNN how she wal –'

'Look, I'm out of time! What aren't you telling me?'

'Okay, okay, the only other thing noted in the reports that was strange was that his bed was made.'

'What are you talking about?'

'His bed. It was made. The way it had to've worked was he got up, made his bed, got dressed and put on his coat and gloves, like he was going to work, but then instead sat down in the chair and put a bullet through his head. Either that or he stayed up all night thinking about it and then did the job.'

I felt depression and fatigue wash over me in a wave. I slid off the chair to the floor, the phone still held to my ear.

'The guy who worked the case is retired but still around. Mo Friedman. We go back. I was just coming up in dicks when he was near the end. But he was a good man. I just got off the line with him a few minutes ago. Lives up in the Poconos. I asked him about this one and what his take on it was. His unofficial take, I told him.'

'And he said?'

'He said he let it go because either way he figured Harvey Wallbanger got what he had coming.'

'But what did he say his take was?'

'He said that he thought that bed was made because it never was slept in. Never used. He said he thought the father was sleeping with the daughter in the king-size and one morning she drew the line. He didn't know about anything after that, none of this stuff that's been going on lately. Mo's seventy-one years old. He does crossword puzzles. He said he doesn't like watching the news. He didn't know the daughter became an FBI agent.'

I couldn't talk. I couldn't even move.

'Jack, you still there?'

'I gotta go.'

The field office operator said Backus had left for the day. When I asked her to double-check, she put me on hold for five minutes while I was sure she was doing her nails or touching up her makeup. When she came back on she said he was definitely gone and that I could try back in the morning. She hung up before I could say anything else.

Backus was the key. I had to get to him, tell him what I had and play it whatever way he wanted. I decided that if he wasn't at the FO, he might be back at the motel on Wilcox. I had to go there anyway to pick up my car. I threw the strap of my computer bag over my shoulder and headed for the door. I opened it and stopped dead. Backus stood there, fist raised, ready to knock.

'Gladden wasn't the Poet. He was a killer, yes, but not the Poet. I can prove it.'

Backus looked at me as if I had just reported that I had seen the Marlboro Man wink at me.

'Jack, look, you've spent the day making some strange calls. First to me, then to Quantico. I came by because I'm wondering if there's something maybe the doctors overlooked last night. I thought maybe we'd take a ride over to –'

'Look, Bob, I don't blame you for thinking that after what I asked you and Hazelton today. But I had to hold things back until I was sure. Now, I'm sure. Pretty sure. I can explain it now. I was going out the door to find you just now.'

'Then sit down here and tell me what you're talking about. You said that I had a fox in the henhouse. What did you mean?'

'What I meant was here you people are, your job is to identify and catch these people. The serial offenders, as you call them. And there was one in your midst all along.'

Backus let out his breath loudly and shook his head.

'Sit down, Bob, and I'll tell you the story. If you think I'm crazy when I'm done, then you can take me to the hospital. But I know you won't think I'm crazy.'

Backus sat down on the end of the bed and I started spinning the story, recounting the moves and calls I had made through the afternoon. It took me nearly a half hour just to tell that part of it. And just when I was ready to begin telling him my interpretation of the facts I had gathered, he interrupted me with something I had already considered and was ready for.

'You're forgetting one thing. You said Gladden admitted killing your brother. At the end. You said this yourself and I read it in your statement this afternoon. You even said he recognized you.'

'But he was wrong. I was wrong. I never told him Sean's name. I just said my brother. I told him he had killed my brother and he thought one of the kids was my brother. You see? That's why he said what he said, that he killed my brother to save him. I think what he meant was that he killed those kids because he knew that once he'd been with them they'd be fucked up for life. Just like he was fucked up by Beltran. So in his mind he thought that by killing them he was saving them from becoming like he was. He wasn't talking about the cops, just those kids. I don't think he even knew about the cops.

'And as far as him recognizing me, I was on TV. CNN, remember? He could've recognized me from that.'

Backus looked down at the floor and I watched him try to compute this and I saw by the expression on his face that he found it plausible. I was getting through to him.

'Okay,' he said. 'What about Phoenix, the hotel rooms, all of that? Where do you see that going?'

'We were getting close. Rachel knew it and needed some way to either derail the investigation or make sure it pointed only to Gladden when we got him. Even though every cop in the country wanted him dead, she couldn't be sure that would happen.

'So she did three things. First, she sent the fax, the one from the Poet, from her computer to the general number at Quantico. She wrote it in a way that she knew the information it contained would become the definitive link between Gladden and the cop killings. Think back, remember the meeting on the fax? She was the one who said it tied all the cases together.'

Backus nodded but said nothing.

'Next,' I said, 'she thought that if she leaked the story to Warren, it would trigger my story and the rest of the whole media stampede. Gladden would have to see the story somewhere and he'd go underground, knowing that he was being blamed not only for the murders he did commit but the cop killings that came after. So she called up Warren and gave him the story. She must've known that he'd gone to L.A. to peddle the story after he got canned at the foundation. Maybe he had called and left her a message about where he was. You follow all of this?'

'You were so sure it was Gordon.'

'I was. And with good reason. The hotel bills. But the drugstore receipt shows he wasn't even in his room when the calls were made and Warren told me today his source wasn't Thorson. By then he had no reason to lie. Thorson was dead.'

'What was the third thing?'

'I think she made a connection by computer to the PTL Network. I don't know how she already knew about it. Maybe it was a tip to the bureau or something. I'm not sure. But she dialed in. I don't know, maybe that was when she shipped one of those Eidolon files that Clearmountain found. Again, it would be evidence linking Gladden to the Poet murders. She was sealing him up tight in a package. Even if I didn't kill him and he lived to deny everything, the evidence would be there and nobody would believe him, especially in light of the killings he did commit.'

I took a breather so Backus could digest everything said so far.

'All three of the calls she made were from Thorson's room,' I said after a half minute. 'It was just one more buffer. If things went wrong there would be no record of her making the calls. They'd be on Thorson's room. But the box of condoms destroys that. See, you know firsthand about the relationship she had with Thorson. They battled but there was still something there. He still had something for her and she knew it. She used it. So I think if she told him to go get a box of condoms and she'd be waiting for him in his bed, he'd've run out the door to the drugstore like a man with his pants on fire. And I think that's exactly what she did do. Only she didn't wait in his bed. She made those calls. Then when Thorson got back she was gone. Thorson didn't exactly tell me all of that but in so many words he did. When we worked together that day.'

Backus nodded. He looked like a man lost. I thought maybe he saw what was to become of his career now. First his command questioned by the fiasco of the Gladden arrest, and now this. His days as an assistant special agent in charge were numbered.

'It seems so ...'

He didn't finish and I didn't finish it for him. There was still more for me to tell him but I waited. Backus got up and paced a little. He looked out the balcony door at the Marlboro Man. He didn't seem to have the same fascination with him that I had.

'Tell me about the moon, Jack.'

'What do you mean?'

'The Poet's moon. You've told me the end of the story. What's the beginning? How does a woman end up at the point we are at now?'

He turned from the door and looked at me, a challenge in his eyes. He was looking for something, anything that he could build a case on for not believing. I cleared my throat before beginning.

'That's the hard part,' I said. 'You should ask Brass.'

'I will. But you try it.'

I thought a moment before starting.

'A young girl, I don't know, twelve, thirteen years old. She's abused by her father. Sexually. Her mother either ... her mother leaves. She either knew what was happening and couldn't stop it or just didn't care. The mother leaves and then the girl is left alone with him. He's a cop. A detective. He threatens her, convinces her she can never tell anyone because he's a detective and he'll find out. He tells her she won't be believed and she believes him.

'So one day she's finally had enough or she'd had enough

451

all along but didn't have the chance or hadn't thought out the right plan. Whatever. But that one day comes and she kills him, makes it look like he did it himself. Suicide. She gets away with it. There's a detective on the case who knows something isn't right but what's he gonna do? He knows the guy had it coming to him. He lets it go.'

Backus was standing in the middle of the room staring at the floor.

'I knew about her father. The official version, I mean.'

'I had a friend find out the details of the unofficial version.'

'What next?'

'What happens next is she blossoms. The power she had in that one moment makes up for a lot of things. She gets past it. Few do, but she makes it. She's a smart girl and she goes on to the university to study psychology, to learn about herself. And then she even gets drafted by the FBI. She's a prize and she moves fast through the bureau until she's in the unit that actually studies people like her father. And like herself. You see, her whole life has been this struggle to understand. And then when her team leader wants to study police suicides he goes to her because he knows the official story about her father. Not the truth. Just the official story. She takes the job, knowing inside that the reason she had been chosen was a sham.'

I stopped there. The more I told of the story the more power I felt. Knowledge of someone's secrets is an intoxicating power. I reveled in my ability to put the story together.

'And so,' Backus whispered then, 'how does it all come apart for her?'

I cleared my throat.

'Things were going good,' I continued. 'She married her partner and things were going good. But then things weren't so good. I don't know if it was pressure from the job, the memories, the breakup of that marriage, maybe all of those things. But she started coming apart. Her husband left her, thinking that she was empty inside. The Painted Desert, he called her, and she hated him for it. And then ... maybe she remembered the day when she killed her tormentor. Her father. And she remembered the peace that came after ... the release.'

I looked at him. He had a far-off look in his eyes, maybe envisioning the story as I conjured it from hell.

'One day,' I continued, 'one day a request for a profile comes in. A boy has been killed and mutilated in Florida. The case detective wants a profile of the person who did this. Only she recognizes the detective, knows his name. Beltran. A name from the past. A name maybe brought up in an old interview and she knows that he, too, was a tormentor, an abuser like her father, and that the victim he is calling about was also probably his victim ...'

'Right,' Backus said, taking up the strand. 'So she goes down to Florida to this man, Beltran, and does it again. Just like with her father. Makes it look like a suicide. She even knew where Beltran kept his shotgun hidden. Gladden had told her that. It was probably an easy thing to get to him. She flies down, goes to him with her bureau credentials and gets inside the house to do it. It brings her peace again. Fills that void. Only thing is it doesn't last. Soon she is empty again and she has to do it again. And then again and again. She follows the killer, Gladden, and kills those who are after him, using him to cover her tracks before she had even made them.'

Backus was staring blankly at some vision as he spoke.

'She knew all the touches, all the moves,' he said. 'Wiping the lubricated condom off inside Orsulak's mouth. The perfect deflection. It was true genius.'

I nodded and took it from there.

'She had seen Gladden's cell and knew there was a photograph in the files that could be found one day,' I said. 'She knew the books about Poe were in the photo. It was all a setup. She followed Gladden around the country. She had a sense. She knew from the cases coming in for profiling which were the ones he did. She had an empathy. She'd follow him. She'd go out and kill the cop that was after him. She made each one look like a suicide, but she had Gladden to put it on if someday someone came along and it unraveled.'

Backus looked at me.

'Someone like you,' he said.

'Yeah. Like me.'

49

········

Backus said the story was like a sheet hanging on a clothes-line in high wind. Barely held on by a few clothespins, it was ready to fly away.

'We need more, Jack.'

I nodded. He was the expert. Besides, the real trial had already been held in my heart and the verdict was in.

'What are you going to do?' I asked.

'I'm thinking. You had – you were beginning a relationship with her, weren't you?'

'It was that obvious?'

'Yes.'

Then he didn't say anything for a full minute. He paced the room, not really looking at anything, all interior dialogue and thought. Finally, he stopped moving and looked at me.

'Would you wear a wire?'

'What do you mean?'

'You know what I mean. I'll bring her back here, put her alone with you and you draw it out. You might be the only one who could.'

I looked down at the floor. I remembered our last phone conversation and how she had seen through my act.

'I don't know. I don't think I could pull it off.'

'She might be suspicious and check,' Backus said, dis-carding the idea and searching the floor with his eyes for another. 'Still, you're the one, Jack. You're not an agent and she knows if need be she can take you.'

'Take me where?'

'Take you out.' He snapped his fingers. 'I've got it. You won't have to wear a wire. We'll put you inside the wire.'

'What are you talking about?'

He raised a finger as if to tell me to hold on. He picked up the phone, wedged the receiver into the crook of his neck and carried it with him while he tapped in a number and waited for an answer. The cord was like a leash, containing his pacing to only a few steps in any direction.

'Pack your things,' he said to me while waiting for the call to be picked up.

I got up and slowly began to follow his order, putting my few things in the computer bag and the pillowcase while listening as he asked for Agent Carter and then began issuing directions. He told Carter to call Quantico communications and to relay a message to the bureau jet with Rachel on it. Call the plane back, Backus ordered.

'Just tell them something's come up that cannot be discussed on the air and that I need her back here,' he said into the phone. 'Nothing more than that. Understand?'

Satisfied with Carter's reply, he pressed on.

'Now, before you do that, put me on hold and call the SAC's office. I need the exact address and key combination for the earthquake house. He'll know what I mean. I'll be going there from here. I want you to grab a sound and video tech and two good agents. I'll fill you in there. Call the SAC now.'

I looked at Backus with a curious expression.

'I'm on hold.'

'Earthquake house?'

'Clearmountain told me about it. It's in the hills over the Valley. Top to bottom it's wired. Sound and video. It was damaged in the quake and the real owners just left it, didn't have insurance. The bureau leased it from the bank and used it for a sting on local building and safety inspectors, contractors and repairmen. A lot of fraud involving the funds from the Federal Emergency Management Agency. That's where the bureau came in. Indictments are pending. The sting's been closed down but the bureau's lease isn't up. So it's –'

He held his hand up. Carter had come back on the line. Backus listened for a few moments and nodded his head.

'Right on Mulholland and then the first left. Easy enough. What's your ETA?'

He hung up after telling Carter we'd get there ahead of him and adding that he needed the agent's best work on this.

As Backus drove away from the hotel I made a secret salute to the Marlboro Man. We went east on Sunset to Laurel Canyon Boulevard and then up the winding cut through the mountains.

'How's this going to work?' I asked him. 'How are you going to get Rachel up to this place we're going?'

'You'll leave a message for Rachel on her voice mail at Quantico. You'll tell her you're at a friend's house – somebody you used to know from the paper who moved out here – and leave the number. Then when I talk to Rachel I'll tell her I called her back from Florida because you've been making calls and strange accusations about her but nobody knows where you are. I'll tell her I think you've popped too many pain pills but that we need to bring you in.'

I was feeling increasingly uncomfortable about the prospect of being used as bait and having to face Rachel. I did not know how I'd be able to bring it off.

'Eventually,' Backus continued, 'Rachel will get the message. But she won't call you. Instead, she'll trace the number to the house and she'll go to you, Jack. Alone. For one of two things.'

'What?' I asked, though I already had a pretty good idea.

'To either try to set you straight ... or to kill you. She'll think you're the only one who knows. She'll need to convince you that you are wrong about these wild-ass ideas. Or she'll need to put you in the ground. My guess is that it will be the ground.'

I nodded. It was my guess, too.

'But we'll be there. Inside with you, close.'

It wasn't comforting.

'I don't know ...'

'Not to worry, Jack,' Backus said, reaching over and giving

457

me a playful punch on the shoulder. 'You'll be all right and this time we're going to do it right. What you *do* have to worry about is getting her to talk. Get her on the tape, Jack. Get her admitting to just one part of the Poet's story and we've got her for the rest. Get her on tape.'

'I'll try.'

'You'll be fine.'

At Mulholland Drive, Backus turned right as Carter had instructed and we followed the road as it snaked along the mountain crest, offering a view through the darkening haze of the Valley below. We serpentined for nearly a mile until we saw Wrightwood Drive and turned left and descended into a neighborhood of small homes built on steel pylons, their weight hanging out over the mountain's edge, precarious testaments to engineering and the desires of developers to leave their mark on every crest in the city.

'Do you believe people live in these things?' Backus asked.

'Hate to be in one during an earthquake.'

Backus drove slowly, checking the address numbers painted on the curb. I let him do that while I watched between the houses for glimpses of the Valley below. It was approaching dusk and many of the lights were coming on down there. Backus finally stopped the car in front of a house on a bend in the road.

'This is it.'

It was a small, wood-frame structure. From the front the pylons that supported it could not be seen and it seemed to be floating above the deep drop-off to the Valley. We both looked at it for a long moment without making a move to get out.

'What if she knows about the house?'

'Rachel? She won't, Jack. I only know because of Clearmountain. It came up during a bit of gossip. Some of the guys from the FO use the place on occasion, if you know what I mean. When they're with someone they can't bring home.'

I looked over at him and he winked at me.

'Let's check it out,' he said. 'Don't forget your stuff.'

There was a lockbox on the front door. Backus knew the

combination and opened it, retrieved the key from the tiny compartment and opened the door.

He entered the house and flicked on the light in an entrance alcove. I followed him in and closed the door. The house was only modestly furnished but I ignored this because my attention was immediately drawn to the rear wall of the living room. The wall was made entirely of thick glass panels offering a spectacular view of the entire Valley sprawling below the house. I crossed the room and gazed out. At the far rim of the Valley I saw the rise of another mountain chain. I stepped close enough to the glass so that I could see my own breath against it and looked down into the dark arroyo directly below. A sense of unease at being at such a precipice licked at me and I stepped back as Backus turned on a lamp behind me.

It was then that I saw the cracks. Three of the five glass panels had fractures spidering through them. I turned to the left and saw the disjointed image of myself and Backus in a mirrored wall that had also been fractured by the earthquake.

'What else happened? Is it safe to be in here?'

'It's safe, Jack. But safety is a relative thing. The next big one could come along and change everything ... As far as other damage, there is a floor below us. Was a floor, I should say. Clearmountain said that is where the damage was. Buckled walls, broken water pipes.'

I put my computer bag and pillowcase down on the floor and turned back to the rear window. My eyes were drawn to the view and I bravely stepped to the glass again. I heard a sharp creaking sound from the direction of the alcove where we had come in. I looked at Backus with alarm.

'Don't worry, they had the pylons checked by an engineer before they even started the sting. The house isn't going anywhere. It just looks like it is and sounds like it is and that's what they wanted for the sting.'

I nodded again but not with a lot of confidence. I looked back at him through the glass.

'The only thing going somewhere is you, Jack.'

I glanced at him in the mirror, not sure what he meant.

And there, quadrupled in the broken reflection, I saw the gun in his hand.

'What is this?' I asked.

'This is the end of the line.'

In a rush it came to me. I'd taken a wrong turn and blamed the wrong one. In that moment I also came to the realization that it was the flaw in my own interior that had led me the wrong way. My inability to believe and accept. I had taken Rachel's emotions and looked for the flaw in them instead of the truth.

'You,' I said. 'You are the Poet.'

He didn't answer. Instead he gave a small smile and a nod. I knew then that Rachel's plane hadn't been recalled and that Agent Carter was not coming with a tech and two good agents. I could see the true plan perfectly, right down to the finger Backus must have kept on the phone while he faked the call in my hotel room. I was alone now with the Poet.

'Bob, why? Why you?'

I was so shocked I was still calling him by his first name like a friend would.

'It's a story as old as any of them,' he replied. 'Too old and forgotten to tell you. You don't need to know it now, anyway. Sit down on the chair, Jack.'

He signaled with the gun toward the stuffed chair opposite the couch. Then he aimed the gun back at me. I didn't move.

'The calls,' I said. 'You made the calls from Thorson's room?'

I said it more to be saying something as a stall for time, though in my gut I knew that time was meaningless to me now. No one knew I was here. No one would be coming. Backus laughed in a forced, scoffing manner at my question.

'The luck of chance,' he said. 'That night I checked in for all of us – Carter, Thorson, me. Then I apparently mixed the keys up. I made those calls from my own room, but the bill had Thorson's name on it. I didn't know that, of course, until I took the bills from your room Monday night while you were with Rachel.'

I thought about what Rachel had said about making your own luck. I guessed it applied to serial killers as well.

'How'd you know I had the bills?'

'I didn't. Not for sure. But you called Michael Warren and told him you had his source by the balls. He then called me because I was his source. Even though he said you accused Gordon of being the source, I had to find out what you knew. That was the reason I let you back into the investigation, Jack. I had to figure out what you knew. It wasn't until I went into your room while you were bedding Rachel that I found out it was the hotel bills.'

'Was that you who followed me later, to the bar?'

'That night you were the one with the luck. If you had gone to that doorway to see who was there, this would all have been over right then.

'But then the next day when you didn't come to me and accuse Thorson of breaking into your room, I thought the threat was over. That you were letting it go. Everything proceeded nicely from there – right according to plan – until you called up today and started asking about condoms and phone calls. I knew what you were up to, Jack. I knew I had to move quickly. Now sit down in that chair. I'm not going to ask you again.'

I moved to the chair and sat down. I rubbed my hands down my thighs and felt my hands shaking. My back was now to the rear wall of glass. I had nothing to look at but Backus.

'How'd you know about Gladden?' I asked. 'Gladden and Beltran.'

'I was there. Remember? I was part of the team. While Rachel and Gordon conducted other interviews I had my own little sit-down with William. From what he was willing to say it was not difficult for me to identify Beltran. Then I waited for Gladden to act once he was set free. I knew he'd act out. It was in his nature. I know about that. And so I used him as cover. I knew that if one day my work was discovered, the evidence would lead to him.'

'And the PTL Network?'

'We're talking too much, Jack. I have work to do here.'

Without taking his eyes off me he stooped to the floor, picked up and then emptied the pillowcase. He reached down and felt around in my belongings, his eyes always on me. Unsatisfied, he did the same with my computer bag, until he came up with the vial of pills I had gotten at the hospital. He glanced down quickly at the label, read it and looked back at me with a smile.

'Tylenol with codeine,' he said and smiled. 'This is going to work out nicely. Take one, Jack. Take two, in fact.'

He tossed the vial to me and I instinctively caught it.

'I can't,' I said. 'I took one a couple hours ago. I can't take any for another two hours.'

'Take two, Jack. Now.'

His voice had stayed in a steady monologue but the look in his eyes chilled me. I fumbled with the cap and finally managed to open the vial.

'I need water.'

'No water, Jack. Take the pills.'

I put two of the pills into my mouth and tried to act as if I had swallowed them as I moved them under my tongue.

'Okay.'

'Open wide, Jack.'

I did and he leaned forward to look but he never came close enough for me to take a swing at the gun. He stayed out of reach.

'Know what I think? I think they're under your tongue, Jack. But that's okay because they'll dissolve. It'll just take a little extra time. I've got the —'

There was another creaking sound and he looked around but then quickly back at me.

'I've got the time.'

'You wrote those PTL files. You're the Eidolon.'

'Yes, I am the Eidolon, thank you. And to answer your earlier questions, I learned of the PTL board from Beltran. He was kind enough to be on-line the night I paid my visit to him. So I took his place on the net, so to speak. I used his passwords and later had the systems operator change them to

Edgar and Perry. I'm afraid Mr Gomble never knew that he had a . . . fox in the henhouse, to use your turn of phrase.'

I looked at the mirror to my right and in it I could see the reflection of the Valley lights behind me. All those lights, all those people, I thought, and no one to see or help me. I felt the shudder of fear move through me, stronger.

'You have to relax, Jack,' Backus said in a calming monotone. 'That's the key. Are you feeling the codeine yet?'

The pills had broken up under my tongue and filled my mouth with an acrid taste.

'What are you going to do to me?'

'I'm going to do for you what I did for all of them. You wanted to know about the Poet? You are going to know all there is to know. Everything. Firsthand knowledge, Jack. You see, you are the choice. Remember what the fax said? The choice has been made, he's in my sights. That was you, Jack. All along.'

'Backus, you sick fuck! You –'

My outburst jarred some of the debris loose in my mouth and I swallowed it before I could stop. Backus, seemingly knowing what had happened, burst out laughing but then abruptly cut it off. He glared at me and I could see a dim light in his unblinking eyes. I realized then how mad he was and it dawned on me that because Rachel was not the one, the thing that I had believed was part of her misdirection might in actuality be part of the real Poet's killing pattern. The condoms, the sexual aspects. It could all be part of his killing program.

'What did you do to my brother?'

'That was between him and me. Personal.'

'Tell me.'

He exhaled.

'Nothing, Jack. Nothing. He was the one who wouldn't go along with the program. He was my one failure. But now I have the closest thing to a second chance. I won't fail this time.'

I looked down at the ground. I could feel the effects of the painkillers beginning to move through me. I squeezed my eyes shut and balled my fists but it was too late. The poison was in my blood.

'There's nothing you can do,' Backus said. 'Just relax, Jack, let it take you. Soon it will all be over.'

'You're not going to get away. There's no way Rachel's not going to see this for what it was.'

'You know, Jack, I think you are one hundred percent correct. She'll know. She may already. That's why I'm leaving after this. You are the last chore on my list, then I take my leave.'

I didn't get it.

'Leaving?'

'I'm sure Rachel already has her suspicions. That's why I've had to keep sending her to Florida. But it's only a temporary deflection. Soon enough she'll know. That's why it's time to shed the skin and move on. I've got to be me, Jack.'

His face lit up with the last line. I thought he was about to sing it but he didn't.

'How's it feeling now, Jack? A little light-headed?'

I didn't reply but he knew the answer was yes. I felt like I was beginning to slip into a void of darkness, a boat going over the falls. All the while Backus just watched, talking in his calm monotone, using my name often.

'Let it work itself through you, Jack. Just enjoy these moments. Think about your brother. Think about what you are going to say to him. I think you should tell him what a great investigator you turned out to be. Two in the family, that's something. Think of Sean's face. Smiling. Smiling at you, Jack. Now let your eyes close until you can see him. Go ahead. Nothing's going to happen. You're safe, Jack.'

I couldn't help it. My eyelids were drooping. I tried to look away from him. I stared at the lights in the mirror but the fatigue still grabbed me and took me under. I closed my eyes.

'That's good, Jack. Excellent. Do you see Sean now?'

I nodded, then I felt his hand on my left wrist. He moved it onto the arm of the chair. Then he did the same with my right arm.

'Perfect, Jack. You're a wonderful subject. So cooperative.

Now I don't want you to feel any pain. No pain, Jack. No matter what happens here, you will not feel any pain, do you understand that?'

'Yes,' I said.

'I don't want you to move, Jack. In fact, Jack, you cannot move. Your arms are like dead weights. You cannot move them. Isn't that right?'

'Yes,' I said.

My eyes were still closed and my chin was resting on my chest but I was totally aware of my surroundings. It was as if my mind and body had separated. It was as if I was looking down from above at myself in the chair.

'Open your eyes now, Jack.'

I did as I was told and saw Backus standing before me. His gun was holstered under his open jacket and in one hand he now held a long steel needle. This was my chance. The gun was in the holster but I could not move from the chair or reach out to him. My mind could no longer send messages to my body. I sat motionless and could only watch as he matter-of-factly pressed the point of the needle into my unbandaged palm. He repeated the procedure with two of my fingers. I made no move to stop it.

'That's good, Jack. I think you are ready for me now. Remember, arms like dead weights. You just can't move them no matter how much you want to. You can't speak, no matter how much you want to. But keep your eyes open, Jack, you don't want to miss this.'

He stepped back and looked at me with an appraising look.

'Who's best now, Jack?' he asked. 'Who's the better man? Who has won and who has lost?'

My mind filled with revulsion. I couldn't move my arms or speak but still felt the energy wave of absolute fear go screaming through me. I felt tears form in my eyes but they didn't fall. I watched as his hands went to his belt buckle and he said, 'I don't even have to use rubbers anymore, Jack.'

Just as he said that the light in the alcove behind him went out. Then I saw movement in the shadows left behind and heard her voice. Rachel.

'Don't move an inch, Bob. Not even an inch.'

She said it calmly and confidently. Backus froze, his eyes on mine, as if he could see her reflection in them. They were dead eyes. His right hand, shielded from Rachel's view, started moving inside his jacket. I wanted to call out a warning but I could not. At once, I strained every muscle of my body to move just an inch and my left leg kicked out from the chair impotently.

But it was enough. The hold Backus had was losing its grip.

'Rachel!' I yelled just as Backus pulled his gun from his holster and spun around on her.

There was an exchange of shots and Backus was launched backward onto the floor. I heard the shattering of one of the glass panels and the cool evening air rushed into the room as Backus scrambled to cover behind the chair I sat in.

Rachel dipped around the corner, grabbed the lamp and jerked it away from the socket. The house plunged into a darkness only interrupted by the stray light from the Valley below. Backus fired twice more at her, the report of his weapon so close to my head it was deafening. I felt him jerk the chair backward to give him better cover. I was like a man coming out of a deep dream, struggling just to move. As I began to pull myself up, his hand clamped over my shoulder and pulled me back down into the chair. It held me in place.

'Rachel,' Backus called out. 'You shoot and you hit him, you want that? Put the gun down and come out. We'll talk about this.'

'Forget it, Rachel,' I called. 'He'll kill us both. Shoot him! Shoot him!'

Rachel swung around the bullet-pocked wall once more. This time she was low to the ground. The barrel of her gun took a bead on a spot just over my right shoulder but she hesitated. Backus didn't. He fired twice more as Rachel dove back to cover and I saw the corner of the alcove entrance explode in plaster dust and debris.

'Rachel!' I yelled.

I dug the heels of both shoes into the carpet and in one

great burst of what strength I could command I shoved the chair back as hard and as quick as I could.

The move surprised Backus. I felt the chair hit him solidly, its impact knocking him away from cover. At that moment Rachel wheeled around the corner of the alcove and the room exploded in the light of another round being fired from her gun.

Behind me I heard a shriek from Backus and then silence. My eyes now adjusted to the dim light, I saw Rachel step out of the alcove and come toward me. She held her gun raised in both hands, her elbows locked. The weapon was pointed past me. I slowly turned as she stepped by. At the precipice, she pointed the gun down toward the darkness into which Backus had fallen. She stood stock still for at least a half a minute before being satisfied that he was gone.

Silence gripped the house. I felt the cool night air against my skin. She finally turned and came to me. Grabbing my arm, she pulled me up until I was standing.

'Come on, Jack,' she said. 'Come out of it. Are you hurt? Are you hit?'

'Sean.'

'What?'

'Nothing. Are you all right?'

'I think so. Are you hit?'

I noticed her looking at the floor behind me and turned around. There was blood on the floor. And shattered glass.

'No, that's not me,' I said. 'You hit him. Or the glass got him.'

I stepped back to the edge with her. There was only blackness below. The only sounds were the breeze through the trees down there and traffic noises filtering up from further down.

'Rachel, I'm sorry,' I said. 'I thought it . . . I thought it was you. I'm sorry.'

'Don't say it, Jack. We'll talk about it later.'

'I thought you were on a plane.'

'After I talked to you I knew something wasn't right. Then Brad Hazelton called and told me what you had called him

467

about. I decided to talk to you before I left. I went to the hotel and saw you leaving with Backus. I don't know why but I followed. I guess it was because Bob had sent me to Florida before when he should have sent Gordon. I didn't trust him anymore.'

'How much did you hear up here?'

'Enough. I just couldn't make a move until he holstered his weapon. I'm sorry you had to go through all of that, Jack.'

She stepped back from the edge but I stayed there, staring into the darkness.

'I didn't ask him about the others. I didn't ask him why.'

'What others?'

'Sean, the others. Beltran got what he deserved. But why Sean? Why the others?'

'There's no explanation, Jack. And if there was, we'll never know it now. My car's down the road a bit. I need to go back and call for backup and a helicopter to search the canyon. To make sure. I better call the hospital, too.'

'Why?'

'To tell them how many of those pills you've taken and to see what we should do about it.'

She started walking toward the entrance alcove.

'Rachel,' I called after her. 'Thanks.'

'Anytime, Jack.'

50
....

Pretty soon after Rachel left I passed out on the couch. The sound of a close helicopter invaded my dreams but not enough to wake me. Finally, when I awoke on my own, it was three in the morning. I was taken to the thirteenth floor of the federal building and placed in a small interview room. Two dour-faced agents I had never met before asked me questions for the next five hours, going over my story again and again until I was sick of regurgitating it. For this interview they did not have a stenographer sit in the corner of the room with her machine because this time we were talking about one of their own and I had the feeling that they wanted to sculpt my story into the form that could best serve them before putting it down on the record.

Sometime after eight they finally said I could go down to the cafeteria for breakfast before they brought the stenographer in and made a formal record. By then we had been over the story so many times I knew exactly how they wanted me to answer nearly every question. I wasn't hungry but I wanted out of that room and away from them so badly I would have said yes to anything. At least they didn't escort me down to the cafeteria like a prisoner.

I found Rachel sitting there, alone at a table. I bought a coffee and a sugar doughnut that looked like it was three days old and went over.

'Can I sit here?'

'It's a free country.'

'Sometimes I wonder. Those guys, Cooper and Kelley, they've held me in that room up there for five hours.'

'You've got to understand something. You're the messenger, Jack. They know you are going to go out from here and tell the story in newspapers, on TV, probably a book. The whole world will know about the FBI's one bad apple. It doesn't matter how much good we do or how many bad guys we stop, the fact that there was a bad guy among us is going to be a big, big story. You are going to be rich and we are going to have to live with what comes after. That, in a nutshell, is why Cooper and Kelley aren't treating you like a prima donna.'

I studied her for a few moments. It looked like she had eaten a full breakfast. I could see egg yolk smeared on her empty plate.

'Good morning, Rachel,' I said. 'Maybe we can start over.'

That just got her mad.

'Look, Jack, I'm not going to treat you gently, either. Just how do you expect me to react to you now?'

'I don't know. The whole time with those guys I've been answering their questions but doing nothing but thinking about you. About us.'

I studied her face for reaction but got none. She was looking down at her plate.

'Look, I could try to explain to you all the reasons I thought it was you but it wouldn't matter. It all comes down to me, Rachel. Something in me is missing and . . . I couldn't accept what you offered without some suspicion, some kind of cynicism. It was from that small doubt that everything grew and got blown out of proportion . . . Rachel, you have my apology and my promise that if I were given a new chance with you I would work to overcome it, to fill that void. And I promise you that I would succeed.'

Still nothing, not even eye contact. I became resigned. It was over.

'Rachel, can I ask you something?'

'What is it?'

'Your father. And you . . . Did he hurt you?'

'Do you mean did he fuck me?'

I just looked at her, silently.

'That's part of me and my life I don't have to talk to anyone about.'

I turned my coffee cup on the table, staring at it like it was the most interesting thing I'd ever seen. Now I was the one who couldn't look up.

'Well, I've got to get back up there,' I finally said. 'They only gave me fifteen minutes.'

I made a move to stand up.

'Have you told them about me?' she asked.

I stopped.

'About us? No, I've been trying to avoid that.'

'Don't hold back with them, Jack. They already know, anyway.'

'You told them?'

'Yes. There was no point in trying to hide anything from them.'

I nodded.

'What if I tell them and they ask if we still are . . . if we still have a relationship?'

'Tell them the jury's still out.'

I nodded again and stood up. Her use of the word jury reminded me of my own thoughts of the night before when in my mind, as the jury of one, I had reached a verdict about her. I thought it was only appropriate now that she should be weighing the evidence against me.

'Let me know when you reach a verdict.'

I dropped the doughnut into the trash can by the cafeteria door on my way out.

It was almost noon before I was finished with Kelley and Cooper. It was also not until then that I heard about Backus. Walking through the field office I noticed how empty it was. The doors to all the group rooms were open and the desks empty. It was like a detective bureau during a cop's funeral, and in a way it was. I almost walked back to the interrogation room where I had left my inquisitors to ask them what was going on. But I knew they didn't like me and wouldn't tell me anything they didn't want or have to tell me.

As I passed the communications room, I heard the chatter of two-way radio talk. I looked in and saw Rachel sitting alone in the room. She had a microphone console in front of her on a desk. I walked in.

'Hey.'

'Hey.'

'I'm done. They told me I could leave. Where is everyone? What's going on?'

'They're all out looking for him.'

'Backus?'

She nodded.

'I thought...' I didn't finish. It was obvious now that he hadn't been found at the bottom of the drop-off. I hadn't asked before because I just assumed that his body had been recovered. 'Jesus. How could he have ...'

'Survived? Who knows? He was gone by the time they got down there with their flashlights and dogs. There was a tall eucalyptus tree. They found blood in the upper branches. The theory is that he fell into the tree. It broke his fall. The dogs lost his scent on the road further down the hill. The helicopter was pretty much useless except for keeping everybody on the hillside up half the night. Everybody but you. They're still out there. We've put everybody out on the street, the hospitals. So far, nothing.'

'Jesus.'

Backus was still out there. Somewhere. I couldn't believe it.

'I wouldn't worry,' she said. 'The possibility that he would go after you, or me for that matter, is considered very remote. His goal now is escape. Survival.'

'That's not what I meant,' I said, though I guess it was. 'It's just scary. Someone like that out there ... Have they come up with anything about ... why?'

'They're working on it. Brass and Brad are on it. But he's going to be a tough one to crack. There was just no sign at all. The wall between his two lives was as thick as a bank vault's door. On some of them we just never get through. The unexplainable ones. All you know is that it was there inside them.

The seed. And then one day it metastasized ... and he began doing what he was probably only fantasizing about before.'

I didn't say anything. I just wanted her to continue, to talk to me.

'They'll start with the father,' she said. 'I heard Brass was going up to New York to see him today. That's one visit I wouldn't want to have to make. Your son follows you into the bureau and turns out to be your worst nightmare. What's that line that Nietzsche said? "Whoever fights monsters..."'

'"Should see to it that in the process he does not become a monster."'

'Yeah.'

We were both quiet for a few moments, thinking about that.

'Why aren't you out there?' I finally asked.

'Because I've been assigned to desk duty until I'm cleared on the shooting ... and my other actions.'

'Isn't that academic? Especially since he isn't even dead.'

'It should be, but there are other factors.'

'Us? Are we one of those factors?'

She nodded.

'You could say my judgment is being questioned. Getting involved with a witness and journalist is not what you'd call standard FBI practice. Then there's this that came in this morning.'

She turned over a sheet of paper and handed it to me. It was a faxed copy of a grainy black-and-white photo. It was a picture of me sitting on a table and Rachel standing between my spread legs, kissing me. It took me a moment to place it and then I realized it was the hospital emergency room suite.

'Remember that doctor you saw looking in on us?' Rachel asked. 'Well, he wasn't a doctor. He was some freelance piece of shit who sold the photo to the *National Enquirer.* Must've snuck in there in his disguise. It will be on the cashier stand at every supermarket in the country by Tuesday. In keeping with their aboveboard journalistic ethics they faxed this over and asked for an interview or at least a comment. What do you think, Jack? How about "fuck you" for a comment? Think they'll print that?'

I put the fax photo down and looked at her.

'I'm sorry, Rachel.'

'You know, that's all you can say now. "Sorry, Rachel. Sorry, Rachel." It doesn't look very good on you, Jack.'

I almost said it again but instead just nodded. I looked at her, brooding for a moment about how I could ever have made the mistake I made. I knew then it had cost me my chance with her. Feeling sorry for myself, my mind ran through all the parts that had made the whole and had convinced me of something my heart should have known was wrong. I was looking for excuses but knew there weren't any.

'Remember that day we met and you took me down to Quantico?'

'Yes, I remember.'

'That was Backus's office you put me in, wasn't it? To make my calls. Why'd you do that? I thought it was your office.'

'I don't have an office. I have a desk and work space. I put you in there so you'd have some privacy. Why?'

'Nothing. It was just one of the parts that seemed ... to fit so well before. The calendar on the desk, it showed he was on vacation when Orsulak ... So I thought you lied to me about not having a vacation in so long.'

'We're not going to talk about this now.'

'Then when? If we don't talk about it now we never will. I made a mistake, Rachel. I've got no acceptable excuse. But I want you to know what I knew. I want you to understand what I –'

'I don't care!'

'Maybe you never cared.'

'Don't try to put it on me. You're the one who fucked up. I wasn't the one who –'

'What did you do that night, the first night, after you left my room? I called and you weren't there. I knocked on your door and you weren't there. I went out in the hall and I saw

Thorson. He was coming from the drugstore. You sent him didn't you?'

She looked down at the desk for the longest time.

'At least answer that, Rachel.'

'I saw him in the hallway, too,' she said softly. 'Earlier. After I left you. It made me so angry that he was there, that Backus brought him out. It all boiled up. I wanted to hurt him. Humiliate him. I needed . . . something.'

So with a promise that she'd be waiting, she sent him out to the drugstore for a condom. But she was gone when he got back.

'I was in my room when you called and knocked. I didn't answer because I thought it was him. He must've done the same because twice people knocked. Twice they called. I never answered.'

I nodded.

'I'm not proud of what I did to him,' she said. 'Especially now.'

'Everybody has things they're not proud of, Rachel. It doesn't stop them from going on. It shouldn't.'

She didn't say anything.

'I'm going now, Rachel. I hope things work out for you. And I hope you'll call me sometime. I'll be waiting.'

'Good-bye, Jack.'

As I moved away from her I brought my hand up. With one finger I traced the line of her jaw. Our eyes briefly met and held. Then I walked out.

51
....

He huddled in the dark of the storm-drainage tunnel, resting and concentrating his mind on mastering the pain. Already he knew there was infection. The wound was minor in terms of damage, a through-and-through shot that tore an upper abdominal muscle but little else before leaving, but it was dirty and he could feel the poisons beginning to move through his body, making him want to lie down and sleep.

He looked down the length of the dark tunnel. Only stray light leaking from somewhere up above made it this far down. Lost light. He pushed himself up the slippery wall until he was standing and then he began moving again. One day, he thought as he moved. Make it through the first day and you'll make it through the rest. It was the mantra he repeated in his mind.

In a sense, there was relief. Despite the pain and now the hunger, there was the relief. No more separation. The facade was gone. Backus was gone. Now there was only Eidolon. And Eidolon would triumph. They were nothing before him and could do nothing now to stop him.

'NOTHING!'

His voice echoed down the tunnel into the blackness and disappeared. With one hand clamped over his wound he headed that way.

52

....

In late spring a city Department of Water and Power inspector, investigating the source of a foul odor that had drawn complaints from the residents living above, found the remains of the body in the tunnels.

The remains of *a* body. It carried his identification and FBI badge and the clothes were his. It was found, what was left of it, laid out on a concrete shelf in an underground intersection of two stormwater drainage culverts. The cause of death was unknown because advanced decomposition – sped along by the damp, fetid surroundings of the drainage culvert – and disturbance of the remains by animals precluded accurate autopsy results. The medical examiner did find what appeared to be a wound channel and a cracked rib in the rotting flesh but no bullet fragments that could conclusively tie the wound to Rachel's gun.

As far as the identification went, it, too, was inconclusive. There was the badge and the ID and the clothing but nothing else that proved that these were indeed the remains of Special Agent Robert Backus Jr. The animals that had attacked the body – if it had truly been animals – had made off with the complete lower mandible and an upper bridge, which precluded a comparison with dental records.

That seemed too convenient to me. And others. Brad Hazelton called me to fill me in on these facts. He said the bureau was officially closing the case but there would be those who would still look for him. Unofficially. He said that some people viewed the discovery in the drainage tunnel as nothing more than a skin Backus had left behind, probably a homeless man he had encountered in the pipes. He said they believed Backus was still out there and so did I.

Brad Hazelton told me that while the official search for Backus might be over, the effort to explore the psychological motivations was continuing. But cracking the nut of Backus's pathology was proving difficult. Agents spent three days in his condominium near Quantico but found nothing remotely indicative of his secret life. No souvenirs of his kills, no clipped newspaper stories, nothing.

There were only little things known, small clues. A perfectionist father who never spared the rod. An obsessive-compulsive fixation on cleanliness – I remembered his desk at Quantico and his straightening of the calendar after I had sat there. An engagement broken off years earlier by a bride-to-be who told Brass Doran that Backus required her to shower immediately before and after they made love. A high school friend who came forward and told Hazelton that once Backus had confided to him that when he wet the bed as a boy, his father would handcuff him to the towel bar in the shower – a story denied by Robert Sr.

But these were only details, not answers. They were fragments of the much larger fabric of personality that they could only guess at. I remembered what Rachel had told me once. That it was like trying to put together a shattered mirror. Each piece reflects a part of the subject. But if the subject moves, so does the reflection.

I have stayed in Los Angeles since it all happened. I had my hand repaired by a Beverly Hills surgeon and it only hurts now at the end of a long day at the computer.

I've rented a small house in the hills and on good days I can see the sun's reflection on the Pacific almost fifteen miles away. On bad days the view is depressing and I keep the blinds closed. Sometimes at night I can hear the coyotes whining and barking at each other in Nichols Canyon. It is warm here and I have not had the desire to return to Colorado. I talk to my mother and father and Riley regularly – more so than when I was there – but I still fear the ghosts back there more than the ones here.

Officially, I am on leave from the *Rocky*. Greg Glenn wants me to come back but I have held off on an answer to him. I have the leverage. I'm now a celebrity journalist – I've been on 'Nightline' and 'Larry King Live' – and Greg wants to keep me on staff. So for now, I am on extended leave without pay while writing my book.

My agent sold the book and film rights to my story for more money than I could make in ten years working at the *Rocky*. But most of the money, when I get it all, will go into a trust fund for Riley's unborn baby. Sean's baby. I don't think I could manage with so much in my own bank account and I don't feel deserving of it anyway. It's blood money. I put aside just enough of the first payment from the publisher for living expenses here in L.A. and the possibility that I might make a trip to Italy after I finished the first draft.

That's where Rachel is. Hazelton told me. When they told her she was being transferred out of the BSS unit, out of Quantico, she took her own leave and went overseas. I've waited to hear from her but there has been no word. I don't think there will be now and I don't think I'll be going to Italy as she once suggested. At night, the ghost that haunts me the most is the thing inside of me that led me to doubt the very thing I wanted most.

53

· · · · · · · ·

Death is my beat. I have made my living from it and forged a professional reputation on it. I have profited by it. It has always been around me but never as close as those moments with Gladden and Backus, when it breathed right into my face, put its eye to mine and made a grab for me.

I remember their eyes the most. I can't sleep without first thinking of their eyes. Not for what was in them but for what was missing, what was not there. Behind them was only darkness. An empty despair so intriguing that I find myself fighting sleep to think about it sometimes. And when I think of them I can't help but think of Sean as well. My twin. I wonder if he looked into the eyes of his killer at the end. I wonder if he saw what I saw. An evil as pure and as scarring as a flame. I still mourn for Sean. I always will. And I wonder as I watch and wait for the Eidolon when I'll see that flame again.

ACKNOWLEDGMENTS

I would like to thank the following people for their fine work and support.

Many thanks to my editor, Michael Pietsch, for long and hard work as always on this manuscript and to his colleagues at Little, Brown, particularly my friend Tom Rusch, for all of their efforts on my behalf. Once again Betty Power came through with a wonderful job of copyediting and more. Also to my agents, Philip Spitzer and Joel Gotler, who were there when it was only an idea, thanks again.

My wife, Linda, and members of my family provided invaluable help to me by reading the early drafts and showing me where I went wrong – repeatedly. And I am most indebted to my father's brother, the Reverend Donald C. Connelly, for his stories about growing up a twin.

I'd like to thank Michele Brustin and David Percelay for their creative advice and, in matters of research, thanks to Bill Ryan and Richard Whittingham, the fine Chicago writer, along with Rick and Kim Garza.

And lastly I would also like to thank the many booksellers I have come to know in the last few years who have put my stories into the hands of the readers.

I think maybe I only know one thing in this world. One thing for sure. And that is that the truth does not set you free. Not like I have heard it said and not like I have said myself the countless times I sat in small rooms and jail cells and urged ragged men to confess their sins to me. I lied to them, tricked them. The truth does not salvage you or make you whole again. It does not allow you to rise above the burden of lies and secrets and wounds to the heart. The truths I have learned hold me down like chains in a dark room, an underworld of ghosts and victims that slither around me like snakes. It is a place where the truth is not something to look at or behold. It is the place where evil waits. Where it blows its breath, every breath, into your mouth and nose until you cannot escape from it. This is what I know. The only thing.

I knew this going in on the day I took the case that would take me into the narrows. I knew that my life's mission would always take me to the places where evil waits, to the places where the truth that I might find would be an ugly and horrible thing. And still I went without pause. And still I went not being ready for the moment when evil would come from its waiting place. When it would grab at me like an animal and take me down into the black water.

I

She was in darkness, floating on a black sea, a starless sky above. She could hear nothing and see nothing. It was a perfect black moment but then Rachel Walling opened her eyes from the dream.

She stared up at the ceiling. She listened to the wind outside and heard the branches of the azaleas scratching against the window. She wondered if it had been the scratching on glass or some other noise from within the house that had awakened her. Then her cell phone rang. She wasn't startled. She calmly reached to the bed table. She brought the phone to hear ear and was fully alert when she answered, her voice showing no indication of sleep.

'Agent Walling,' she said.

'Rachel? It's Cherie Dei.'

Rachel knew right away that this would not be a Rez call. Cherie Dei meant Quantico. It had been four years since the last time. Rachel had been waiting.

'Where are you, Rachel?'

'I'm at home. Where do you think I'd be?'

'I know you cover a lot of territory now. I thought maybe you –'

'I'm in Rapid City, Cherie. What is it?'

She answered after a long moment of silence.

'He's resurfaced. He's back.'

Rachel felt an invisible fist punch into her chest and then hold there. Her mind conjured memories and images. Bad ones. She closed her eyes. Cherie Dei didn't have to use a name. Rachel knew it was Backus. The Poet had resurfaced. Just as they knew he would. Like a virulent infection that moves through the body, hidden from the outside for years, then breaking the skin as reminder of its ugliness.

'Tell me.'

'Three days ago we got something in Quantico. A package in the mail. It contained –'

'Three days? You sat on it for three –'

'We didn't sit on anything. We took our time with it. It was addressed to you. At Behavioral Sciences. The mailroom brought it down to us and we had it X-rayed and then we opened it. Carefully.'

'What was in it?'

'A GPS reader. Do you know what that is, Rachel?'

A global positioning system reader. Rachel had encountered one on a case the previous year. An abduction out in the Badlands where the missing camper had marked her trail with a handheld GPS. They found it in her pack and traced her steps back to a camp where she had encountered a man and he had followed her. They got there too late to save her but they would have never gotten there at all if it hadn't been for the GPS.

'Yes, I know what it is. Longitude and latitude coordinates. What was on it?'

Rachael sat up and brought her legs over the side of the bed. She brought her free hand to her stomach and closed it like a dead flower. She waited and soon Cherie Dei continued. Rachel remembered her as once being so green, just an observer and learner on the go team, assigned to her under the bureau's mentoring program. Ten years later and the cases, all the cases, had etched deep grooves into her voice. Cherie Dei wasn't green anymore and she needed no mentor.

'The device had one waypoint in its record. The Mojave. Just inside the California border at Nevada. We flew out yesterday and we went to the marker. We've been using thermal imaging and gas probes. Late yesterday we found the first body, Rachel.'

'Who is it?'

'We don't know yet. It's old. It had been there a long time. We're just starting with it. The excavation work is slow.'

'You said the *first* body. How many more are there?'

'As of when I left the scene last we were up to four. We think there's more.'

'Cause of death?'

'Too early.'

Rachel was silent as she thought about this. The first questions that ran through her filters were why there and why now.

'Rachel, I'm not calling just to tell you. The point is the Poet is back in play and we want you out there.'

Rachel nodded. It was a given that she would go there.

'Cherie?'

'What?'

'Why do you think he was the one who sent the package?'

'We don't think it. We know it. We got a match a little while ago on a fingerprint from the GPS. He replaced the batteries on it and we got a thumb off of one of them. Robert Backus. It's him. He's back.'

Rachel slowly opened her fist and studied her hand. It was as still as a statue's. The dread she had felt just a moment before was changing. She could admit it to herself but no one else. She could feel the juice begin moving in her blood again, turning it a darker red. Almost black. She had been waiting for this call. She slept every night with the cell phone near her ear. Yes, it was part of the job. The call outs. But this was the only call she had truly been waiting for.

'You can name the way points,' Dei said in the silence. 'On the GPS. Up to twelve characters and spaces. He named this point "Hello Rachel." An exact fit. I guess he still has something for you. It's like he's calling you out, has some sort of plan.'

Rachel's memory dredged up an image of a man falling backward through glass and into darkness. Disappearing into the dark void below.

'I'm on my way,' she said.

'We're running it out of the Vegas field office. It will be easier to keep a blanket on it. Just be careful, Rachel. We don't know what he has in mind with this, you know? Watch your back.'

'I will. I always do.'

'Call me with the details and I'll pick you up.'

'I will.' She repeated.

Then she pushed the button that disconnected the call. She reached to the bed table and turned on the light. For a moment she remembered the dream, the stillness of the black water and the sky above, like black mirrors facing each other. And her in the middle, just floating.

from Chapter

6

Backus stayed at least a hundred feet behind her. Even in the crowded Chicago airport he knew she would be on what they always called 'Six Alert' when he had been with the bureau. Watching her back – her six – and always checking for a trailer. It had been tricky enough traveling with her so far. The plane from South Dakota had been small and less than forty people had been on board. The random assignment of seats had put him only two rows from her. So close he thought he could actually smell her scent – the one beneath the perfume and the makeup. The one the dogs could pick up.

It was intoxicating, to be so close and still such a long distance apart. He wanted the whole time to turn and look back at her, maybe catch a glimpse of her face between the seats, see what she was doing. But he didn't dare. He had to bide his time. He knew that good things came to those who plan carefully and then wait. That was the thing, the secret. Darkness waits. All things come to the dark.

He followed her through half of the American Airlines terminal until she took a seat at Gate K9. It was empty. No travelers were waiting here. No American employees were behind the gate counter waiting and ready to work the computers and check tickets. But Backus knew that this was only because she was early. They both were early. The flight to Las Vegas would not leave from Gate K9 for another two hours. He knew this because he was on the flight as well. In a way he was Rachel Walling's guardian angel, a silent escort who would be with her until she reached her final destination.

He walked on by the gate, careful not to be obvious about glancing at her but curious to see how she was going to pass the time waiting for the next flight. He hooked the strap of his large cowhide carry-on bag over his right shoulder so that if she happened to look up her eyes might be drawn to it instead of his face. He wasn't worried about her recognizing him for who he was. All the pain and the surgeries had taken care of that. But she might recognize him from the flight from Rapid City. And he didn't want that. He didn't want her to get suspicious.

His heart jumped in his chest like a baby kicking under a blanket as he made the one furtive glance while passing by. She had her head down and was reading a book. It was old and worn from many readings. There was a profusion of yellow Post-Its poking out from its pages. But he recognized the cover design and the title. *The Poet*. She was reading about him!

He hurried on by before she could sense she had a watcher and looked up. He went down two more gates and into the restroom. He went into a stall and carefully locked the door. He hung his bag on the door hook and quickly went to work. Off came the cowboy hat and vest. He sat down on the toilet and took off the boots, too.

In five minutes Backus transformed himself from a South Dakota cowboy to a Las Vegas gambler. He put on the silk clothes. He put on the gold. He put on the earring and the shades. He clipped the gaudy chrome cell phone to his belt even though there was no one who would call him and no one he would call. From the bag he took out another bag, much smaller and with the figure of the MGM lion emblazoned on it.

The components of his first skin were pushed into the new bag and he stepped out of the stall, the strap of the MGM bag over his shoulder. Backus admired himself for the preparation he had taken. It was the planning and attention to the small details like that that made him who he was, that made him a success at his craft.

He checked his look in the mirror as he walked toward the restroom's exit door. He smiled. He was a new man. Rachel would not recognize him. Nobody would. Feeling confident, he unzipped the MGM bag and checked on his digital camera. It was there and ready to go. He decided he would take the risk and shoot some photos of Rachel. Just some keepsakes, a few secret shots he could admire and enjoy after she was gone and this was all over.

All Orion/Phoenix titles are available at your local bookshop or from the following address:

Mail Order Department
Littlehampton Book Services
FREEPOST BR535
Worthing, West Sussex, BN13 3BR
telephone 01903 828503, *facsimile* 01903 828802
e-mail MailOrders@lbsltd.co.uk
(Please ensure that you include full postal address details)

Payment can be made either by credit/debit card (Visa, Mastercard, Access and Switch accepted) or by sending a £ Sterling cheque or postal order made payable to *Littlehampton Book Services*.
DO NOT SEND CASH OR CURRENCY.

Please add the following to cover postage and packing

UK and BFPO:
£1.50 for the first book, and 50p for each additional book to a maximum of £3.50

Overseas and Eire:
£2.50 for the first book plus £1.00 for the second book and 50p for each additional book ordered

---

BLOCK CAPITALS PLEASE

name of cardholder ....

delivery address
(if different from cardholder)

address of cardholder ....

....

....

....

....

....

....

postcode ....

postcode ....

☐ I enclose my remittance for £...............................

☐ please debit my Mastercard/Visa/Access/Switch (delete as appropriate)

card number ☐☐☐☐☐☐☐☐☐☐☐☐☐☐☐☐

expiry date ☐☐☐☐   Switch issue no. ☐☐

signature ....

prices and availability are subject to change without notice.